action

ac•tion (ak´shen) *n.* **1.** To initiate or proceed. **2.** A responsibility, mission, or duty. **3.** To move or advance towards change, as in an attempt to better a situation or environment. **4.** A call to battle between good and evil. **5.** A graphic novel line from VIZ.

Also available from VIZ: **Editor's Choice**
Shôjo
Shojo Beat
SHONEN JUMP
SHONEN JUMP Advanced
Studio Ghibli Library

VIZ action

THE ALL-NEW TENCHI MUYŌ!™

Pet Peeves

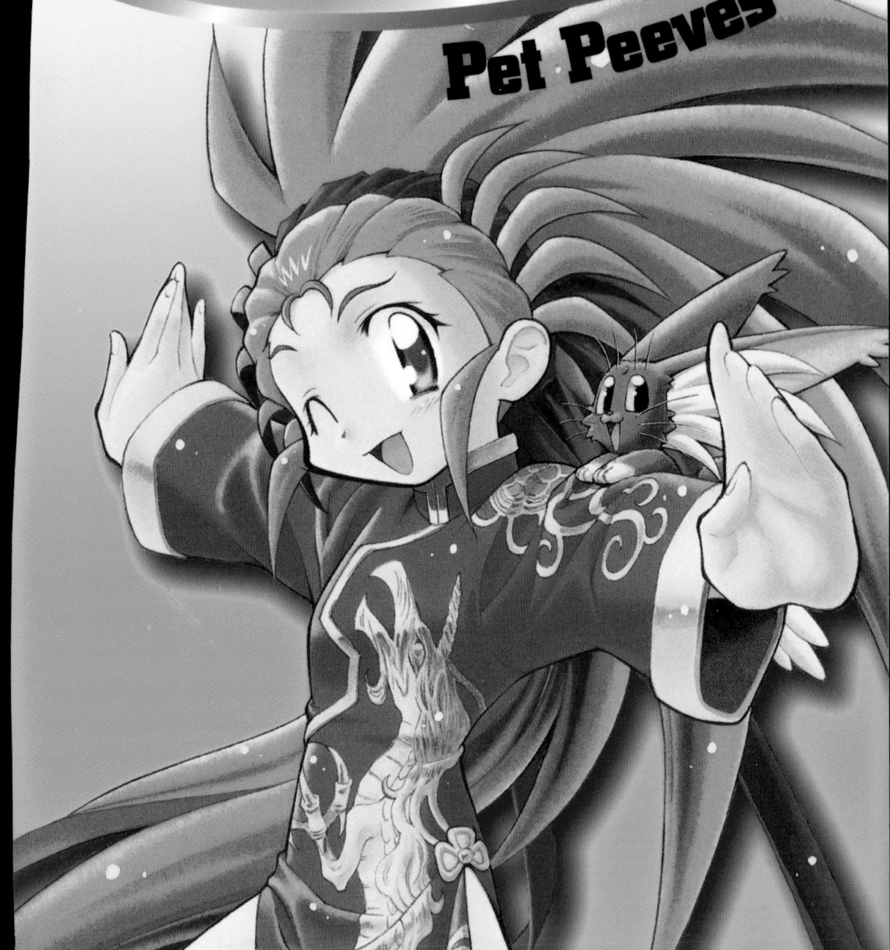

STORY AND ART BY
HITOSHI OKUDA

Vol. 6

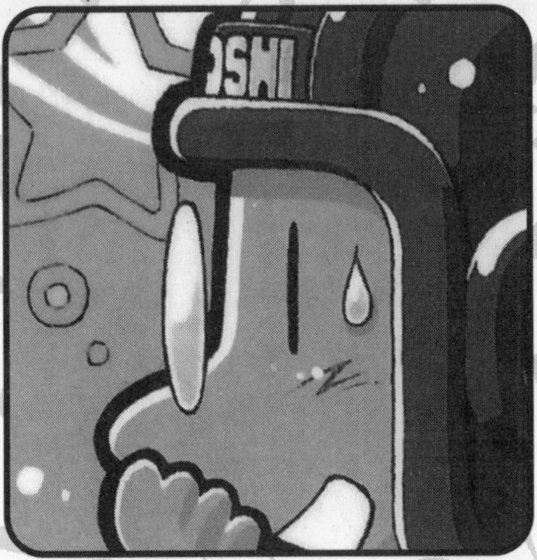
OSHI

Hitoshi Okuda was famous in Japanese amateur manga (*doujinshi*) under a pen name long before he made his professional debut. He studied under Nobuteru Yuki and Yutaka Izubuchi, two of Japan's top animators. His older works include **Radical Guardian**, published in Japan by Fujimi Shobo. His recent works include **The All-New Tenchi Muyô!**, **Ranto Mashoroku**, and **Little Dragon Restaurant**, all published in Japan by Kadokawa Shoten.

The All-New Tenchi Muyô!

Volume 6: Pet Peeves
Action Edition

STORY AND ART BY HITOSHI OKUDA

English Adaptation/Fred Burke
Translation/Aisei Japanese Language Services, Inc.
Touch-up Art & Lettering/Curtis Yee
Design/Hidemi Sahara
Editor/Shaenon K. Garrity

Managing Editor/Annette Roman
Director of Production/Noboru Watanabe
Vice President of Publishing/Alvin Lu
Sr. Director of Acquisitions/Rika Inouye
VP of Sales & Marketing/Liza Coppola
Publisher/Hyoe Narita

© 2001 HITOSHI OKUDA © AIC/VAP • NTV. Originally published in Japan in 2001 by KADOKAWA SHOTEN PUBLISHING CO., LTD.,
Tokyo. English translation rights arranged with KADOKAWA SHOTEN PUBLISHING CO., LTD., Tokyo.
New and adapted artwork and text © 2005 VIZ, LLC. All rights reserved.
The ALL-NEW TENCHI MUYÔ! logo is a trademark of VIZ, LLC.

The stories, characters and incidents mentioned in this publication are entirely fictional. For purposes of publication in
English, the artwork in this publication is generally printed in reverse from the original Japanese version.

Printed in Canada.

Published by VIZ, LLC
P.O. Box 77010
San Francisco, CA 94107

Action Edition
10 9 8 7 6 5 4 3 2 1
First printing, June 2005

For advertising rates or media kit, e-mail advertising@viz.com

store.viz.com

www.animerica-mag.com

www.viz.com

VIZ GRAPHIC NOVEL

THE ALL-NEW
TENCHI MUYŌ!™
PET PEEVES

STORY AND ART BY
HITOSHI OKUDA

CONTENTS

Chapter 1: Longing

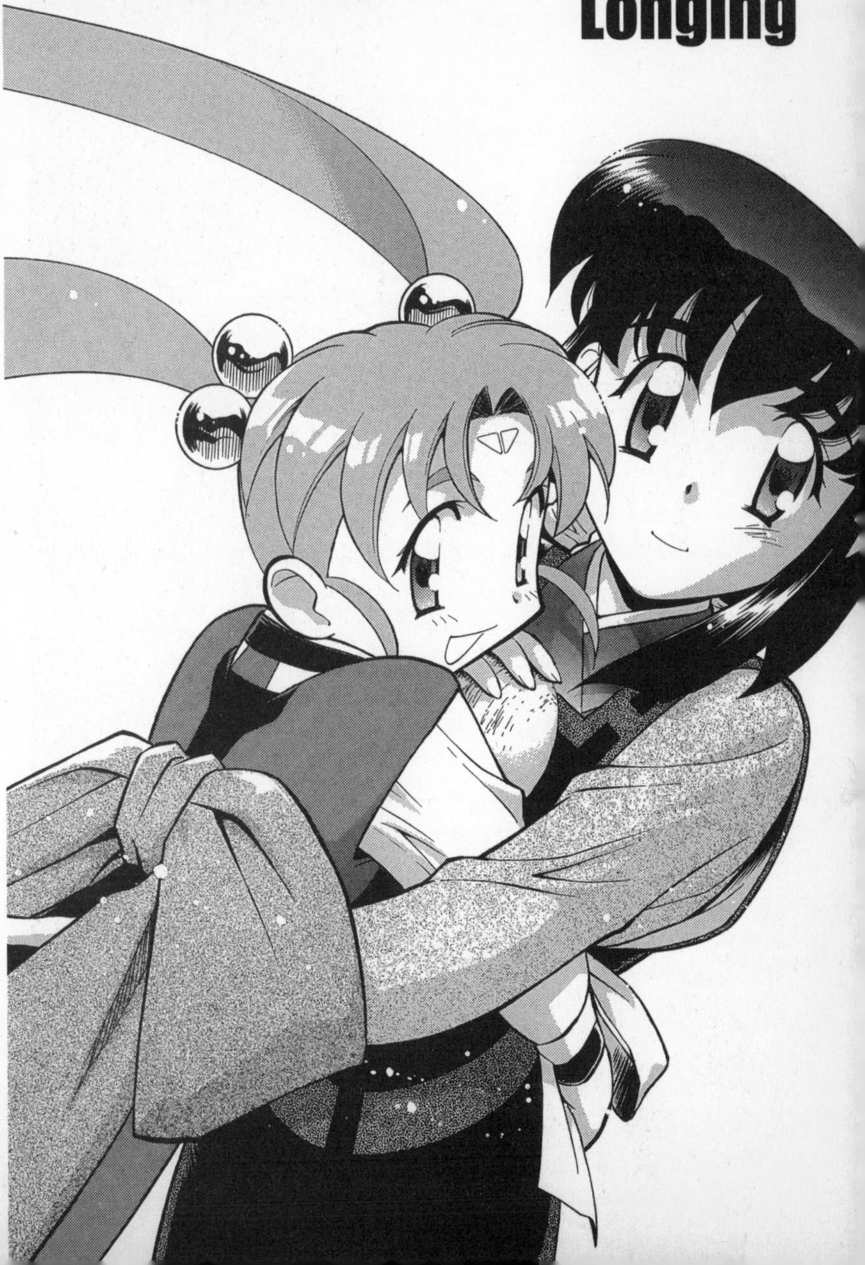

AYEKA AND SASAMI HAVE MADE THEIR WAY TO MIHOSHI'S SPACESHIP, IN ORBIT NEAR SATURN, TO OBTAIN PERMISSION TO EXTEND THEIR STAY ON EARTH...

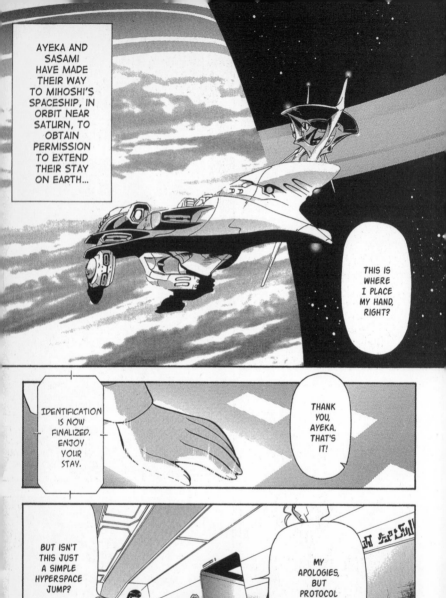

THIS IS WHERE I PLACE MY HAND, RIGHT?

IDENTIFICATION IS NOW FINALIZED. ENJOY YOUR STAY.

THANK YOU, AYEKA. THAT'S IT!

BUT ISN'T THIS JUST A SIMPLE HYPERSPACE JUMP?

MY APOLOGIES, BUT PROTOCOL IS MOST IMPORTANT IN THIS SITUATION.

YES!

THE SYSTEM WILL NOW VERIFY YOUR IDENTITY, SASAMI.

SO FATHER HAS...

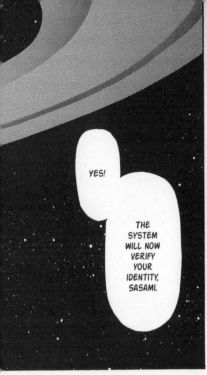

YOU SEE, I HAVE INSTRUCTIONS FROM THE EMPEROR OF JURAI TO GIVE THIS TO YOU *PERSONALLY*.

WHAT?

IS IT SOME SORT OF *SECRET*?

TEE HEE

NO...

...HE SAID IT WAS JUST A NOTE.

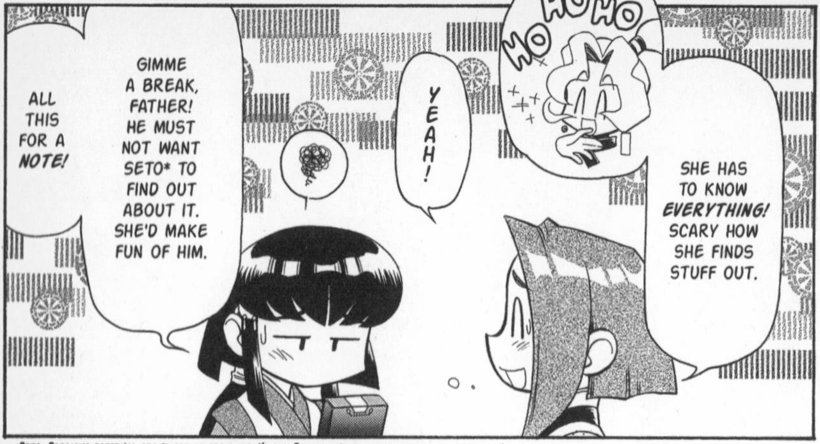
ALL THIS FOR A NOTE!
GIMME A BREAK, FATHER! HE MUST NOT WANT SETO* TO FIND OUT ABOUT IT. SHE'D MAKE FUN OF HIM.
YEAH!
HO HO HO HO
SHE HAS TO KNOW EVERYTHING! SCARY HOW SHE FINDS STUFF OUT.

*Seto: Sasami's paternal grandmother from the Kamiki Family, one of the four royal families of Jurai. Her information-gathering skills have lent her the name "Demonic Princess of Jurai."

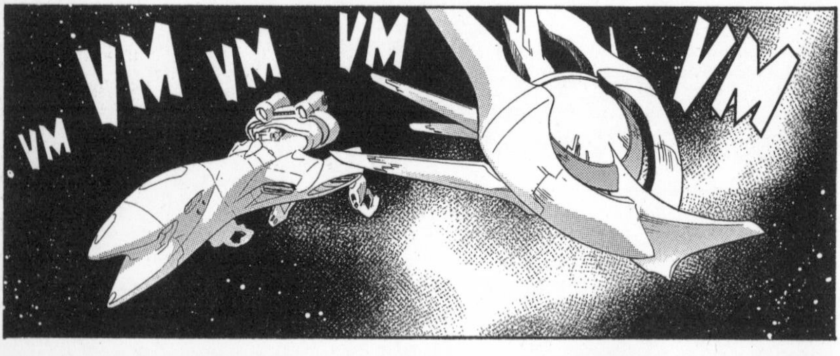
VM VM VM VM VM

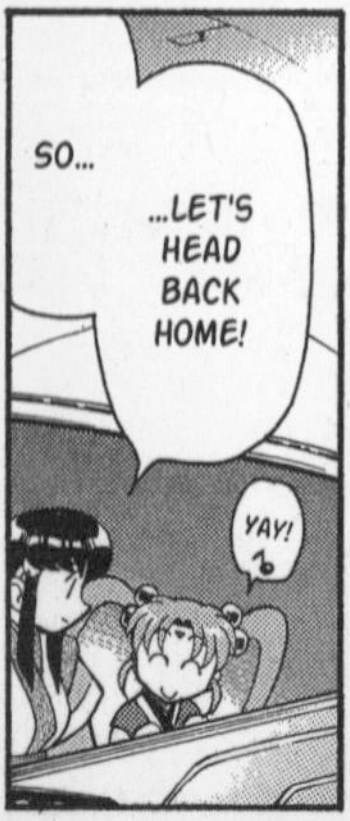
SO...
...LET'S HEAD BACK HOME!
YAY!

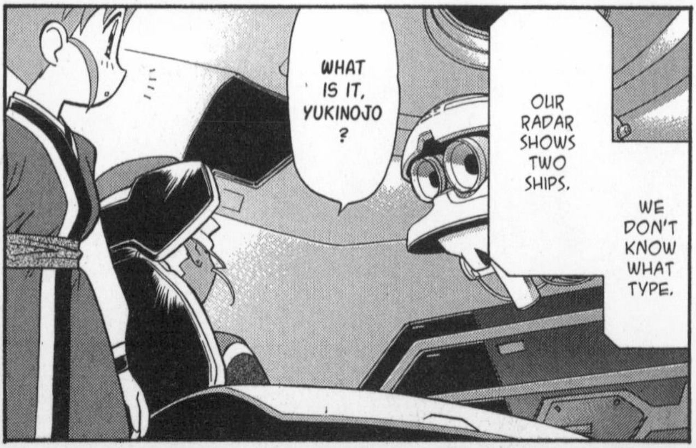
WHAT IS IT, YUKINOJO?
OUR RADAR SHOWS TWO SHIPS.
WE DON'T KNOW WHAT TYPE.

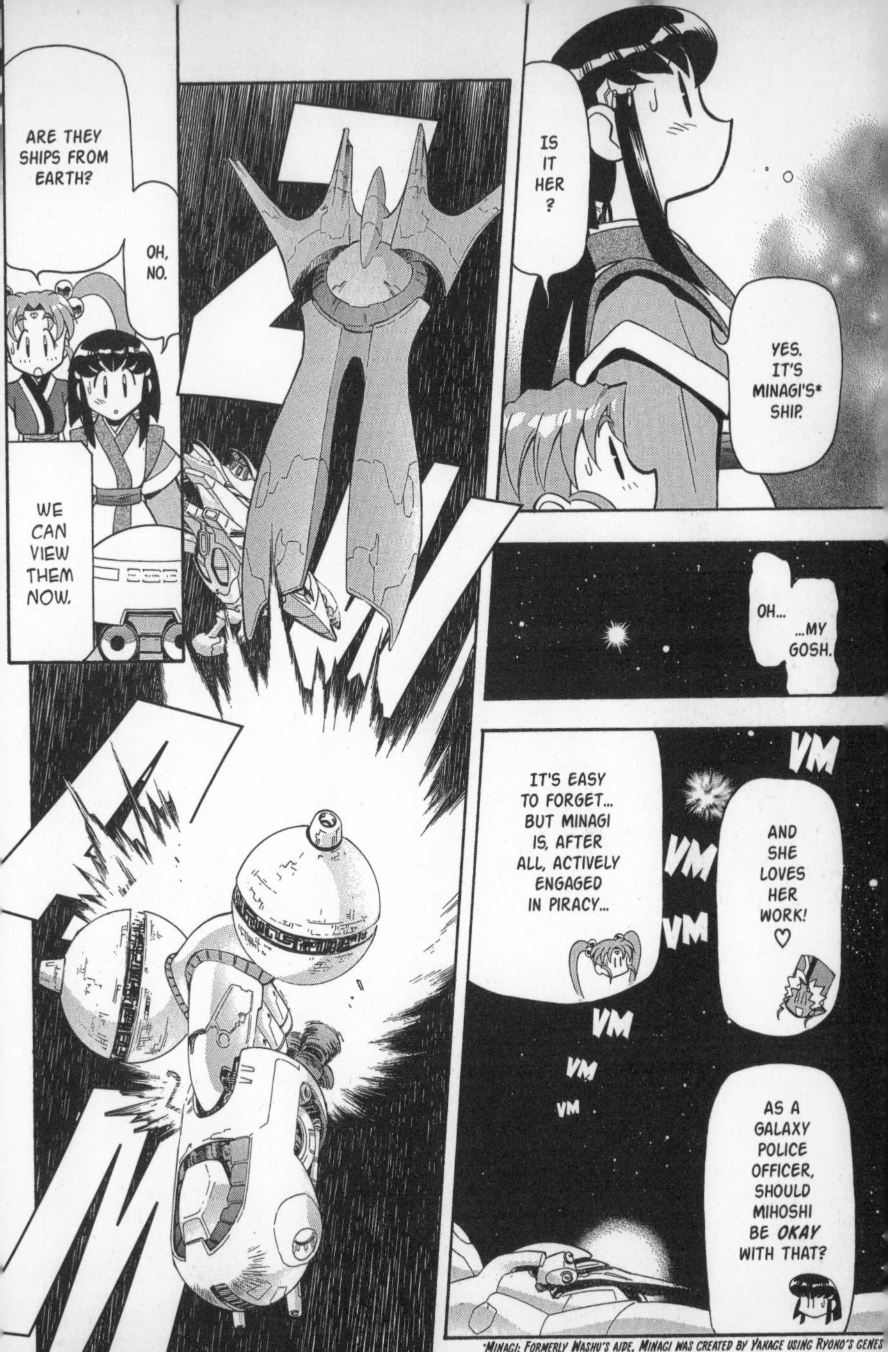
ARE THEY SHIPS FROM EARTH?
OH, NO.
WE CAN VIEW THEM NOW.
IS IT HER?
YES. IT'S MINAGI'S* SHIP.
OH...
...MY GOSH.
IT'S EASY TO FORGET... BUT MINAGI IS, AFTER ALL, ACTIVELY ENGAGED IN PIRACY...
VM
VM
VM
VM
VM
VM
AND SHE LOVES HER WORK! ♡
AS A GALAXY POLICE OFFICER, SHOULD MIHOSHI BE *OKAY* WITH THAT?

*MINAGI: FORMERLY WASHU'S AIDE, MINAGI WAS CREATED BY YAKAGE USING RYOKO'S GENES

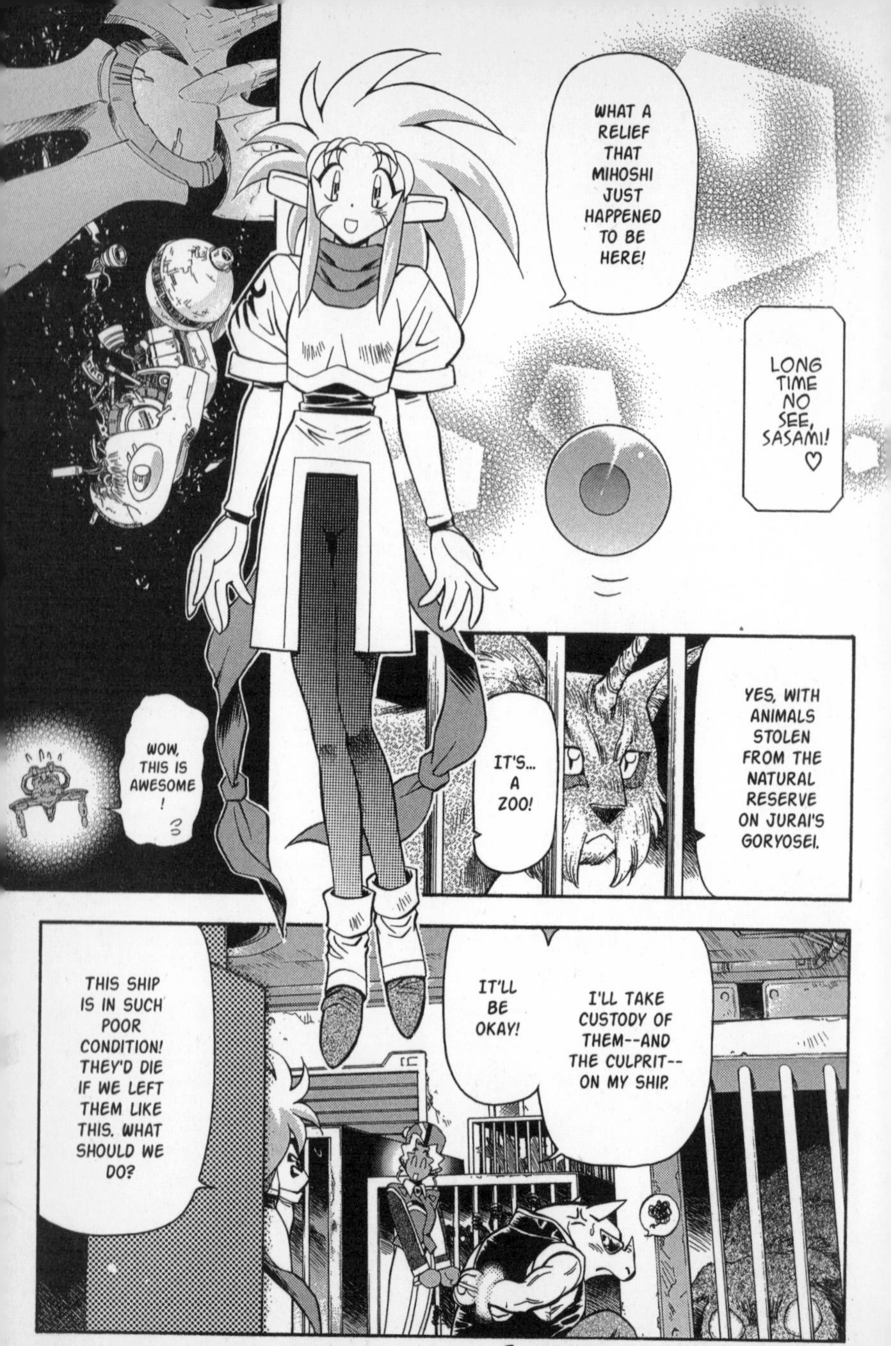
WHAT A RELIEF THAT MIHOSHI JUST HAPPENED TO BE HERE!
LONG TIME NO SEE, SASAMI! ♡
WOW, THIS IS AWESOME!
IT'S... A ZOO!
YES, WITH ANIMALS STOLEN FROM THE NATURAL RESERVE ON JURAI'S GORYOSEI.
THIS SHIP IS IN SUCH POOR CONDITION! THEY'D DIE IF WE LEFT THEM LIKE THIS. WHAT SHOULD WE DO?
IT'LL BE OKAY!
I'LL TAKE CUSTODY OF THEM--AND THE CULPRIT--ON MY SHIP.
THE CULPRIT ▲

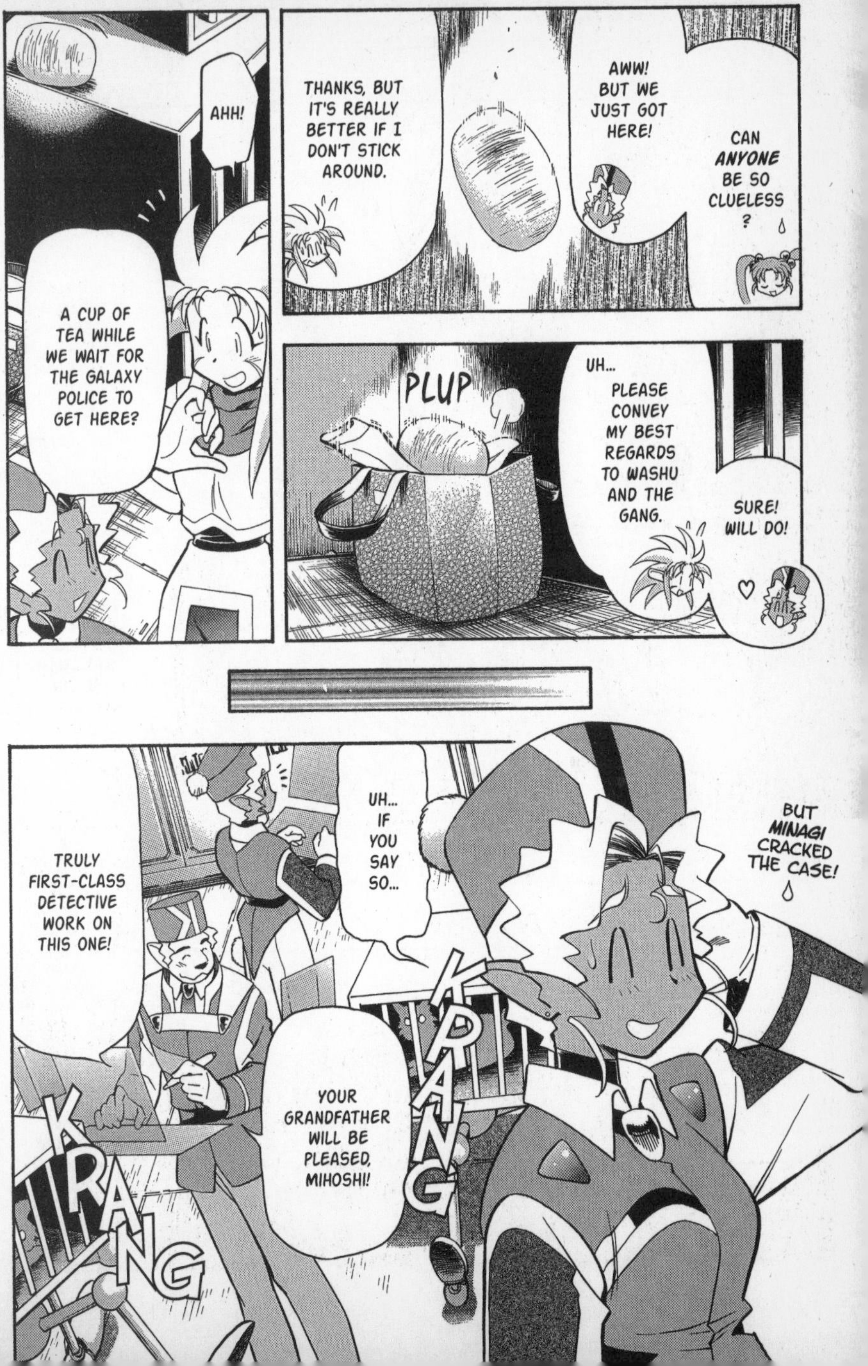
AHH!
A CUP OF TEA WHILE WE WAIT FOR THE GALAXY POLICE TO GET HERE?
THANKS, BUT IT'S REALLY BETTER IF I DON'T STICK AROUND.
AWW! BUT WE JUST GOT HERE!
CAN ANYONE BE SO CLUELESS ?
PLUP
UH... PLEASE CONVEY MY BEST REGARDS TO WASHU AND THE GANG.
SURE! WILL DO!
TRULY FIRST-CLASS DETECTIVE WORK ON THIS ONE!
UH... IF YOU SAY SO...
BUT MINAGI CRACKED THE CASE!
YOUR GRANDFATHER WILL BE PLEASED, MIHOSHI!
KRANG
KRANG

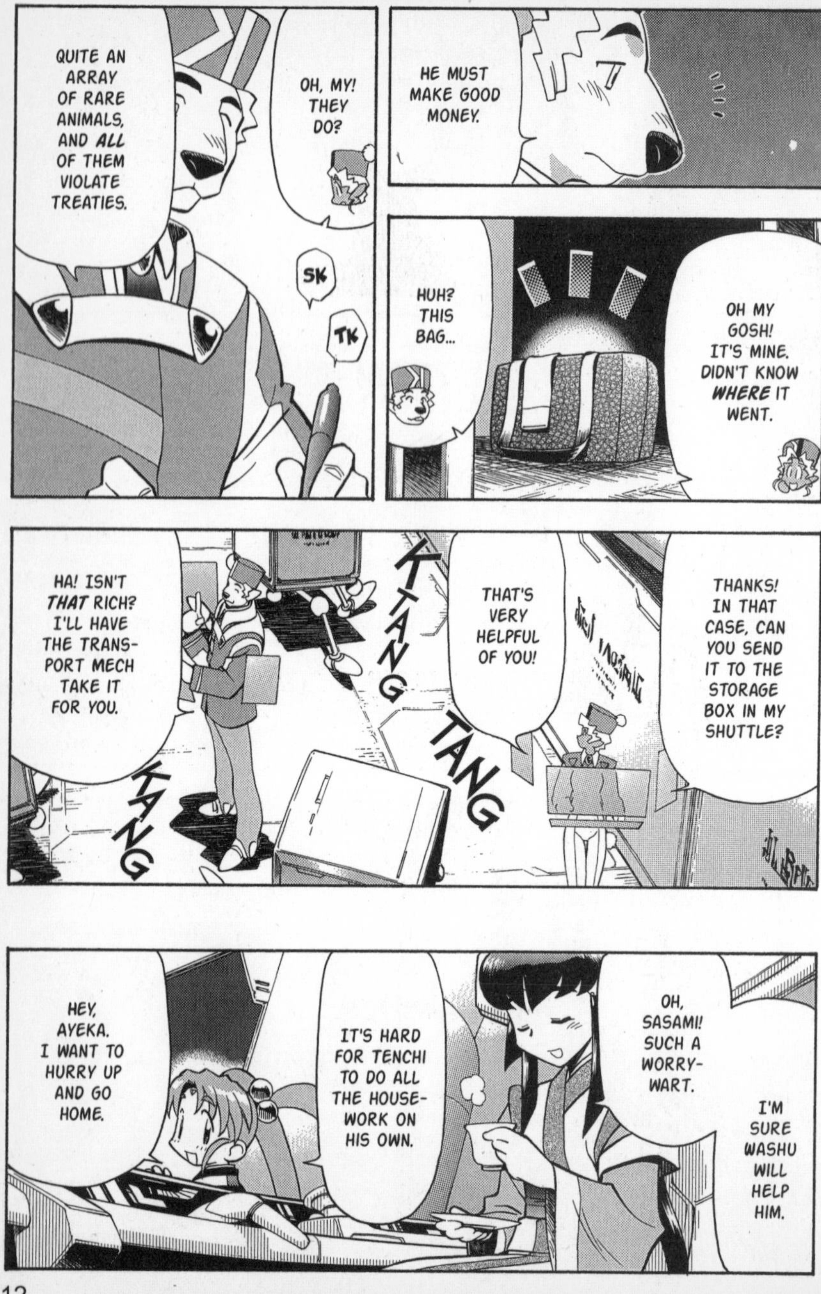
QUITE AN ARRAY OF RARE ANIMALS, AND *ALL* OF THEM VIOLATE TREATIES.
OH, MY! THEY DO?
SK
TK
HE MUST MAKE GOOD MONEY.
HUH? THIS BAG...
OH MY GOSH! IT'S MINE. DIDN'T KNOW *WHERE* IT WENT.
HA! ISN'T *THAT* RICH? I'LL HAVE THE TRANSPORT MECH TAKE IT FOR YOU.
KTANG
KANG
THAT'S VERY HELPFUL OF YOU!
TANG
THANKS! IN THAT CASE, CAN YOU SEND IT TO THE STORAGE BOX IN MY SHUTTLE?
HEY, AYEKA. I WANT TO HURRY UP AND GO HOME.
IT'S HARD FOR TENCHI TO DO ALL THE HOUSEWORK ON HIS OWN.
OH, SASAMI! SUCH A WORRYWART.
I'M SURE WASHU WILL HELP HIM.

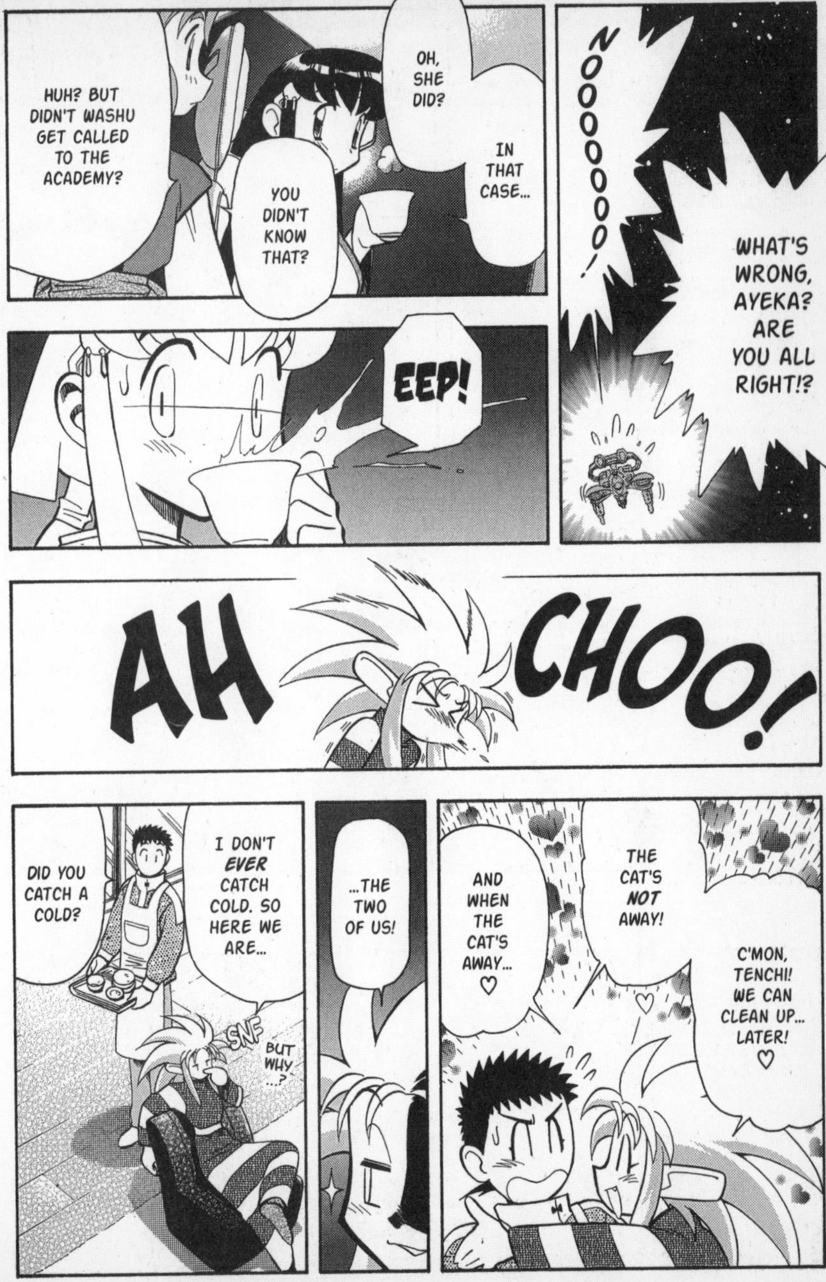
HUH? BUT DIDN'T WASHU GET CALLED TO THE ACADEMY?
OH, SHE DID?
YOU DIDN'T KNOW THAT?
IN THAT CASE...
EEP!
NOOOOOOOO!
WHAT'S WRONG, AYEKA? ARE YOU ALL RIGHT!?
AH CHOO!
DID YOU CATCH A COLD?
I DON'T EVER CATCH COLD. SO HERE WE ARE...
SNF
BUT WHY...?
...THE TWO OF US!
AND WHEN THE CAT'S AWAY... ♡
THE CAT'S NOT AWAY!
C'MON, TENCHI! WE CAN CLEAN UP... LATER! ♡

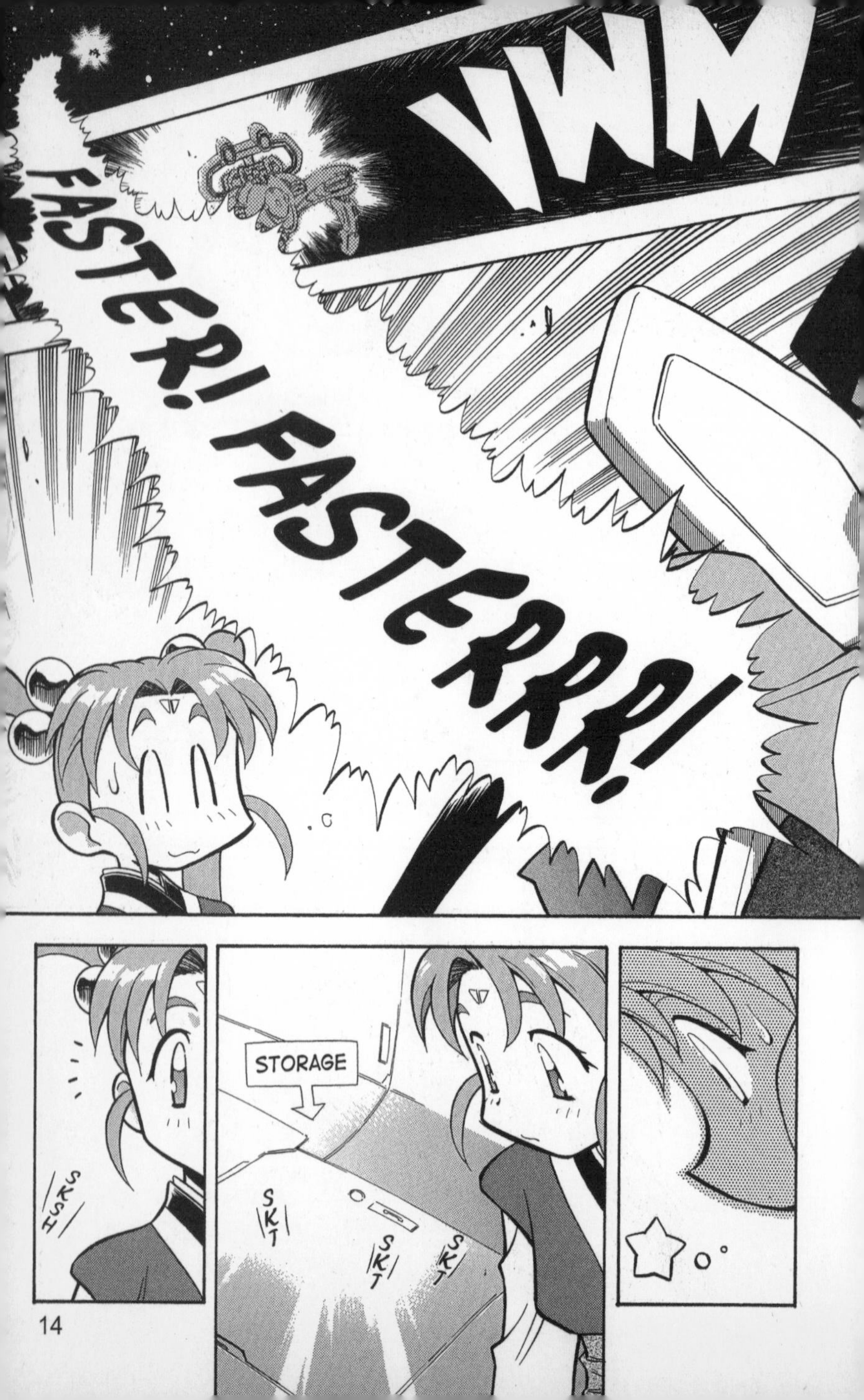
VWM
FASTER! FASTER! FASTERRR!
STORAGE
SKSH
SKT
SKT
SKT

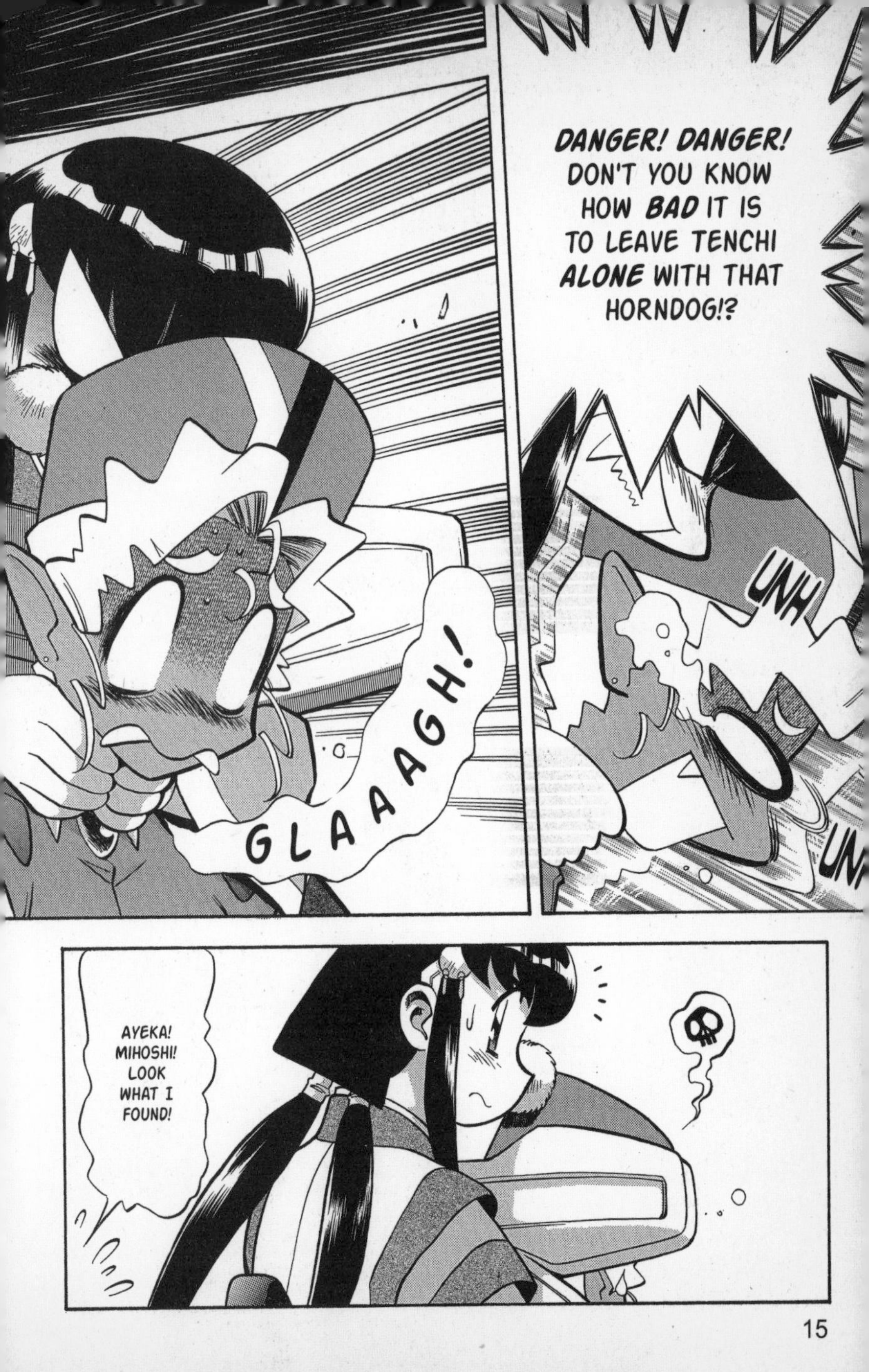
GLAAAGH!
DANGER! DANGER! DON'T YOU KNOW HOW BAD IT IS TO LEAVE TENCHI ALONE WITH THAT HORNDOG!?
UNH
UN
AYEKA! MIHOSHI! LOOK WHAT I FOUND!

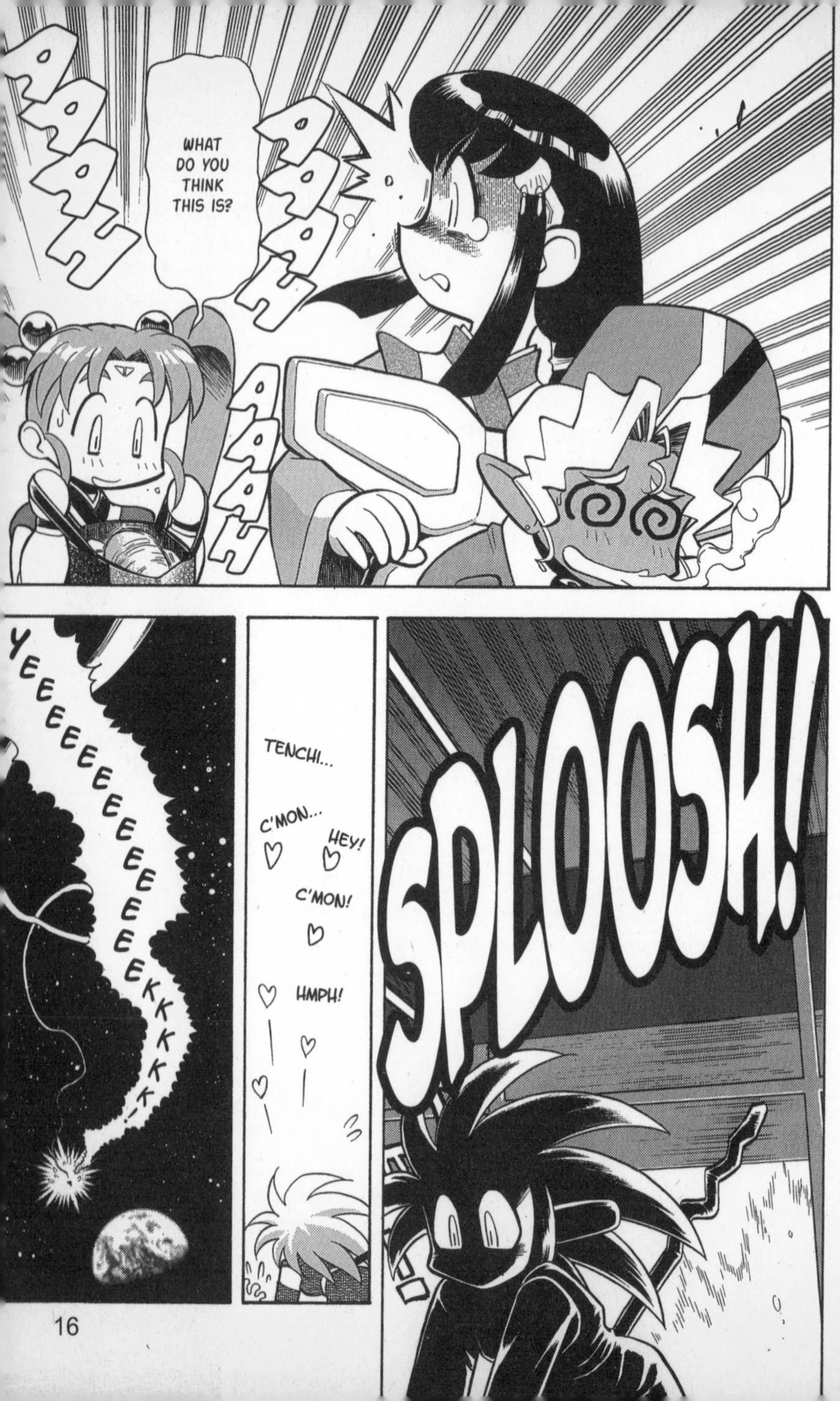
AAAAAH
WHAT DO YOU THINK THIS IS?
AAAAAH
AAAAH
YEEEEEEEEEEEEEEEKKKKKK!
TENCHI...
C'MON...
HEY!
C'MON!
HMPH!
SPLOOSH!

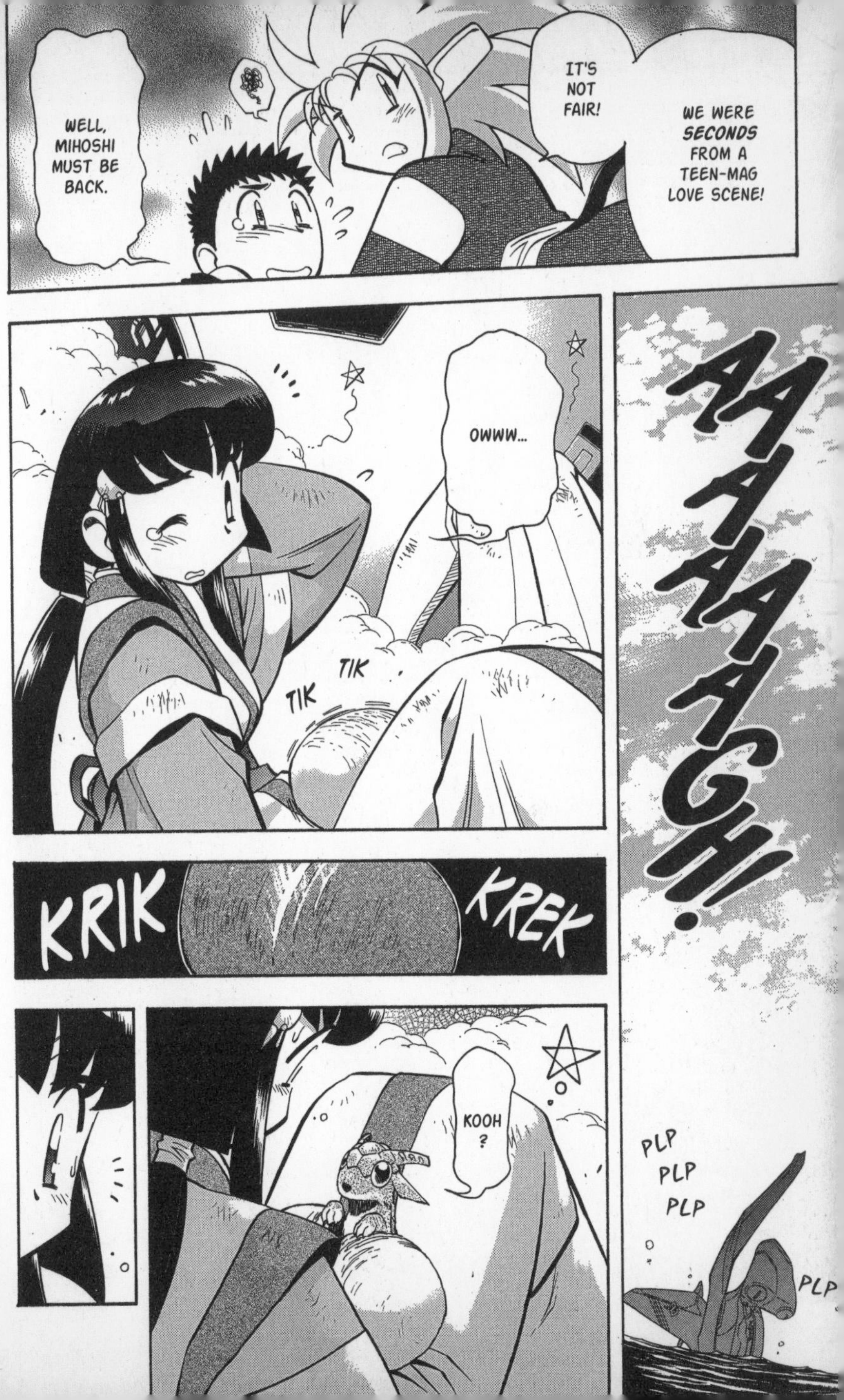

WELL, MIHOSHI MUST BE BACK.
IT'S NOT FAIR!
WE WERE SECONDS FROM A TEEN-MAG LOVE SCENE!
OWWW...
TIK
TIK
KRIK
KREK
KOOH ?
AAAAAAGH!!!
PLP
PLP
PLP
PLP

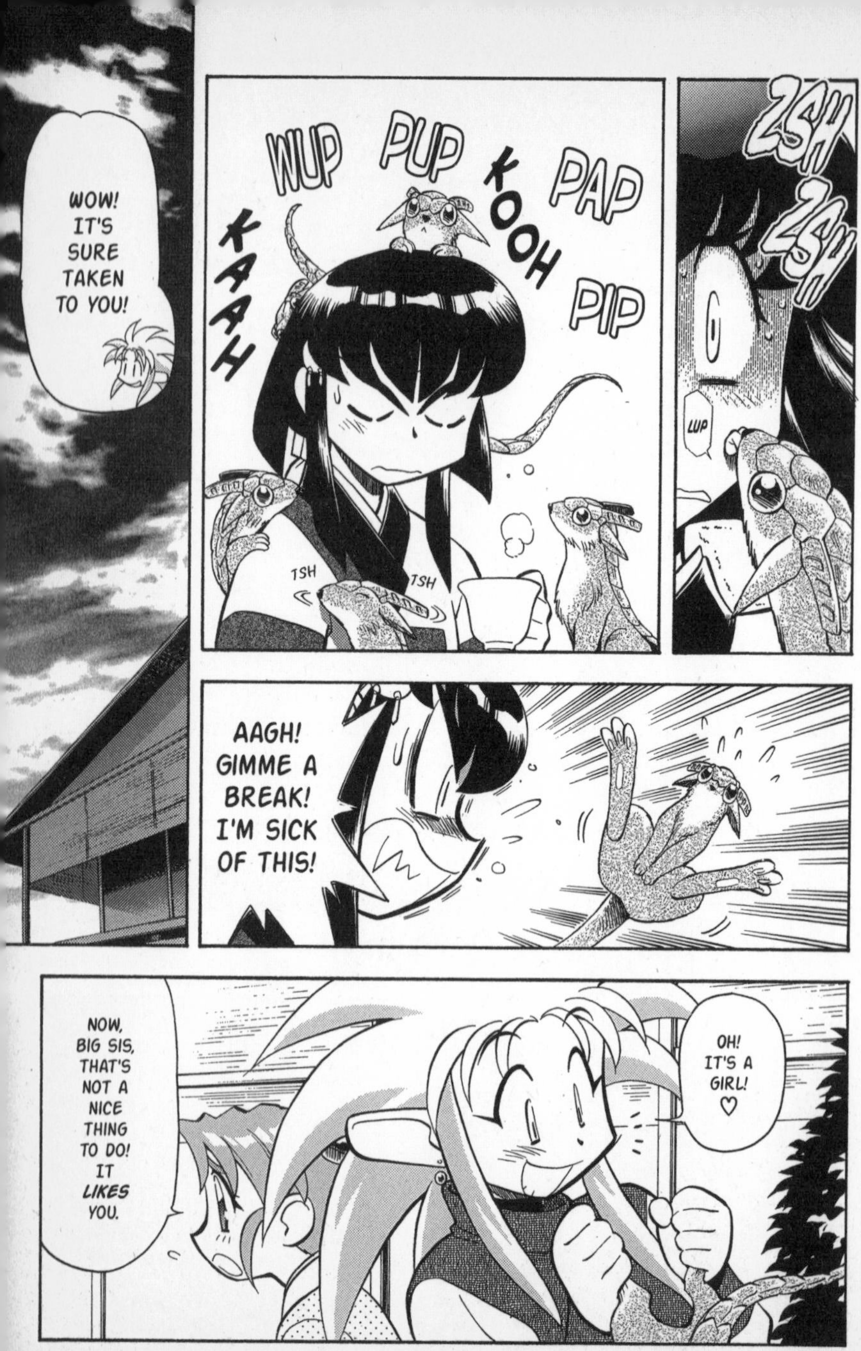

WOW! IT'S SURE TAKEN TO YOU!
WUP
PUP
PAP
KOOH
KAAAH
PIP
TSH
TSH
ZSH
ZSH
LUP
AAGH! GIMME A BREAK! I'M SICK OF THIS!
NOW, BIG SIS, THAT'S NOT A NICE THING TO DO! IT *LIKES* YOU.
OH! IT'S A GIRL! ♡

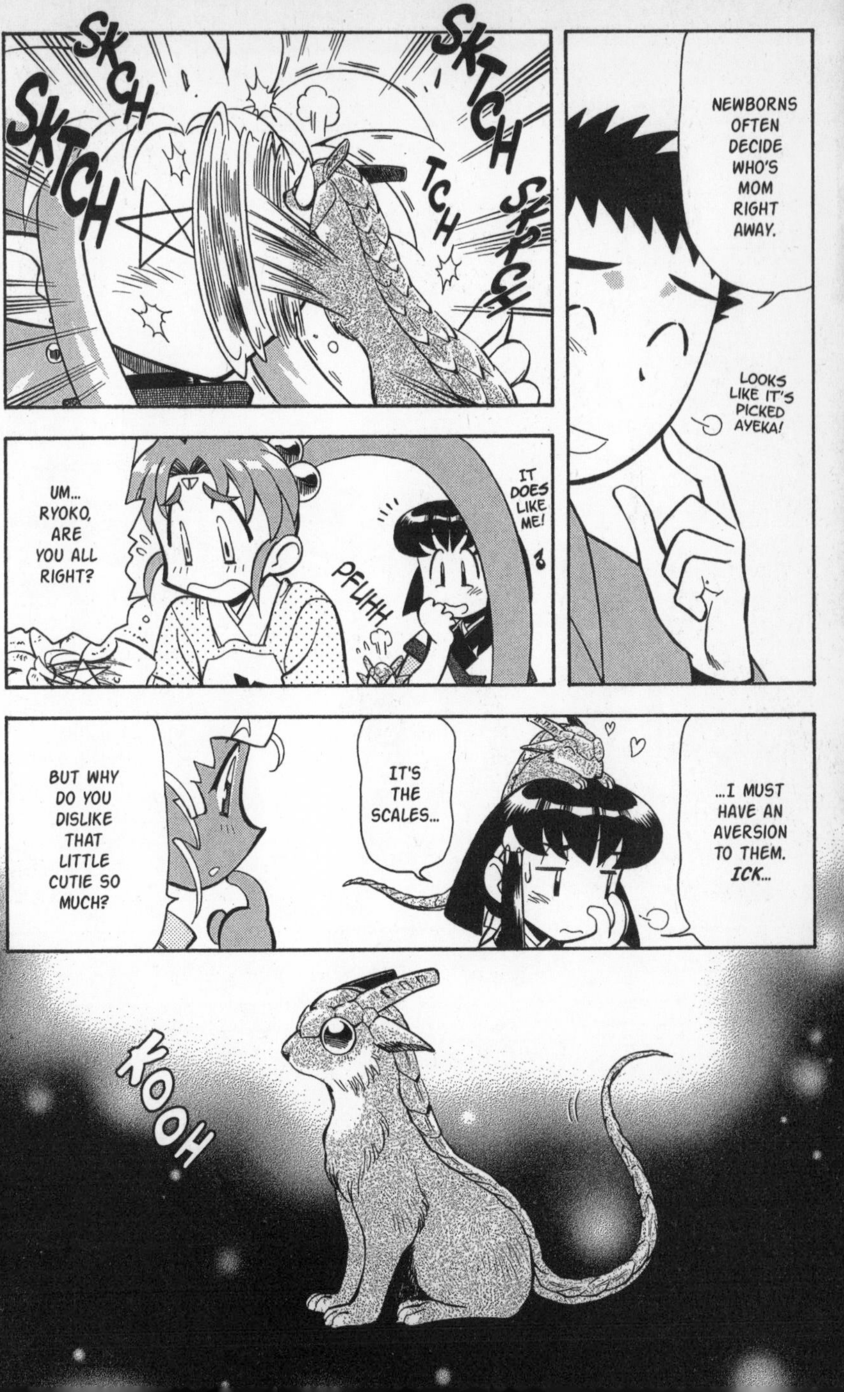
SKCH
SKTCH
SKTCH
TCH
SKPCH
UM... RYOKO, ARE YOU ALL RIGHT?
IT DOES LIKE ME!
PFUHH
NEWBORNS OFTEN DECIDE WHO'S MOM RIGHT AWAY.
LOOKS LIKE IT'S PICKED AYEKA!
BUT WHY DO YOU DISLIKE THAT LITTLE CUTIE SO MUCH?
IT'S THE SCALES...
...I MUST HAVE AN AVERSION TO THEM. *ICK*...
KOOH

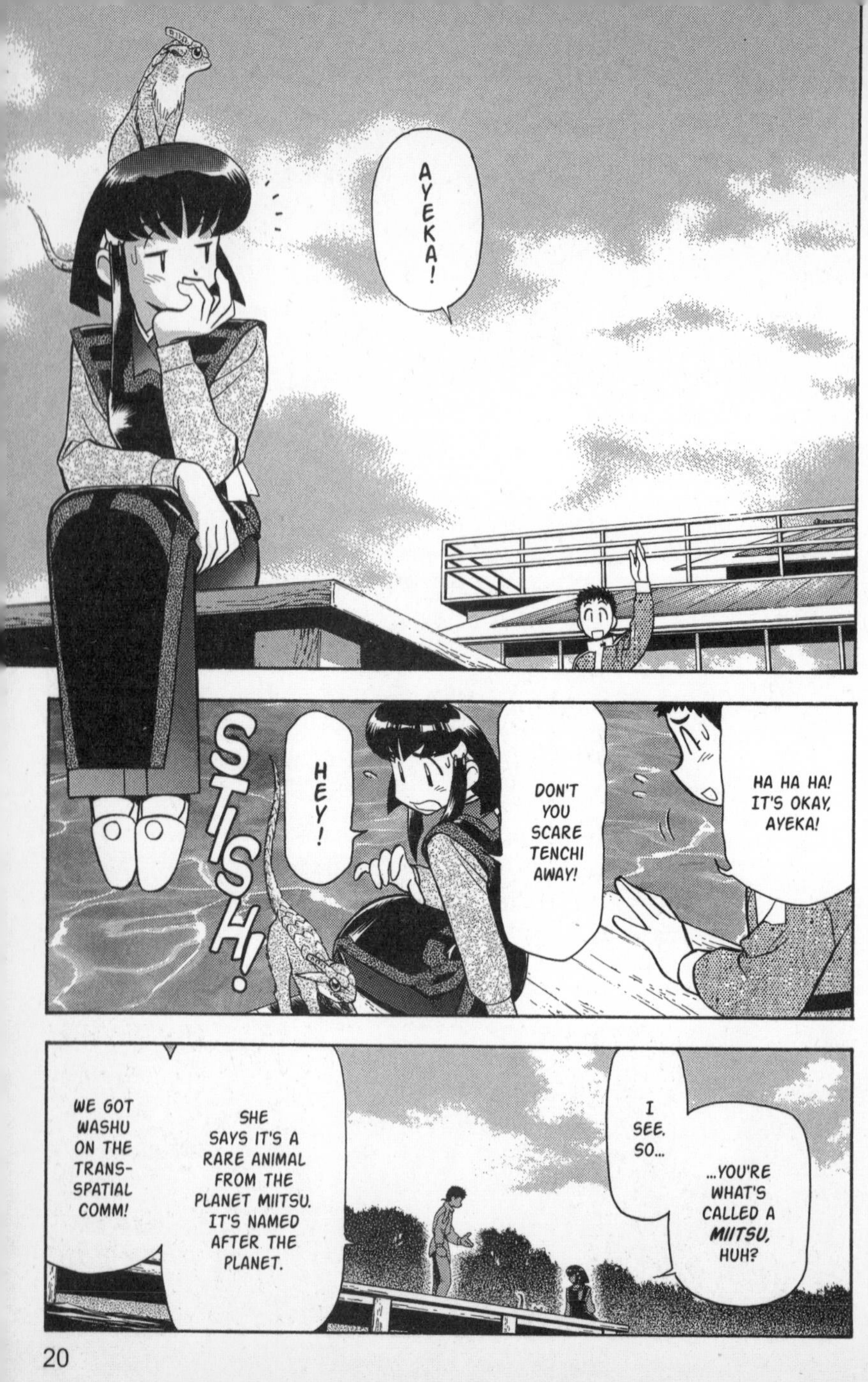

AYEKA!
STISH!
HEY!
DON'T YOU SCARE TENCHI AWAY!
HA HA HA! IT'S OKAY, AYEKA!
WE GOT WASHU ON THE TRANS-SPATIAL COMM!
SHE SAYS IT'S A RARE ANIMAL FROM THE PLANET MIITSU. IT'S NAMED AFTER THE PLANET.
I SEE. SO...
...YOU'RE WHAT'S CALLED A *MIITSU*, HUH?

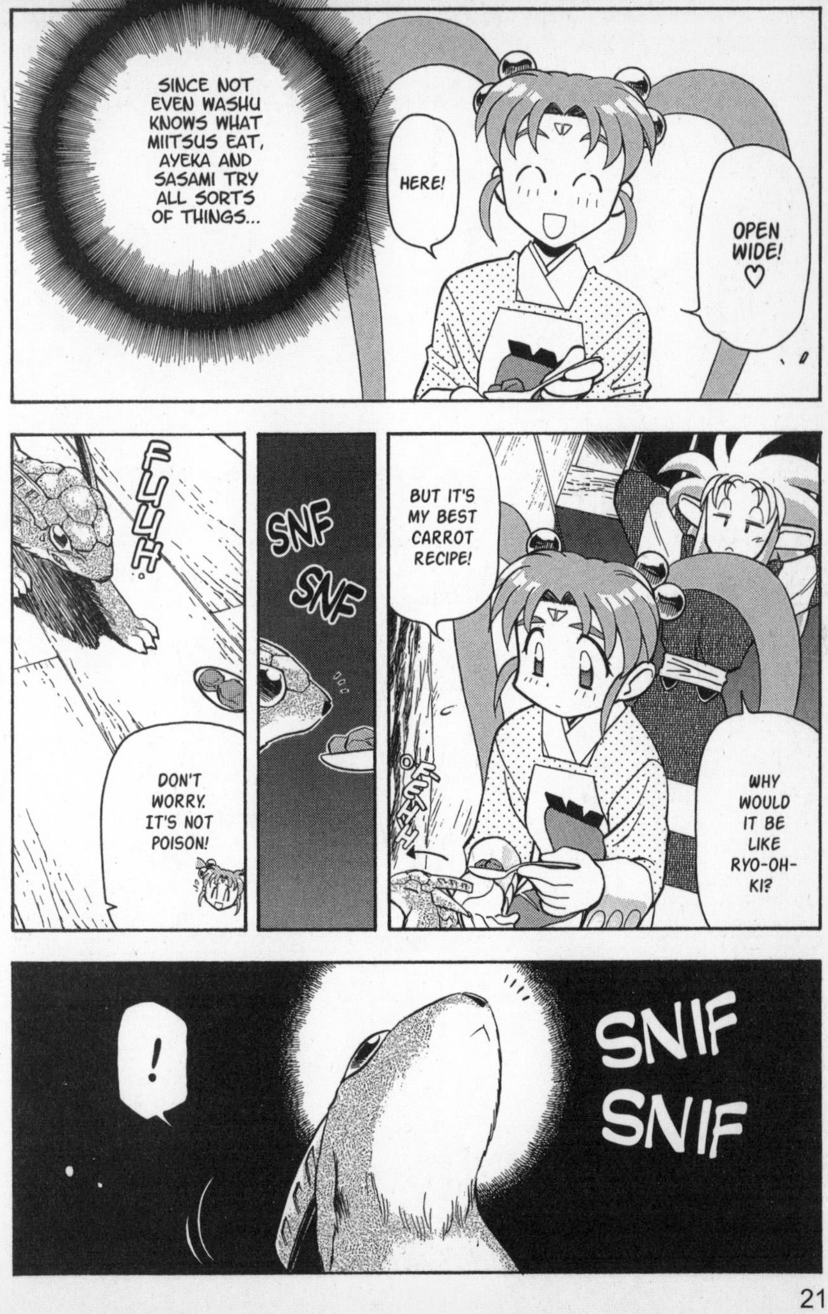
SINCE NOT EVEN WASHU KNOWS WHAT MIITSUS EAT, AYEKA AND SASAMI TRY ALL SORTS OF THINGS...
HERE!
OPEN WIDE! ♡
FLUUH
DON'T WORRY. IT'S NOT POISON!
SNF
SNF
BUT IT'S MY BEST CARROT RECIPE!
WHY WOULD IT BE LIKE RYO-OH-KI?
!
SNIF
SNIF

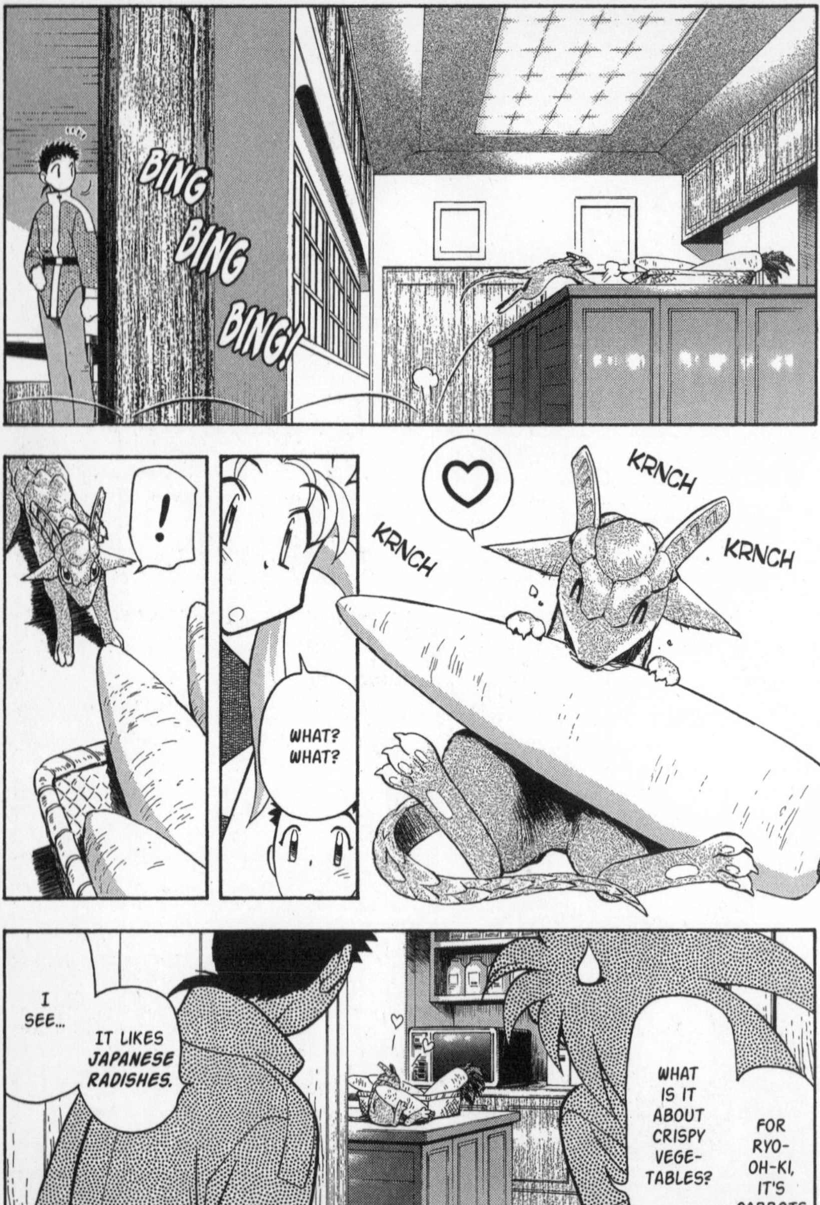
BING
BING
BING!
!
WHAT? WHAT?
KRNCH
KRNCH
KRNCH
I SEE...
IT LIKES JAPANESE RADISHES.
WHAT IS IT ABOUT CRISPY VEGE-TABLES?
FOR RYO-OH-KI, IT'S CARROTS ...

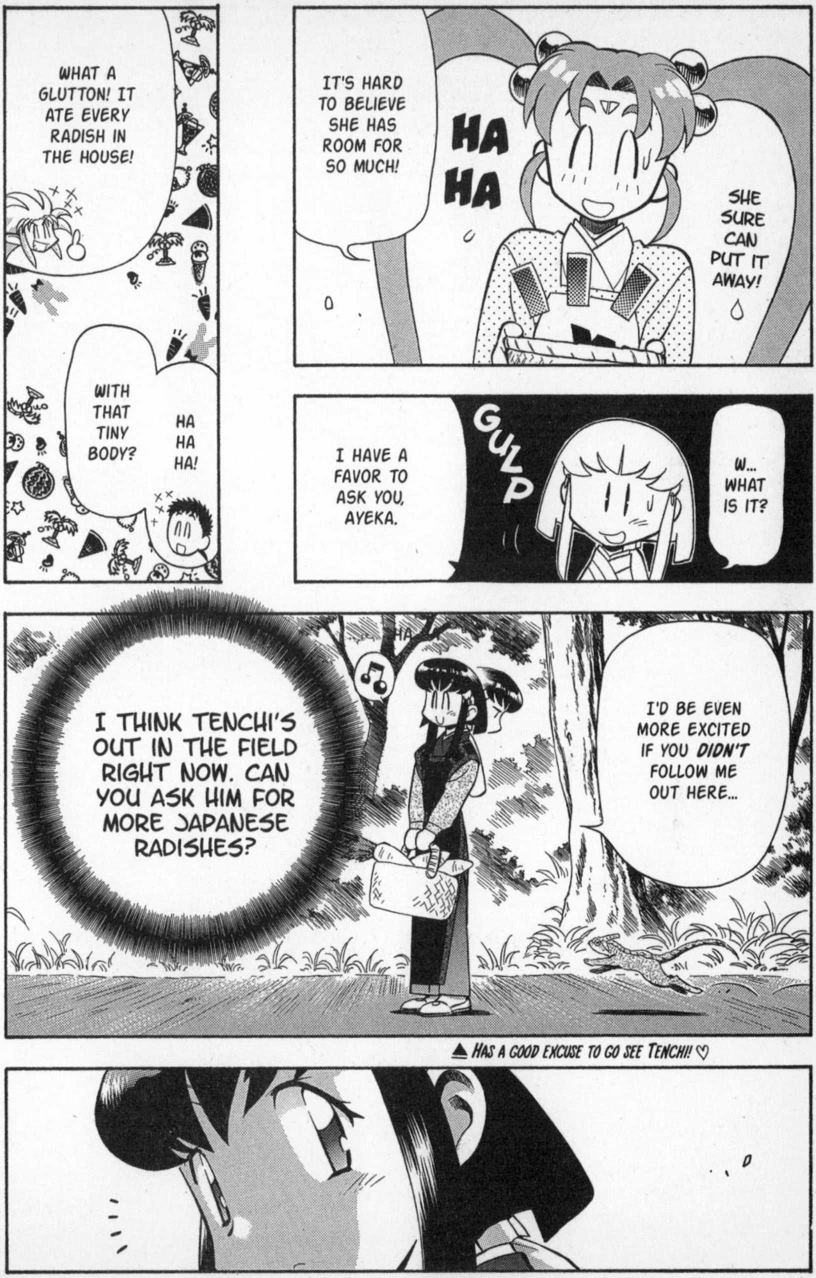
WHAT A GLUTTON! IT ATE EVERY RADISH IN THE HOUSE!
WITH THAT TINY BODY?
HA HA HA!
IT'S HARD TO BELIEVE SHE HAS ROOM FOR SO MUCH!
HA HA
SHE SURE CAN PUT IT AWAY!
I HAVE A FAVOR TO ASK YOU, AYEKA.
GULP
W... WHAT IS IT?
I THINK TENCHI'S OUT IN THE FIELD RIGHT NOW. CAN YOU ASK HIM FOR MORE JAPANESE RADISHES?
HA
I'D BE EVEN MORE EXCITED IF YOU *DIDN'T* FOLLOW ME OUT HERE...
▲ HAS A GOOD EXCUSE TO GO SEE TENCHI! ♡

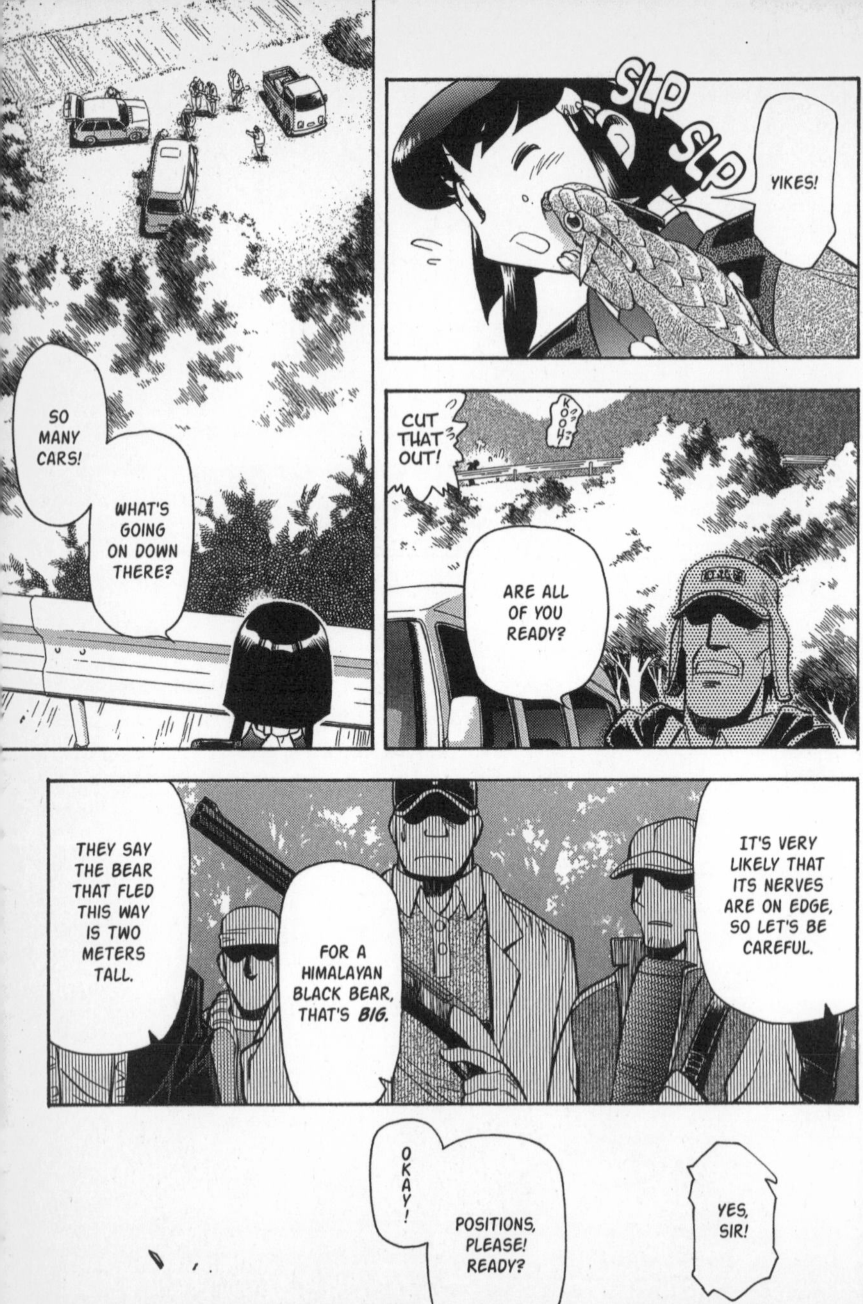

SO MANY CARS!
WHAT'S GOING ON DOWN THERE?
SLP SLP
YIKES!
CUT THAT OUT!
KOOH
ARE ALL OF YOU READY?
THEY SAY THE BEAR THAT FLED THIS WAY IS TWO METERS TALL.
FOR A HIMALAYAN BLACK BEAR, THAT'S *BIG.*
IT'S VERY LIKELY THAT ITS NERVES ARE ON EDGE, SO LET'S BE CAREFUL.
OKAY!
POSITIONS, PLEASE! READY?
YES, SIR!

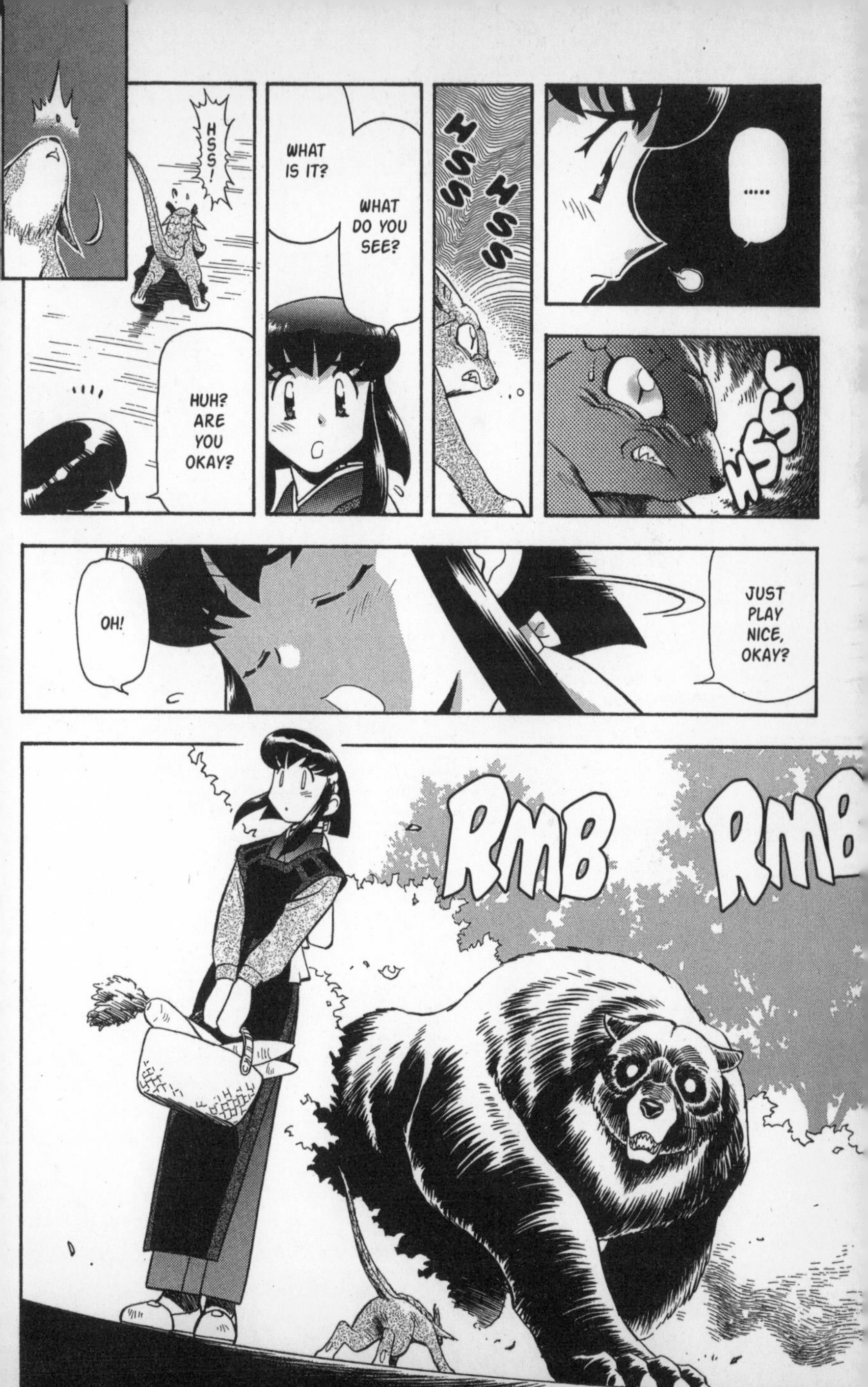
HSS!
HUH? ARE YOU OKAY?
WHAT IS IT?
WHAT DO YOU SEE?
HSS HSS
.....
HSSS
OH!
JUST PLAY NICE, OKAY?
RMB RMB

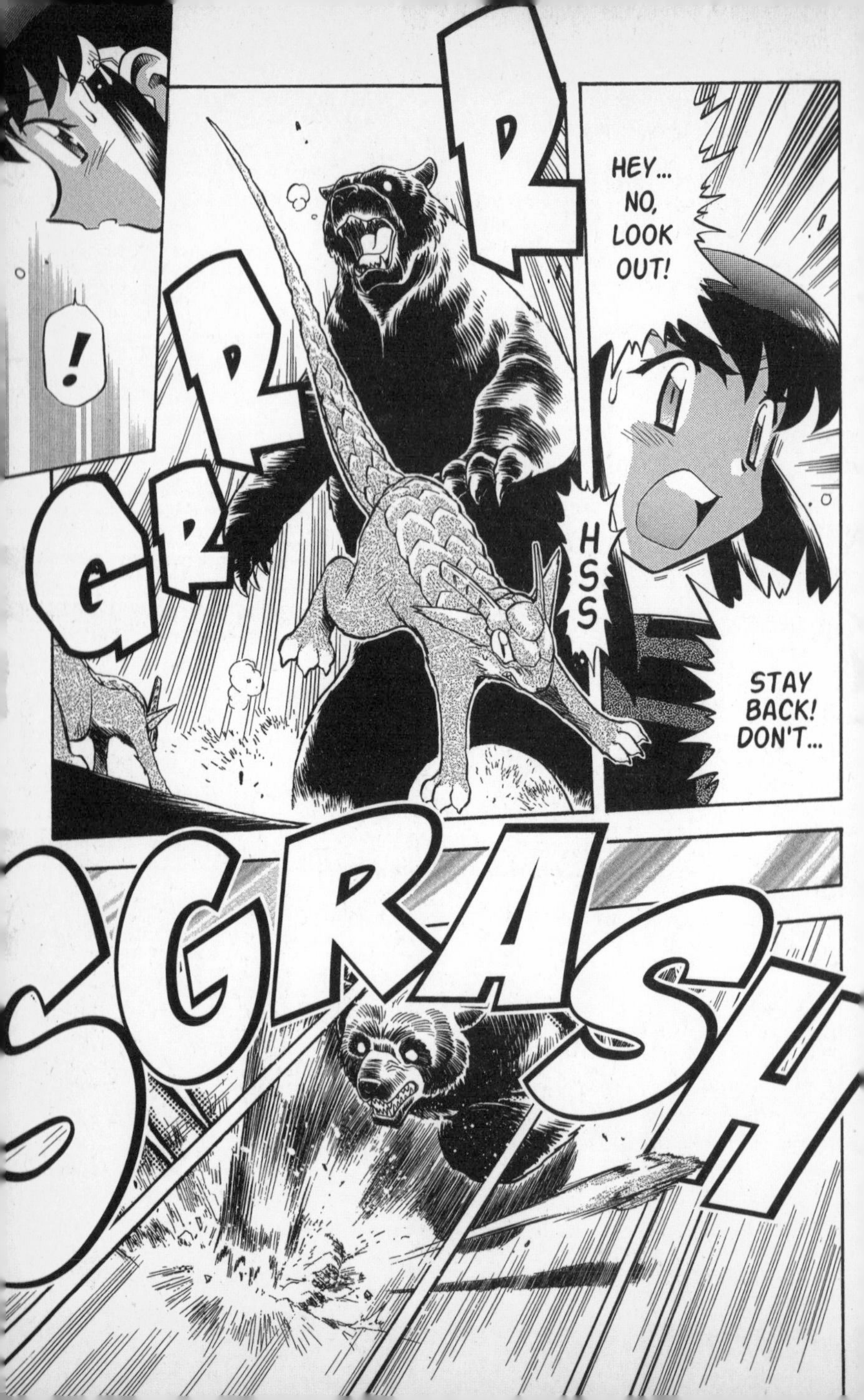
!
GRRR
HSS
HEY... NO, LOOK OUT!
STAY BACK! DON'T...
SCRASH

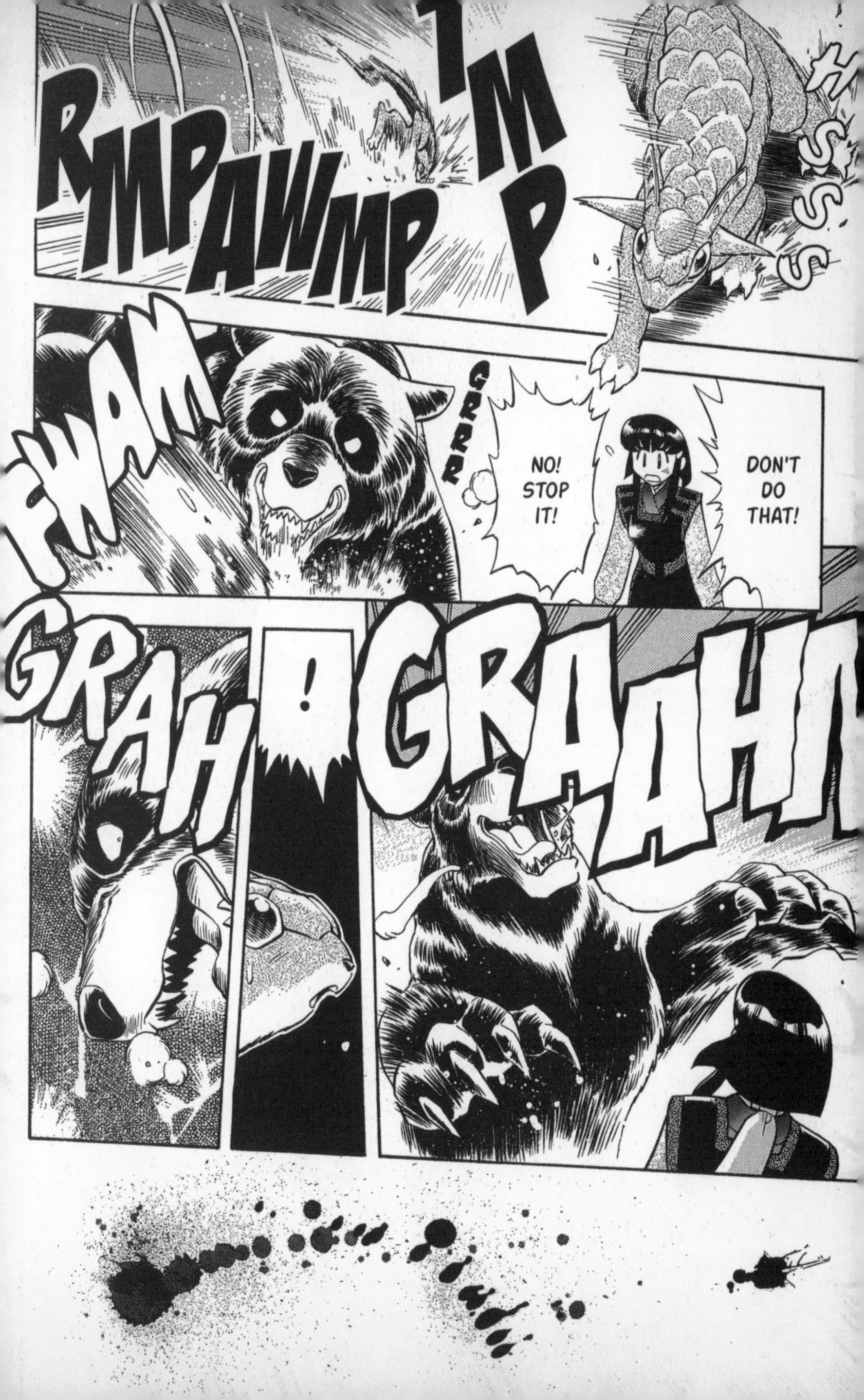
RMP
AWMP
MP
SSS
FWAM
GRRR
NO! STOP IT!
DON'T DO THAT!
GRAH
!
GRAAH

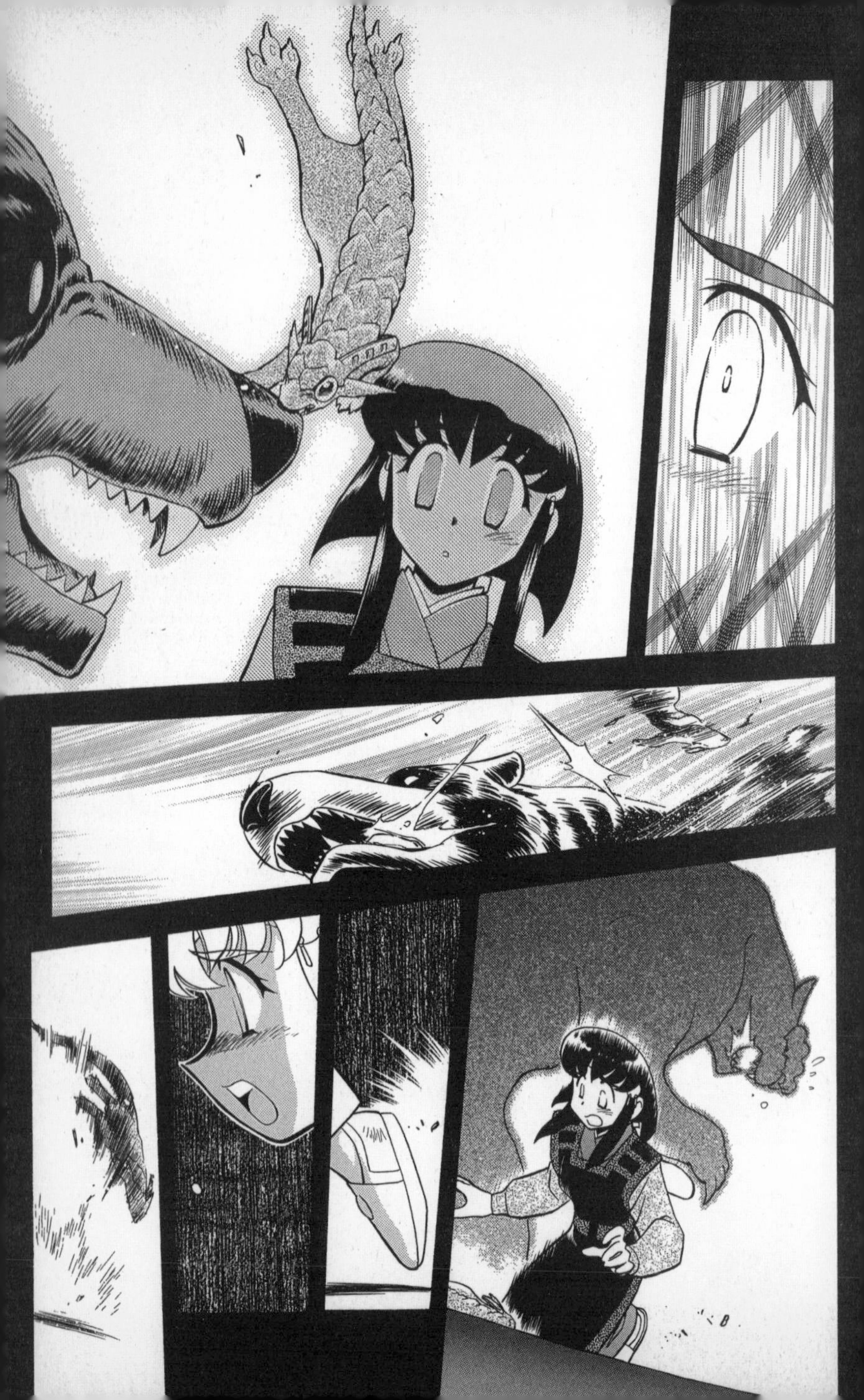

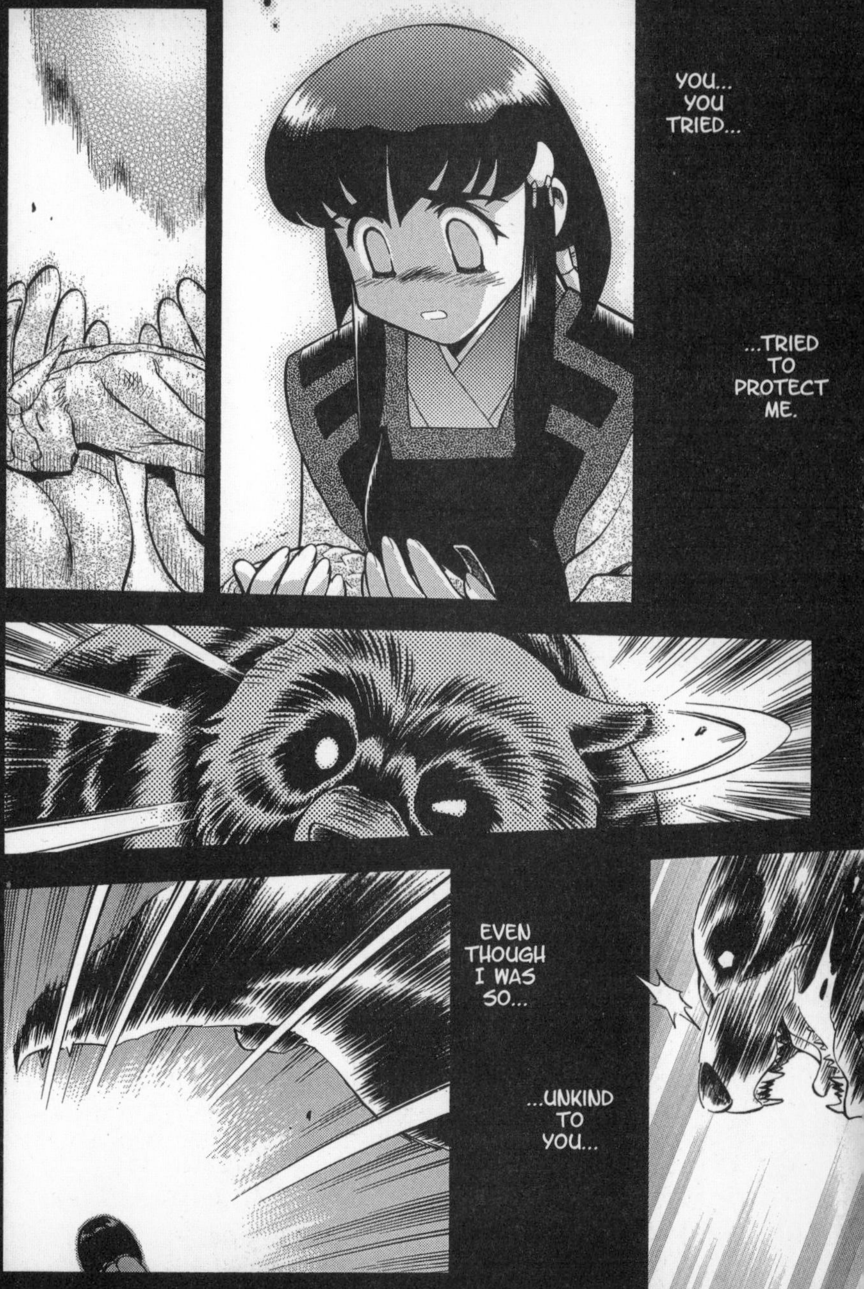
YOU... YOU TRIED...
...TRIED TO PROTECT ME.
EVEN THOUGH I WAS SO...
...UNKIND TO YOU...

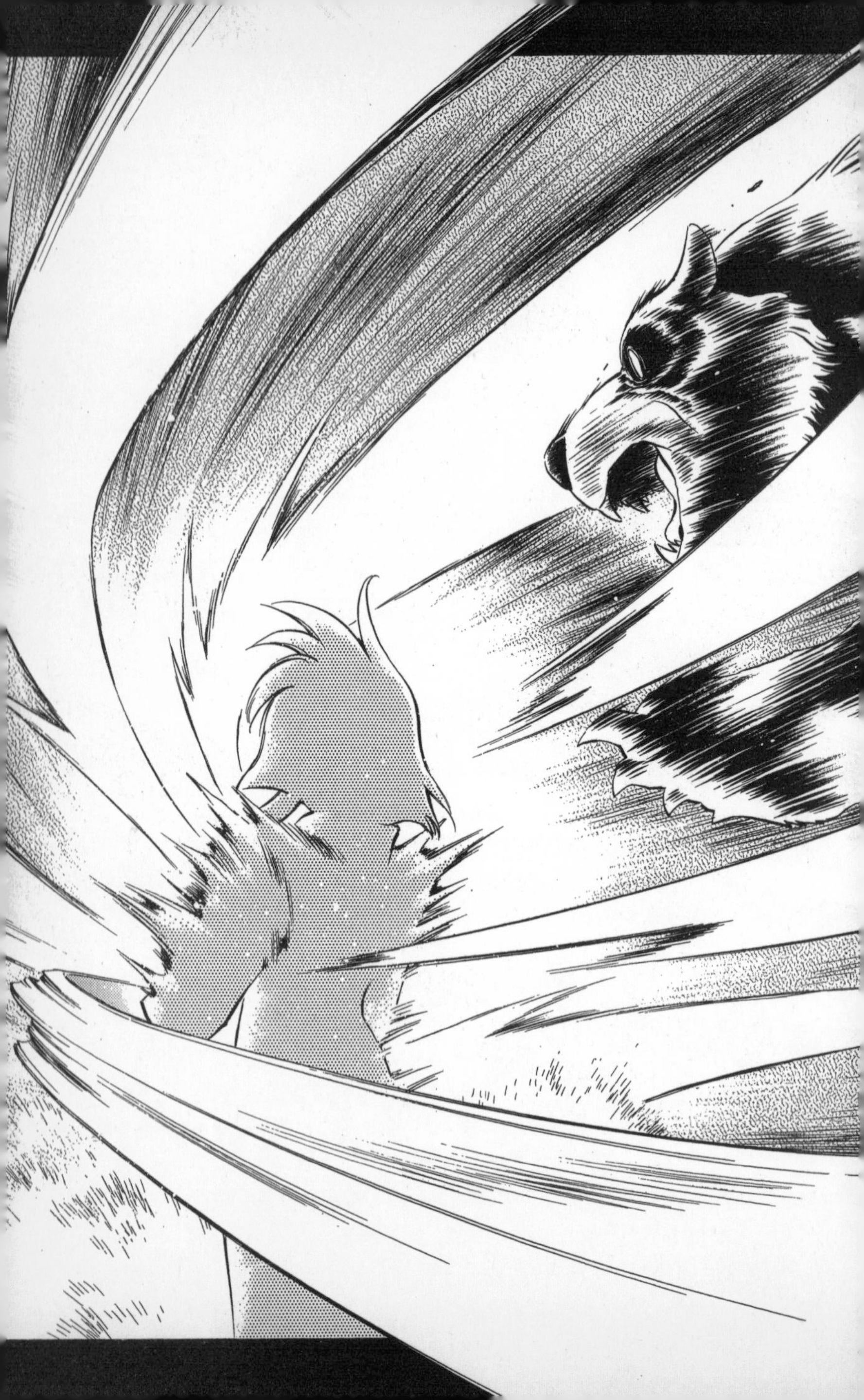

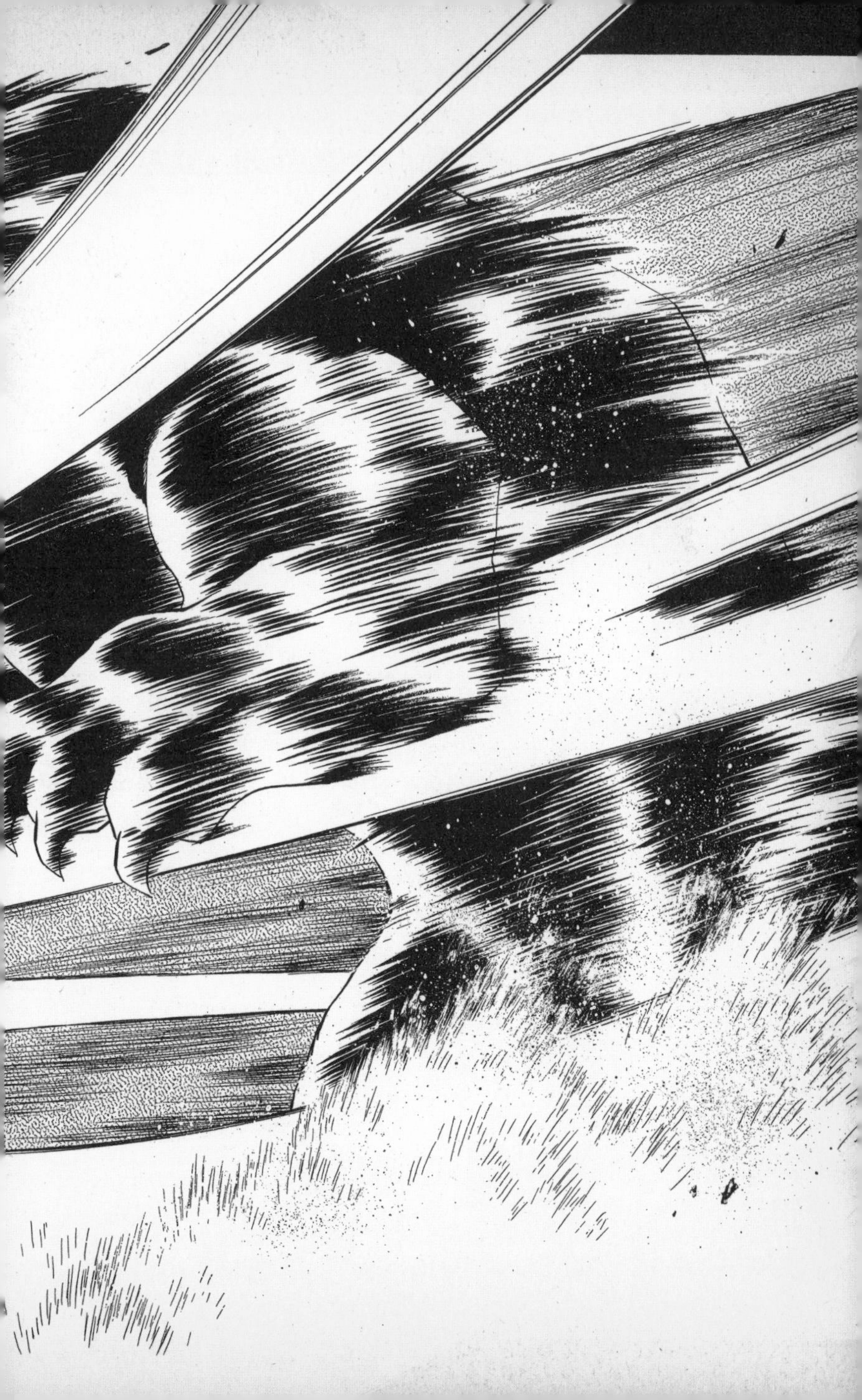

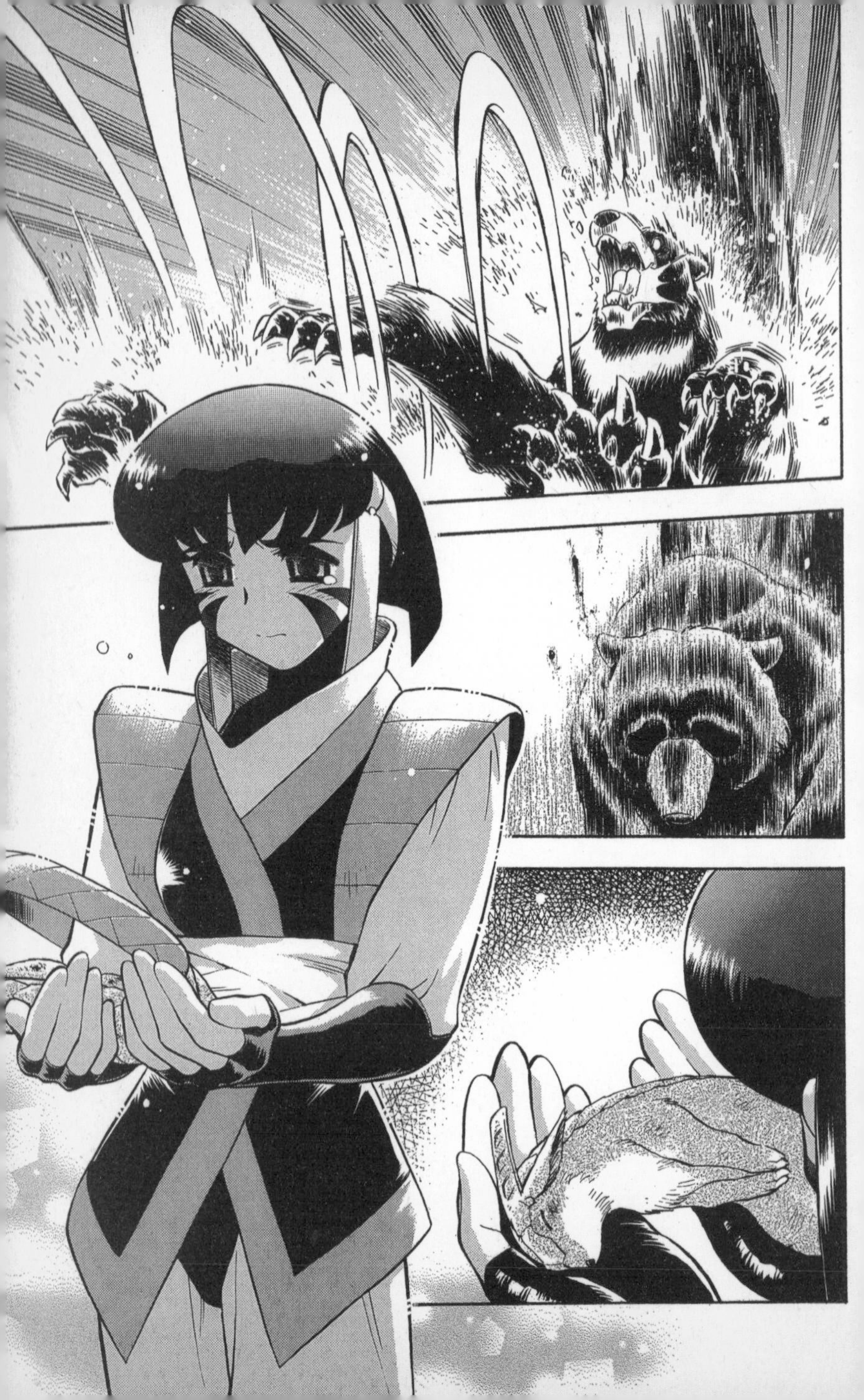

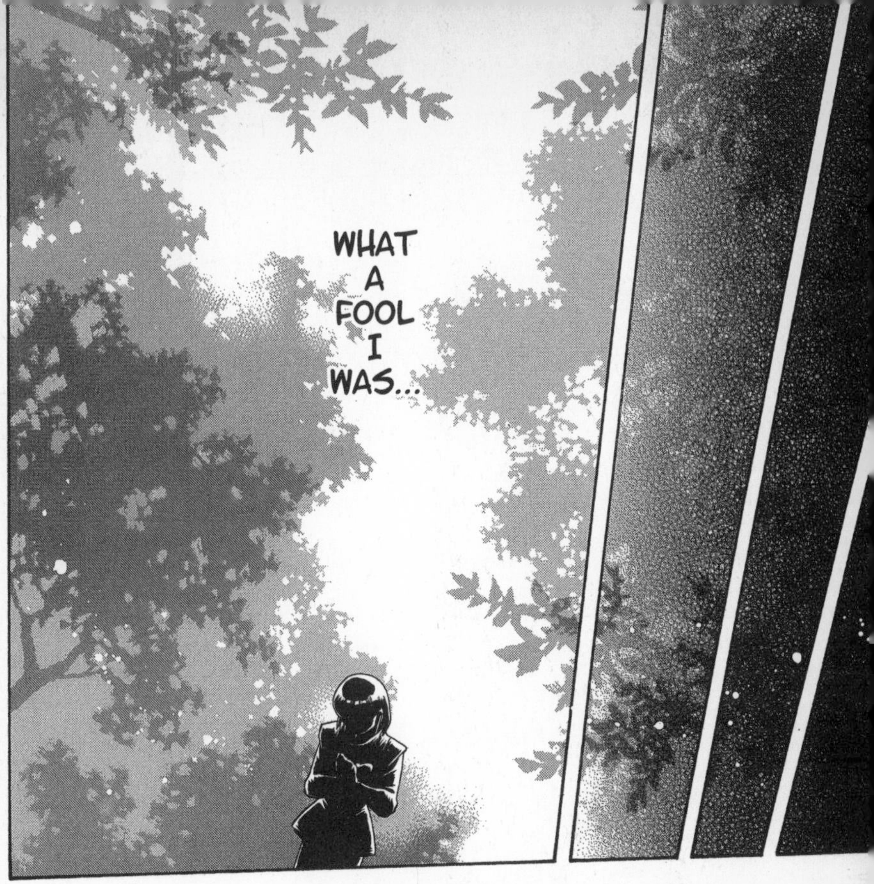
WHAT A FOOL I WAS...

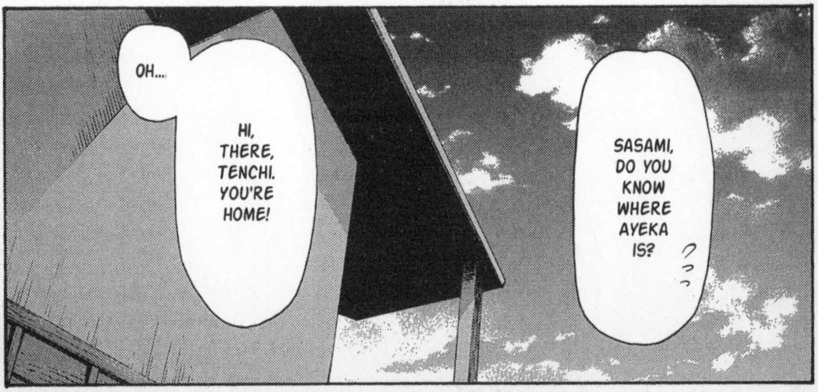
OH...
HI, THERE, TENCHI. YOU'RE HOME!
SASAMI, DO YOU KNOW WHERE AYEKA IS?

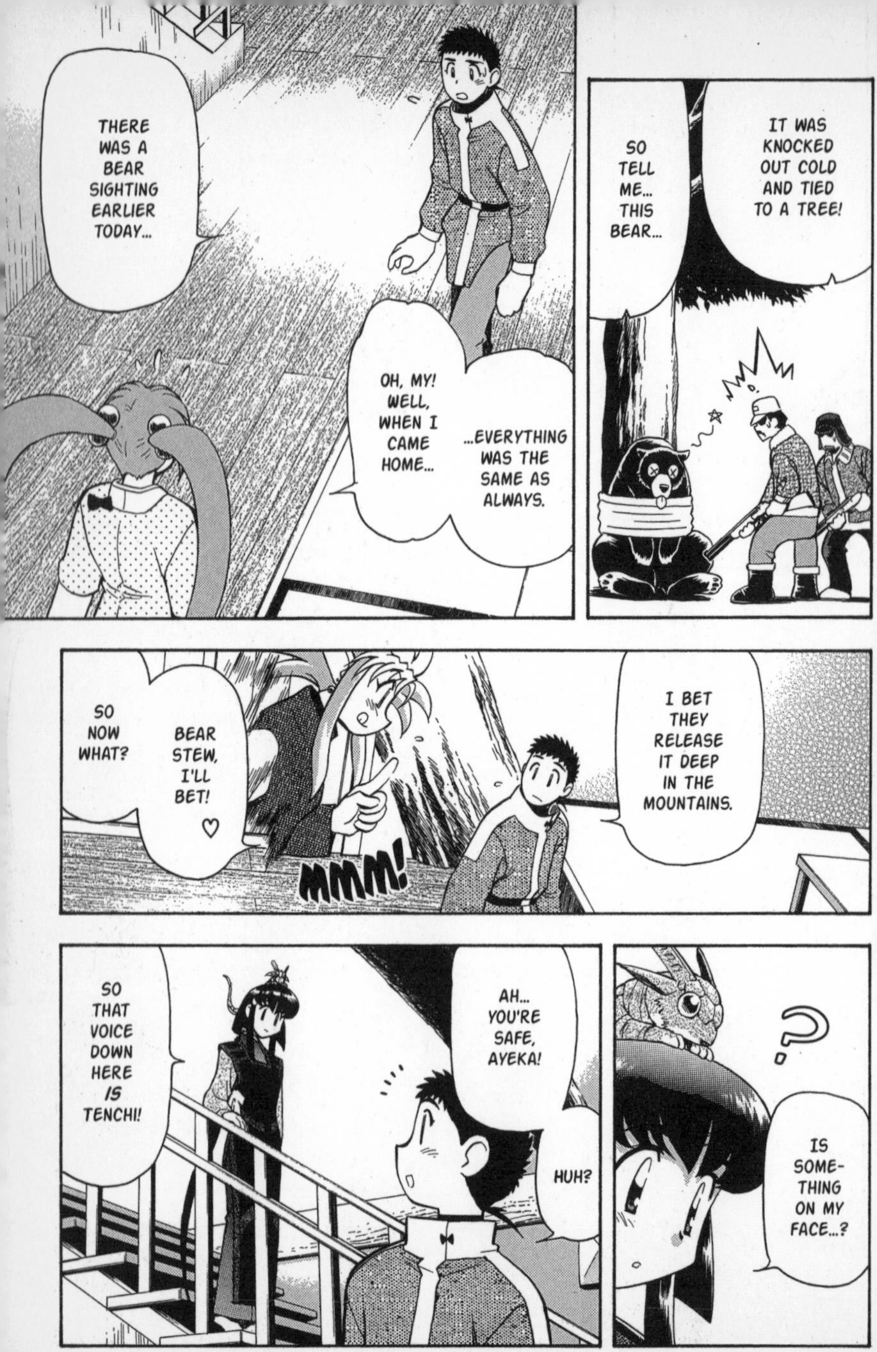
THERE WAS A BEAR SIGHTING EARLIER TODAY...
OH, MY! WELL, WHEN I CAME HOME...
...EVERYTHING WAS THE SAME AS ALWAYS.
SO TELL ME... THIS BEAR...
IT WAS KNOCKED OUT COLD AND TIED TO A TREE!
SO NOW WHAT?
BEAR STEW, I'LL BET! ♡
MMM!
I BET THEY RELEASE IT DEEP IN THE MOUNTAINS.
SO THAT VOICE DOWN HERE *IS* TENCHI!
AH... YOU'RE SAFE, AYEKA!
HUH?
?
IS SOME-THING ON MY FACE...?

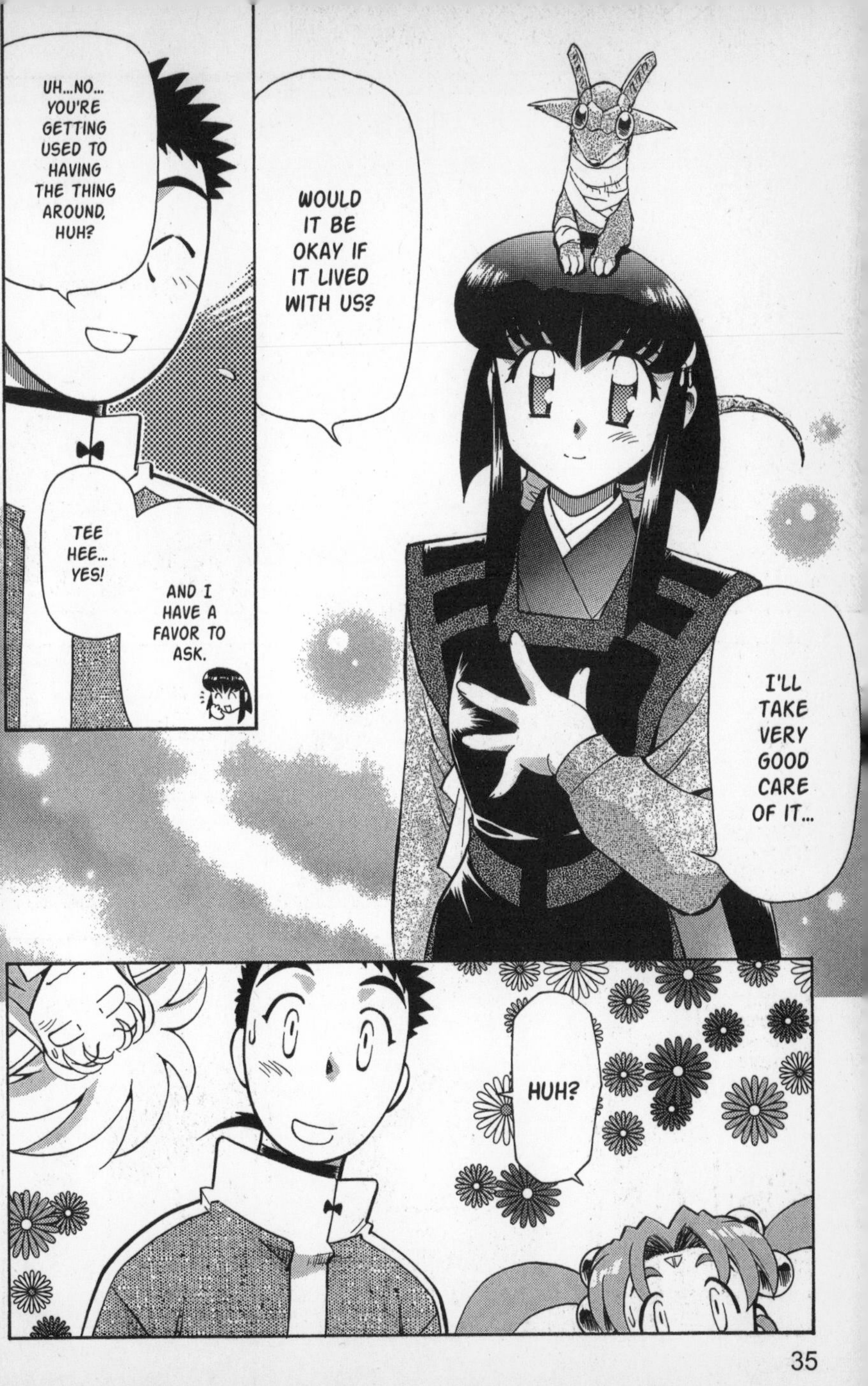
UH...NO... YOU'RE GETTING USED TO HAVING THE THING AROUND, HUH?
TEE HEE... YES!
AND I HAVE A FAVOR TO ASK.
WOULD IT BE OKAY IF IT LIVED WITH US?
I'LL TAKE VERY GOOD CARE OF IT...
HUH?

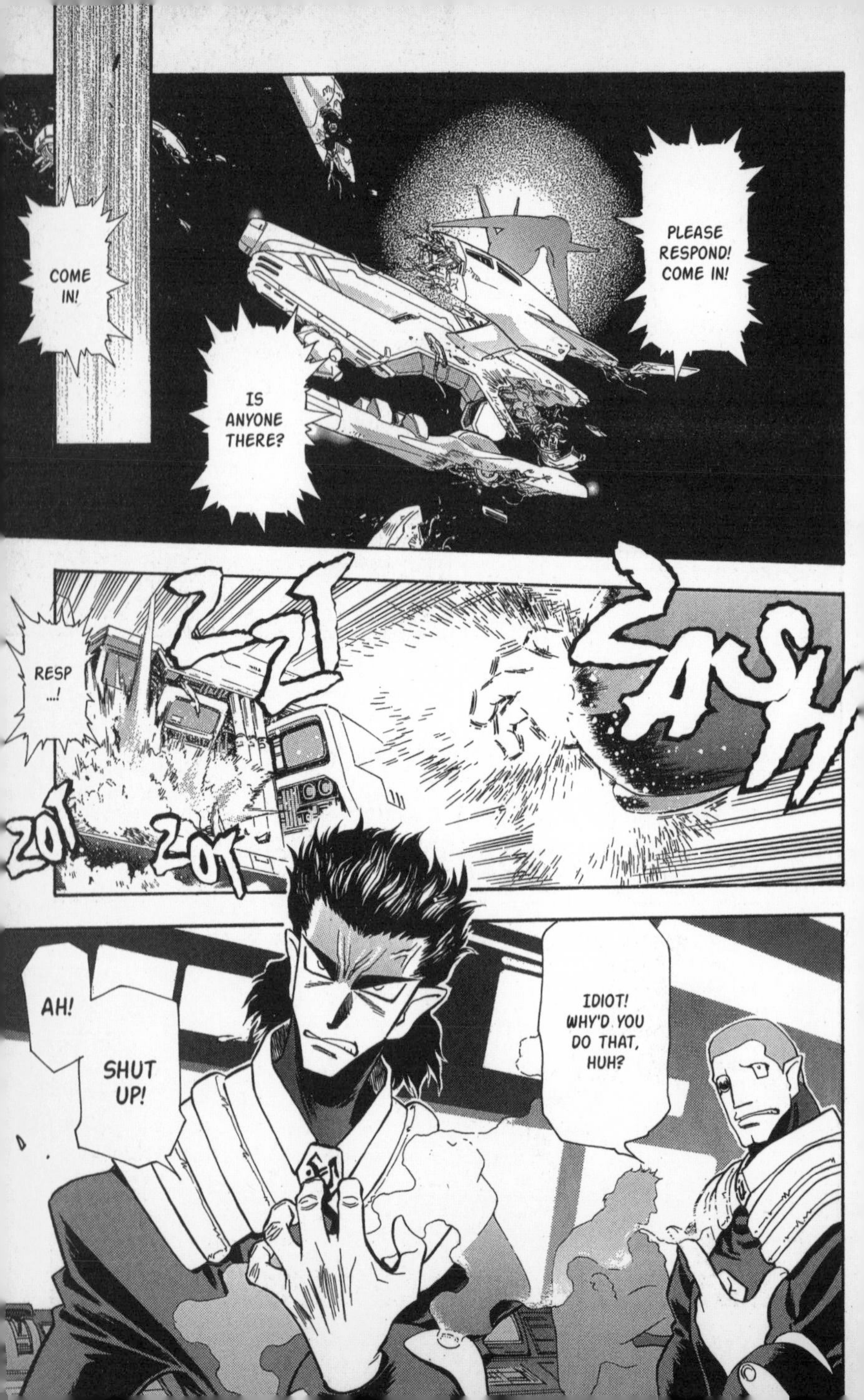
COME IN!
IS ANYONE THERE?
PLEASE RESPOND! COME IN!
RESP ...!
ZZT
ZASH
ZOT
ZOT
AH!
SHUT UP!
IDIOT! WHY'D YOU DO THAT, HUH?

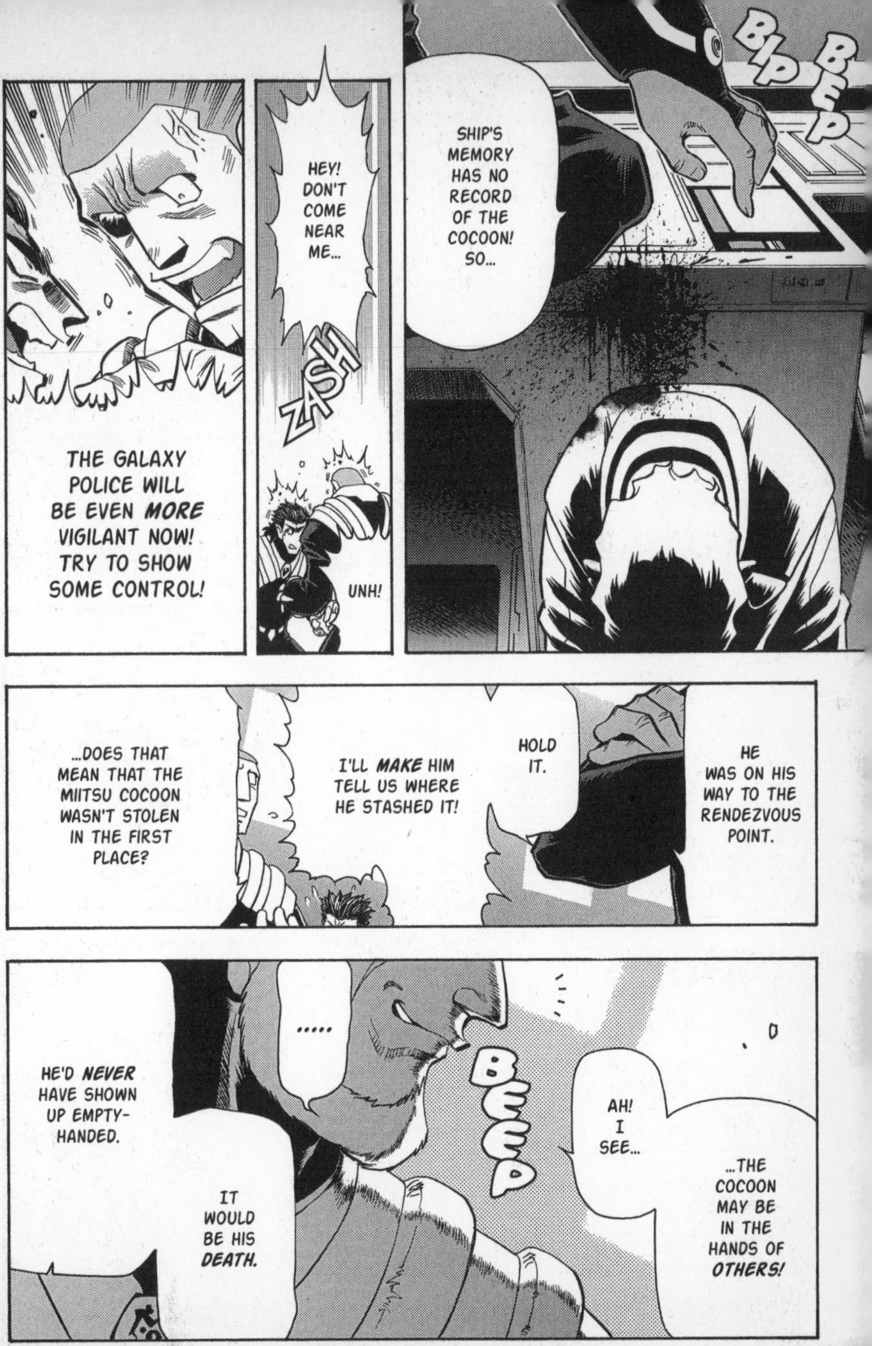
THE GALAXY POLICE WILL BE EVEN MORE VIGILANT NOW! TRY TO SHOW SOME CONTROL!
HEY! DON'T COME NEAR ME...
ZASH
UNH!
SHIP'S MEMORY HAS NO RECORD OF THE COCOON! SO...
BIP
BEEP
...DOES THAT MEAN THAT THE MIITSU COCOON WASN'T STOLEN IN THE FIRST PLACE?
I'LL MAKE HIM TELL US WHERE HE STASHED IT!
HOLD IT.
HE WAS ON HIS WAY TO THE RENDEZVOUS POINT.
HE'D NEVER HAVE SHOWN UP EMPTY-HANDED.
.....
IT WOULD BE HIS DEATH.
BEEP
AH! I SEE...
...THE COCOON MAY BE IN THE HANDS OF OTHERS!

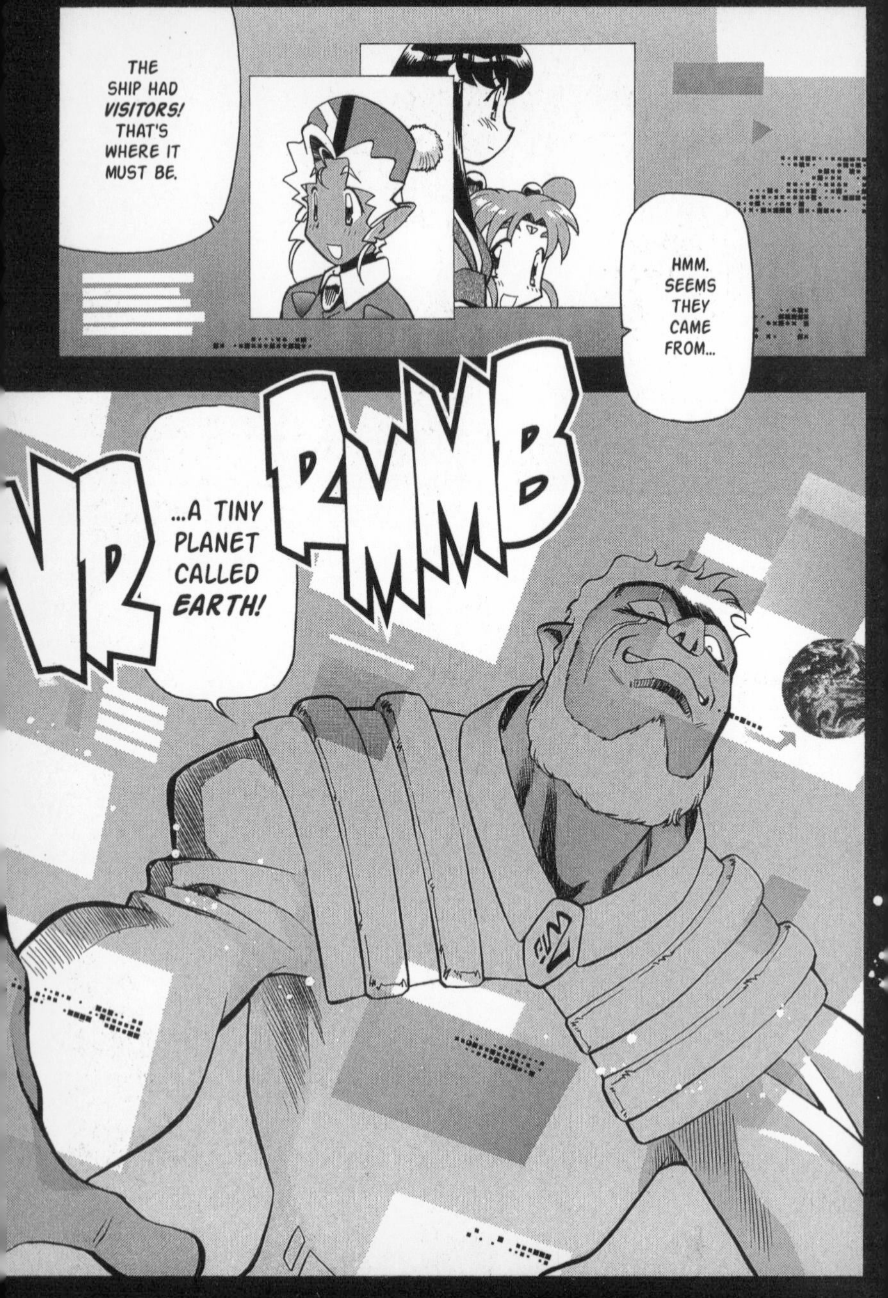
THE SHIP HAD VISITORS! THAT'S WHERE IT MUST BE.
HMM. SEEMS THEY CAME FROM...
VR
RMMB
...A TINY PLANET CALLED EARTH!

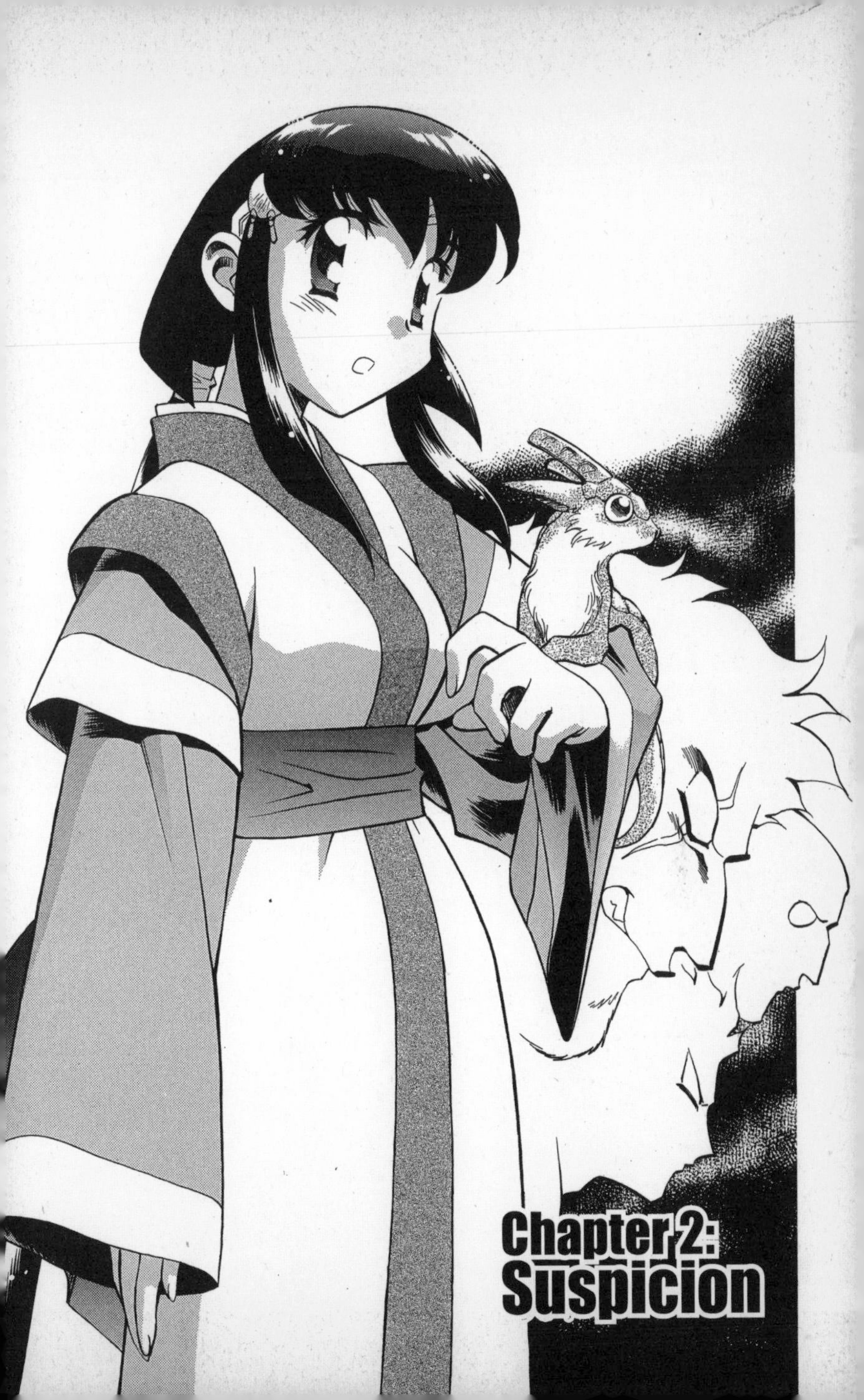
Chapter 2:
Suspicion

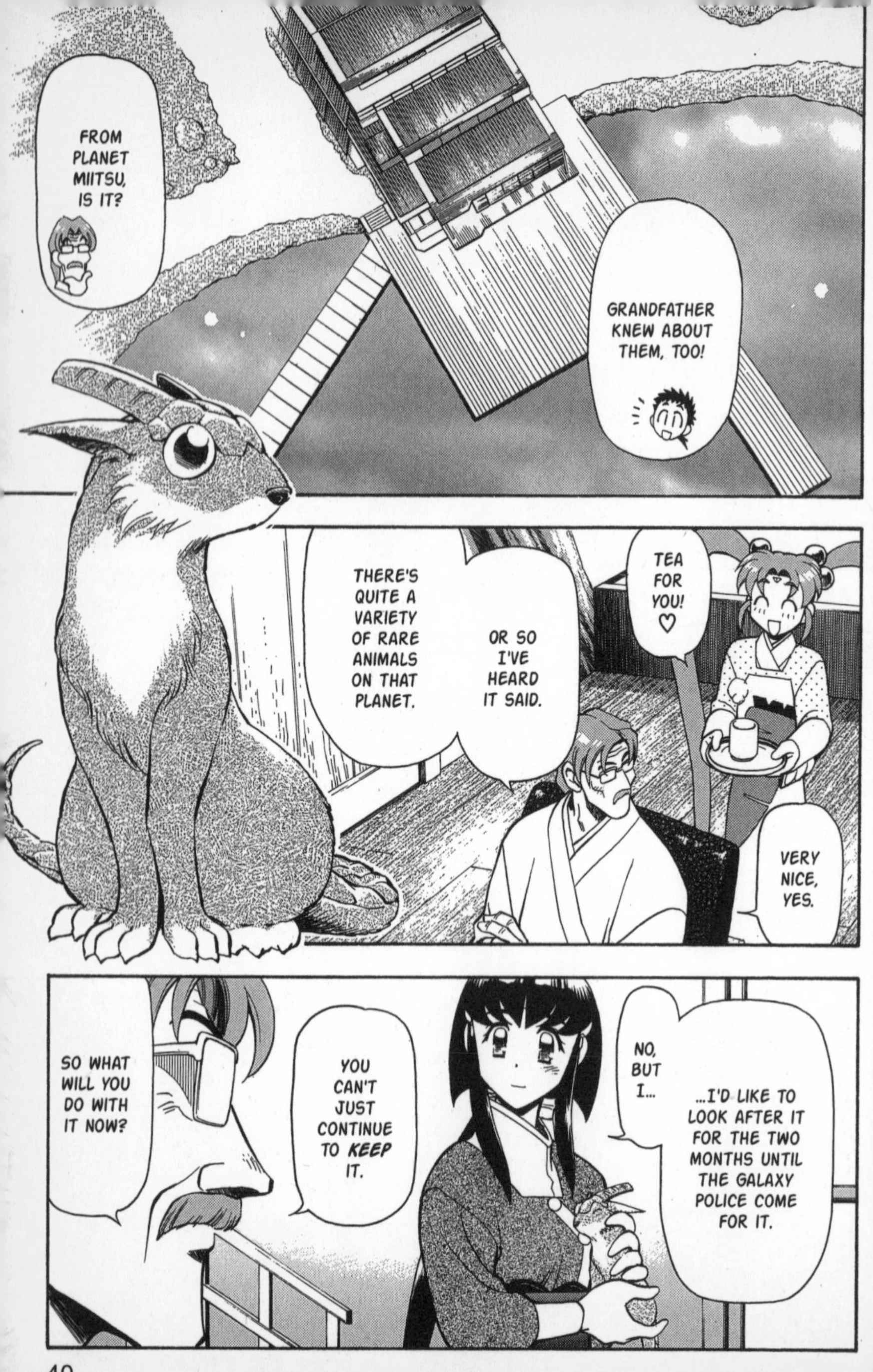
FROM PLANET MIITSU, IS IT?
GRANDFATHER KNEW ABOUT THEM, TOO!
THERE'S QUITE A VARIETY OF RARE ANIMALS ON THAT PLANET.
OR SO I'VE HEARD IT SAID.
TEA FOR YOU! ♡
VERY NICE, YES.
SO WHAT WILL YOU DO WITH IT NOW?
YOU CAN'T JUST CONTINUE TO *KEEP* IT.
NO, BUT I...
...I'D LIKE TO LOOK AFTER IT FOR THE TWO MONTHS UNTIL THE GALAXY POLICE COME FOR IT.

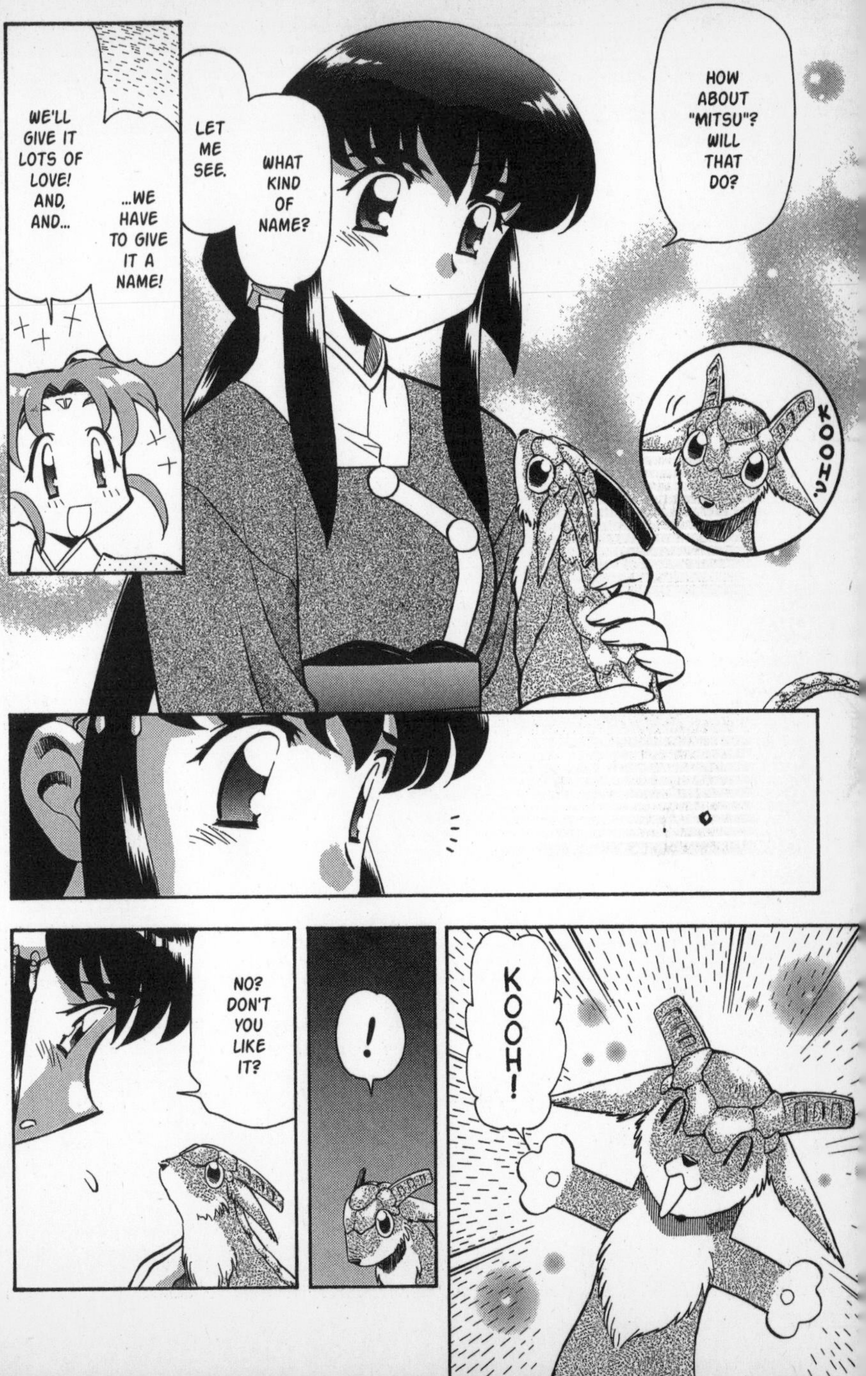
WE'LL GIVE IT LOTS OF LOVE! AND, AND...
...WE HAVE TO GIVE IT A NAME!
LET ME SEE.
WHAT KIND OF NAME?
HOW ABOUT "MITSU"? WILL THAT DO?
KOOH?
NO? DON'T YOU LIKE IT?
!
KOOH!

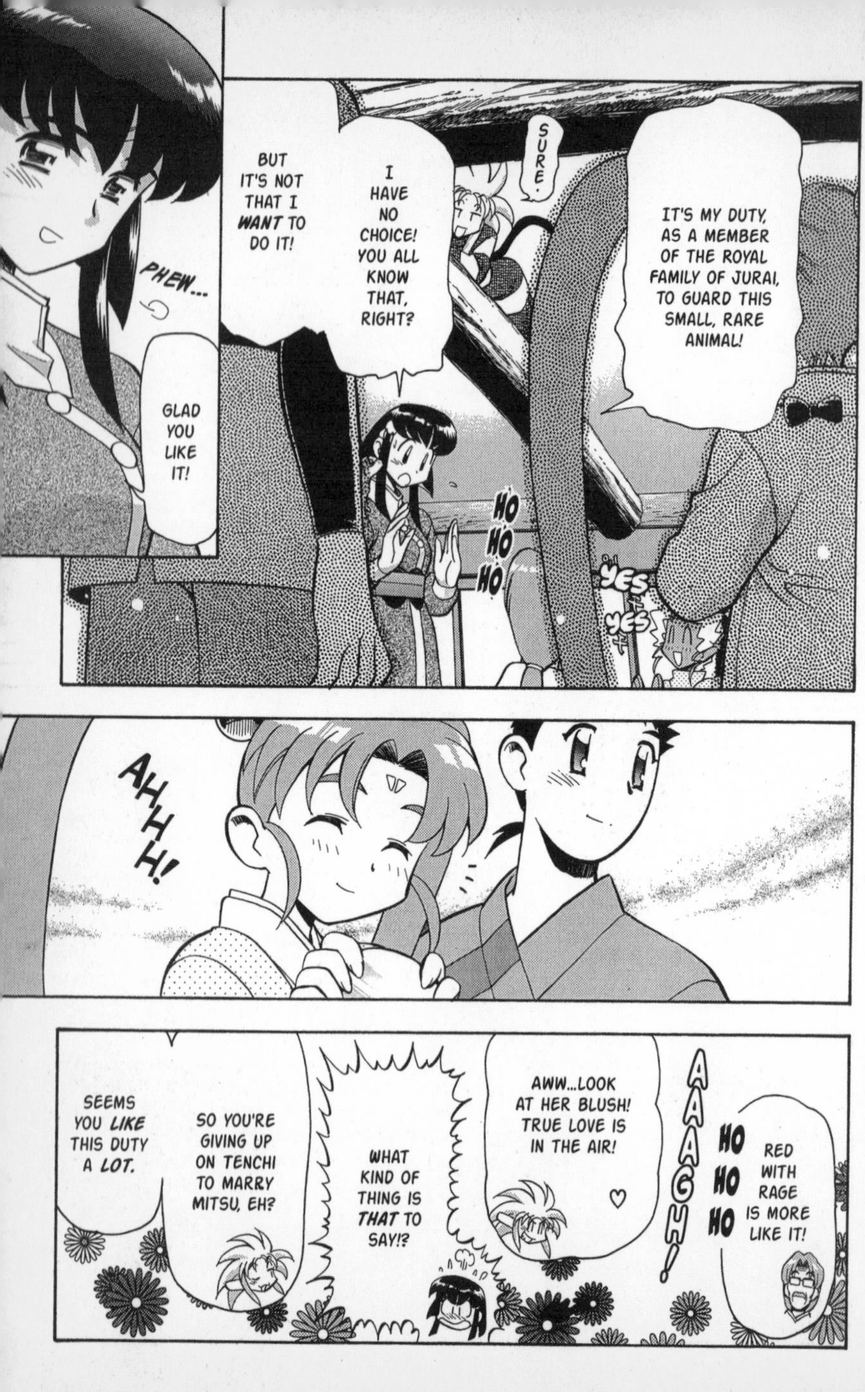
PHEW...
GLAD YOU LIKE IT!
BUT IT'S NOT THAT I *WANT* TO DO IT!
I HAVE NO CHOICE! YOU ALL KNOW THAT, RIGHT?
SURE.
IT'S MY DUTY, AS A MEMBER OF THE ROYAL FAMILY OF JURAI, TO GUARD THIS SMALL, RARE ANIMAL!
HO HO HO
YES YES
AHHHH!
SEEMS YOU *LIKE* THIS DUTY A *LOT.*
SO YOU'RE GIVING UP ON TENCHI TO MARRY MITSU, EH?
WHAT KIND OF THING IS *THAT* TO SAY!?
AWW...LOOK AT HER BLUSH! TRUE LOVE IS IN THE AIR!
AAAGH!
HO HO HO
RED WITH RAGE IS MORE LIKE IT!

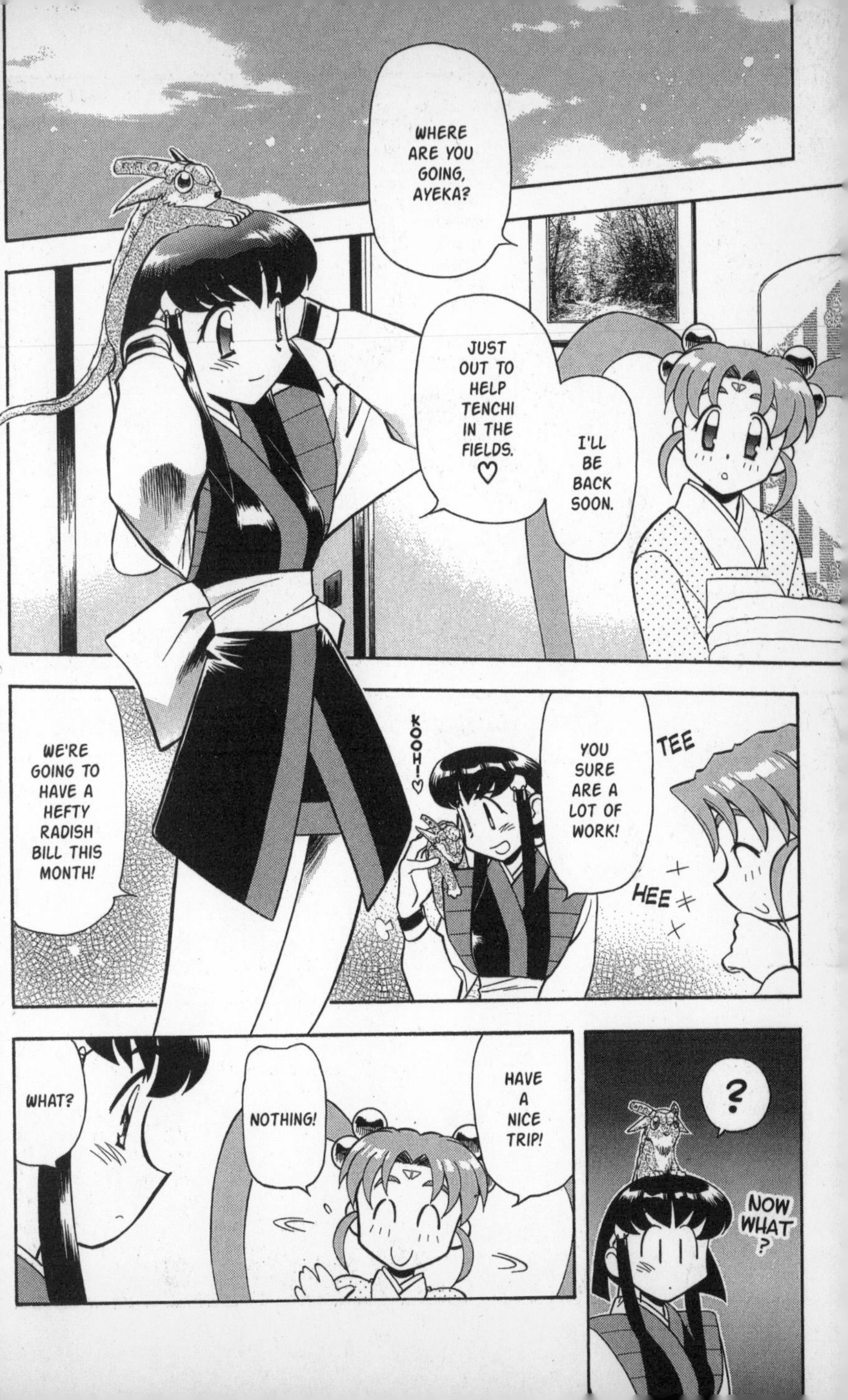
WHERE ARE YOU GOING, AYEKA?
JUST OUT TO HELP TENCHI IN THE FIELDS. ♡
I'LL BE BACK SOON.
WE'RE GOING TO HAVE A HEFTY RADISH BILL THIS MONTH!
KOOH!♡
YOU SURE ARE A LOT OF WORK!
TEE
HEE
WHAT?
NOTHING!
HAVE A NICE TRIP!
?
NOW WHAT?

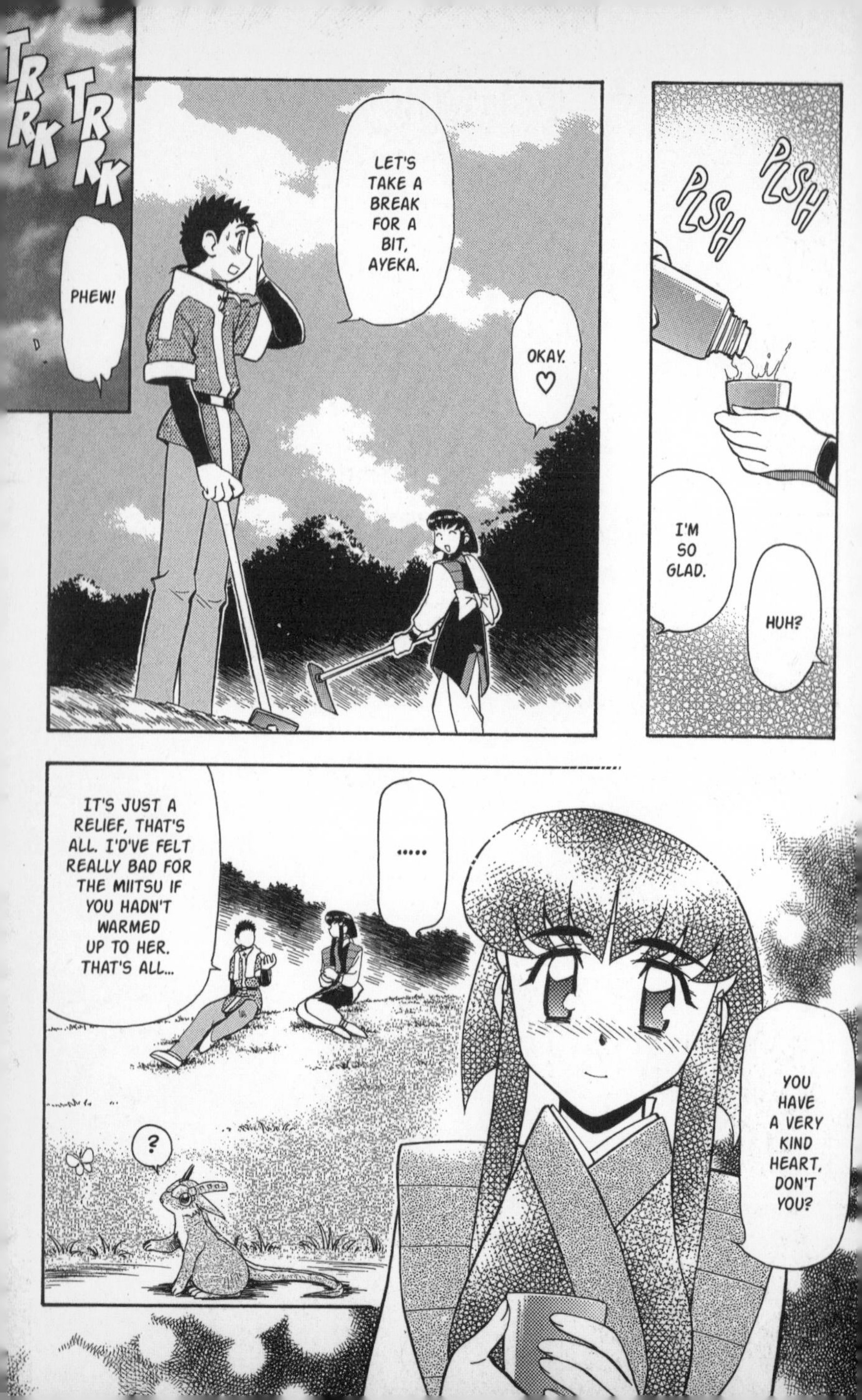
TRRK TRRK
PHEW!
LET'S TAKE A BREAK FOR A BIT, AYEKA.
OKAY. ♡
PLSH PLSH
I'M SO GLAD.
HUH?
IT'S JUST A RELIEF, THAT'S ALL. I'D'VE FELT REALLY BAD FOR THE MIITSU IF YOU HADN'T WARMED UP TO HER. THAT'S ALL...
.....
?
YOU HAVE A VERY KIND HEART, DON'T YOU?

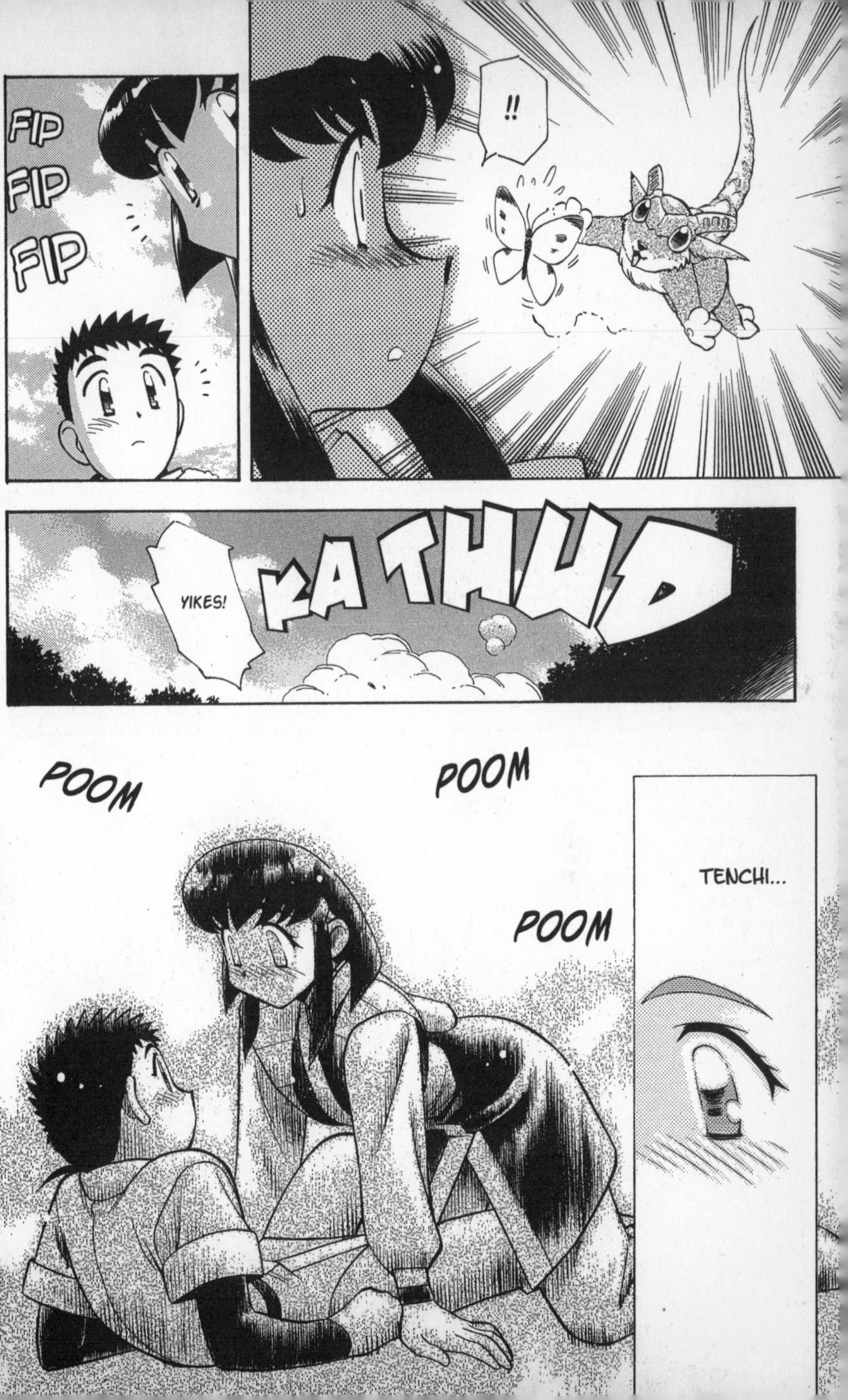
FIP
FIP
FIP
!!
YIKES!
KA THUD
POOM
POOM
POOM
TENCHI...

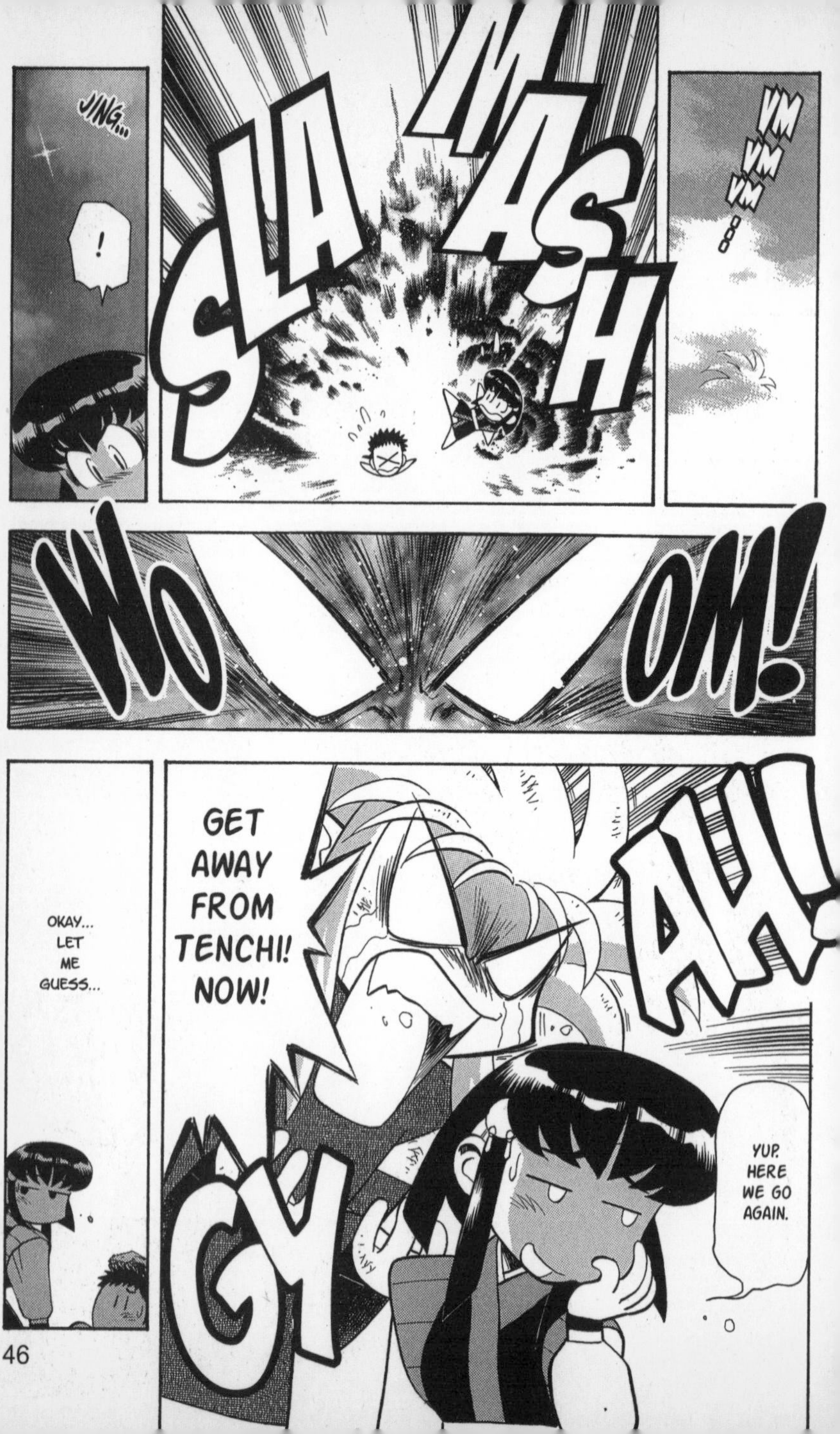
JING...
!
SLAAASH
VM VM VM...
WO OM!
OKAY... LET ME GUESS...
GET AWAY FROM TENCHI! NOW!
AH!
GY
YUP. HERE WE GO AGAIN.

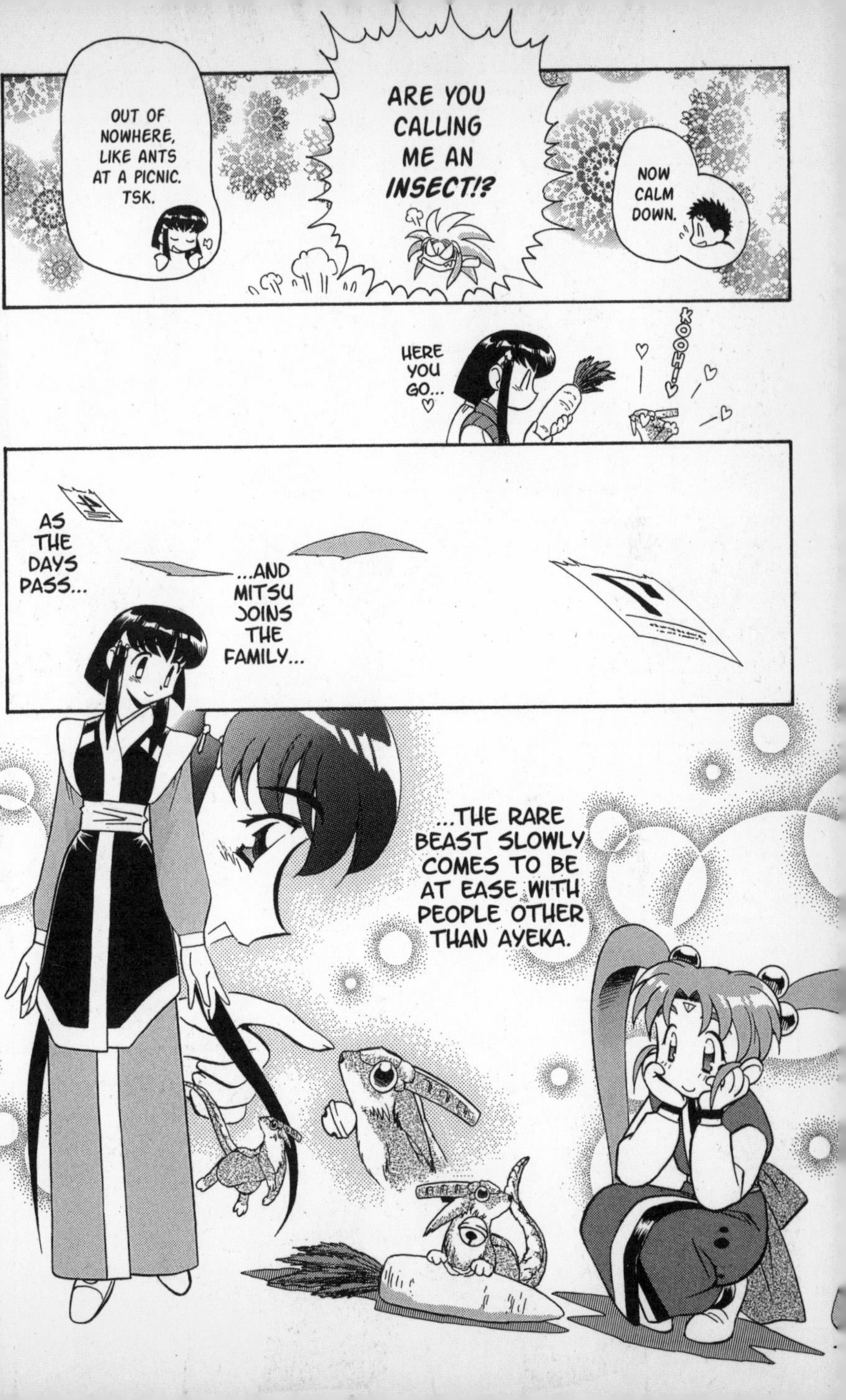
OUT OF NOWHERE, LIKE ANTS AT A PICNIC. TSK.
ARE YOU CALLING ME AN *INSECT!?*
NOW CALM DOWN.
HERE YOU GO... ♡
KOOHI
AS THE DAYS PASS...
...AND MITSU JOINS THE FAMILY...
...THE RARE BEAST SLOWLY COMES TO BE AT EASE WITH PEOPLE OTHER THAN AYEKA.

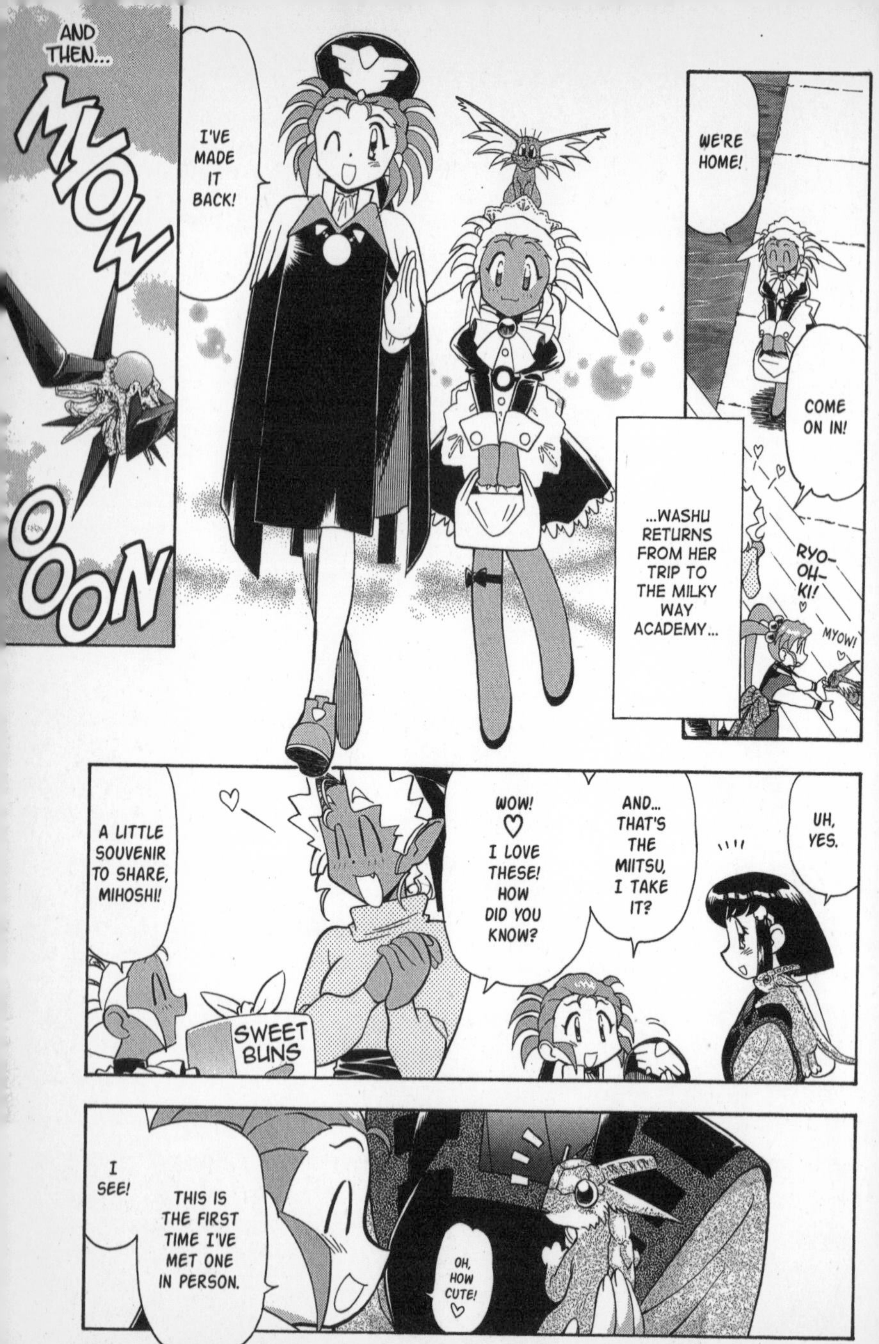
AND THEN...
MYOW OOON
I'VE MADE IT BACK!
WE'RE HOME!
...WASHU RETURNS FROM HER TRIP TO THE MILKY WAY ACADEMY...
COME ON IN!
RYO-OH-KI! ♡
MYOW! ♡
A LITTLE SOUVENIR TO SHARE, MIHOSHI!
WOW! ♡ I LOVE THESE! HOW DID YOU KNOW?
SWEET BUNS
AND... THAT'S THE MIITSU, I TAKE IT?
UH, YES.
I SEE!
THIS IS THE FIRST TIME I'VE MET ONE IN PERSON.
OH, HOW CUTE! ♡

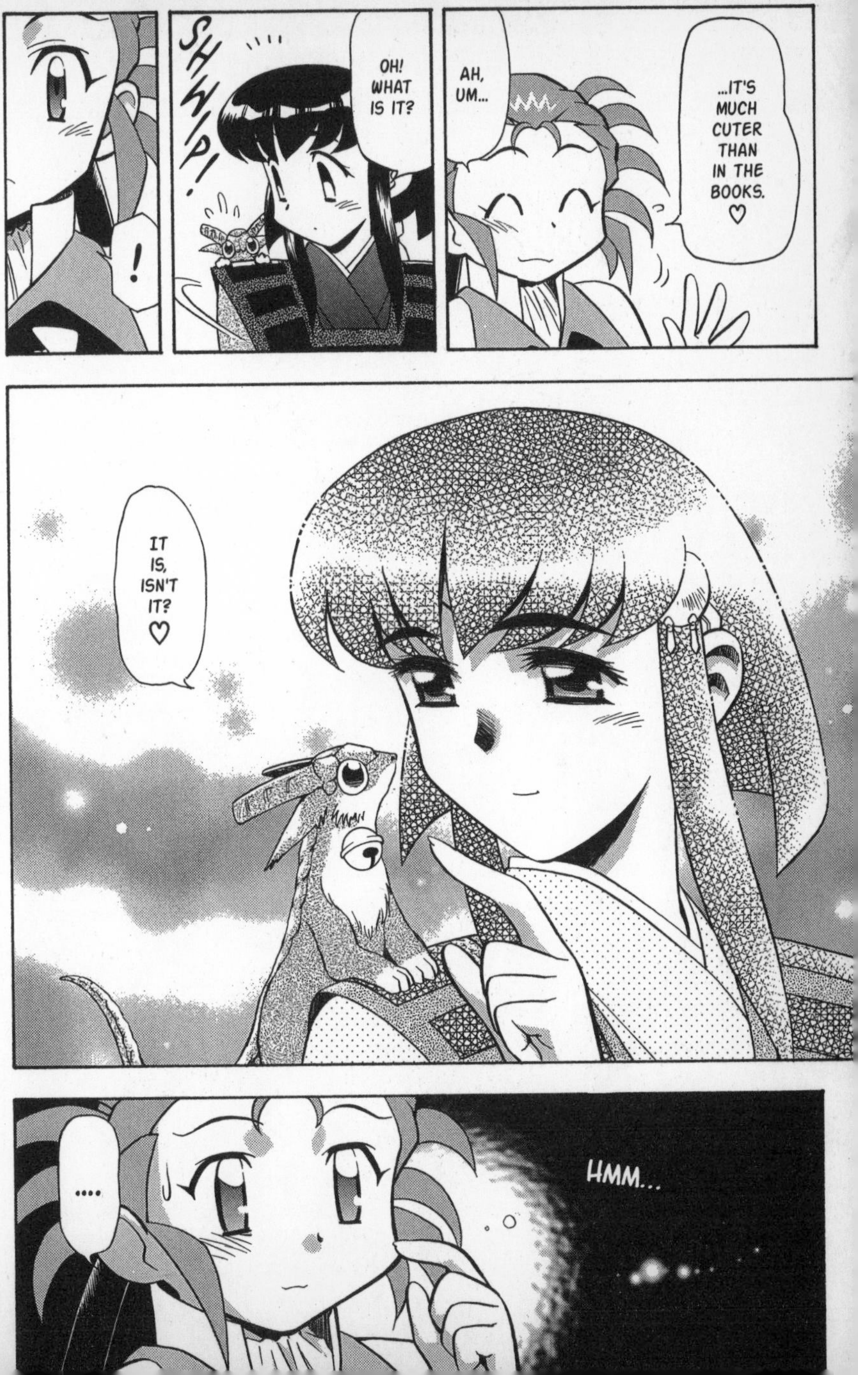
!
SHWIP!
OH! WHAT IS IT?
AH, UM...
...IT'S MUCH CUTER THAN IN THE BOOKS. ♡
IT IS, ISN'T IT? ♡
....
HMM...

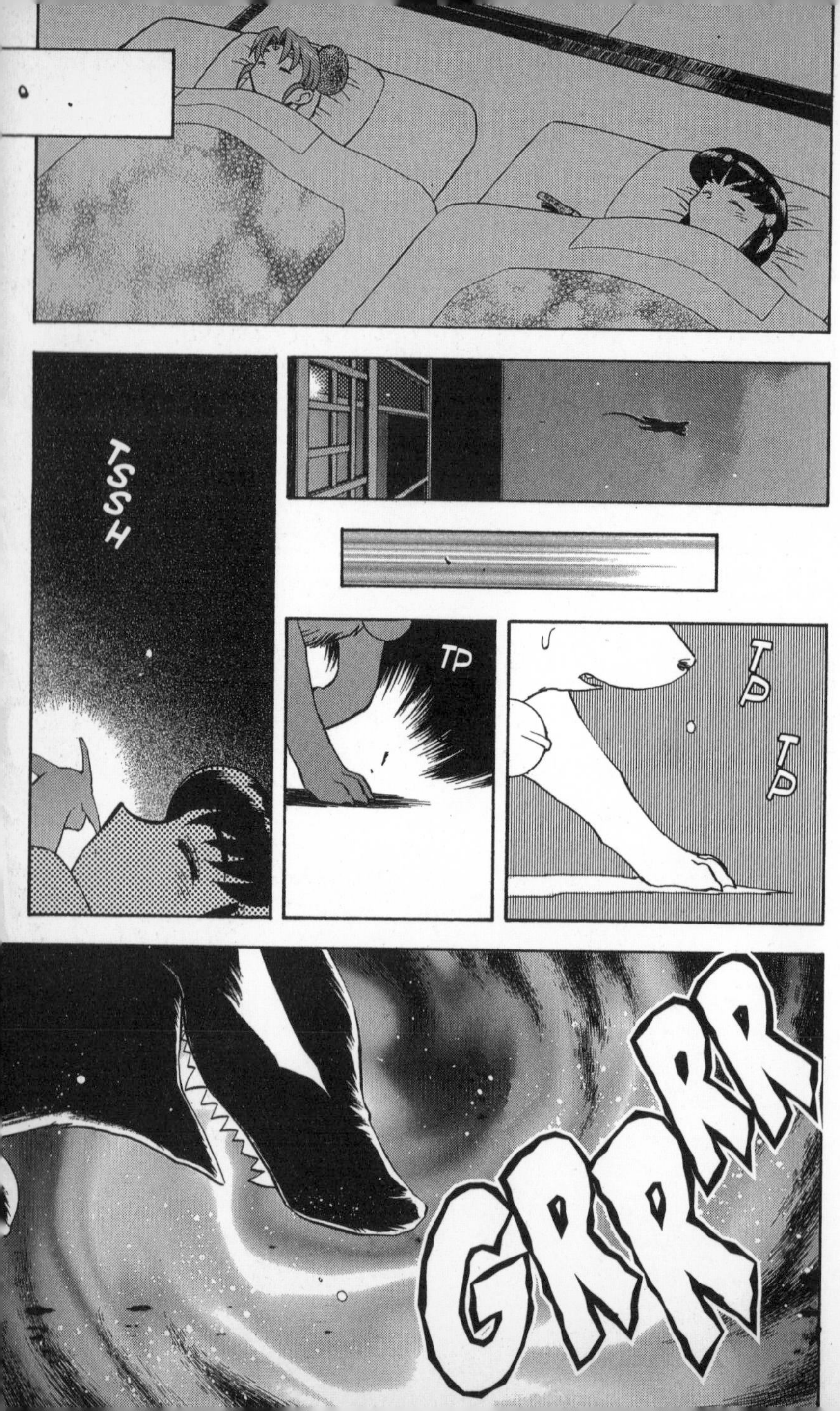

TSSH
TP
TP
TP
GRRRR

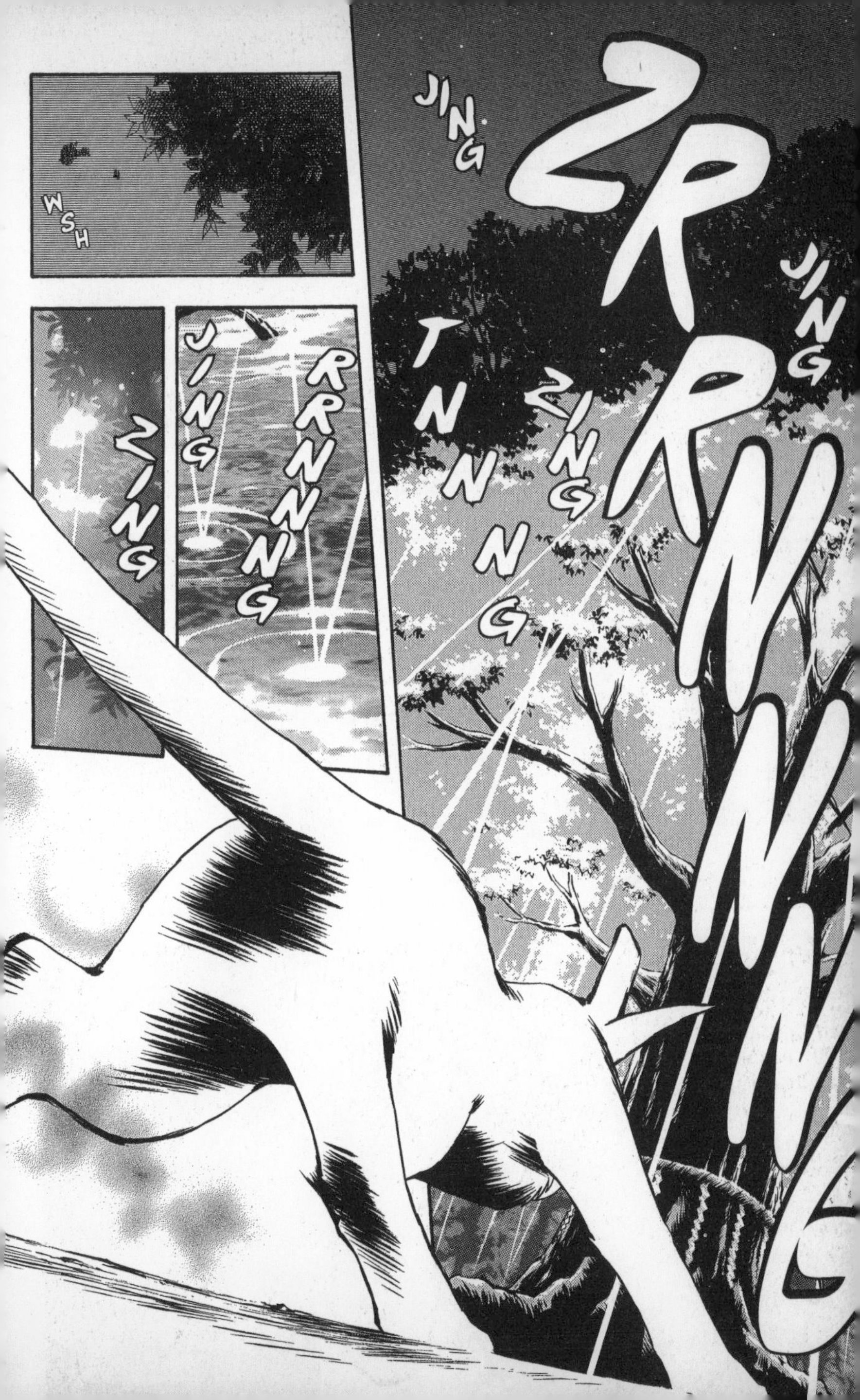
JING
ZRRNNNNG
JING
ZING
TNNNG
WSH
RRNNNG
JING
ZING

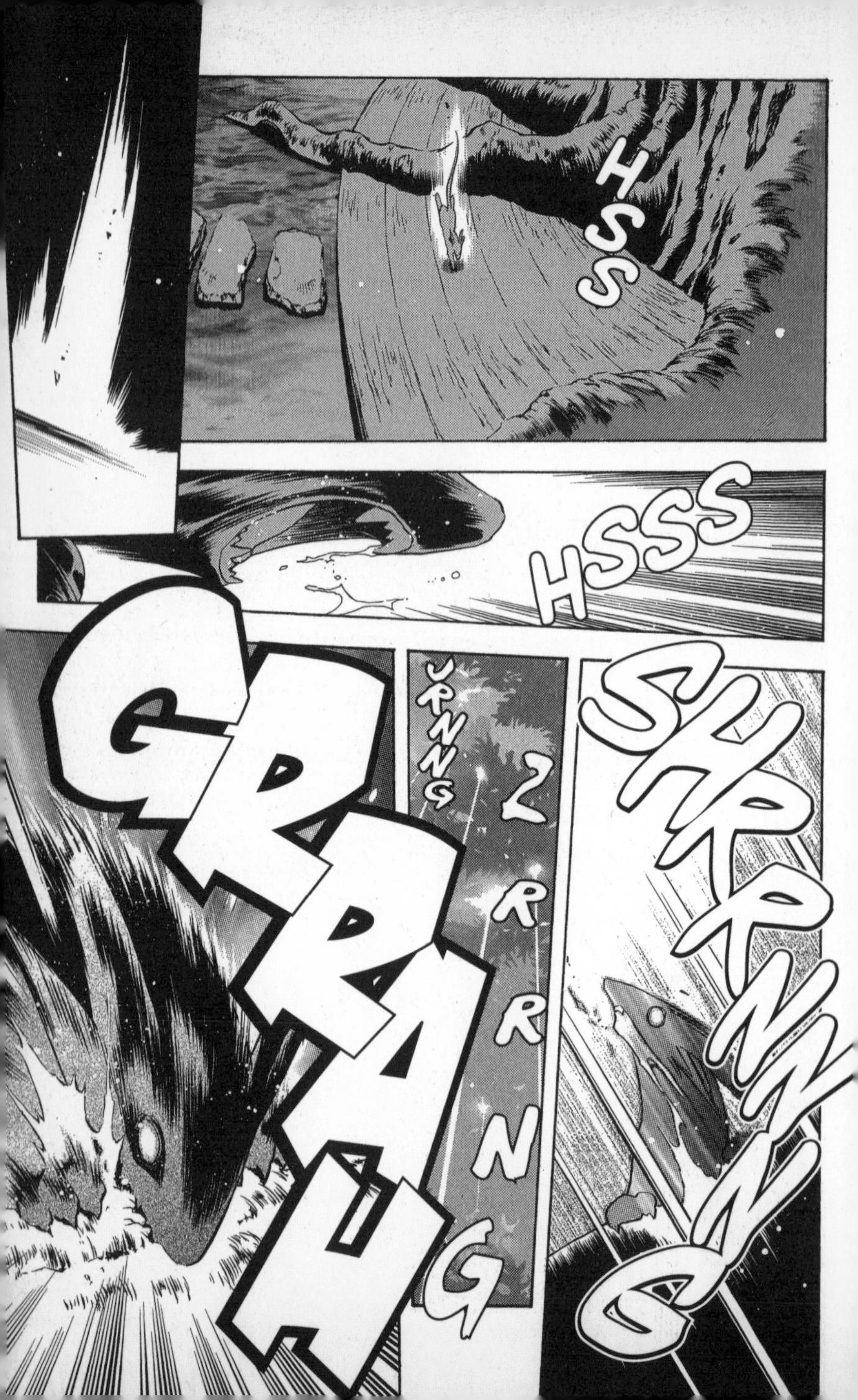
HSS
HSSSS
GRRAHH
JRNNG
ZRRNG
SHRRNNNG

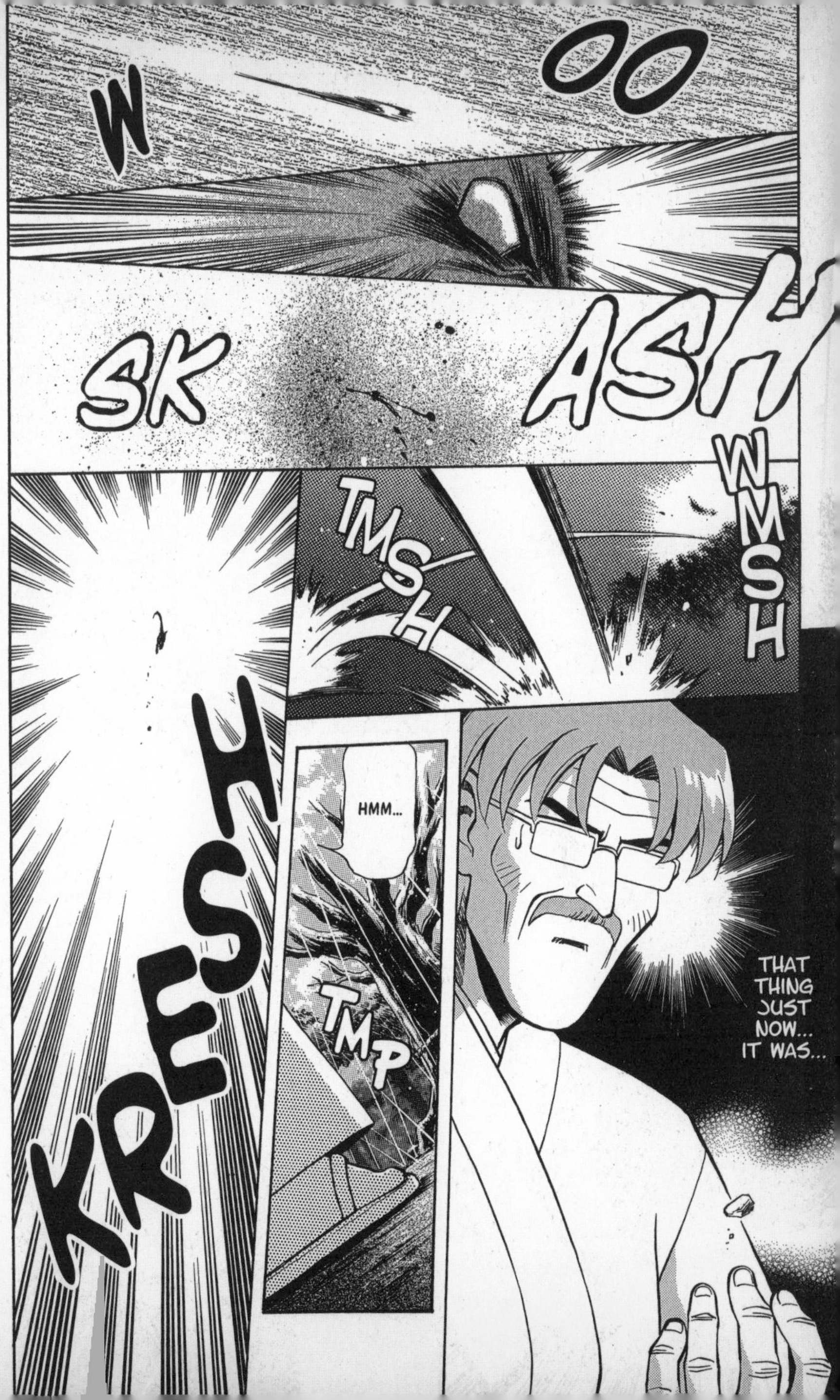

W
OO
SK
ASH
WMSH
KRESH
TMSH
HMM...
TMP
THAT THING JUST NOW... IT WAS...

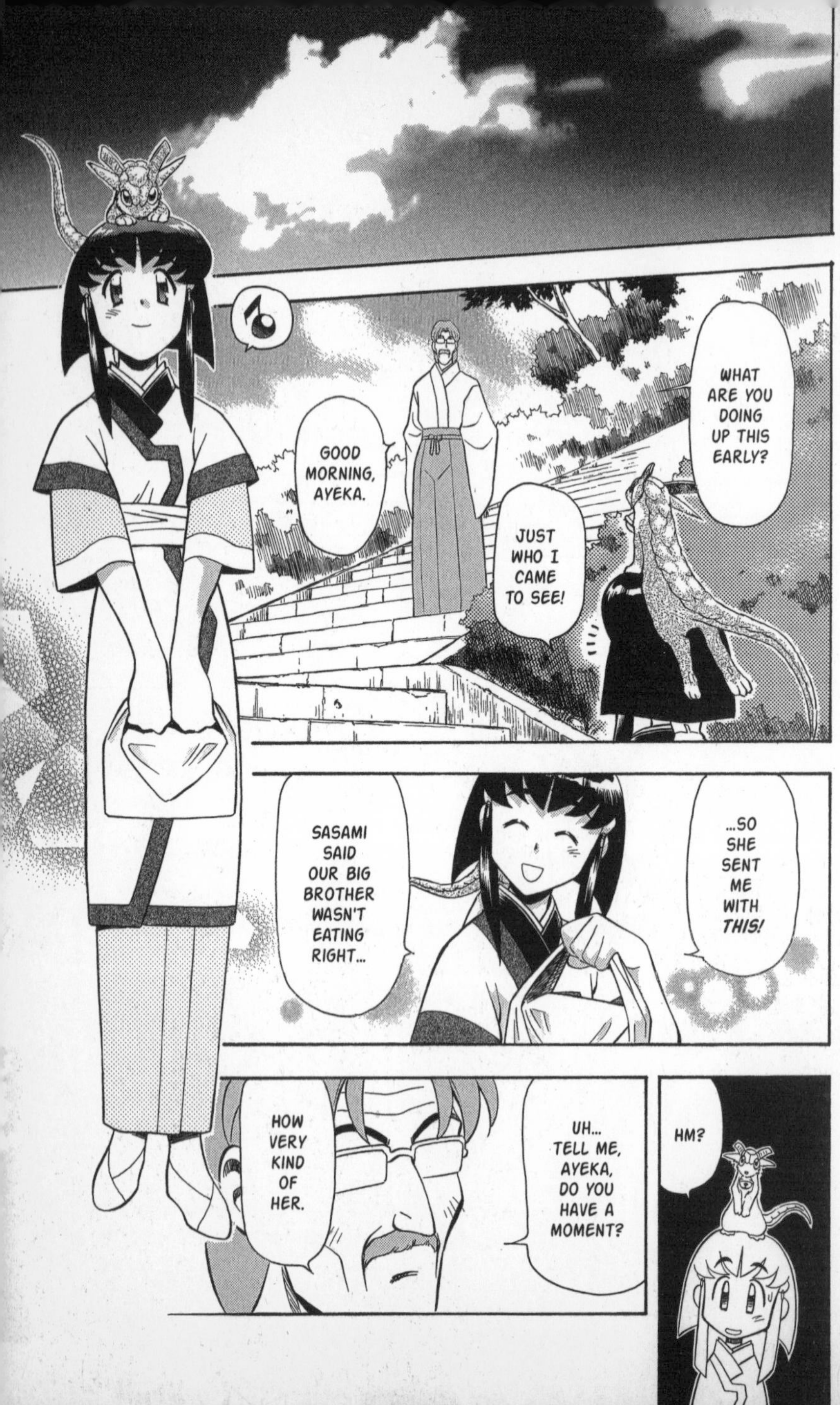
GOOD MORNING, AYEKA.
WHAT ARE YOU DOING UP THIS EARLY?
JUST WHO I CAME TO SEE!
SASAMI SAID OUR BIG BROTHER WASN'T EATING RIGHT...
...SO SHE SENT ME WITH *THIS!*
HOW VERY KIND OF HER.
UH... TELL ME, AYEKA, DO YOU HAVE A MOMENT?
HM?

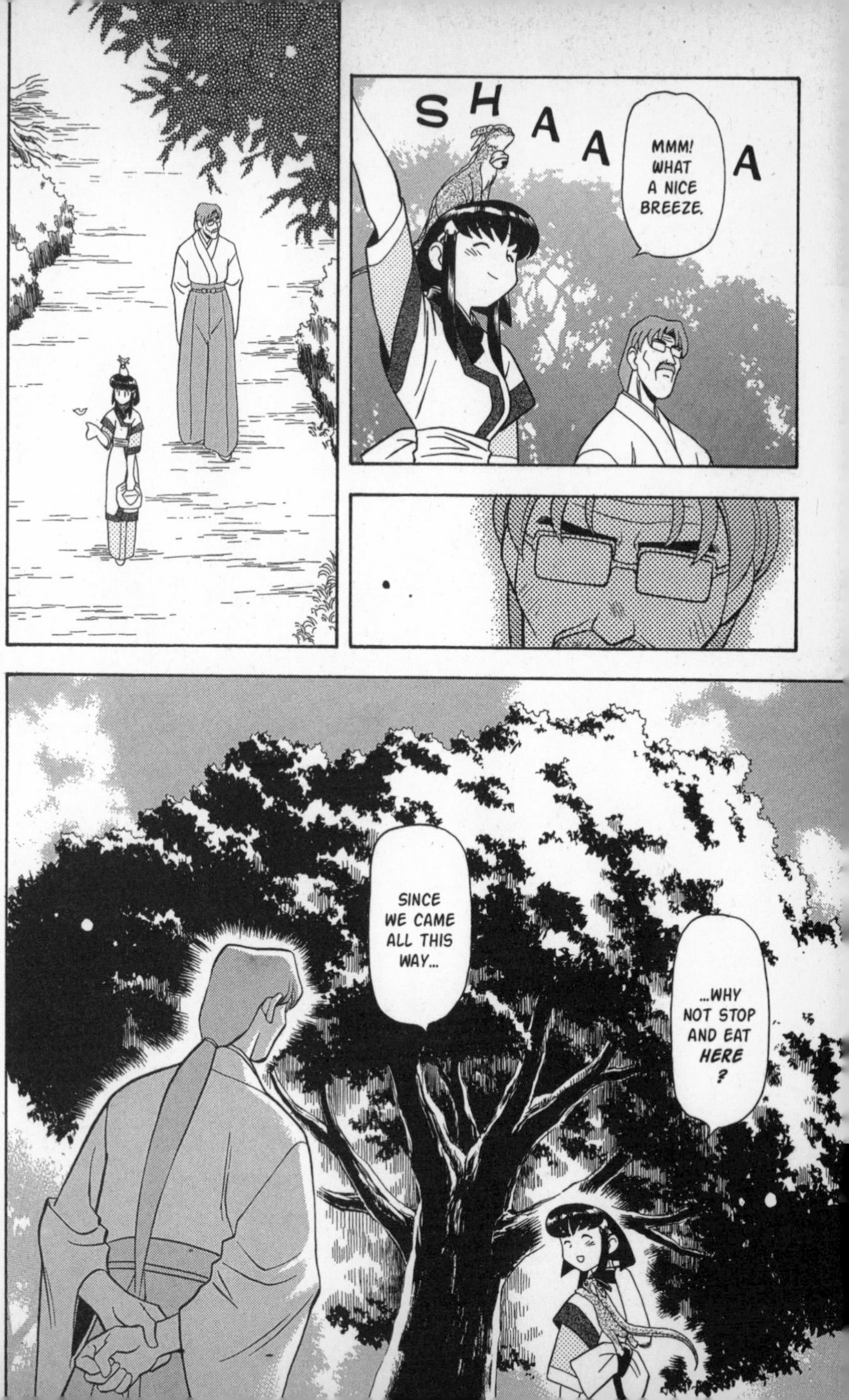
SHAAAA
MMM! WHAT A NICE BREEZE.
SINCE WE CAME ALL THIS WAY...
...WHY NOT STOP AND EAT *HERE*?

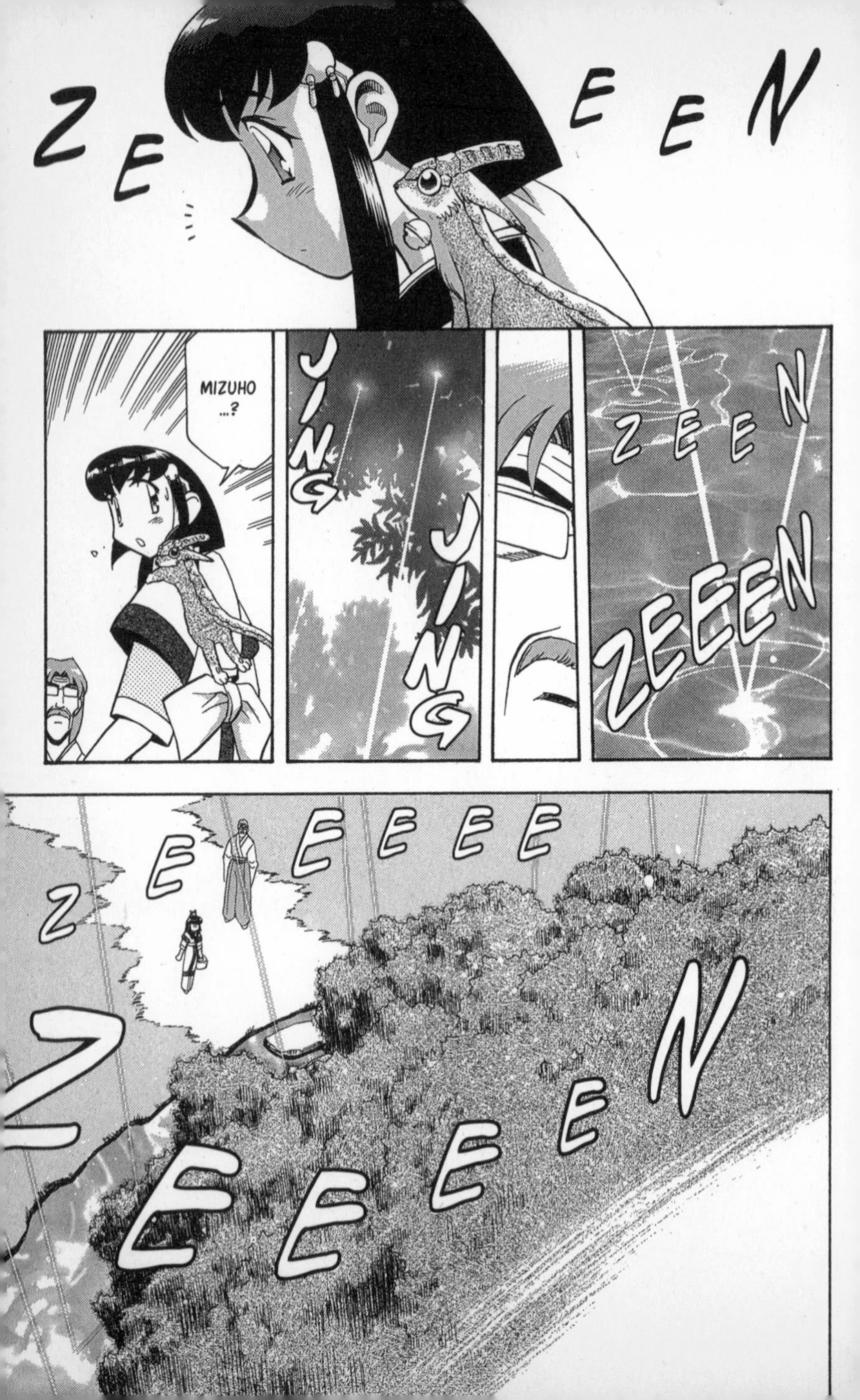
ZEEEN
MIZUHO ...?
JING
JING
ZEEEN
ZEEEN
ZEEEEE
ZEEEEEN

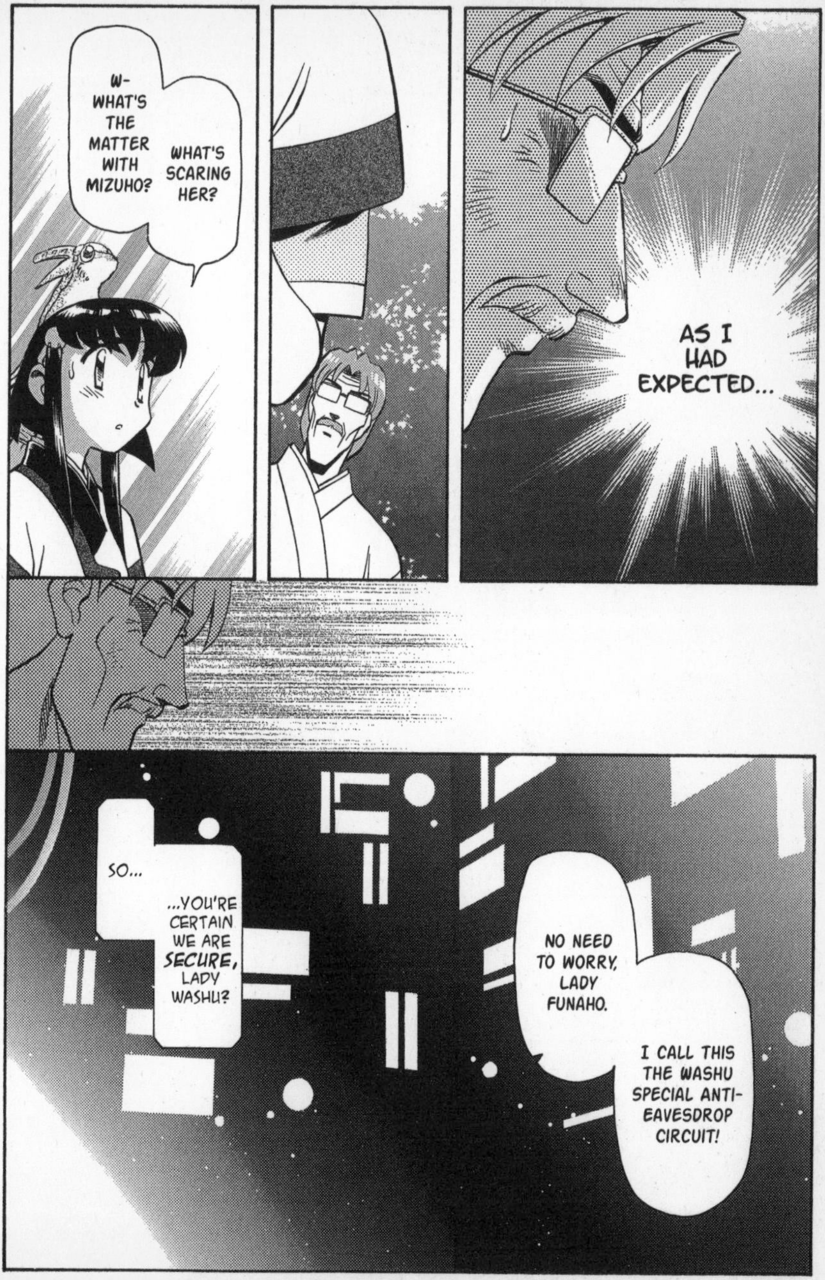

W- WHAT'S THE MATTER WITH MIZUHO?
WHAT'S SCARING HER?
AS I HAD EXPECTED...
SO...
...YOU'RE CERTAIN WE ARE SECURE, LADY WASHU?
NO NEED TO WORRY, LADY FUNAHO.
I CALL THIS THE WASHU SPECIAL ANTI-EAVESDROP CIRCUIT!

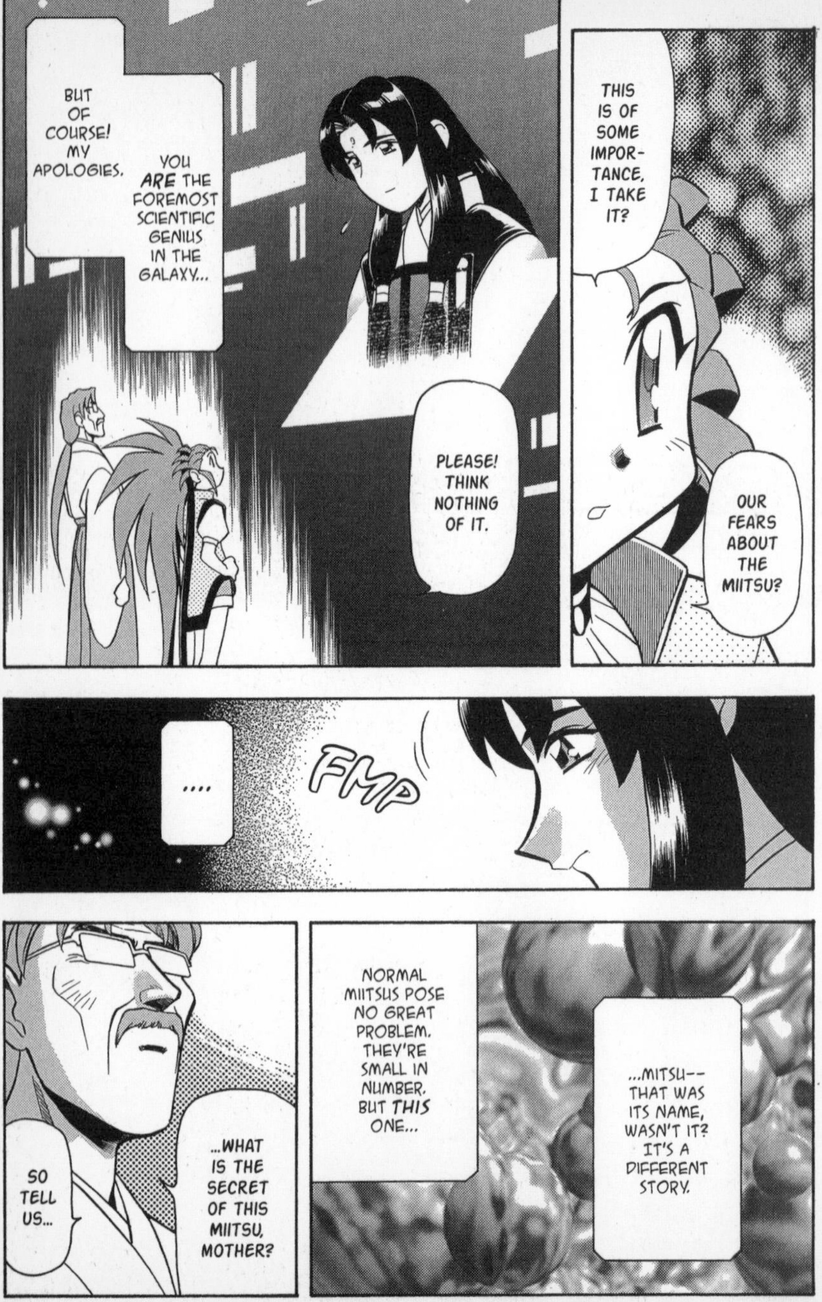
BUT OF COURSE! MY APOLOGIES.
YOU ARE THE FOREMOST SCIENTIFIC GENIUS IN THE GALAXY...
PLEASE! THINK NOTHING OF IT.
THIS IS OF SOME IMPORTANCE, I TAKE IT?
OUR FEARS ABOUT THE MIITSU?
....
FMP
SO TELL US...
...WHAT IS THE SECRET OF THIS MIITSU, MOTHER?
NORMAL MIITSUS POSE NO GREAT PROBLEM. THEY'RE SMALL IN NUMBER. BUT THIS ONE...
...MITSU-- THAT WAS ITS NAME, WASN'T IT? IT'S A DIFFERENT STORY.

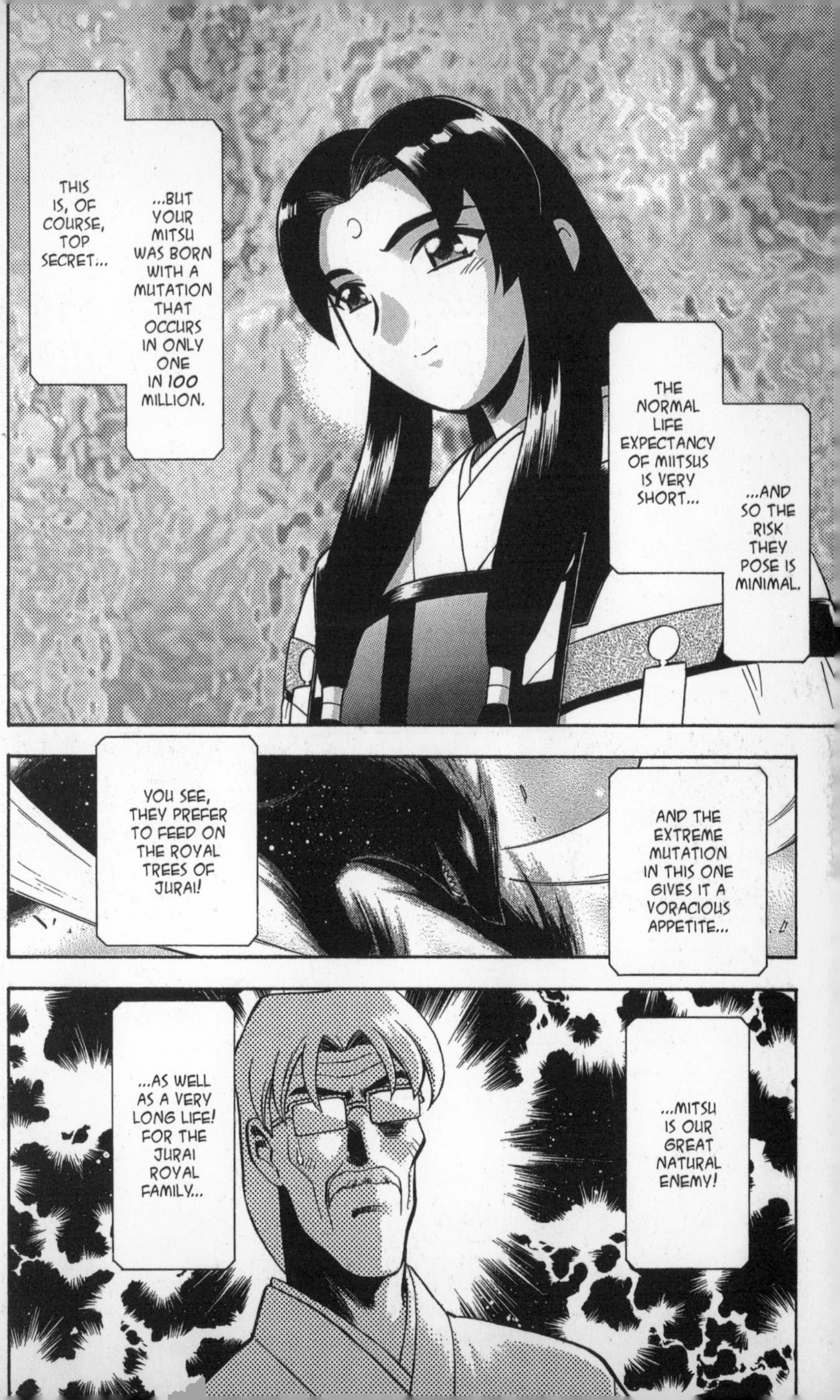
THIS IS, OF COURSE, TOP SECRET...
...BUT YOUR MITSU WAS BORN WITH A MUTATION THAT OCCURS IN ONLY ONE IN 100 MILLION.
THE NORMAL LIFE EXPECTANCY OF MIITSUS IS VERY SHORT...
...AND SO THE RISK THEY POSE IS MINIMAL.
YOU SEE, THEY PREFER TO FEED ON THE ROYAL TREES OF JURAI!
AND THE EXTREME MUTATION IN THIS ONE GIVES IT A VORACIOUS APPETITE...
...AS WELL AS A VERY LONG LIFE! FOR THE JURAI ROYAL FAMILY...
...MITSU IS OUR GREAT NATURAL ENEMY!

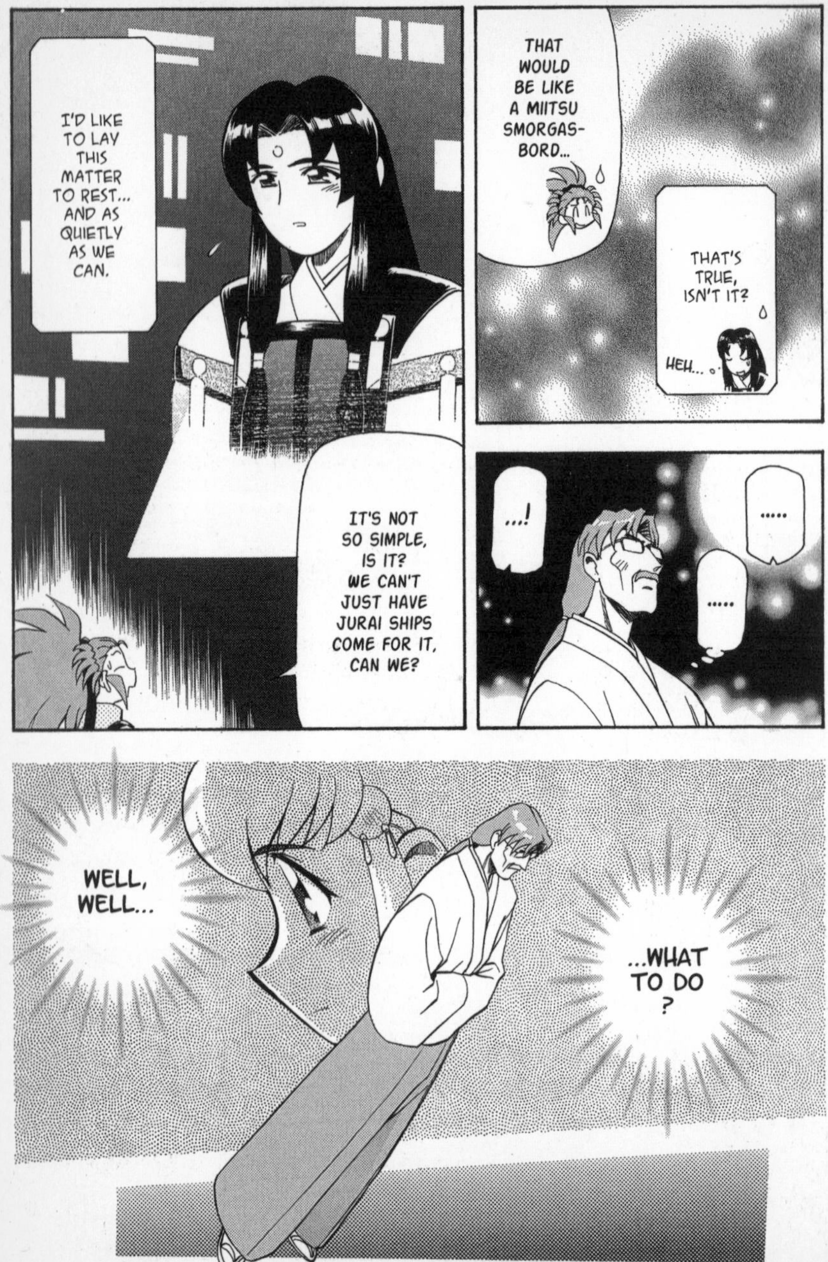
I'D LIKE TO LAY THIS MATTER TO REST... AND AS QUIETLY AS WE CAN.
IT'S NOT SO SIMPLE, IS IT? WE CAN'T JUST HAVE JURAI SHIPS COME FOR IT, CAN WE?
THAT WOULD BE LIKE A MIITSU SMORGAS-BORD...
THAT'S TRUE, ISN'T IT?
HEH...
...!
.....
.....
WELL, WELL...
...WHAT TO DO ?

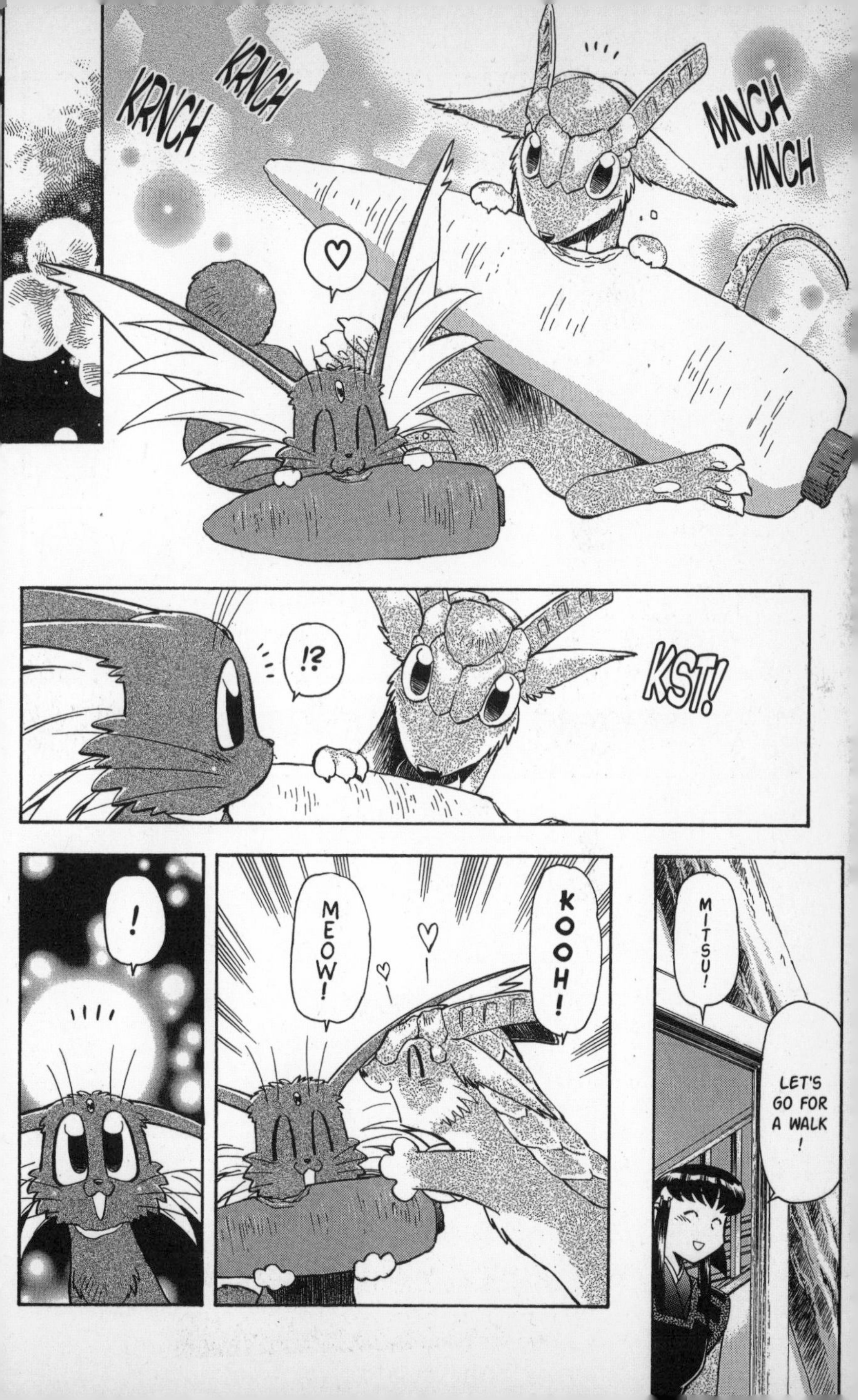
KRNCH
KRNCH
♡
MNCH
MNCH
!?
KST!
!
MEOW!
♡
♡
KOOH!
MITSU!
LET'S GO FOR A WALK!

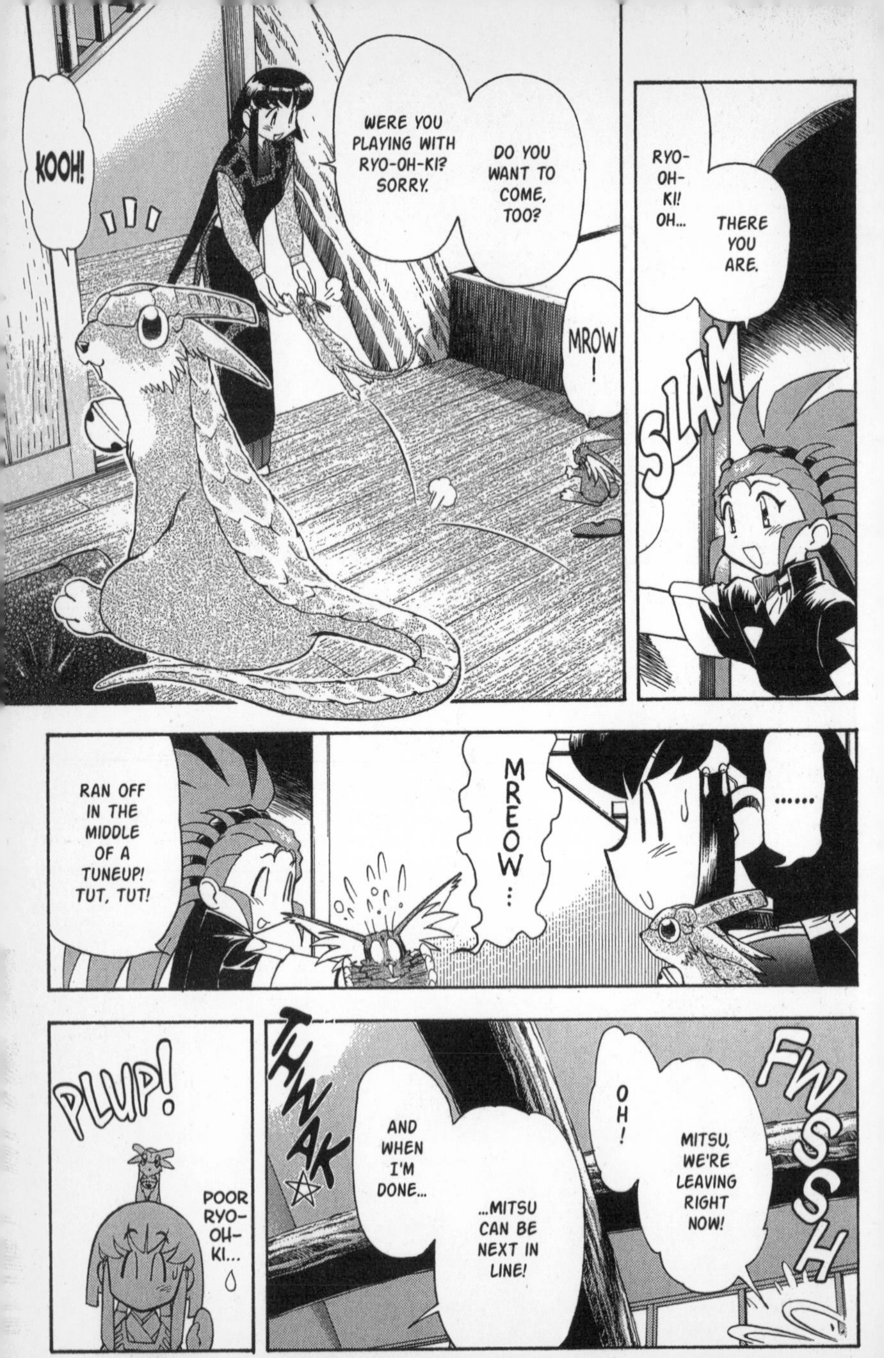
KOOH!
WERE YOU PLAYING WITH RYO-OH-KI? SORRY.
DO YOU WANT TO COME, TOO?
MROW!
RYO-OH-KI! OH...
THERE YOU ARE.
SLAM
RAN OFF IN THE MIDDLE OF A TUNEUP! TUT, TUT!
MREOW...
......
PLUP!
POOR RYO-OH-KI...
THWAK
AND WHEN I'M DONE...
...MITSU CAN BE NEXT IN LINE!
OH!
MITSU, WE'RE LEAVING RIGHT NOW!
FWSSH

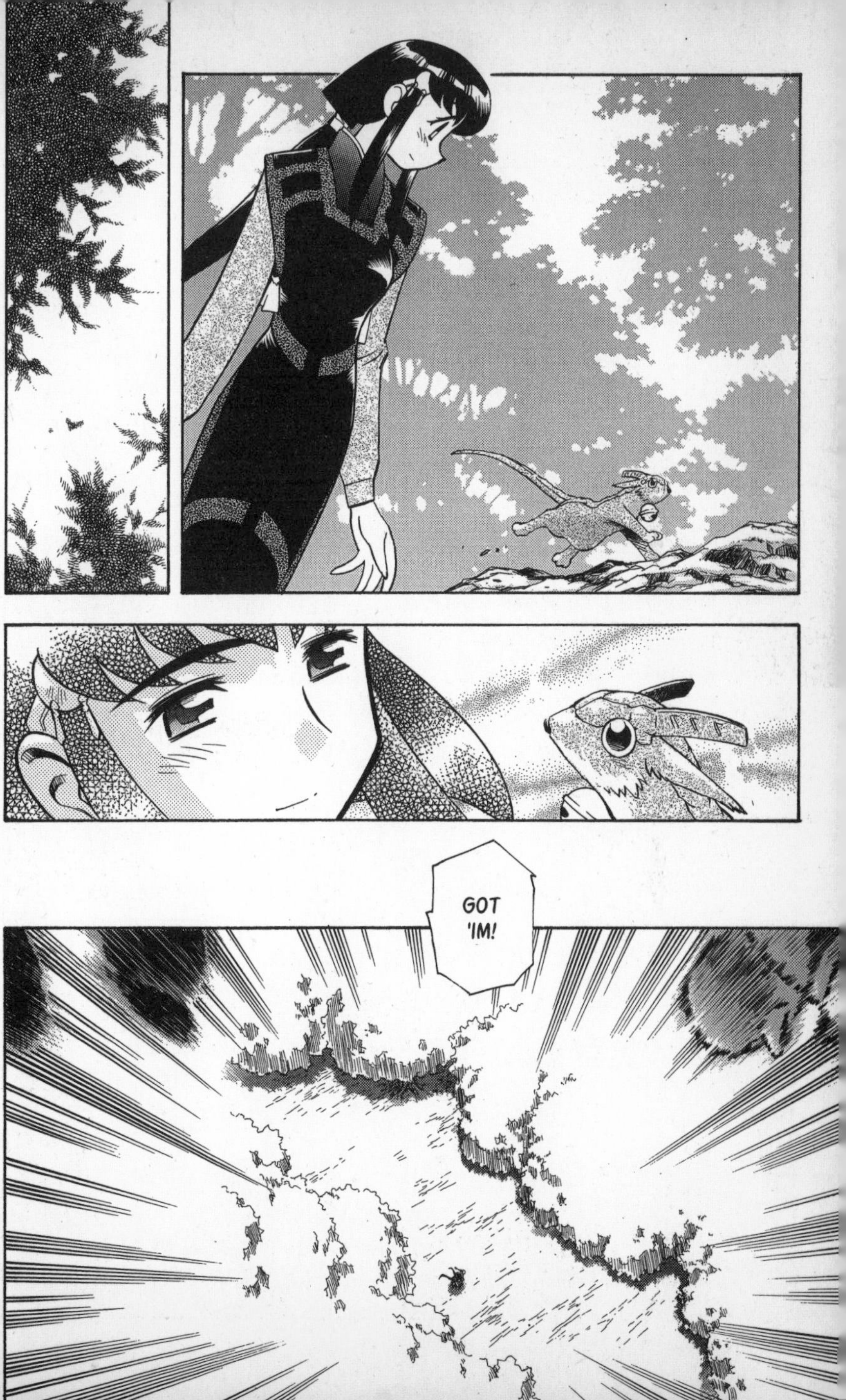
GOT 'IM!

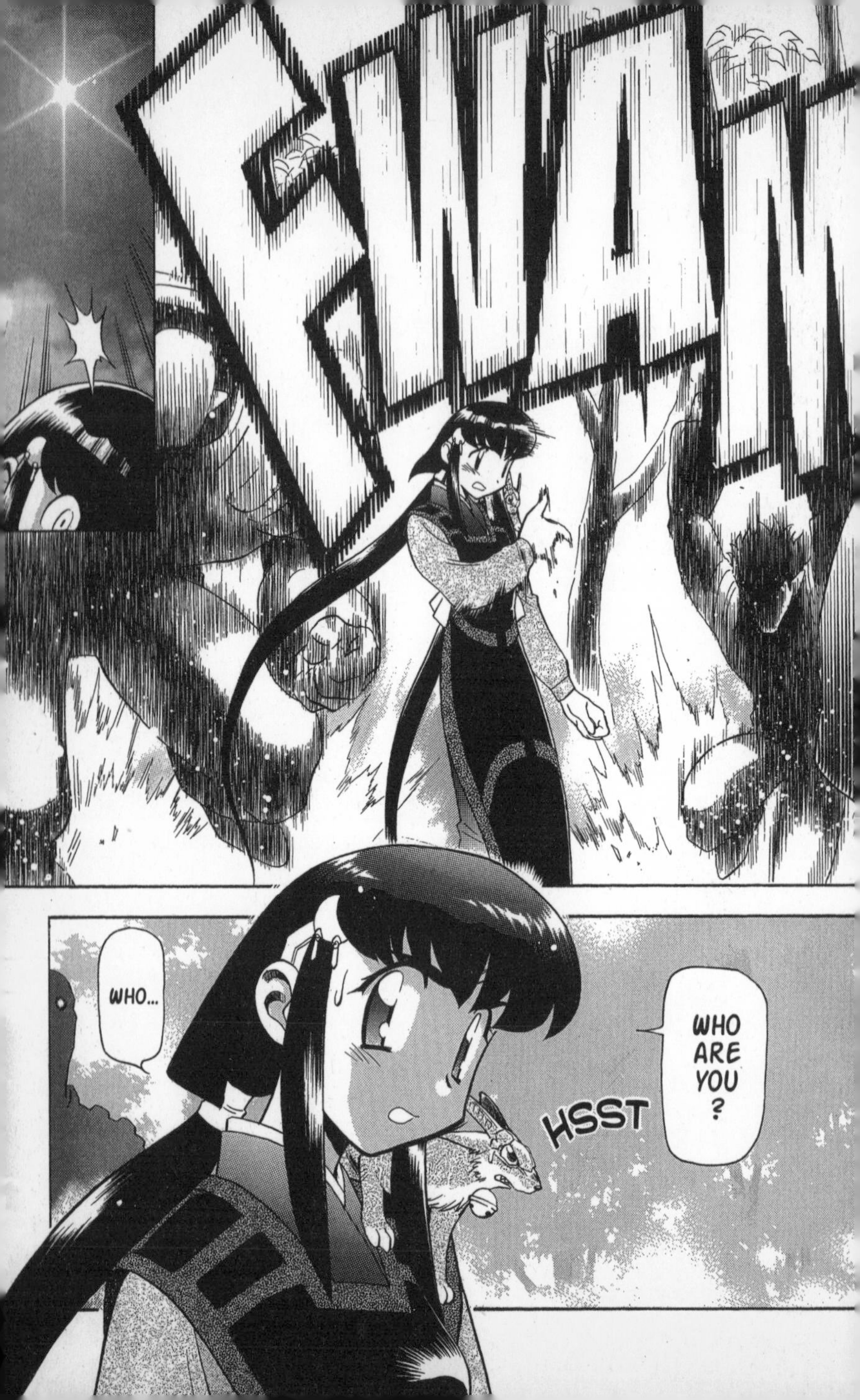
WHO...
WHO ARE YOU?
HSST

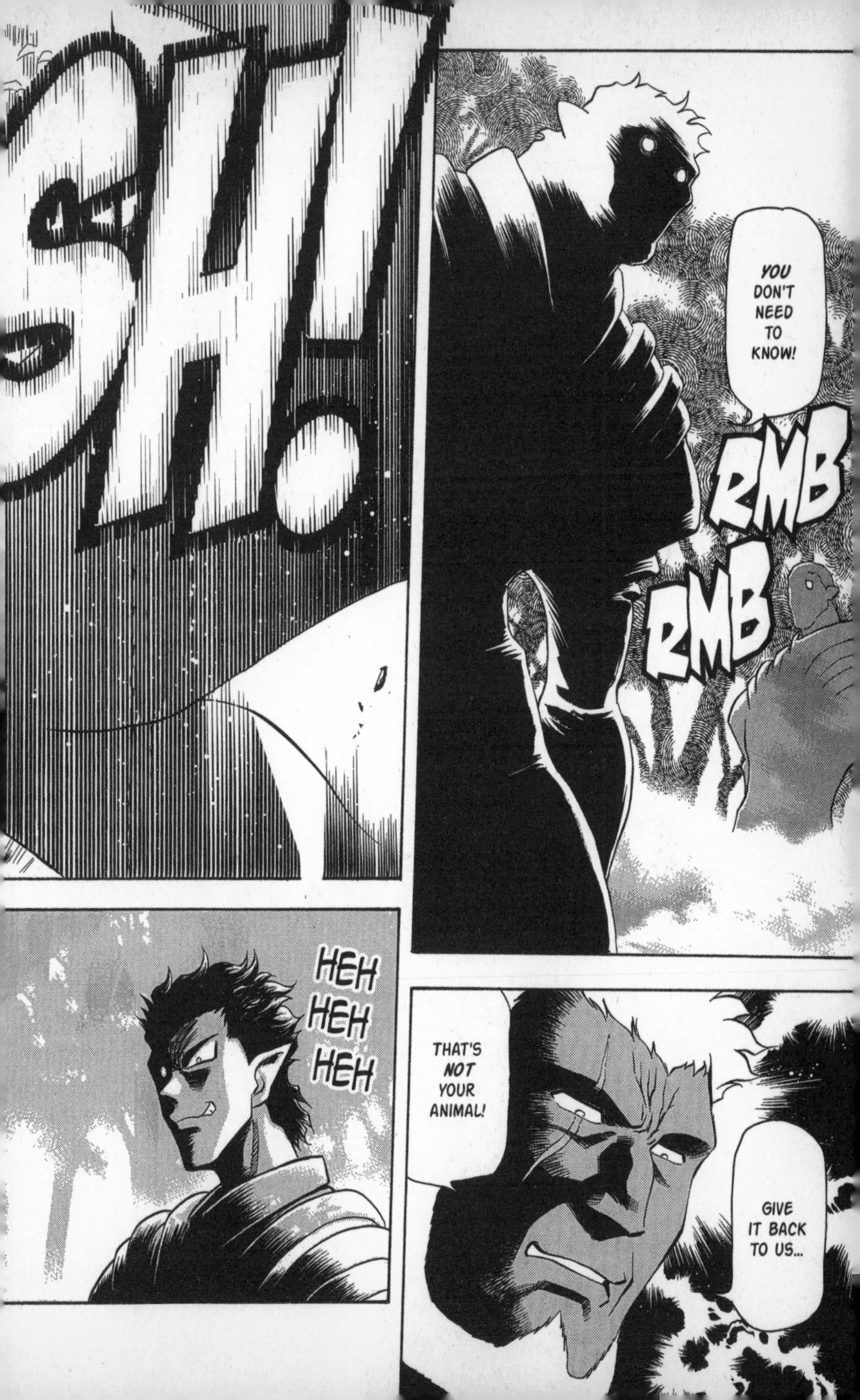
YOU DON'T NEED TO KNOW!
RMB
RMB
HEH HEH HEH
THAT'S *NOT* YOUR ANIMAL!
GIVE IT BACK TO US...

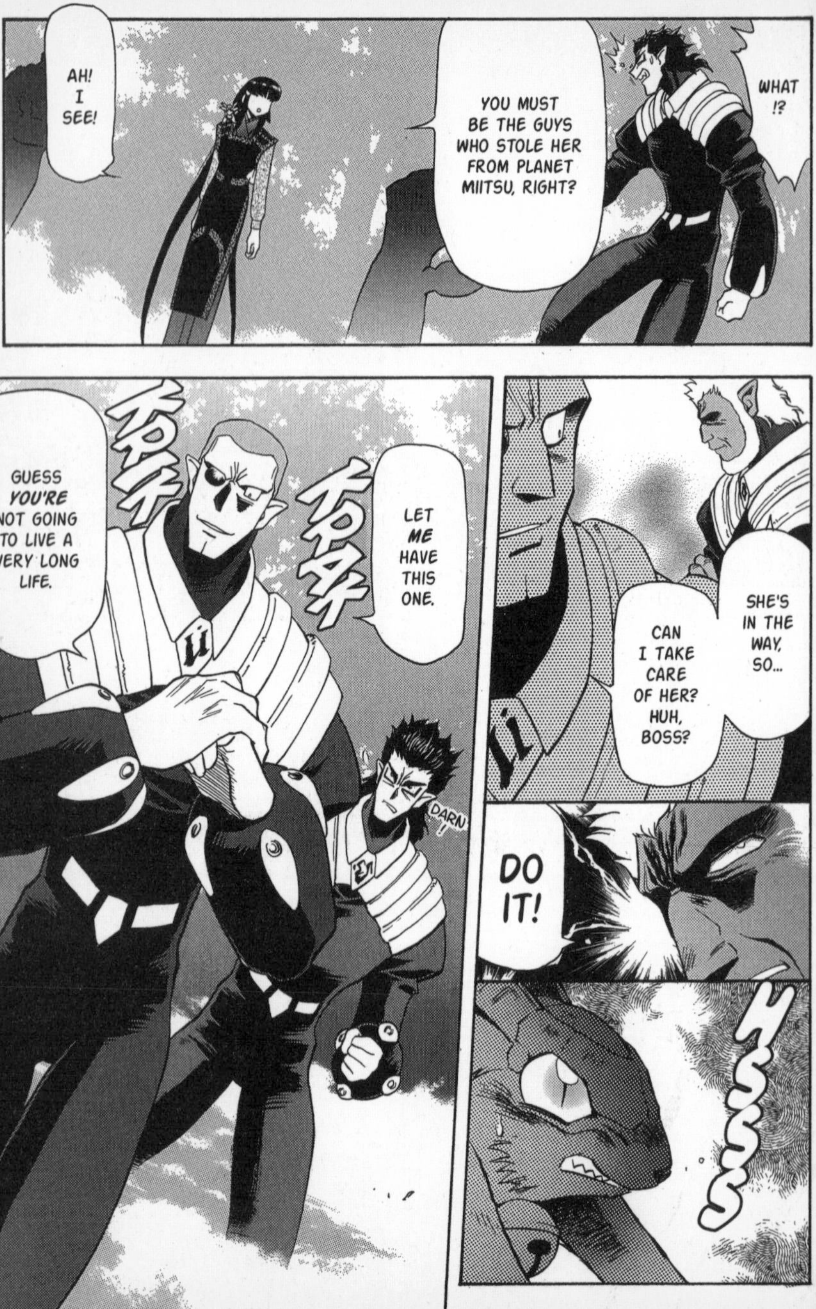
AH! I SEE!
YOU MUST BE THE GUYS WHO STOLE HER FROM PLANET MIITSU, RIGHT?
WHAT !?
GUESS *YOU'RE* NOT GOING TO LIVE A VERY LONG LIFE.
KRAK
KRAK
LET *ME* HAVE THIS ONE.
DARN!
SHE'S IN THE WAY, SO...
CAN I TAKE CARE OF HER? HUH, BOSS?
DO IT!
HSSSS

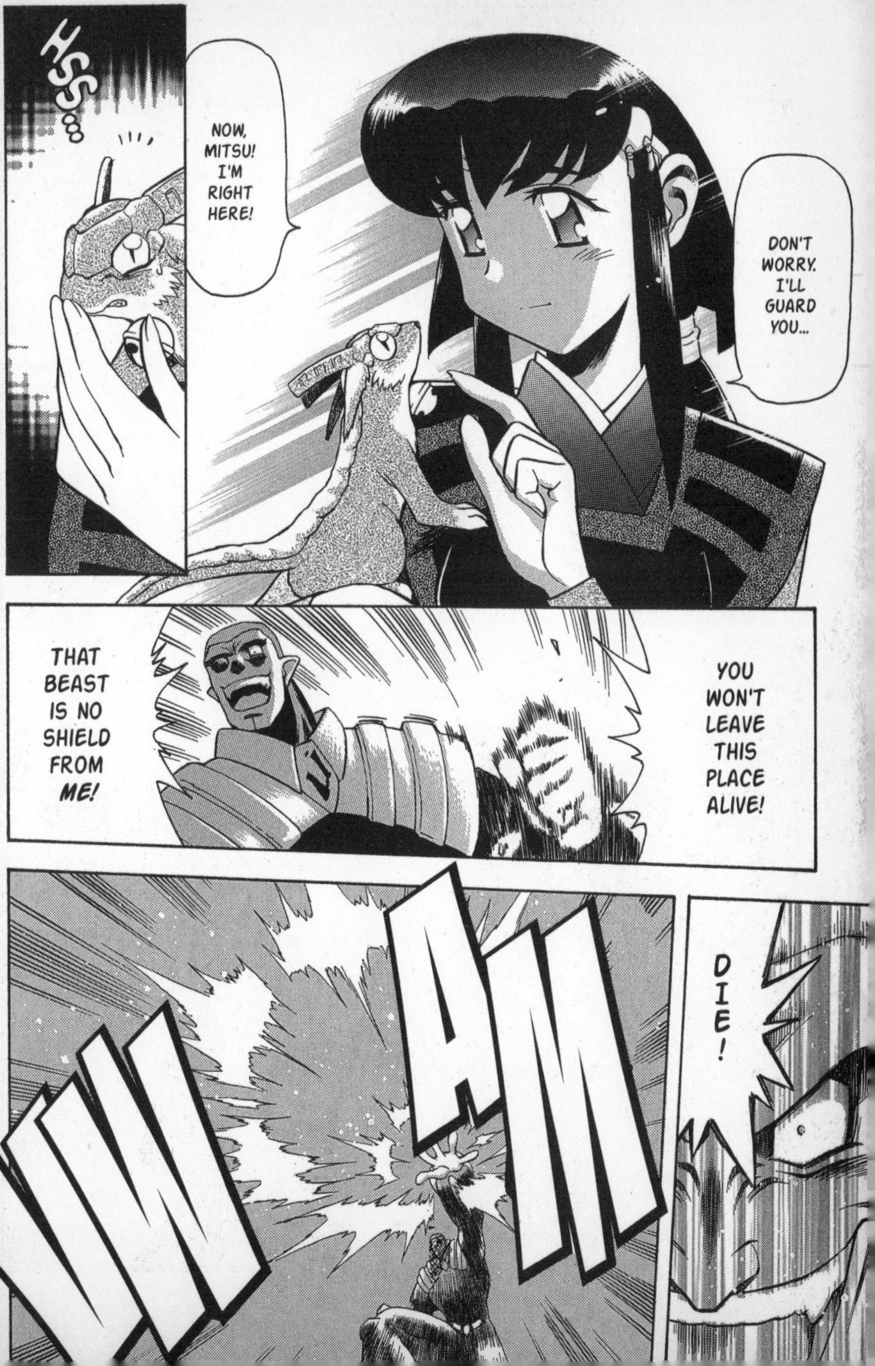
HSS...
NOW, MITSU! I'M RIGHT HERE!
DON'T WORRY. I'LL GUARD YOU...
THAT BEAST IS NO SHIELD FROM *ME!*
YOU WON'T LEAVE THIS PLACE ALIVE!
WHAM
DIE!

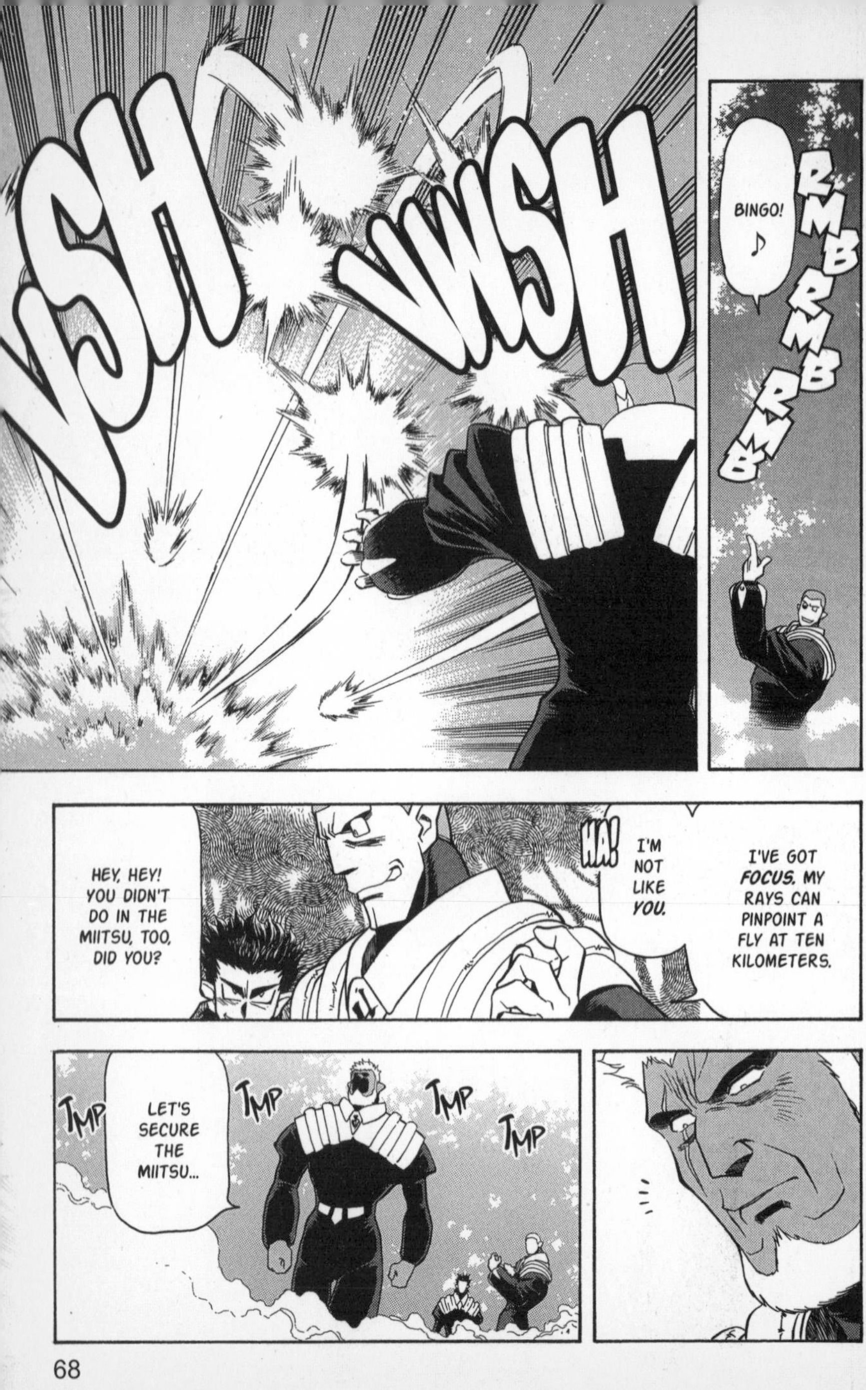
VSH
VWSH
BINGO! ♪
RMB RMB RMB
HEY, HEY! YOU DIDN'T DO IN THE MIITSU, TOO, DID YOU?
HA!
I'M NOT LIKE *YOU.*
I'VE GOT *FOCUS.* MY RAYS CAN PINPOINT A FLY AT TEN KILOMETERS.
TMP
LET'S SECURE THE MIITSU...
TMP
TMP
TMP

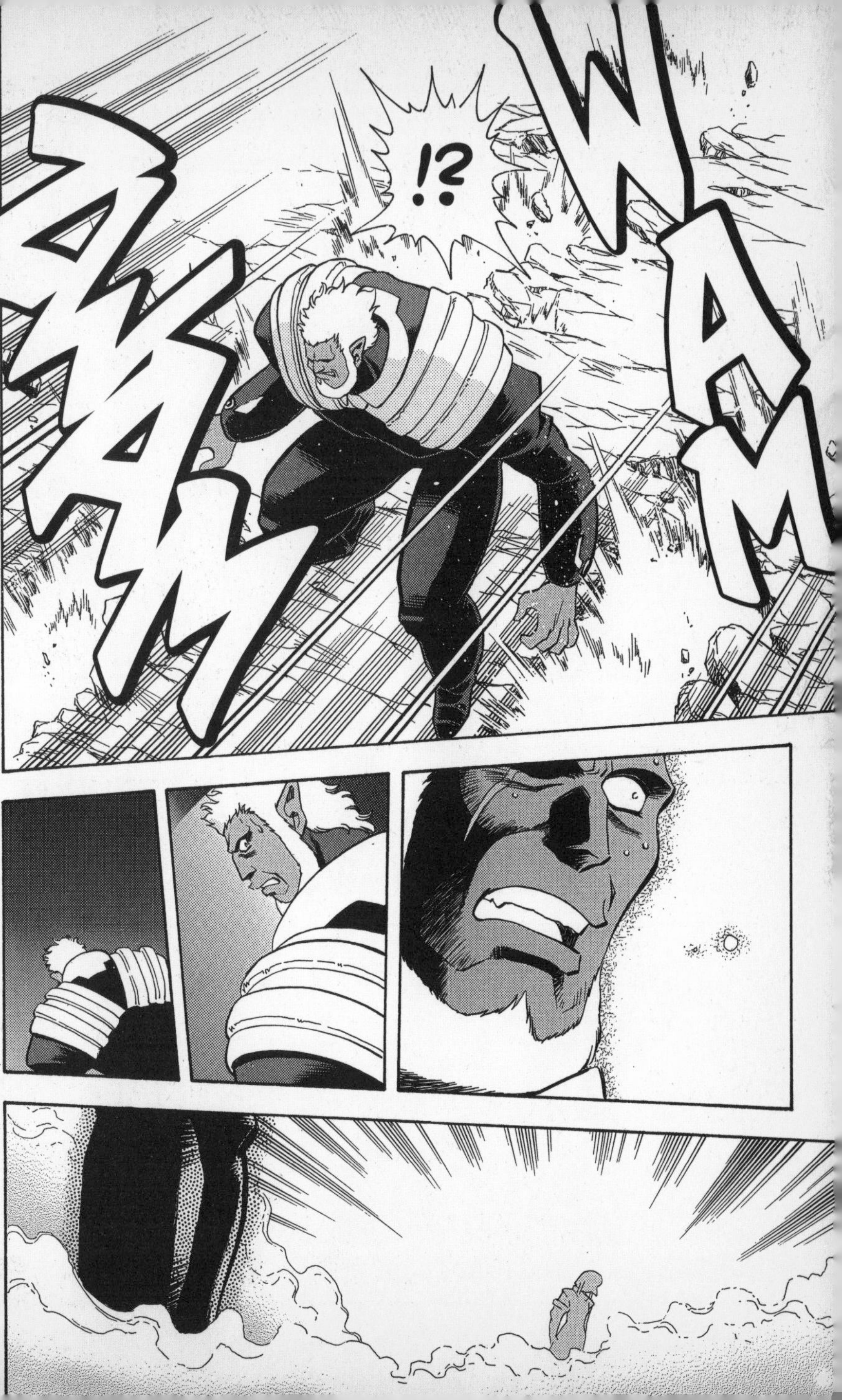
ZAAM
!?
WAM

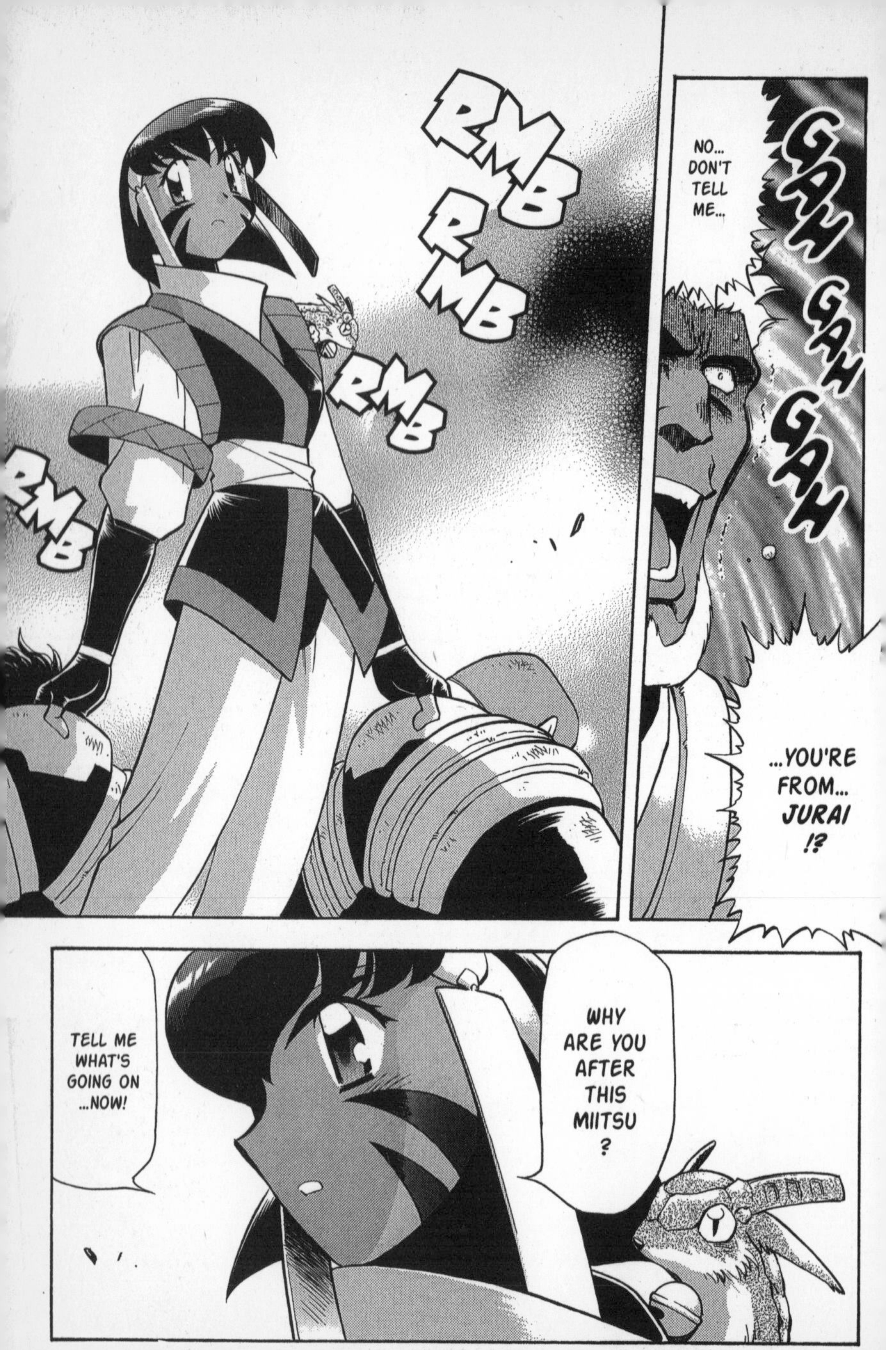
RMB
RMB
RMB
RMB
NO... DON'T TELL ME...
GAH GAH GAH GAH
...YOU'RE FROM... JURAI !?
TELL ME WHAT'S GOING ON ...NOW!
WHY ARE YOU AFTER THIS MIITSU ?

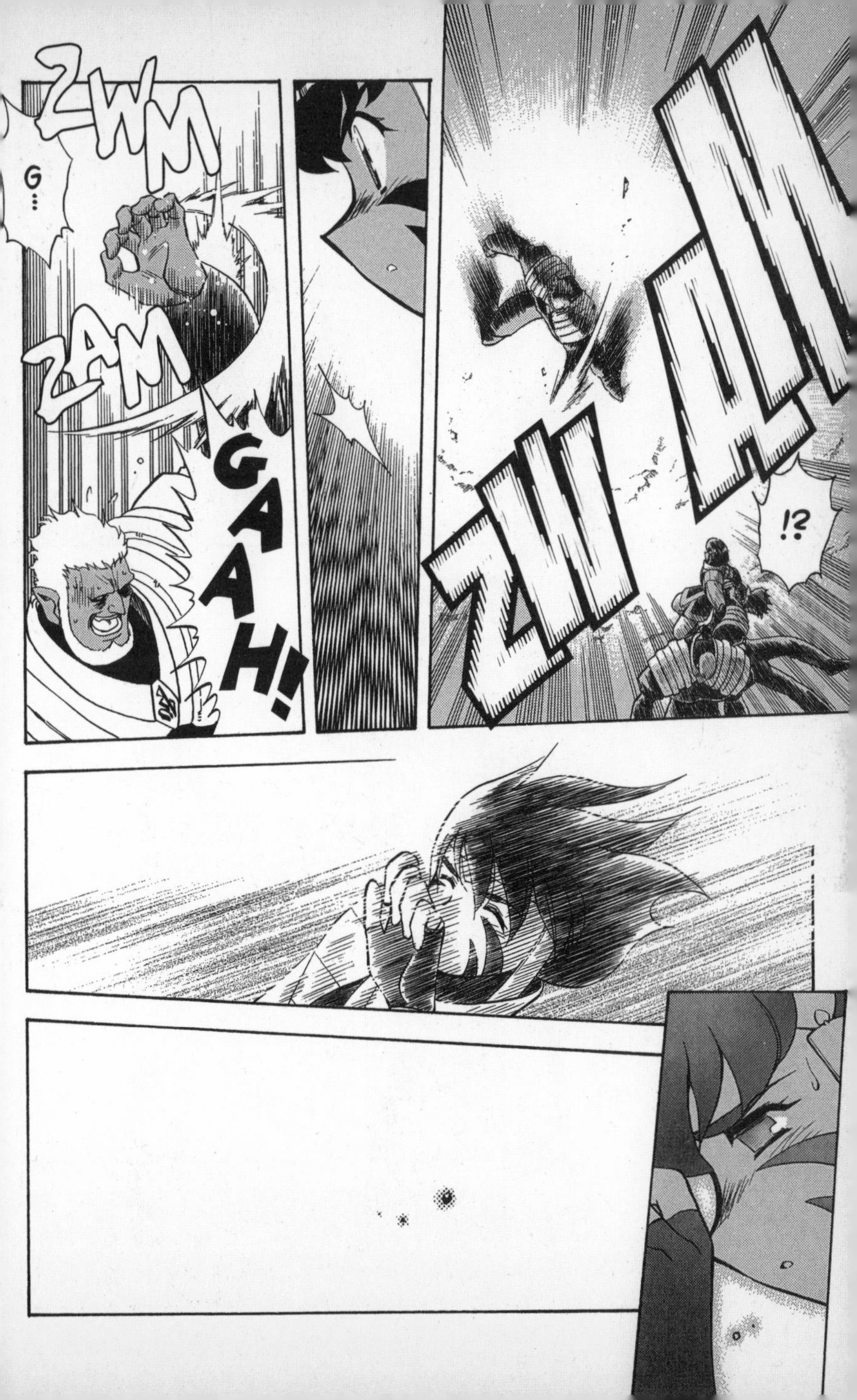
ZWM
G...
ZAM
GAAAH!
ZHUAAH
!?

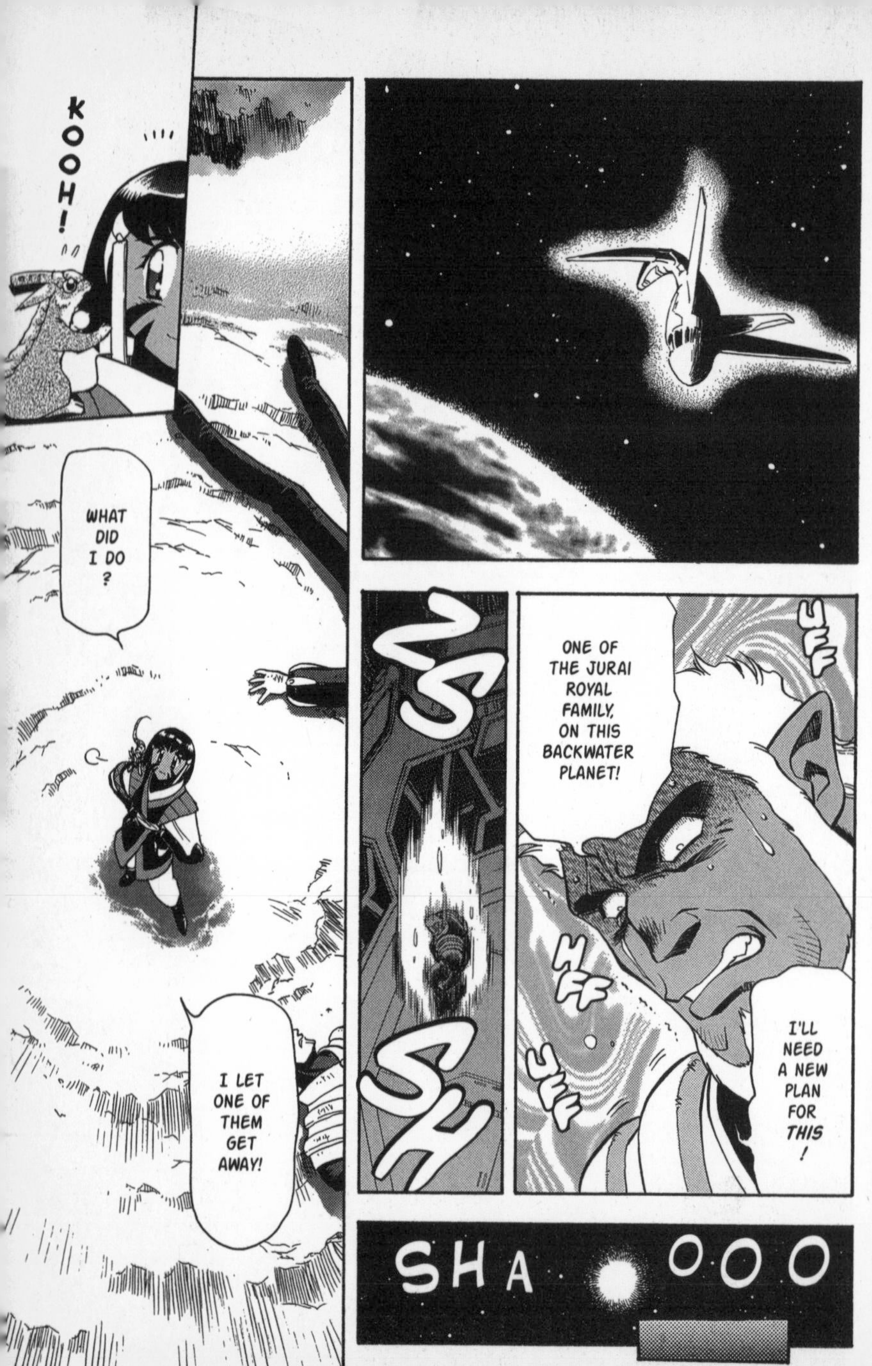
KOOOH!
WHAT DID I DO?
I LET ONE OF THEM GET AWAY!
ZZSSH
ONE OF THE JURAI ROYAL FAMILY, ON THIS BACKWATER PLANET!
UFF
HFF
UFF
I'LL NEED A NEW PLAN FOR THIS!
SHAOOO

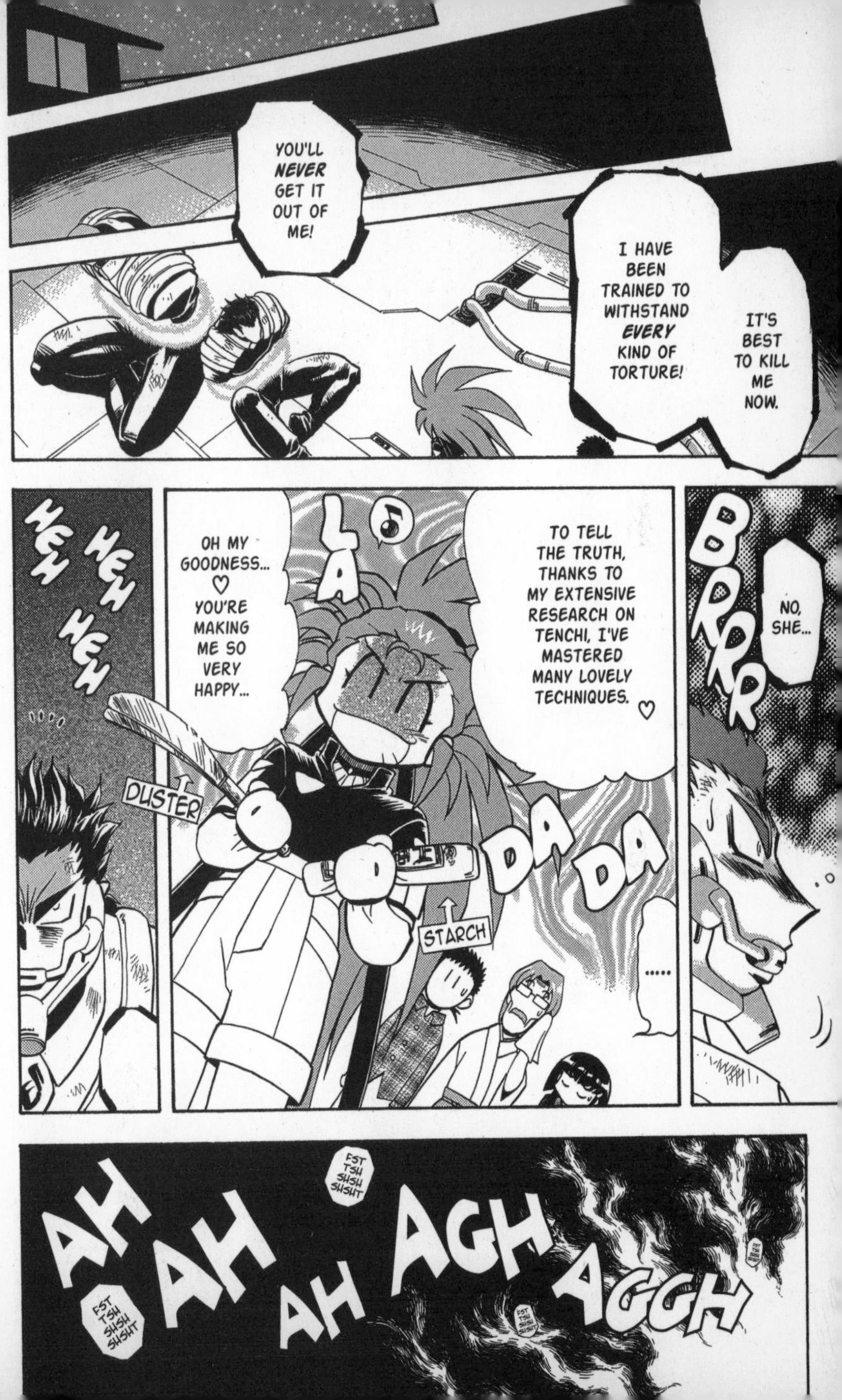
YOU'LL NEVER GET IT OUT OF ME!
I HAVE BEEN TRAINED TO WITHSTAND EVERY KIND OF TORTURE!
IT'S BEST TO KILL ME NOW.
HEH HEH HEH HEH
LA
OH MY GOODNESS... ♡ YOU'RE MAKING ME SO VERY HAPPY...
TO TELL THE TRUTH, THANKS TO MY EXTENSIVE RESEARCH ON TENCHI, I'VE MASTERED MANY LOVELY TECHNIQUES. ♡
DUSTER
DA DA
STARCH
.....
BRRRR
NO, SHE...
AH AH AH AGH AGGH
FST TSH SHSH SHSHT
FST TSH SHSH SHSHT
FST TSH SHSH SHSHT

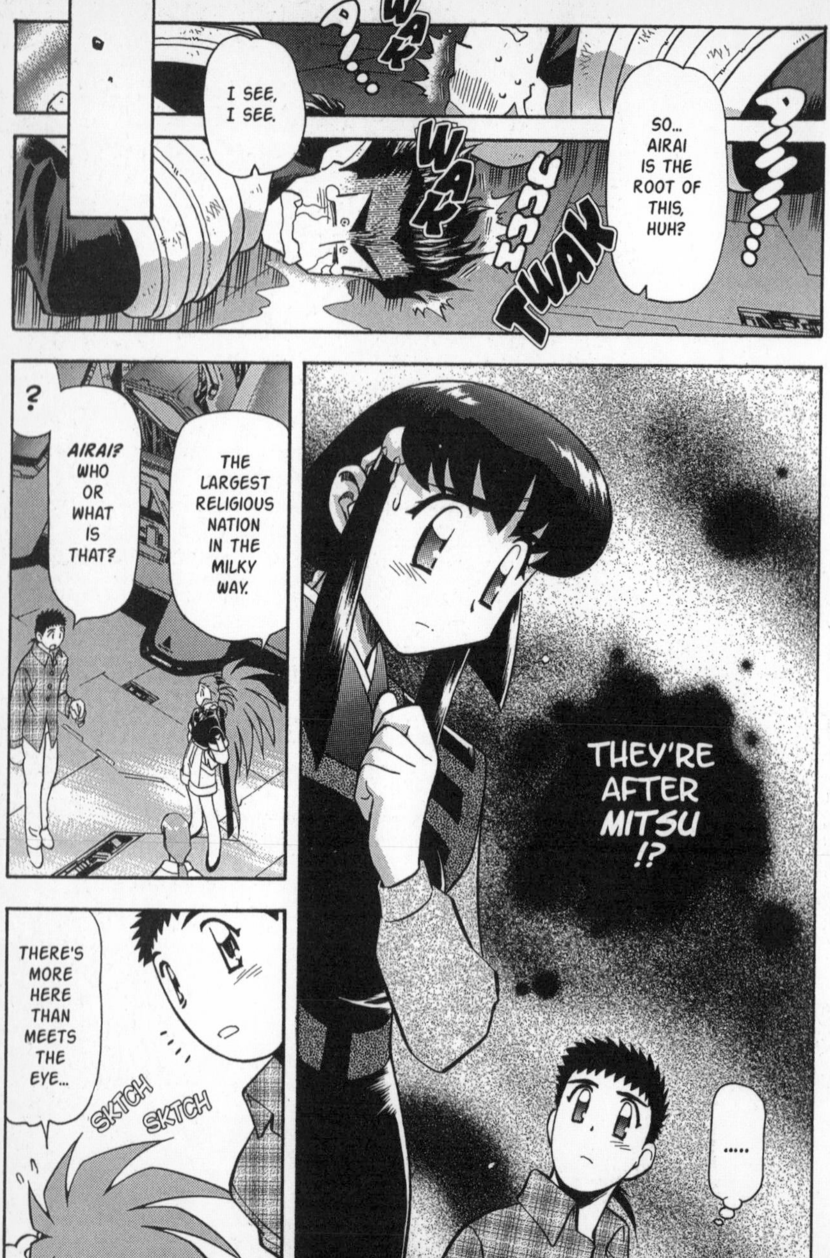
AI...
WAK
I SEE, I SEE.
WAK
TWAK
SO... AIRAI IS THE ROOT OF THIS, HUH?
AIII......
?
AIRAI? WHO OR WHAT IS THAT?
THE LARGEST RELIGIOUS NATION IN THE MILKY WAY.
THERE'S MORE HERE THAN MEETS THE EYE...
SKTCH SKTCH
THEY'RE AFTER MITSU !?
......

Chapter 3: Sacrifice

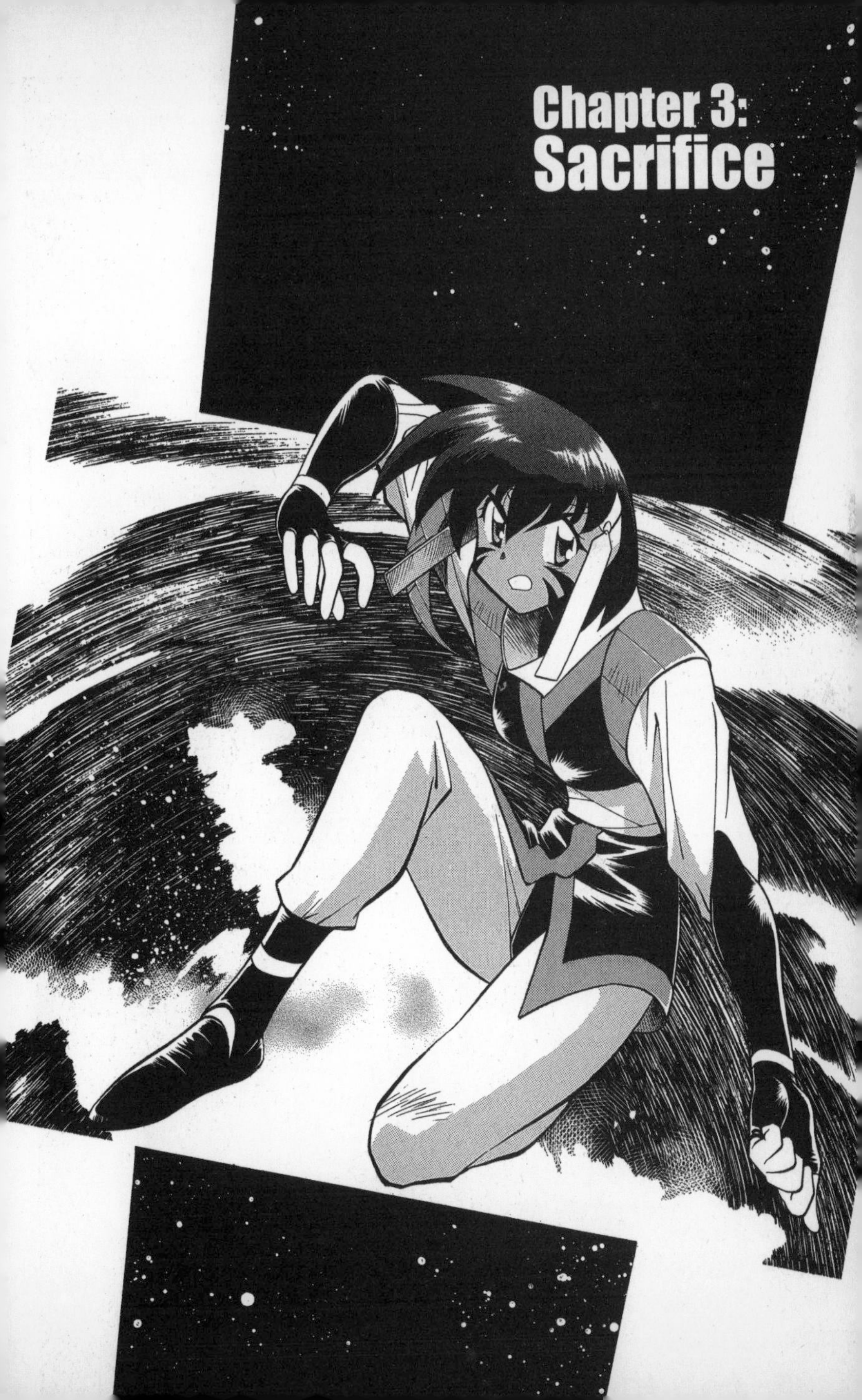

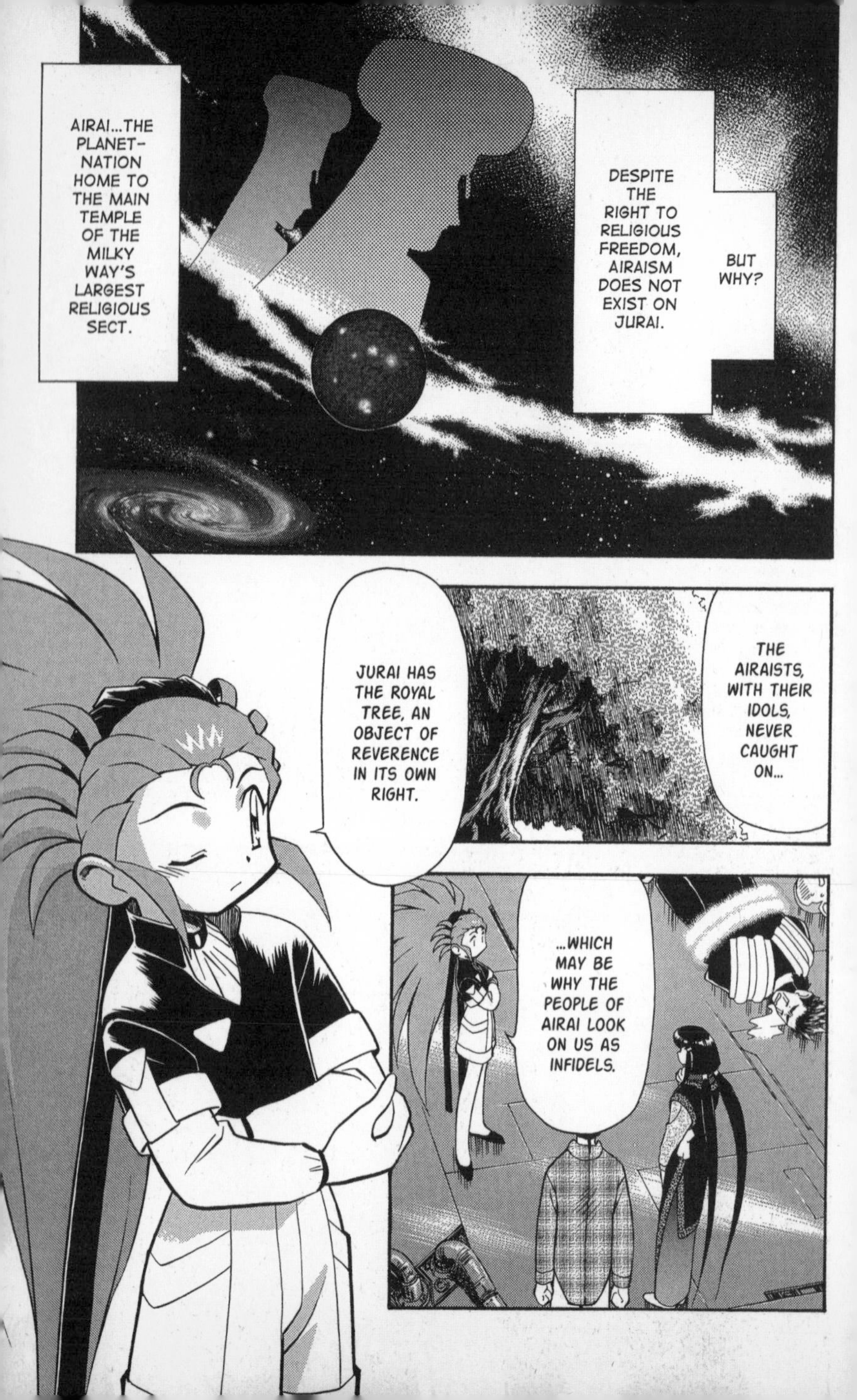
AIRAI...THE PLANET-NATION HOME TO THE MAIN TEMPLE OF THE MILKY WAY'S LARGEST RELIGIOUS SECT.
DESPITE THE RIGHT TO RELIGIOUS FREEDOM, AIRAISM DOES NOT EXIST ON JURAI.
BUT WHY?
JURAI HAS THE ROYAL TREE, AN OBJECT OF REVERENCE IN ITS OWN RIGHT.
THE AIRAISTS, WITH THEIR IDOLS, NEVER CAUGHT ON...
...WHICH MAY BE WHY THE PEOPLE OF AIRAI LOOK ON US AS INFIDELS.

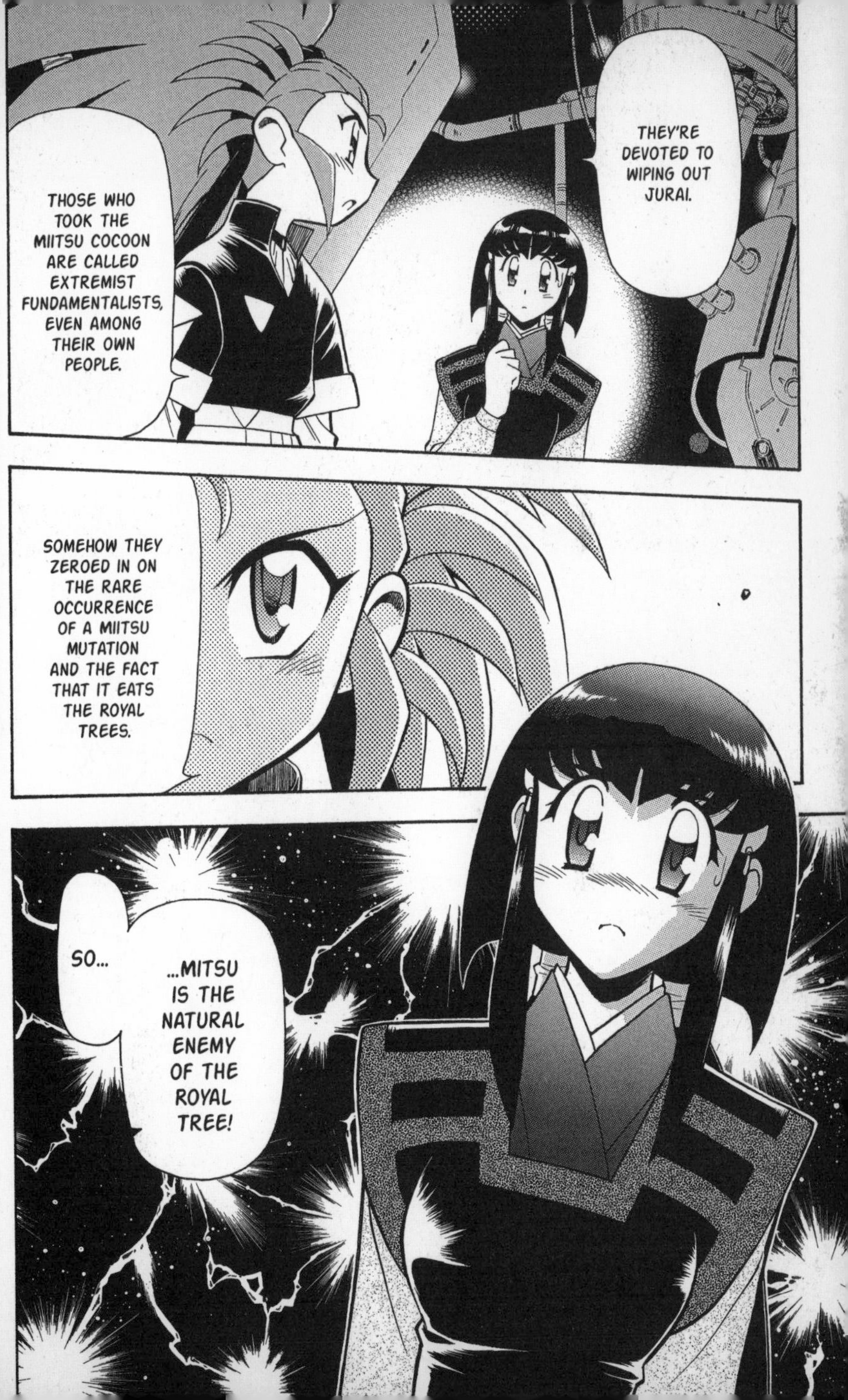
THOSE WHO TOOK THE MIITSU COCOON ARE CALLED EXTREMIST FUNDAMENTALISTS, EVEN AMONG THEIR OWN PEOPLE.
THEY'RE DEVOTED TO WIPING OUT JURAI.
SOMEHOW THEY ZEROED IN ON THE RARE OCCURRENCE OF A MIITSU MUTATION AND THE FACT THAT IT EATS THE ROYAL TREES.
SO...
...MITSU IS THE NATURAL ENEMY OF THE ROYAL TREE!

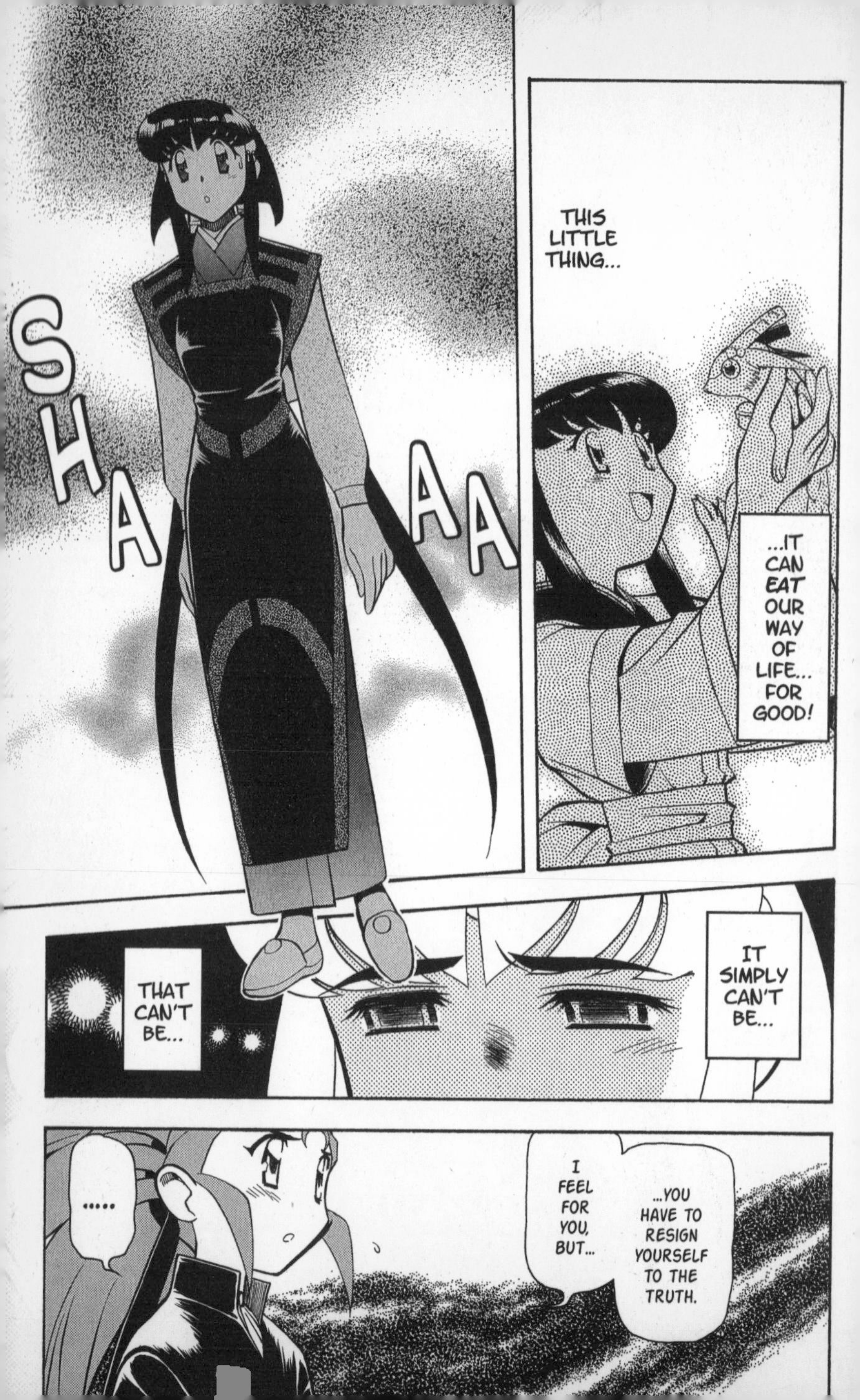
SHAAAA
THIS LITTLE THING...
...IT CAN EAT OUR WAY OF LIFE... FOR GOOD!
THAT CAN'T BE...
IT SIMPLY CAN'T BE...
......
I FEEL FOR YOU, BUT...
...YOU HAVE TO RESIGN YOURSELF TO THE TRUTH.

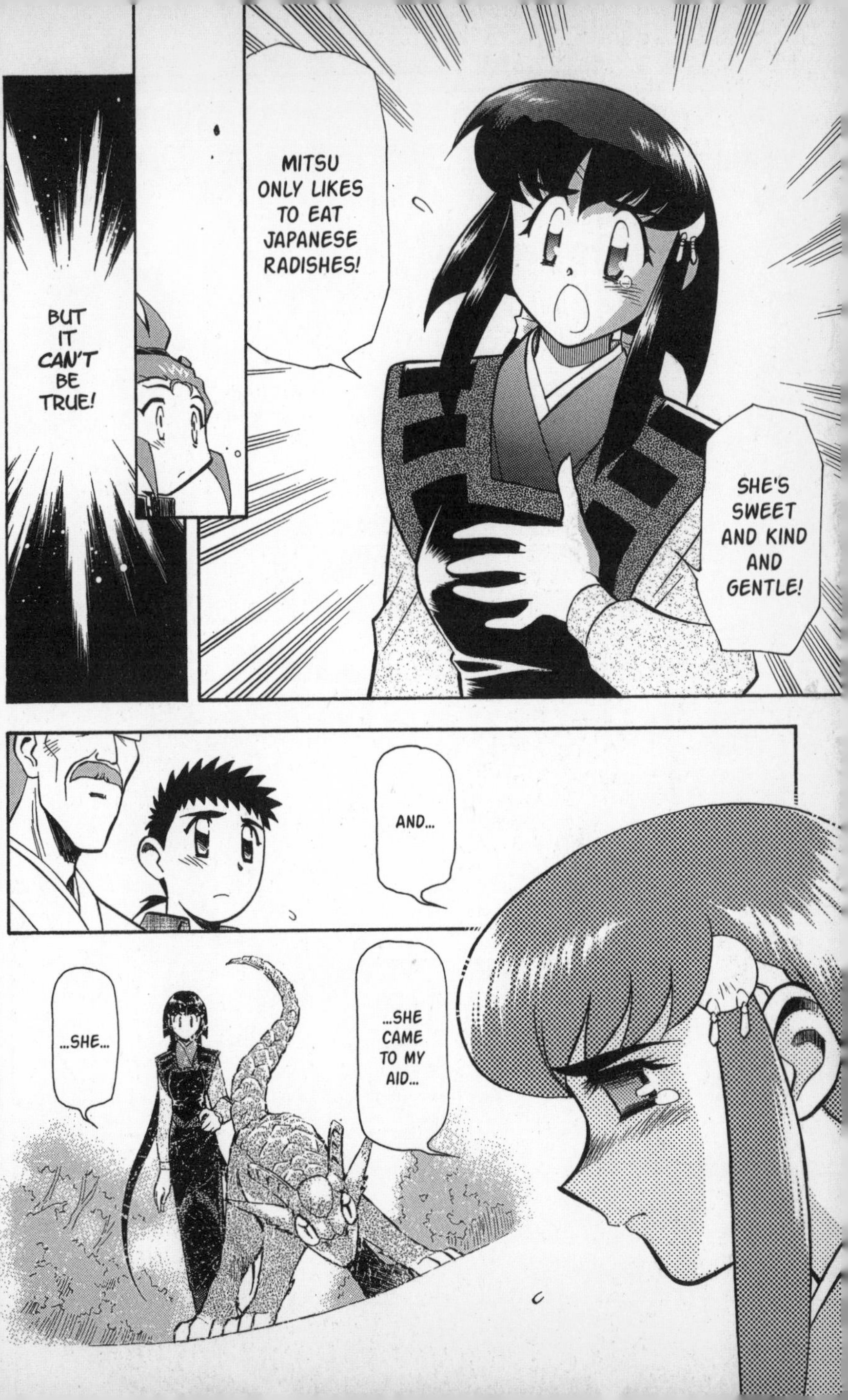
BUT IT CAN'T BE TRUE!
MITSU ONLY LIKES TO EAT JAPANESE RADISHES!
SHE'S SWEET AND KIND AND GENTLE!
AND...
...SHE...
...SHE CAME TO MY AID...

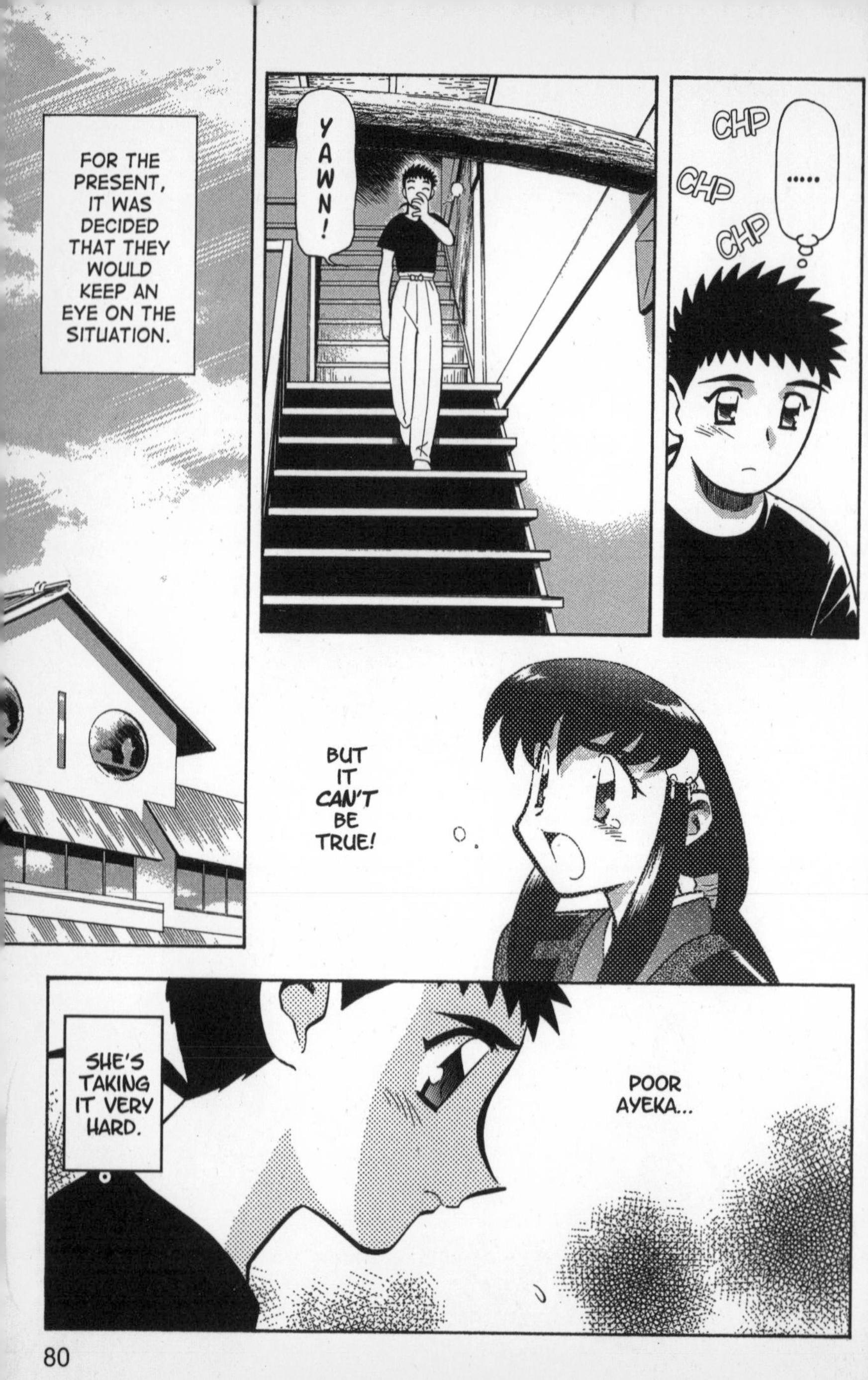
FOR THE PRESENT, IT WAS DECIDED THAT THEY WOULD KEEP AN EYE ON THE SITUATION.
YAWN!
CHP
CHP
CHP
......
BUT IT CAN'T BE TRUE!
SHE'S TAKING IT VERY HARD.
POOR AYEKA...

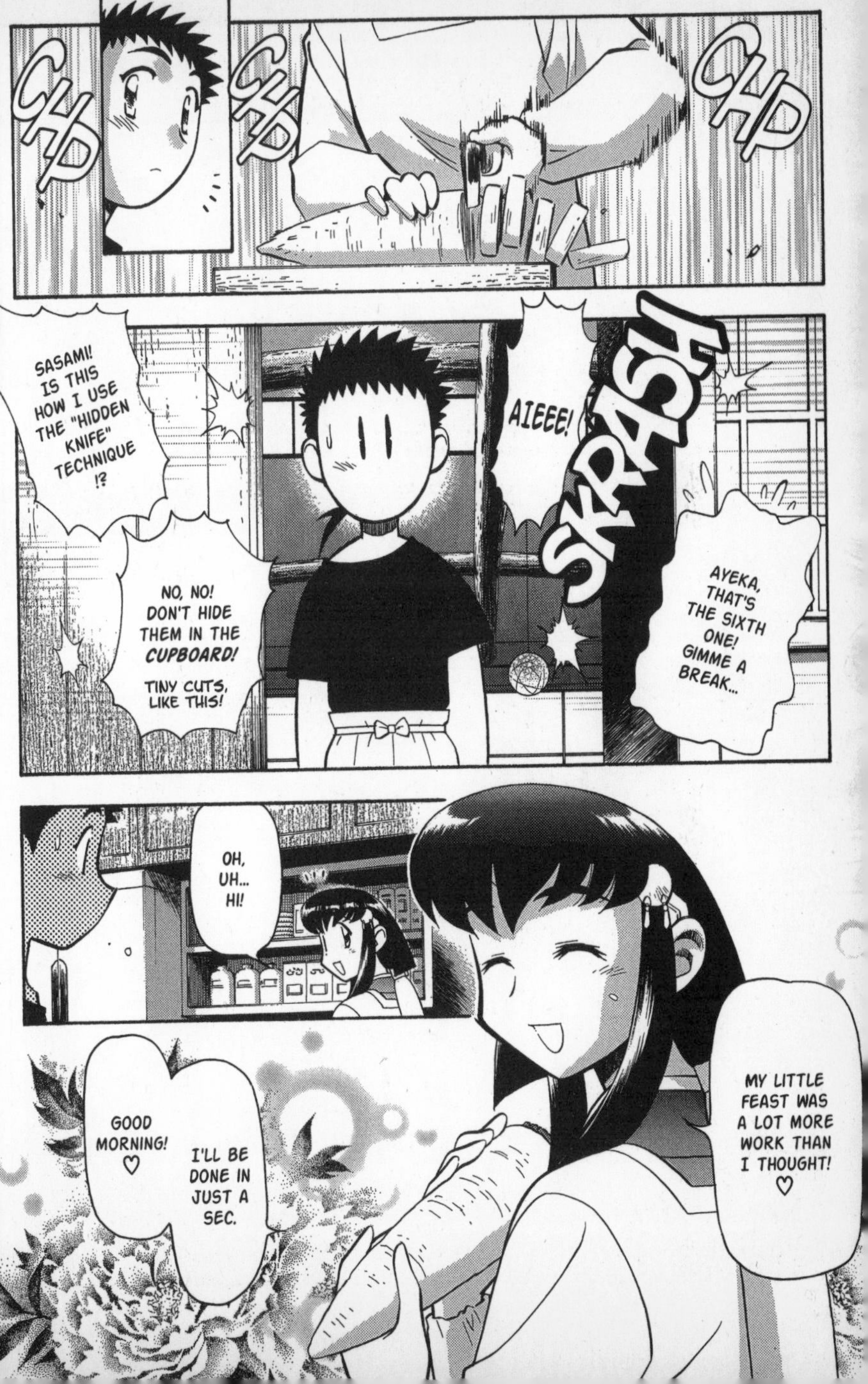
CHP
CHP
CHP
SASAMI! IS THIS HOW I USE THE "HIDDEN KNIFE" TECHNIQUE !?
NO, NO! DON'T HIDE THEM IN THE *CUPBOARD!*
TINY CUTS, LIKE THIS!
AIEEE!
SKRASH
AYEKA, THAT'S THE SIXTH ONE! GIMME A BREAK...
OH, UH... HI!
GOOD MORNING! ♡
I'LL BE DONE IN JUST A SEC.
MY LITTLE FEAST WAS A LOT MORE WORK THAN I THOUGHT! ♡

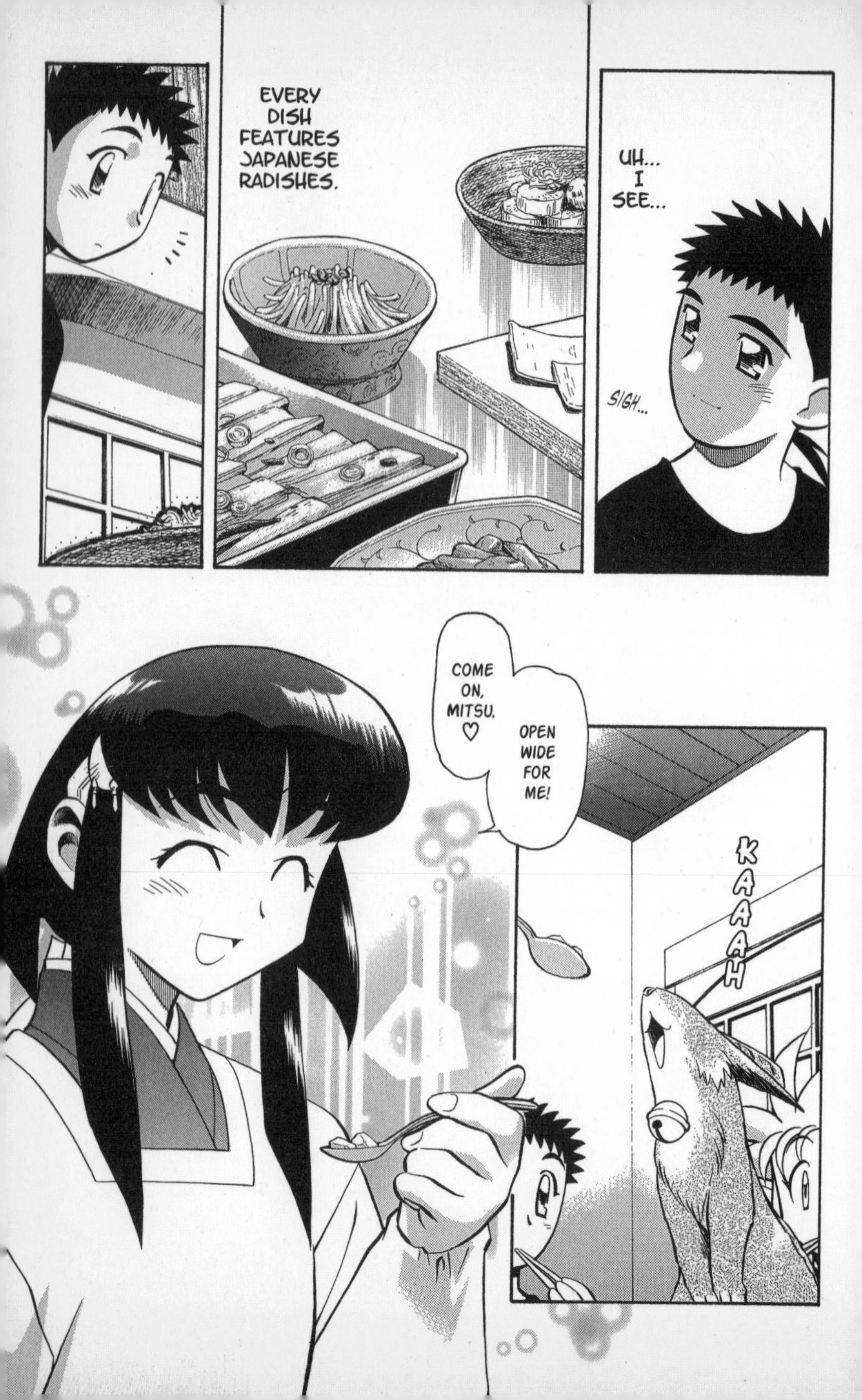
EVERY DISH FEATURES JAPANESE RADISHES.
UH... I SEE...
SIGH...
COME ON, MITSU. ♡
OPEN WIDE FOR ME!
KAAAAH

DOES IT TASTE GOOD?
I'M SO GLAD. ♡ YOU JUST EAT AS MUCH AS YOU LIKE, MITSU!
KOOOH! ♡
MRNCH ♡
ZLRRP
SHE'S GONE *MOM* ON US.
JAPANESE RADISHES...
SHE CAN'T HAVE ANYTHING ELSE!
BUT SOON...
MITSU!
MITSU!
WHERE HAVE YOU GONE?
BIG SIS! LOOK OVER *THERE!*
WHAT A SPOT FOR A NAP!
!?

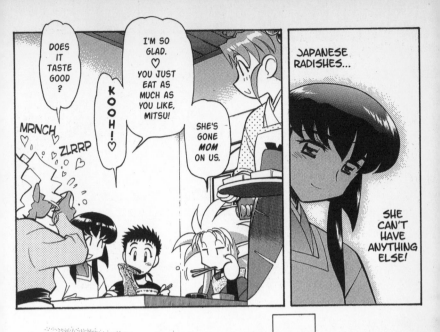

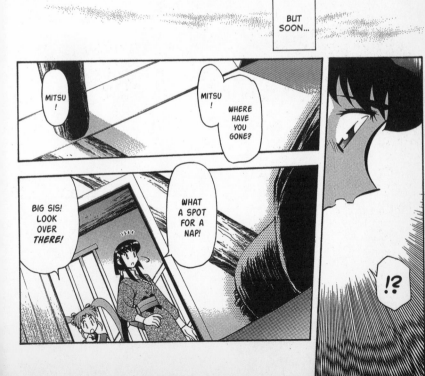

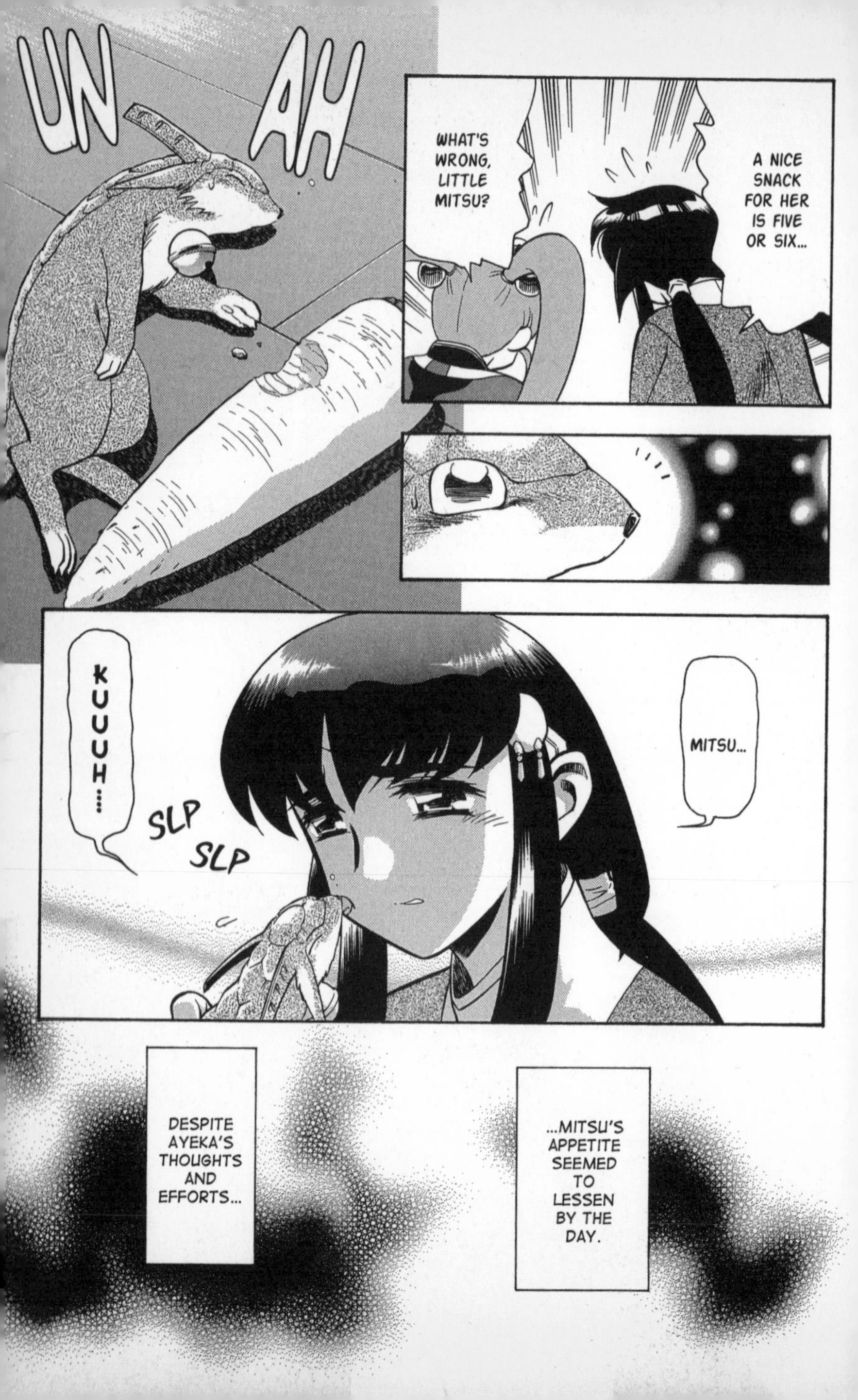
UN
AH
WHAT'S WRONG, LITTLE MITSU?
A NICE SNACK FOR HER IS FIVE OR SIX...
KUUUH...
SLP SLP
MITSU...
DESPITE AYEKA'S THOUGHTS AND EFFORTS...
...MITSU'S APPETITE SEEMED TO LESSEN BY THE DAY.

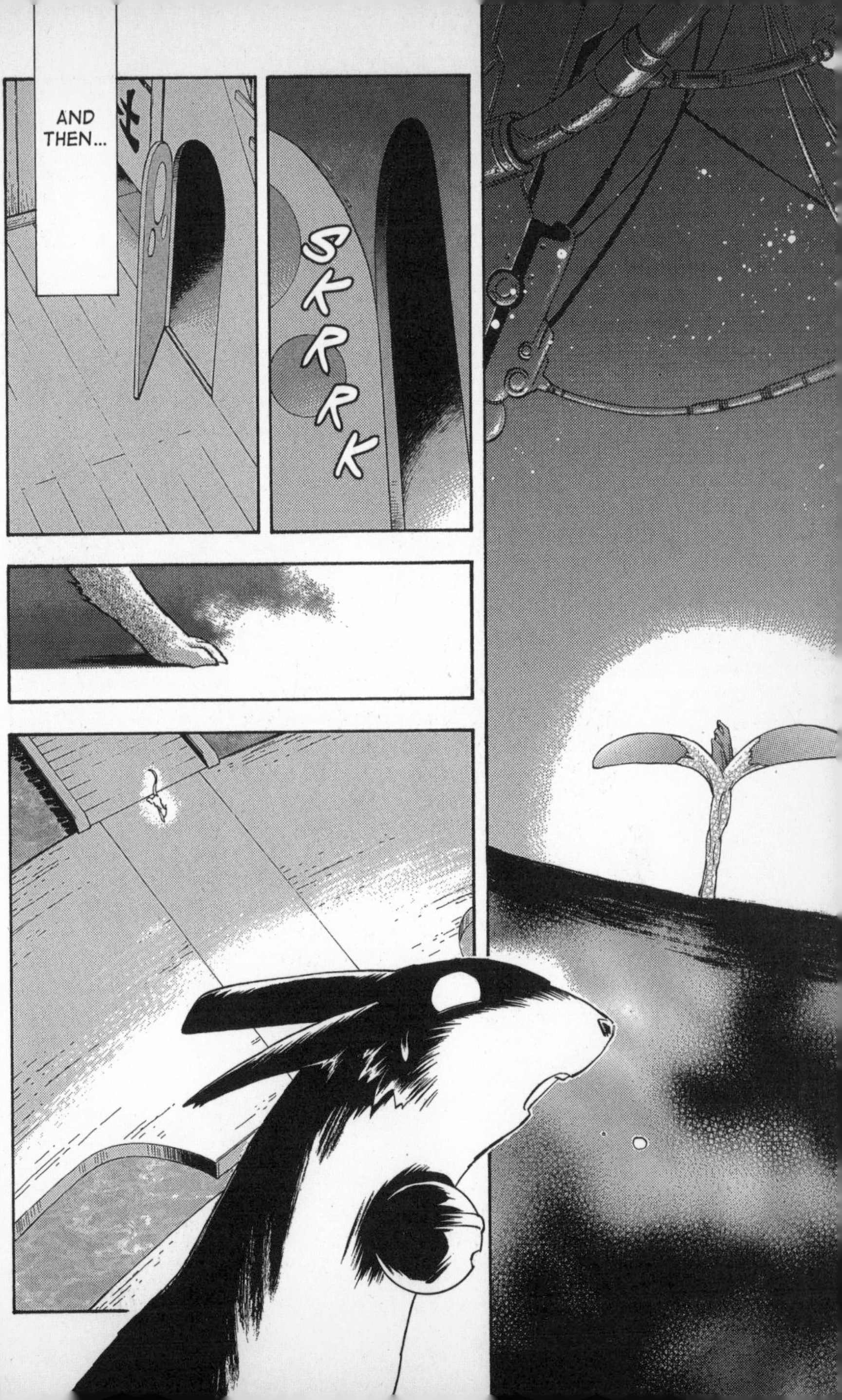
AND THEN...
SKRRK

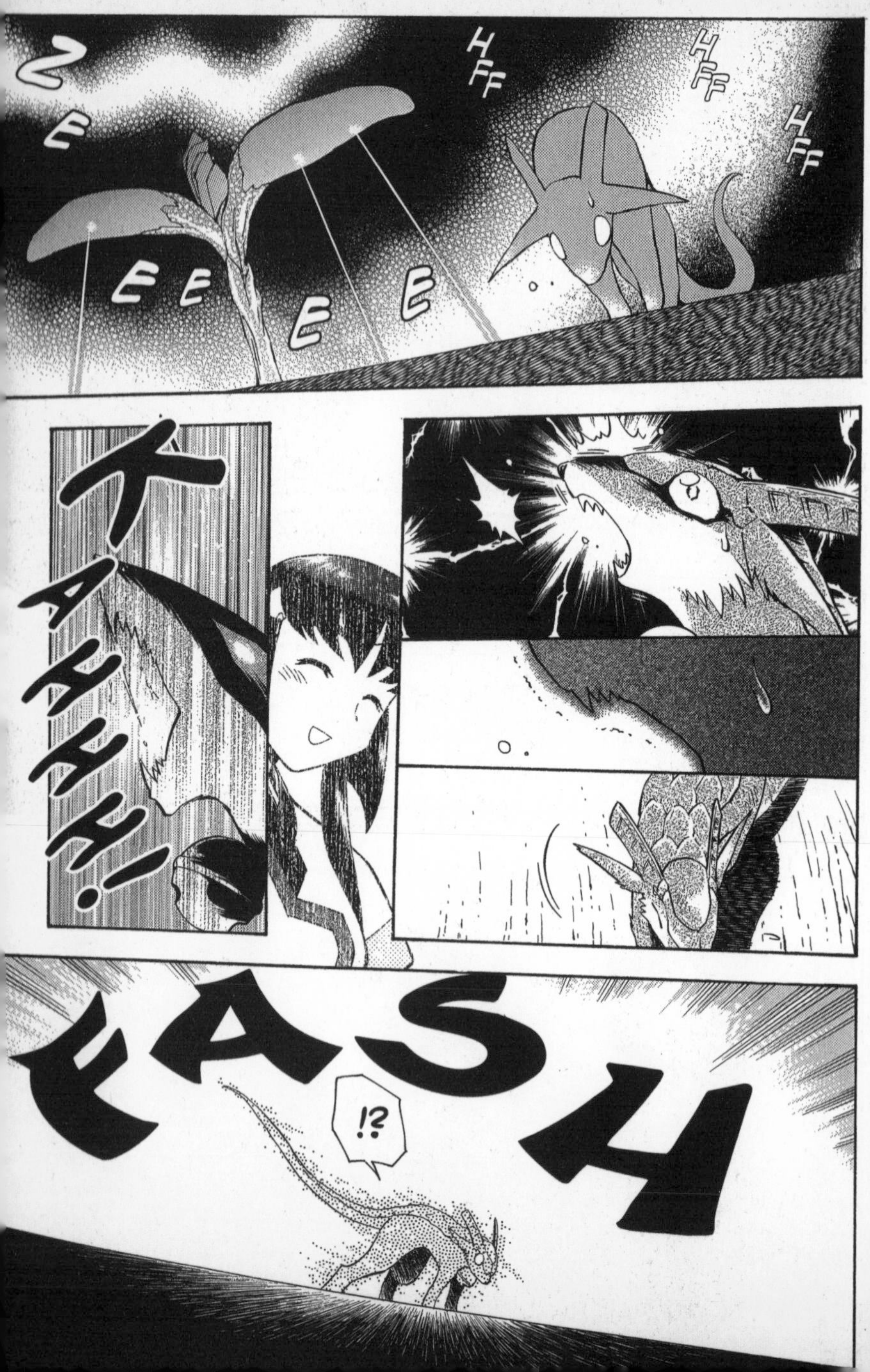
ZEEEEE
HFF
HFF
HFF
KYAHHHH!
FASH
!?

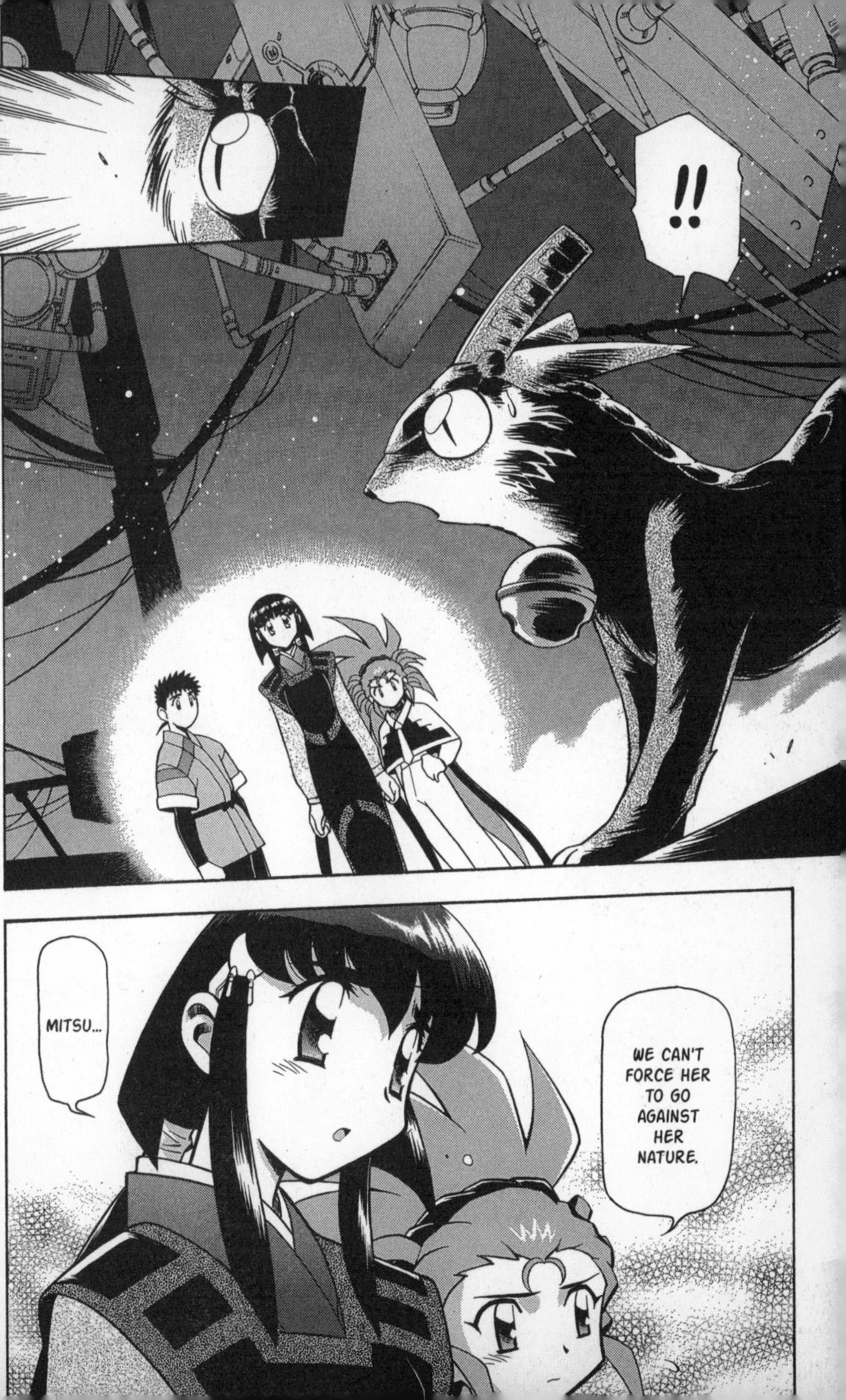
!!
MITSU...
WE CAN'T FORCE HER TO GO AGAINST HER NATURE.

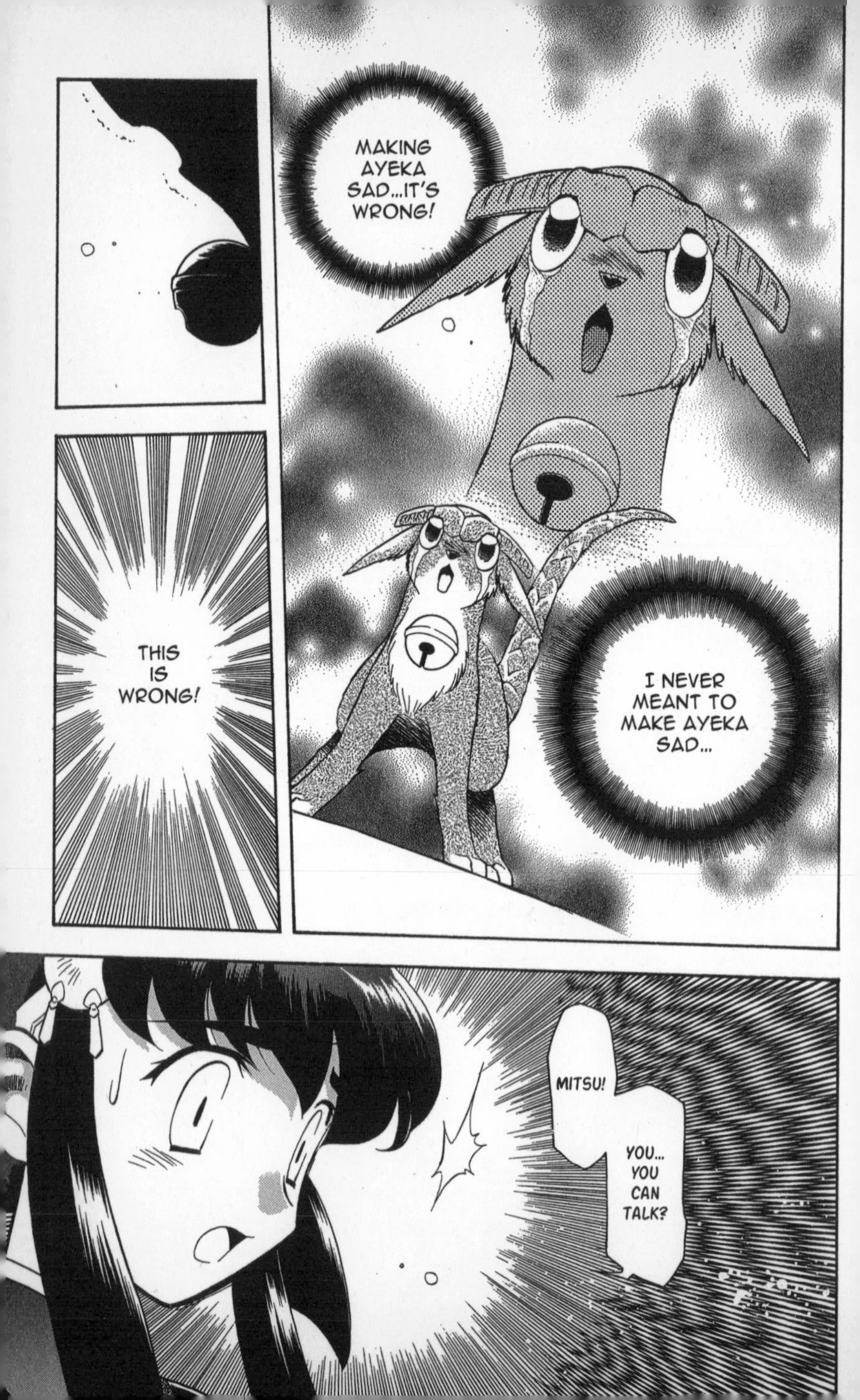
THIS IS WRONG!
MAKING AYEKA SAD...IT'S WRONG!
I NEVER MEANT TO MAKE AYEKA SAD...
MITSU!
YOU... YOU CAN TALK?

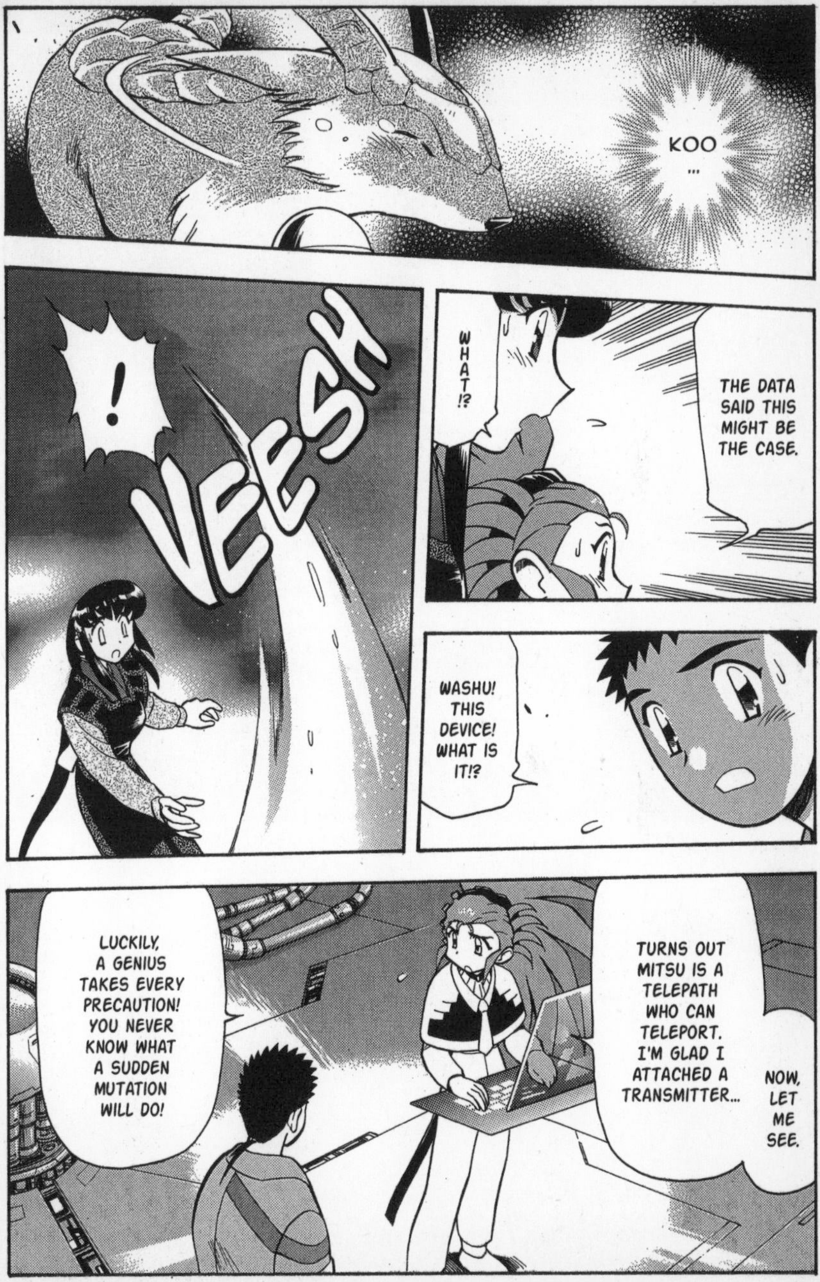
KOO
...
!
VEESH
WHAT!?
THE DATA SAID THIS MIGHT BE THE CASE.
WASHU! THIS DEVICE! WHAT IS IT!?
LUCKILY, A GENIUS TAKES EVERY PRECAUTION! YOU NEVER KNOW WHAT A SUDDEN MUTATION WILL DO!
TURNS OUT MITSU IS A TELEPATH WHO CAN TELEPORT. I'M GLAD I ATTACHED A TRANSMITTER...
NOW, LET ME SEE.

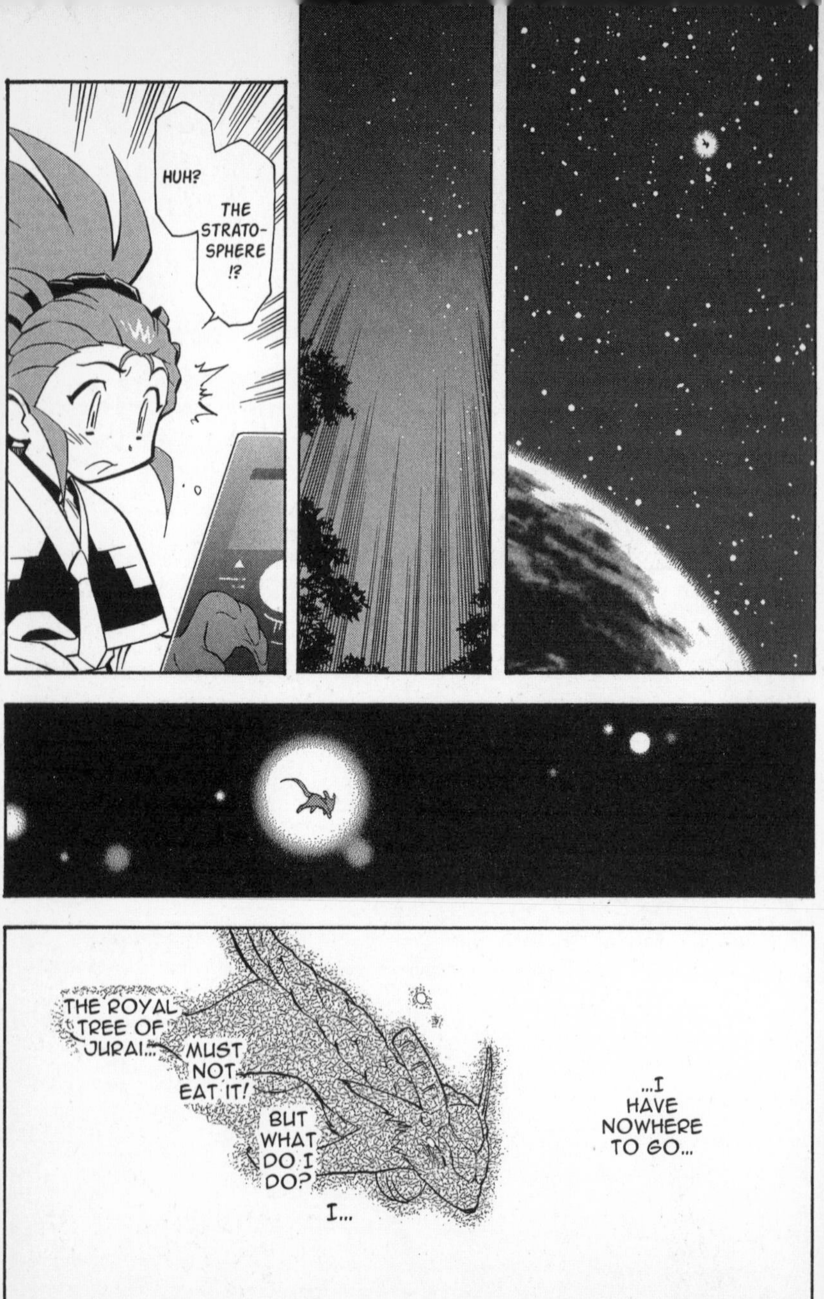
HUH?
THE STRATOSPHERE!?
THE ROYAL TREE OF JURAI...
MUST NOT EAT IT!
BUT WHAT DO I DO?
I...
...I HAVE NOWHERE TO GO...

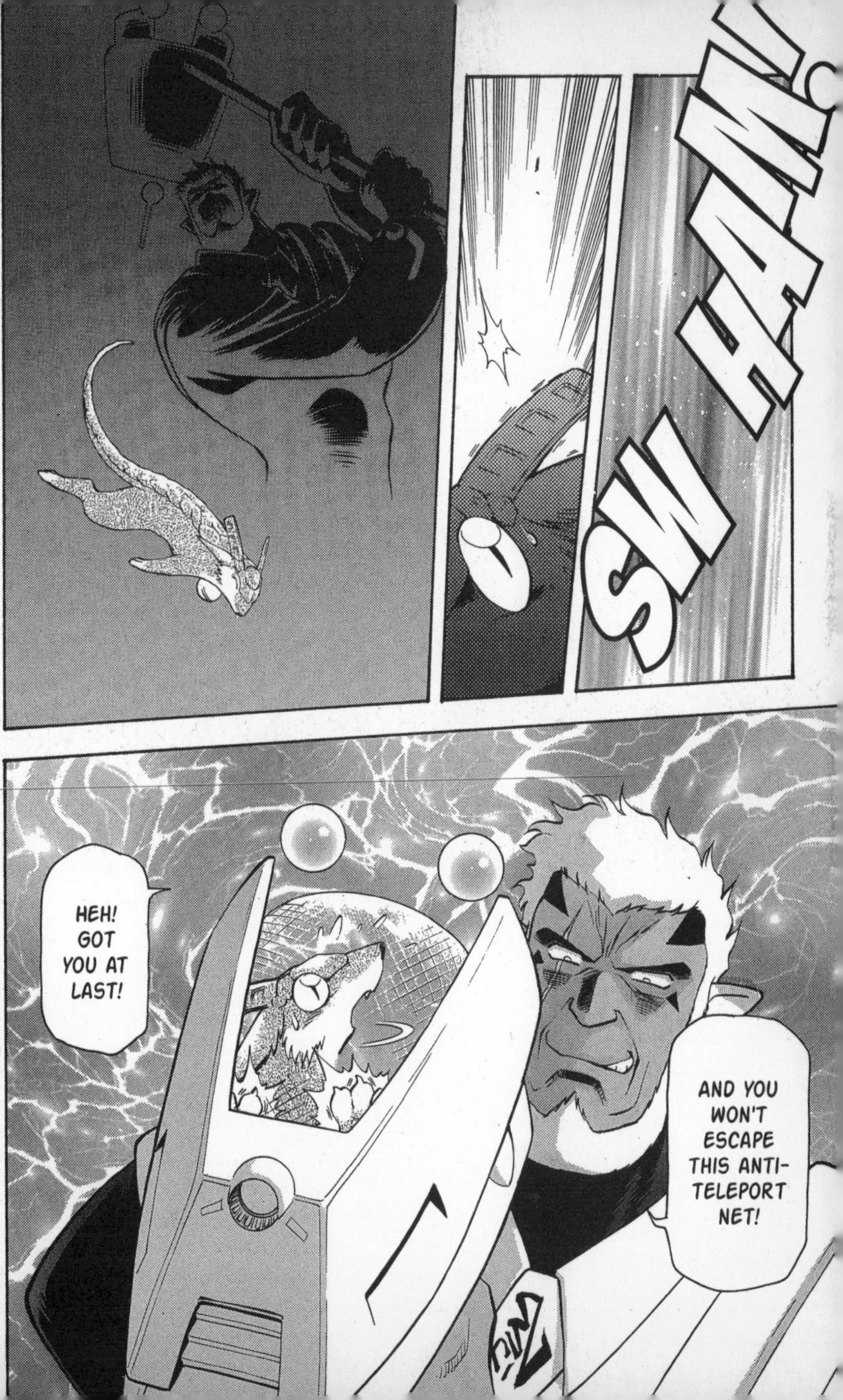
SWHAN!
HEH! GOT YOU AT LAST!
AND YOU WON'T ESCAPE THIS ANTI-TELEPORT NET!

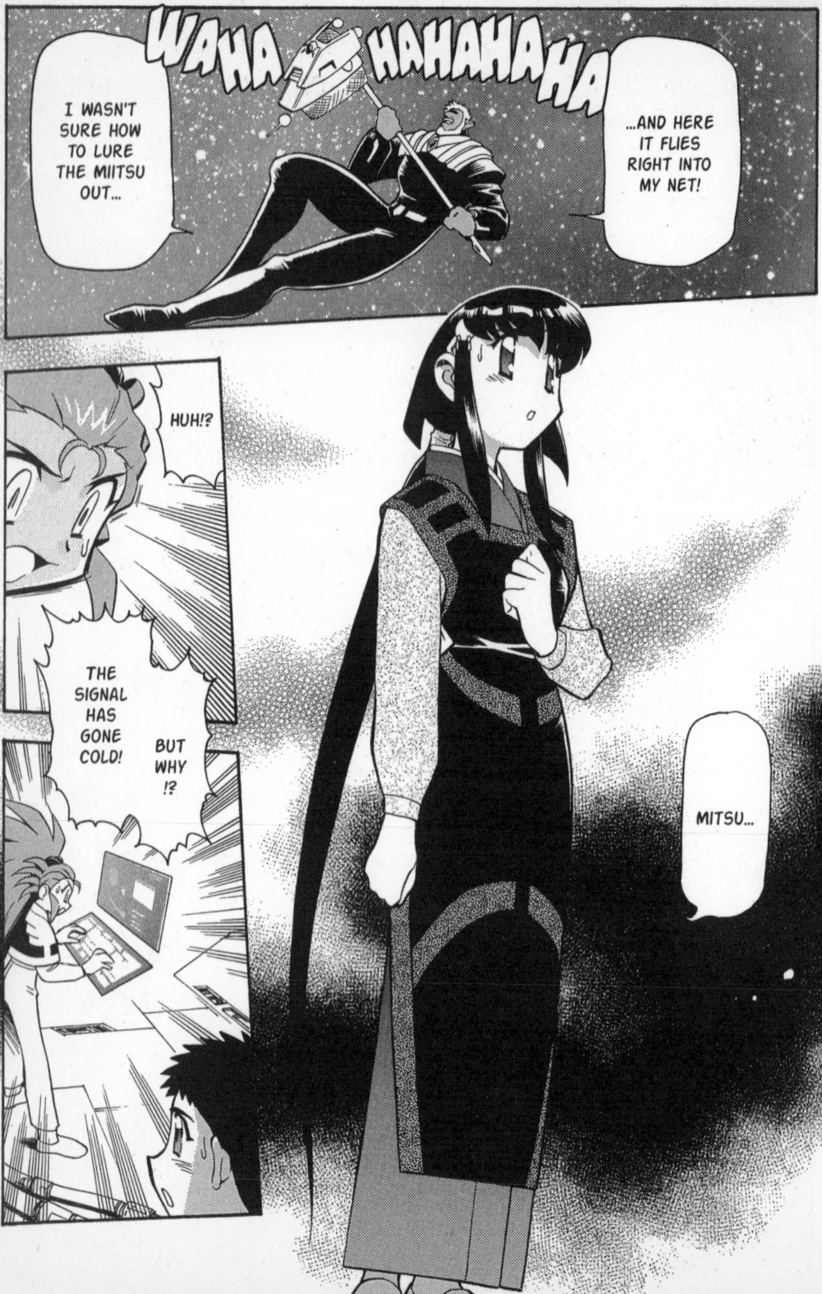
I WASN'T SURE HOW TO LURE THE MIITSU OUT...
WAHA HAHAHAHA
...AND HERE IT FLIES RIGHT INTO MY NET!
HUH!?
THE SIGNAL HAS GONE COLD!
BUT WHY !?
MITSU...

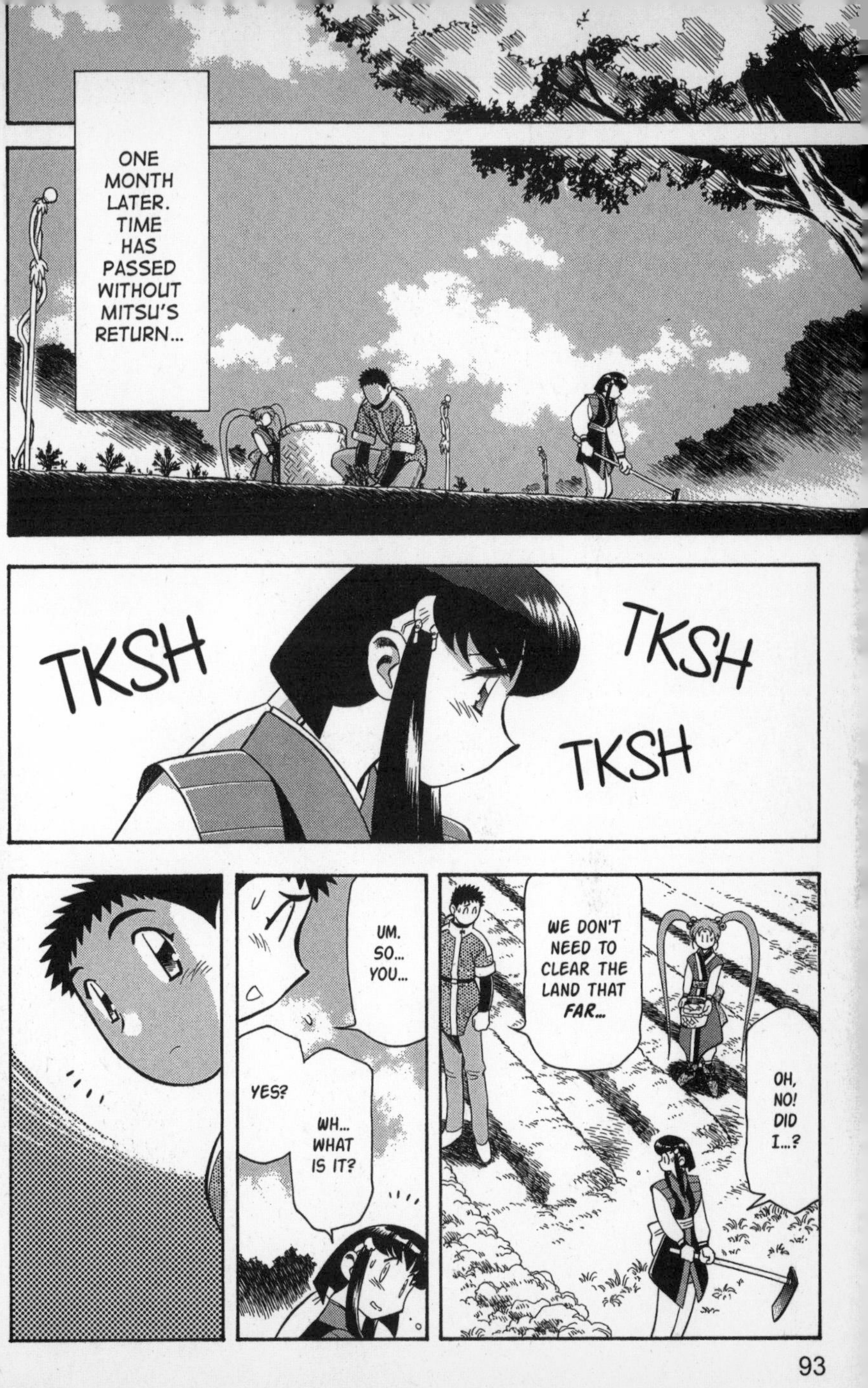
ONE MONTH LATER. TIME HAS PASSED WITHOUT MITSU'S RETURN...
TKSH
TKSH
TKSH
UM. SO... YOU...
YES?
WH... WHAT IS IT?
WE DON'T NEED TO CLEAR THE LAND THAT *FAR*...
OH, NO! DID I...?

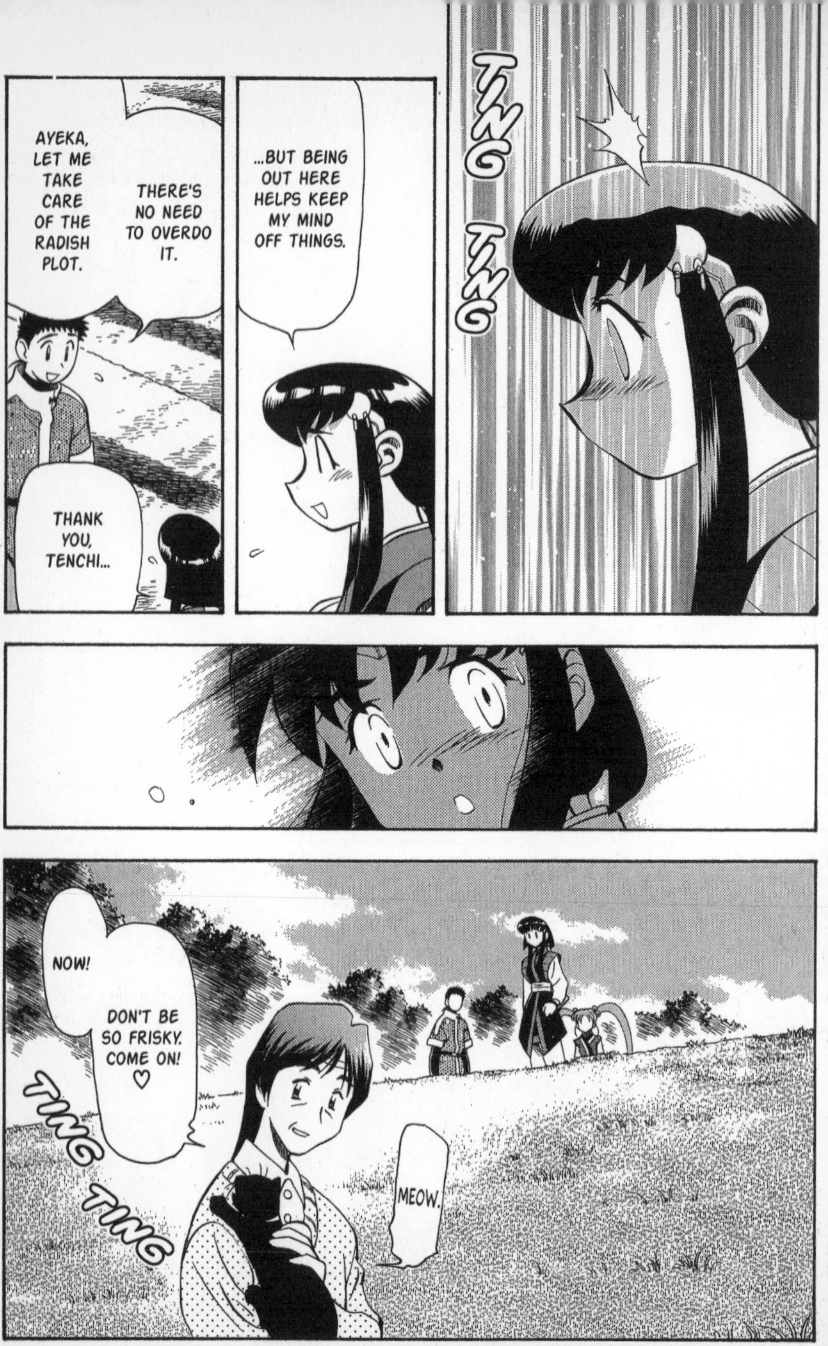
AYEKA, LET ME TAKE CARE OF THE RADISH PLOT.
THERE'S NO NEED TO OVERDO IT.
THANK YOU, TENCHI...
...BUT BEING OUT HERE HELPS KEEP MY MIND OFF THINGS.
TING TING TING
NOW!
DON'T BE SO FRISKY. COME ON! ♡
MEOW.
TING TING TING

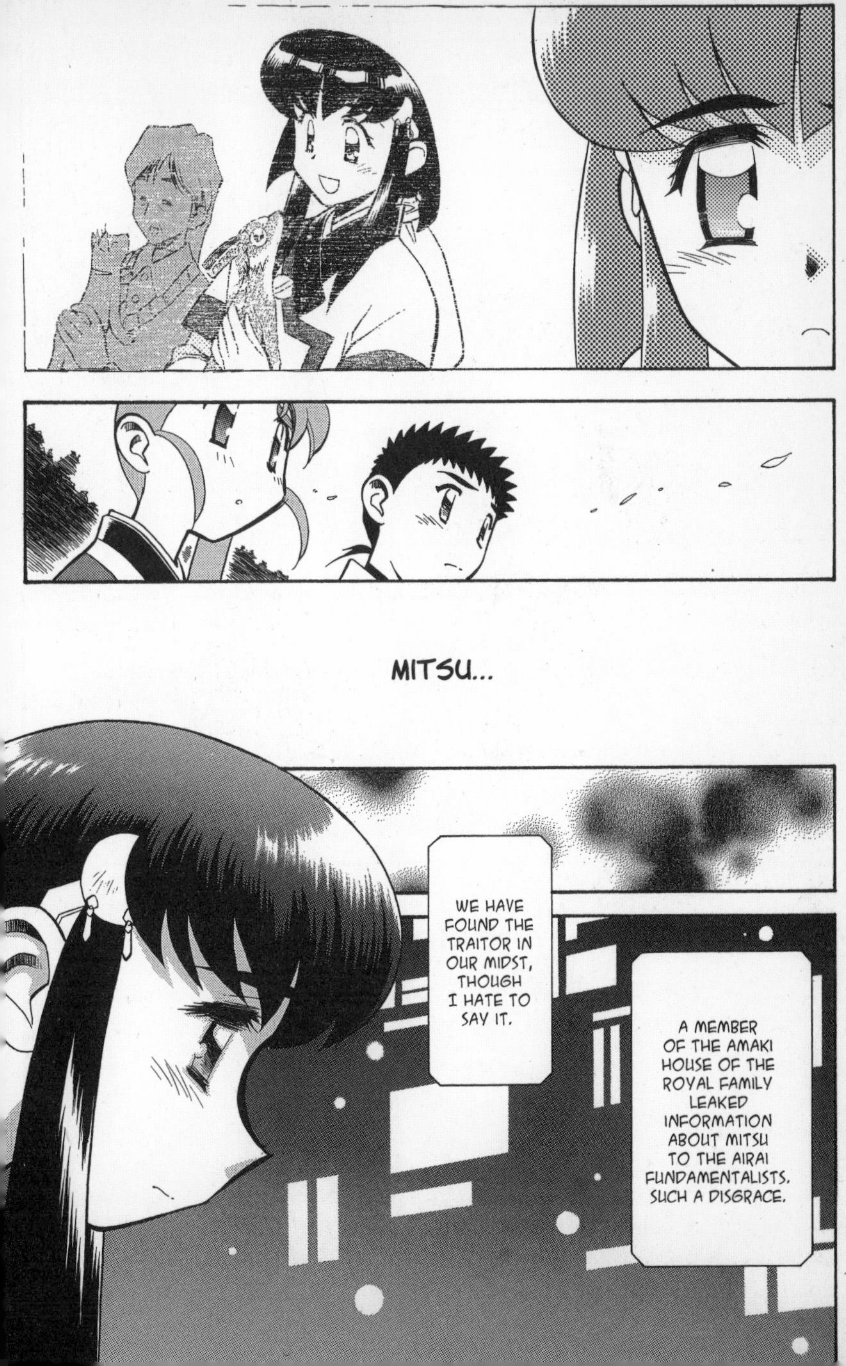
MITSU...
WE HAVE FOUND THE TRAITOR IN OUR MIDST, THOUGH I HATE TO SAY IT.
A MEMBER OF THE AMAKI HOUSE OF THE ROYAL FAMILY LEAKED INFORMATION ABOUT MITSU TO THE AIRAI FUNDAMENTALISTS. SUCH A DISGRACE.

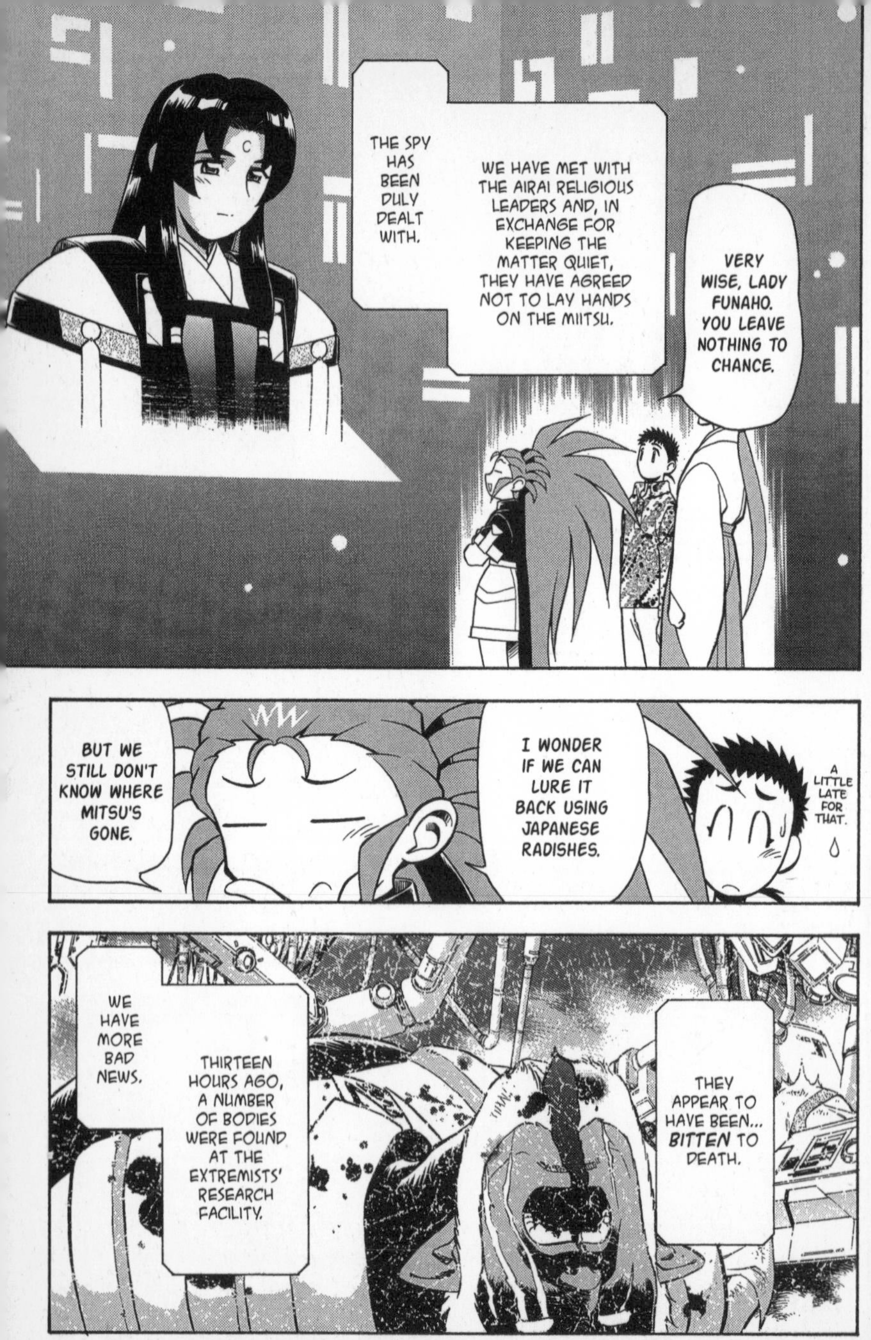
THE SPY HAS BEEN DULY DEALT WITH.
WE HAVE MET WITH THE AIRAI RELIGIOUS LEADERS AND, IN EXCHANGE FOR KEEPING THE MATTER QUIET, THEY HAVE AGREED NOT TO LAY HANDS ON THE MIITSU.
VERY WISE, LADY FUNAHO. YOU LEAVE NOTHING TO CHANCE.
BUT WE STILL DON'T KNOW WHERE MITSU'S GONE.
I WONDER IF WE CAN LURE IT BACK USING JAPANESE RADISHES.
A LITTLE LATE FOR THAT.
WE HAVE MORE BAD NEWS.
THIRTEEN HOURS AGO, A NUMBER OF BODIES WERE FOUND AT THE EXTREMISTS' RESEARCH FACILITY.
THEY APPEAR TO HAVE BEEN... *BITTEN* TO DEATH.

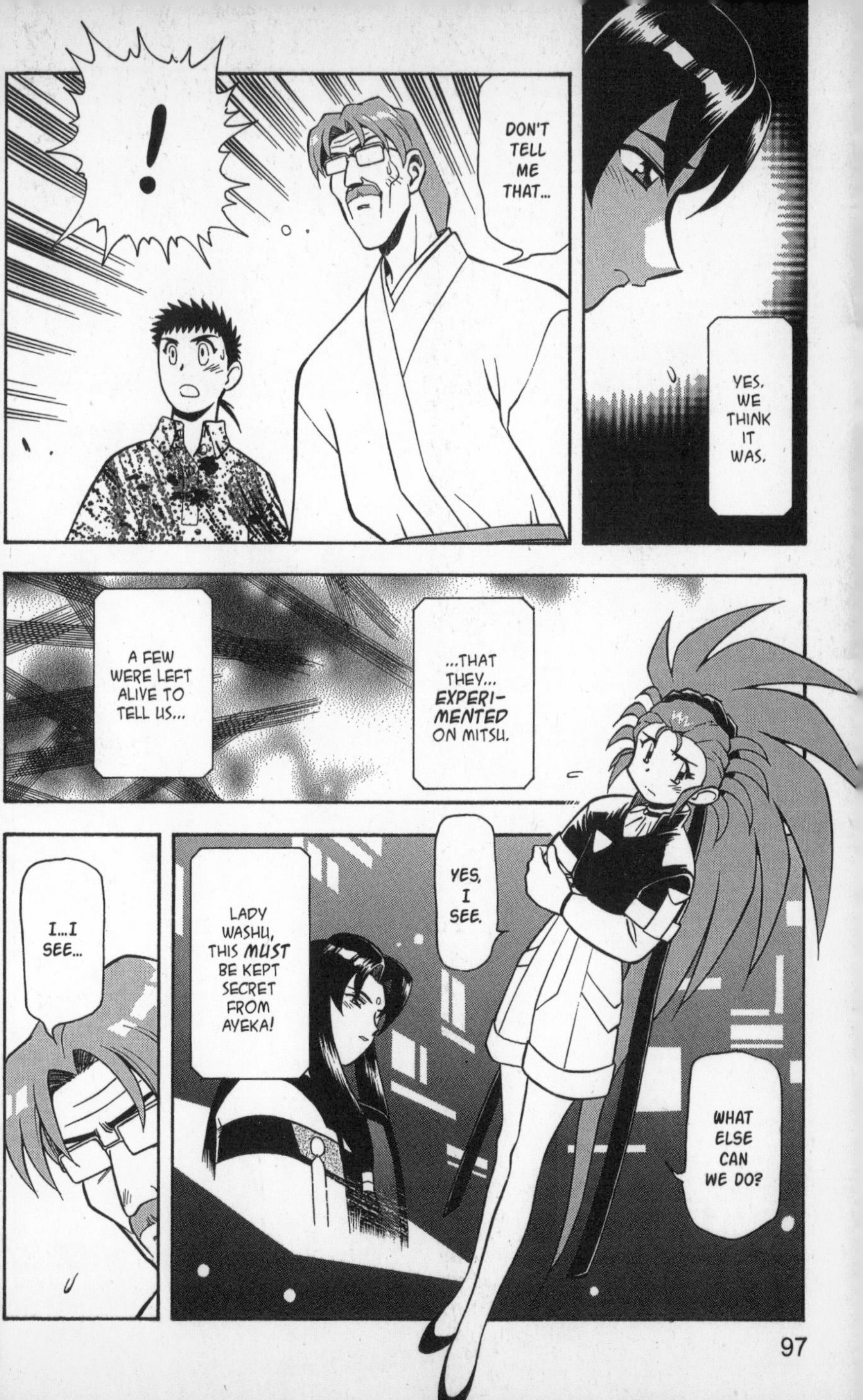
!
DON'T TELL ME THAT...
YES. WE THINK IT WAS.
A FEW WERE LEFT ALIVE TO TELL US...
...THAT THEY... EXPERIMENTED ON MITSU.
I...I SEE...
LADY WASHU, THIS MUST BE KEPT SECRET FROM AYEKA!
YES, I SEE.
WHAT ELSE CAN WE DO?

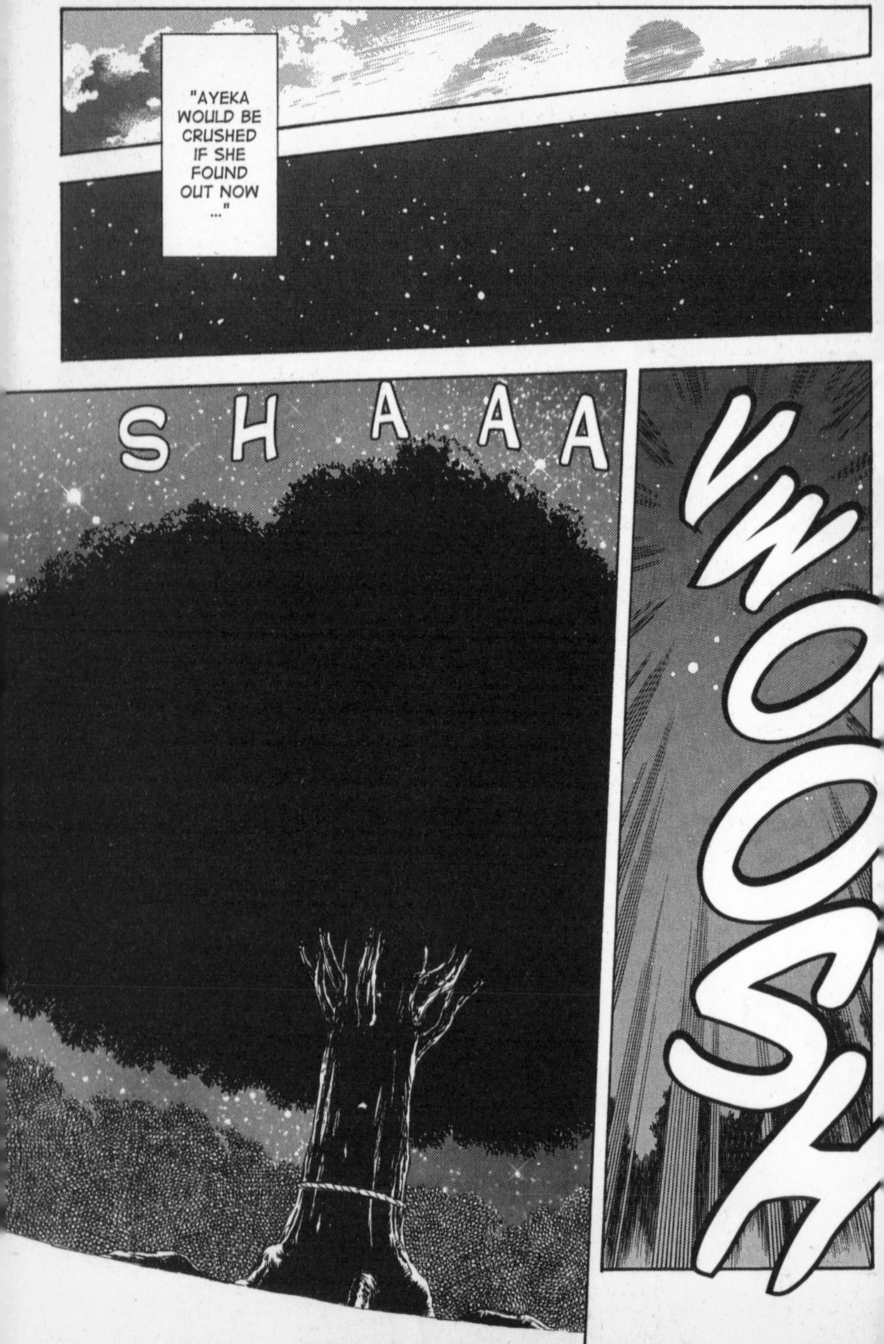
"AYEKA WOULD BE CRUSHED IF SHE FOUND OUT NOW ..."
SHAAA
WOOOSH

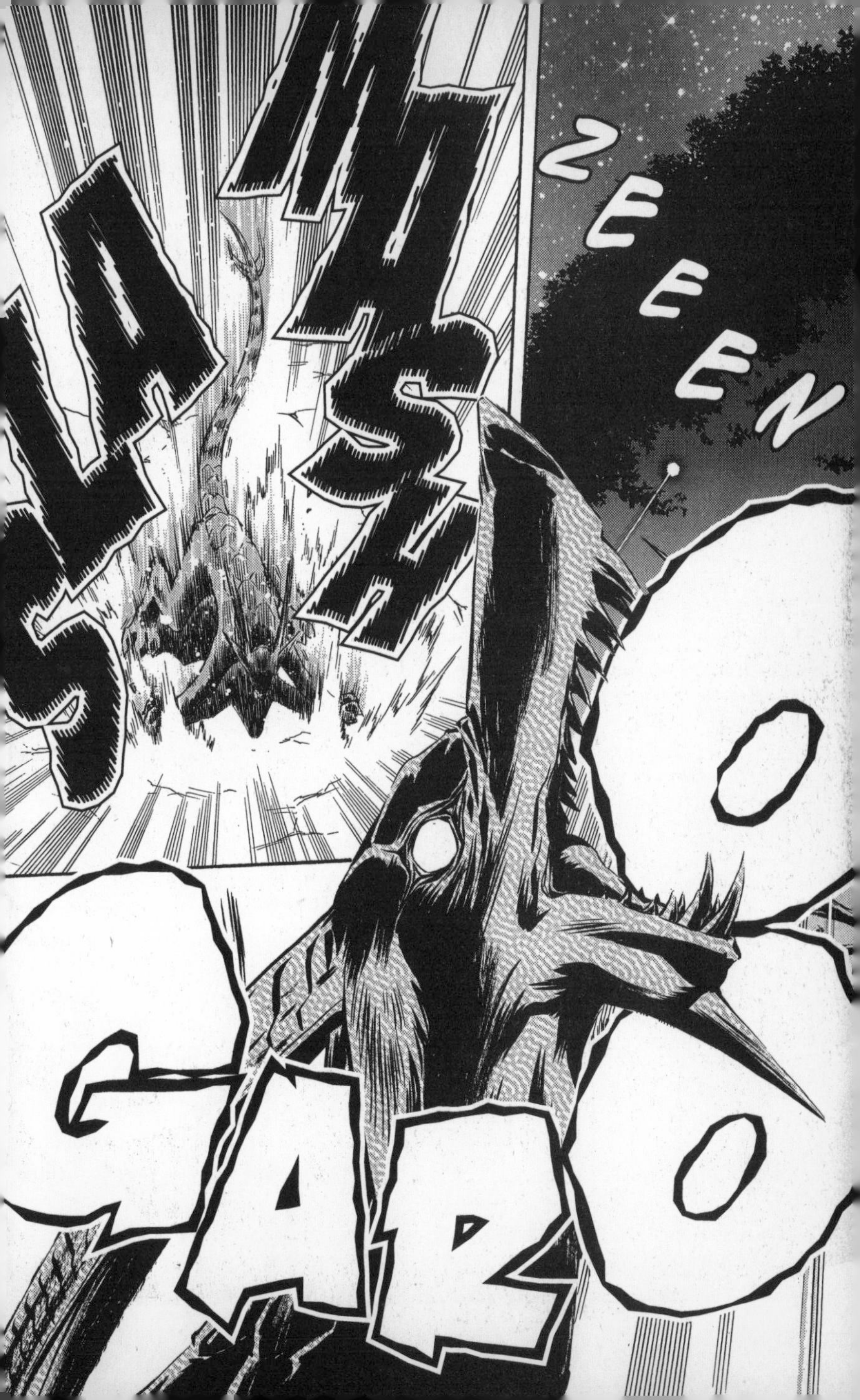
SLASH
ZEEEN
GAROO

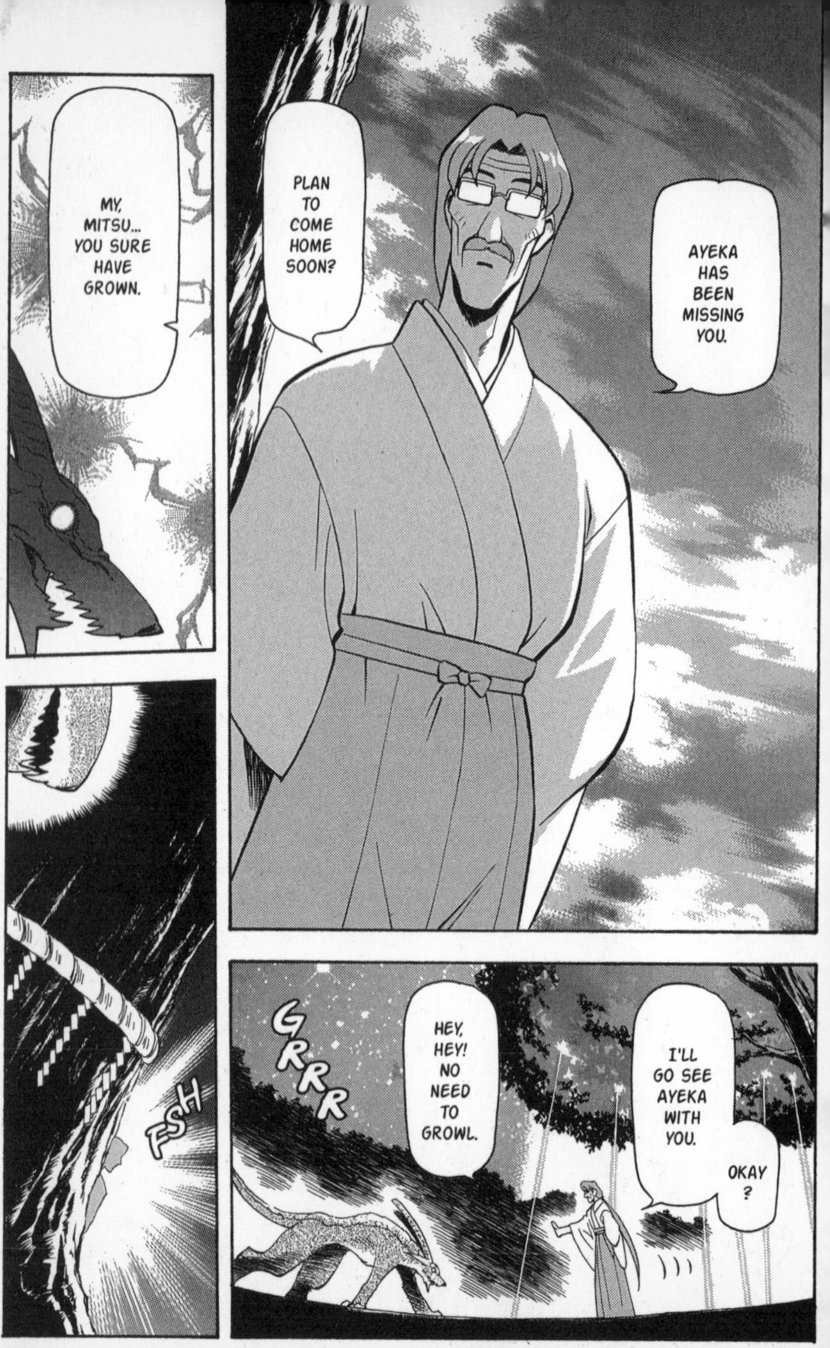
MY, MITSU... YOU SURE HAVE GROWN.
PLAN TO COME HOME SOON?
AYEKA HAS BEEN MISSING YOU.
FSH
GRRR
HEY, HEY! NO NEED TO GROWL.
I'LL GO SEE AYEKA WITH YOU.
OKAY?

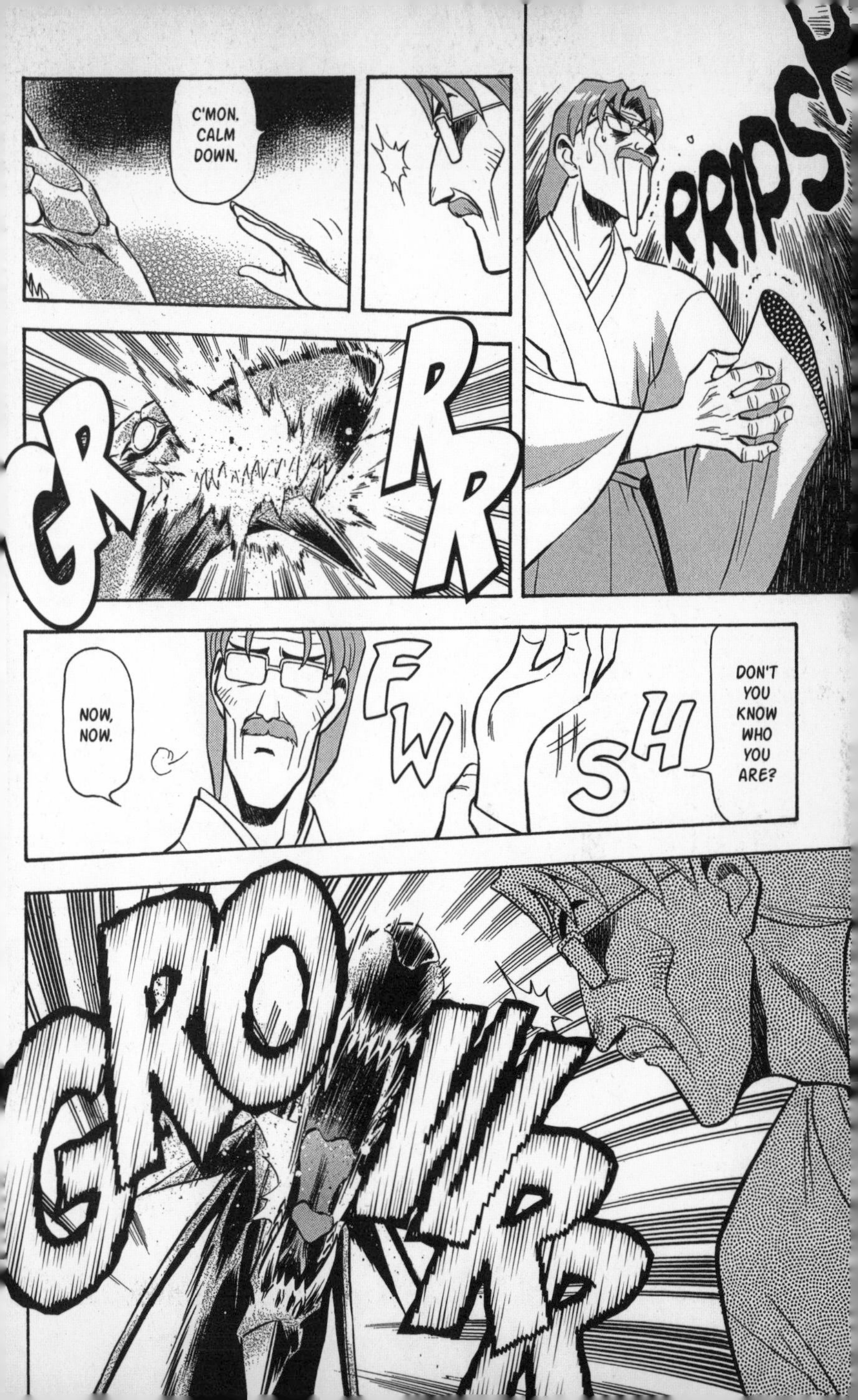
RRIPS
C'MON. CALM DOWN.
GRRR
DON'T YOU KNOW WHO YOU ARE?
FWSH
NOW, NOW.

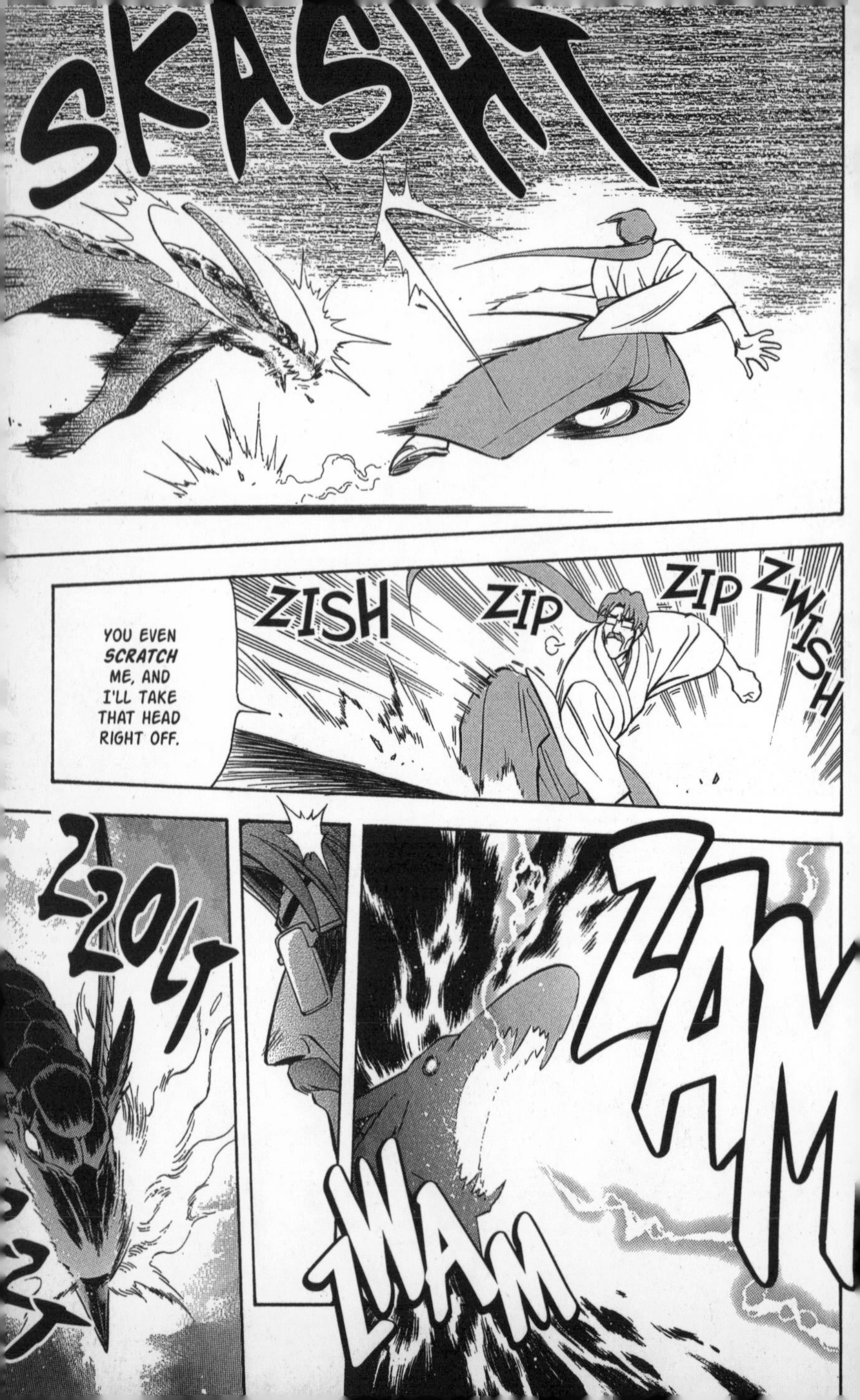
SKASHT
YOU EVEN *SCRATCH* ME, AND I'LL TAKE THAT HEAD RIGHT OFF.
ZISH
ZIP
ZIP
ZWISH
ZZOT
ZAM
WAM

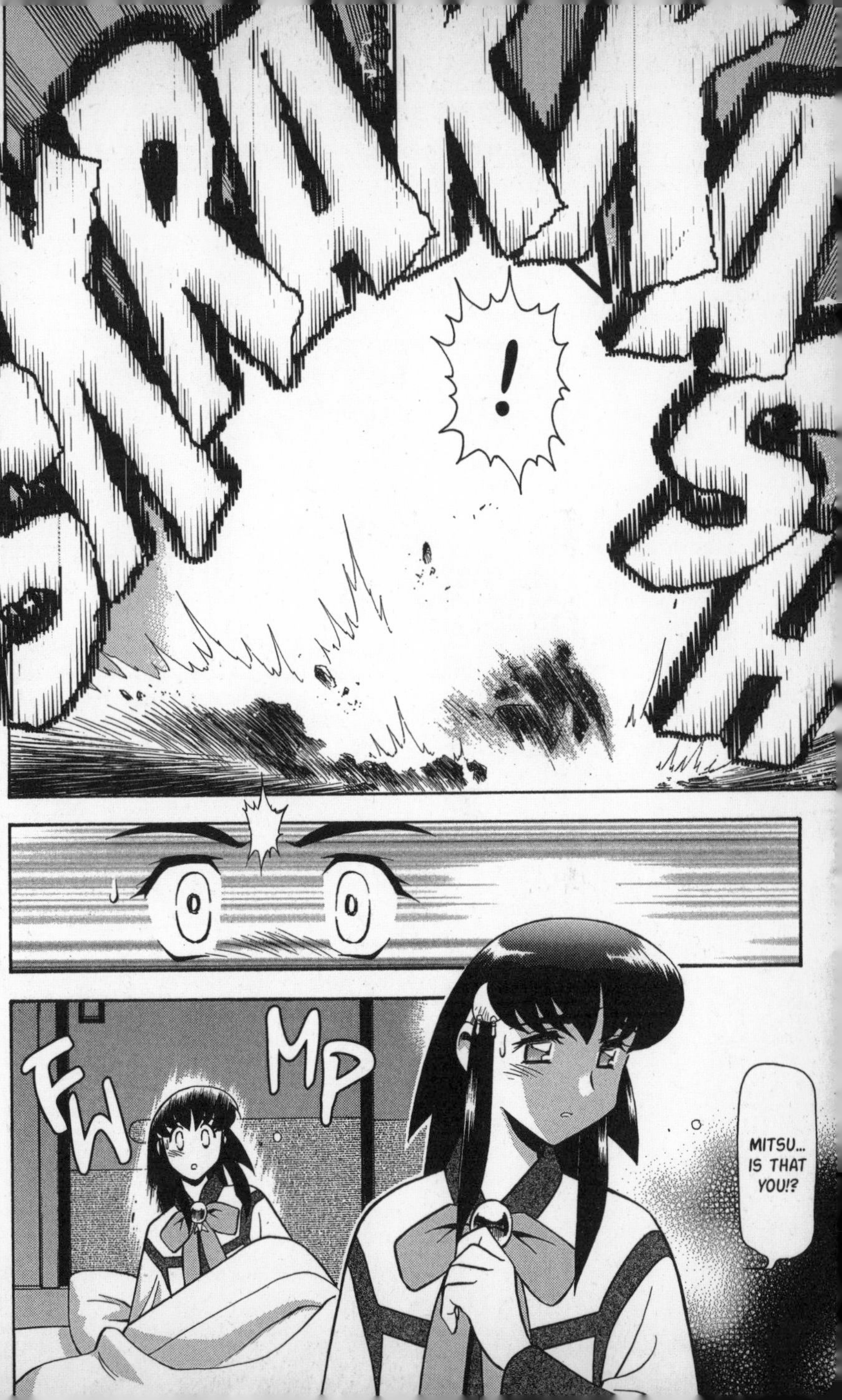
!
FWMP
MITSU... IS THAT YOU!?

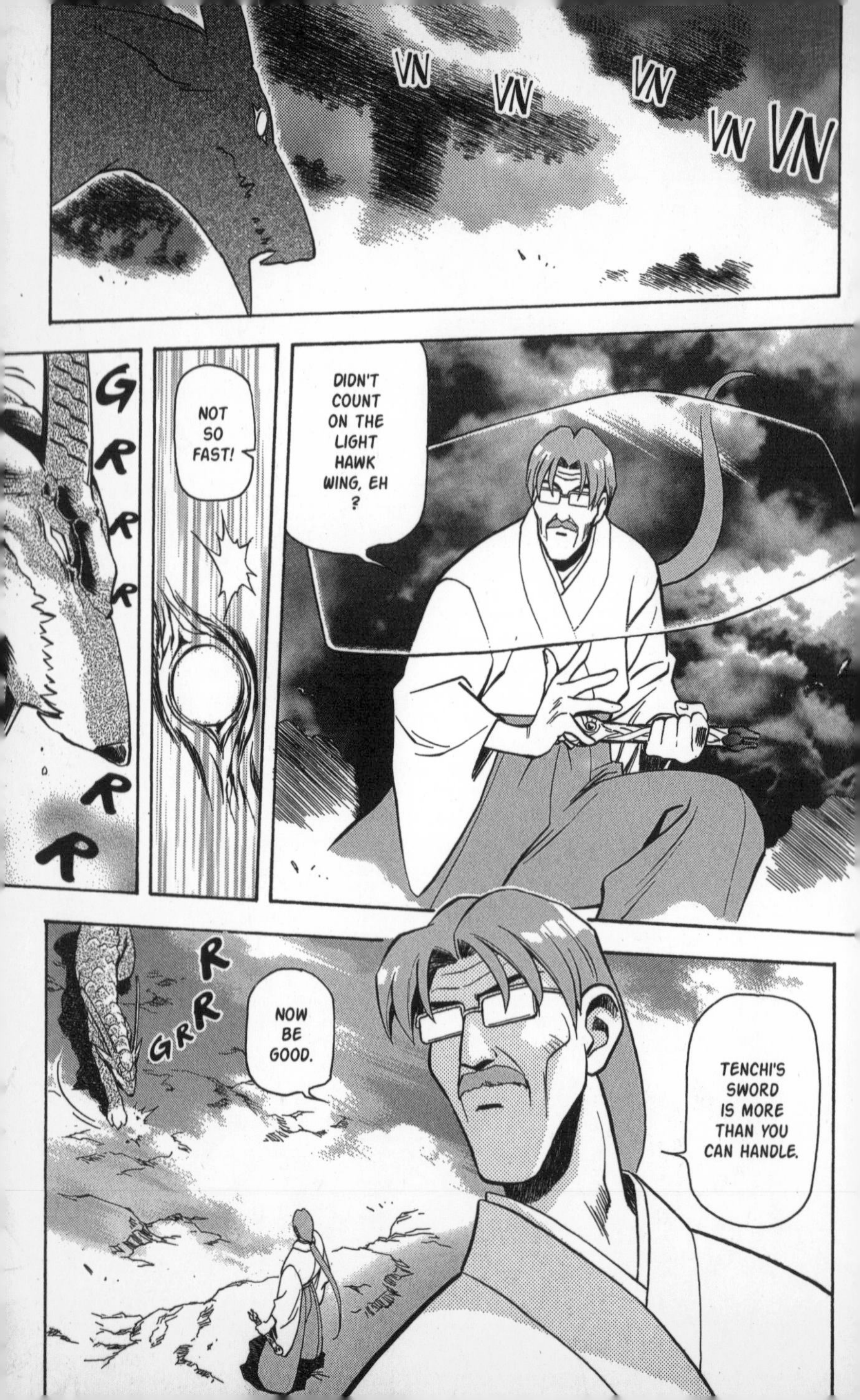
VN
VN
VN
VN
VN
G
R
R
R
R
R
NOT SO FAST!
DIDN'T COUNT ON THE LIGHT HAWK WING, EH ?
R
GRR
NOW BE GOOD.
TENCHI'S SWORD IS MORE THAN YOU CAN HANDLE.

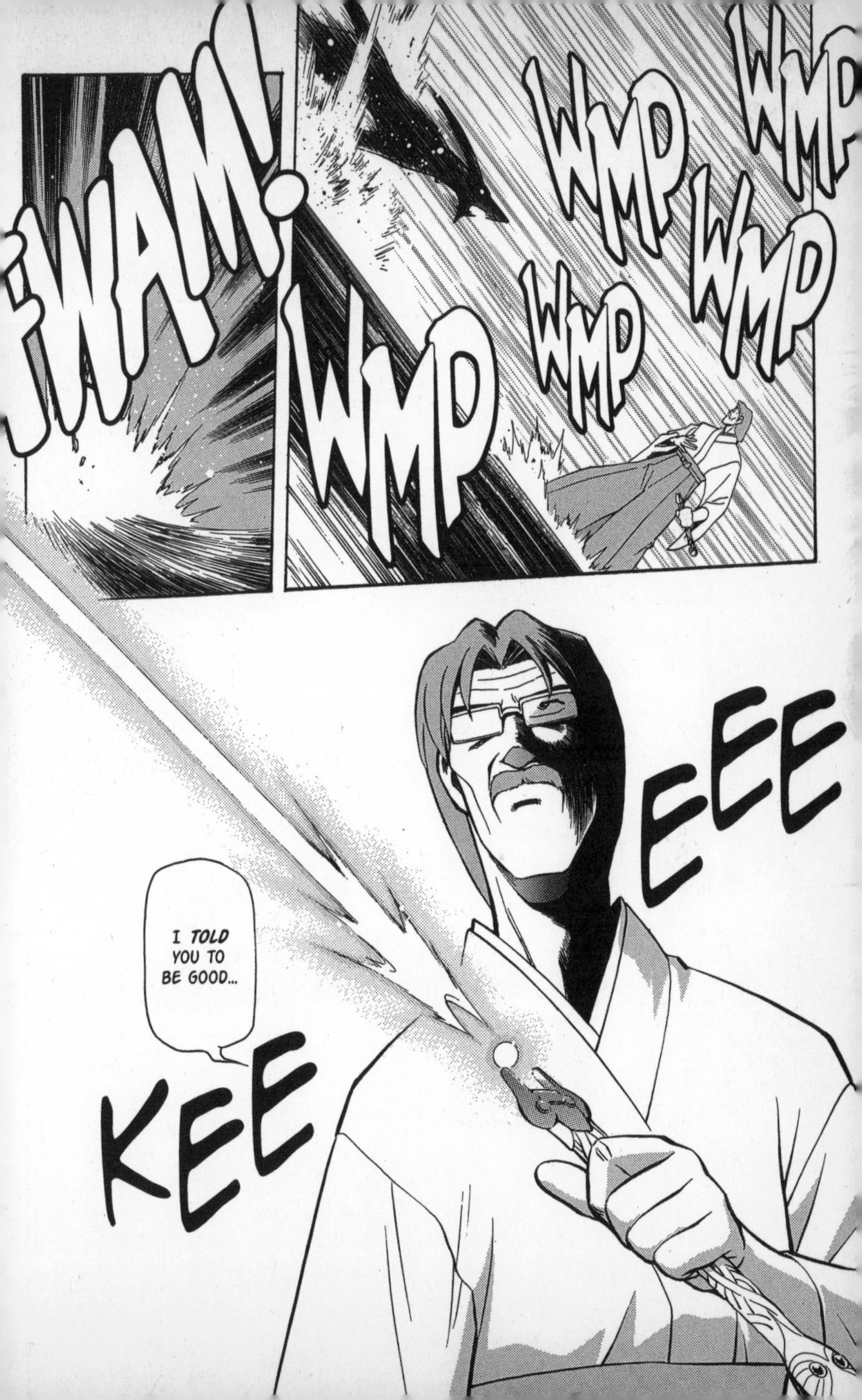
WAM!
WMP
WMP
WMP
WMP
WMP
EEE
I TOLD YOU TO BE GOOD...
KEE

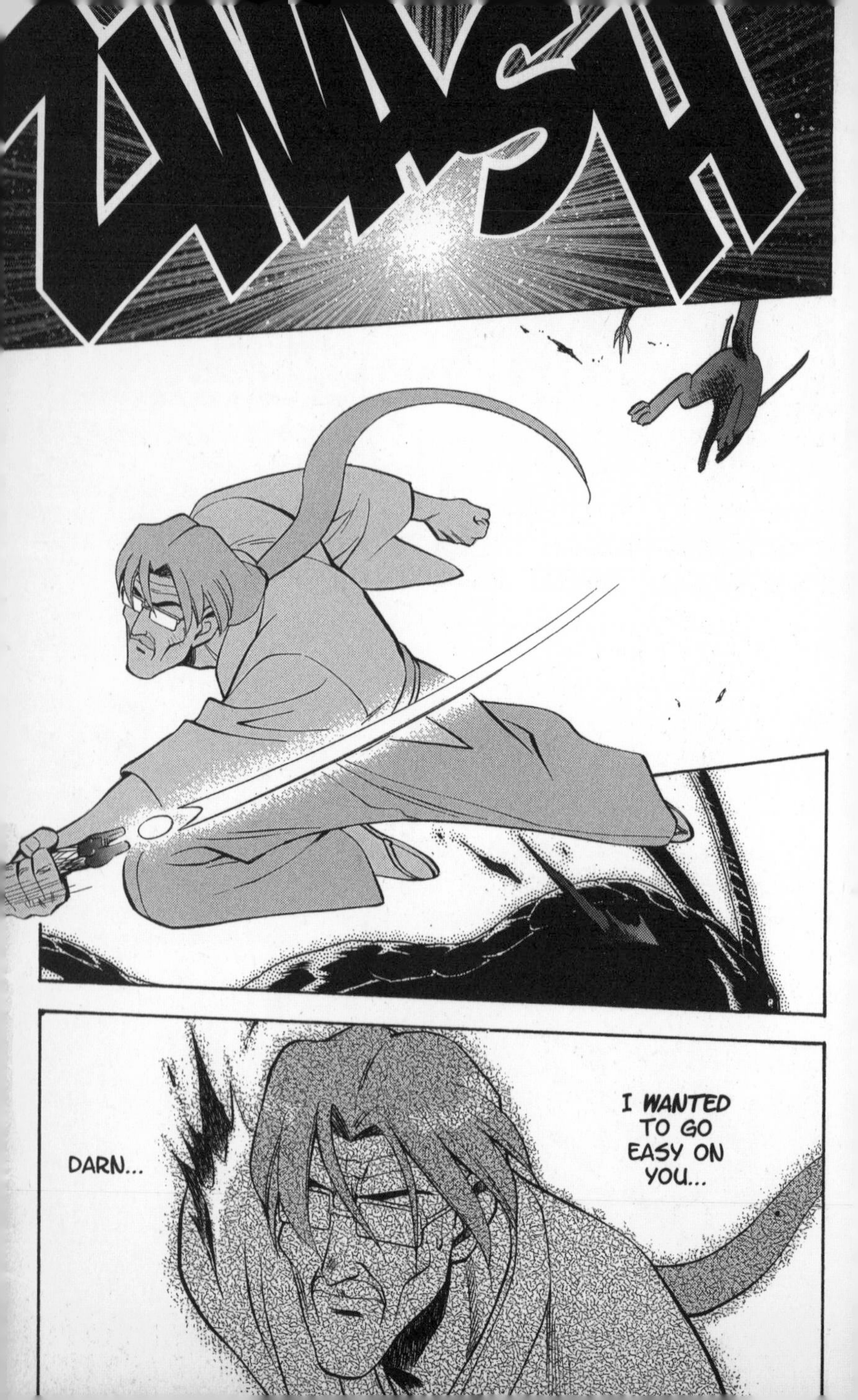
ZWASH
DARN...
I WANTED TO GO EASY ON YOU...

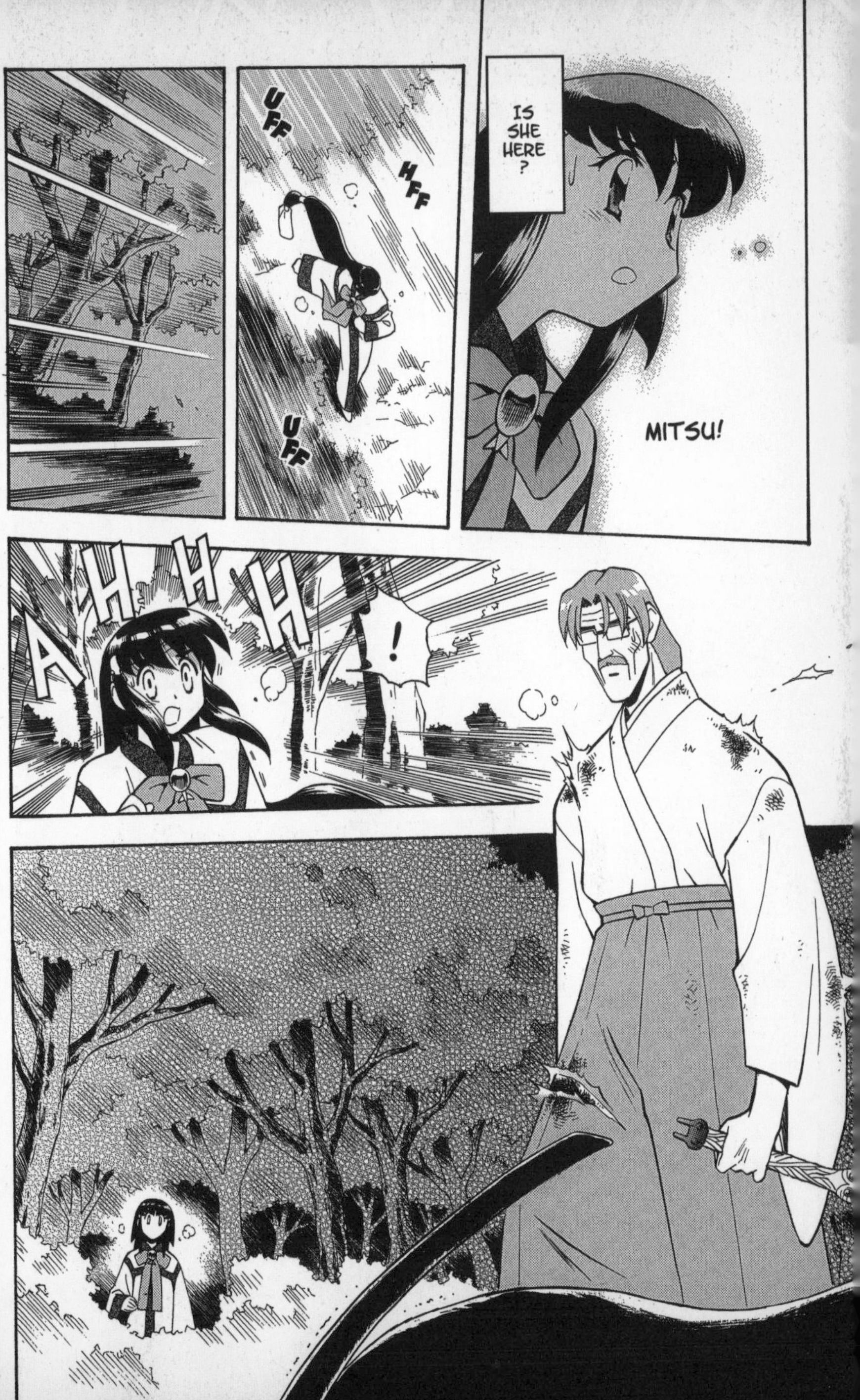
UFF
HFF
UFF
IS SHE HERE?
MITSU!
AHHH
!

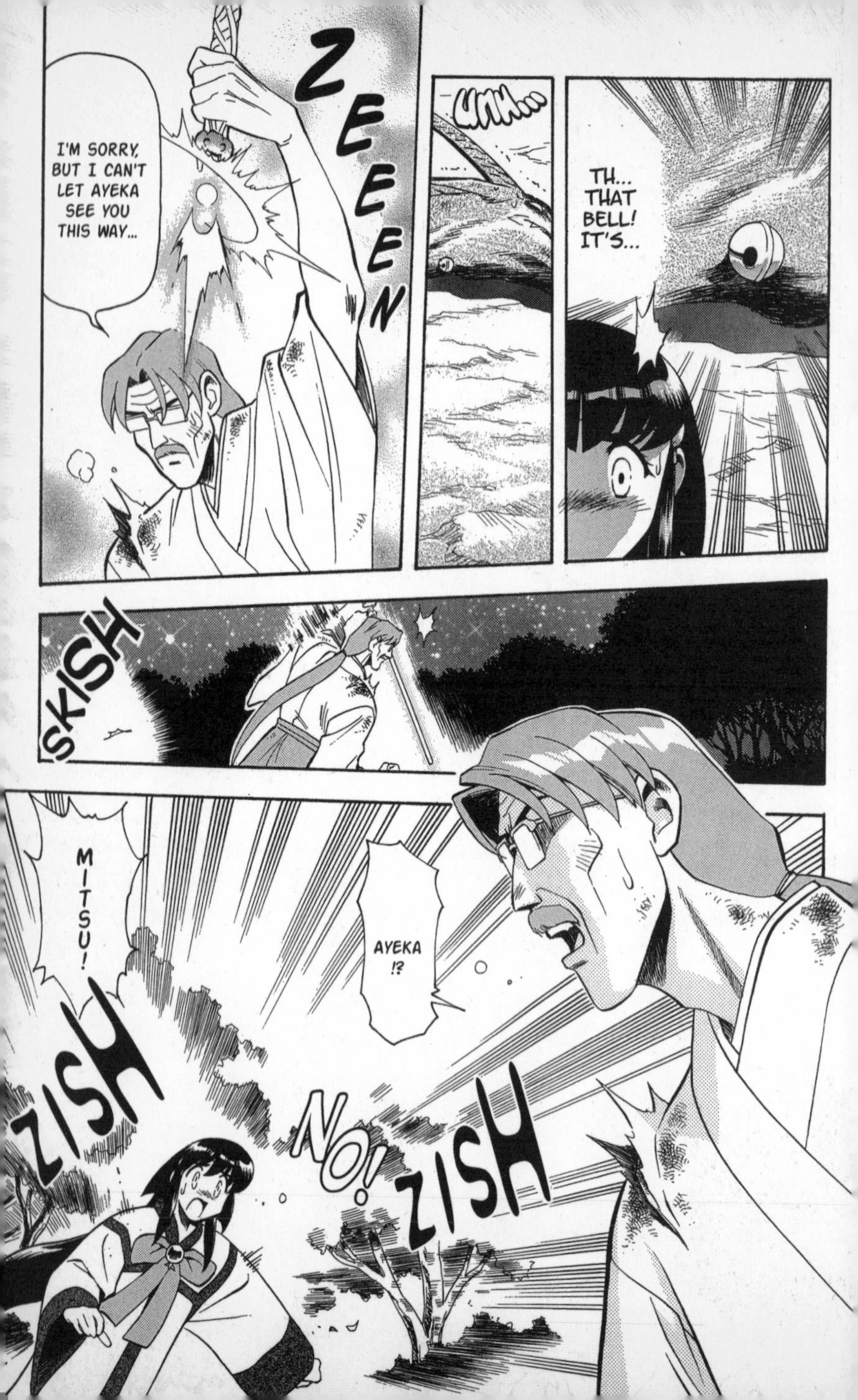
I'M SORRY, BUT I CAN'T LET AYEKA SEE YOU THIS WAY...
ZEEEEN
UNH...
TH... THAT BELL! IT'S...
SKISH
MITSU!
AYEKA!?
ZISH
NO!
ZISH

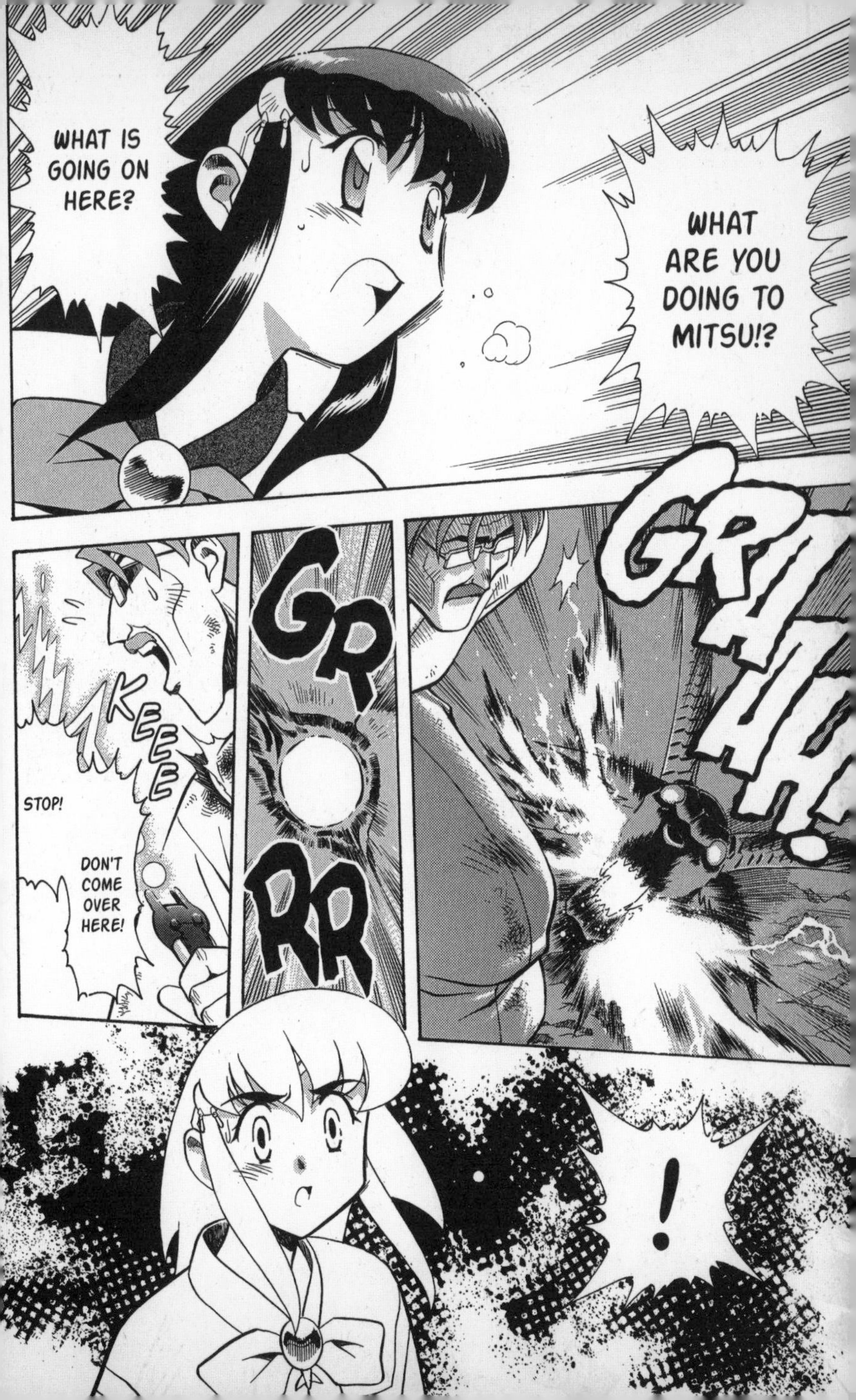
WHAT IS GOING ON HERE?
WHAT ARE YOU DOING TO MITSU!?
KEEEE
STOP!
DON'T COME OVER HERE!
GRRR
GRAHH!
!

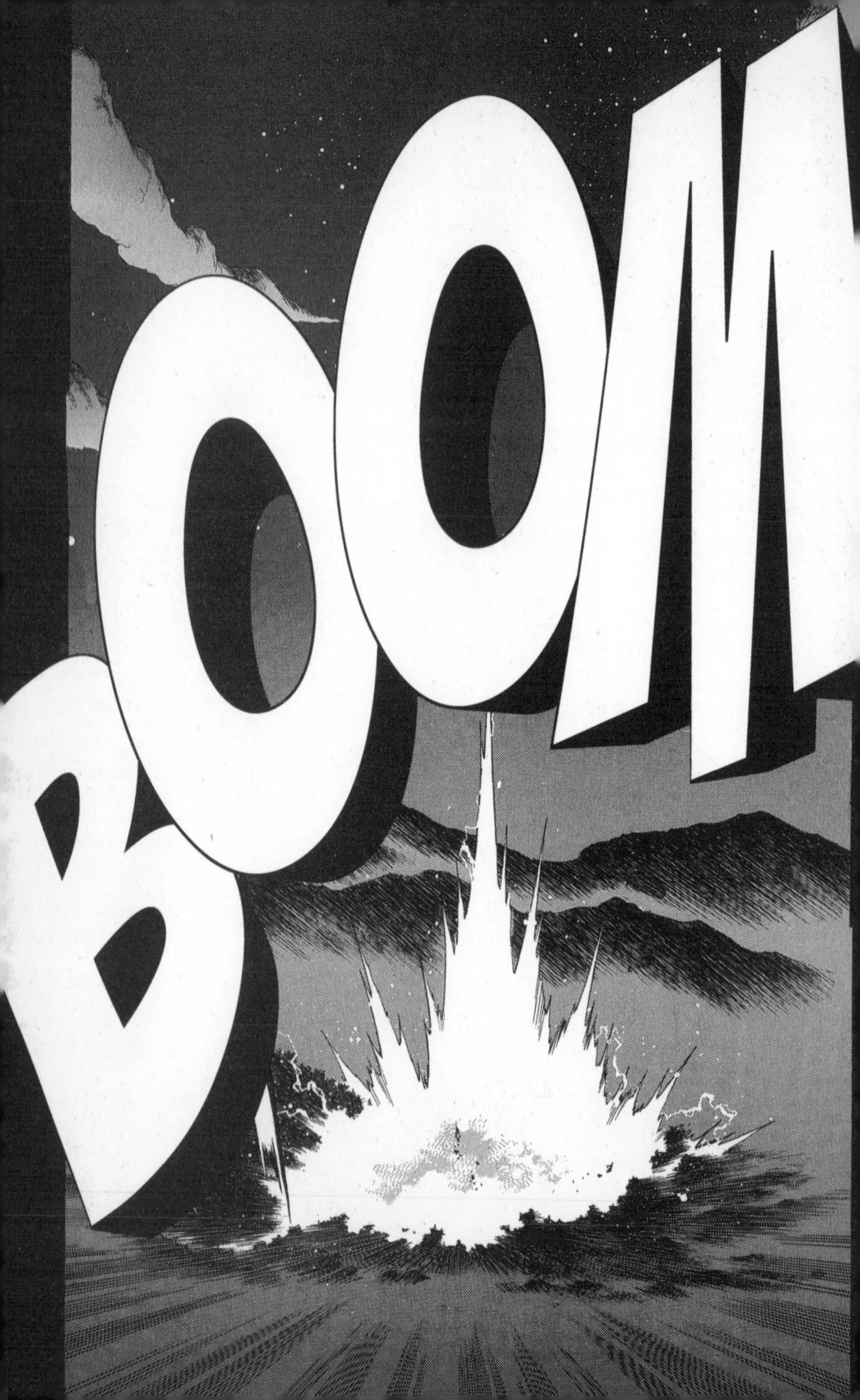
BOOM

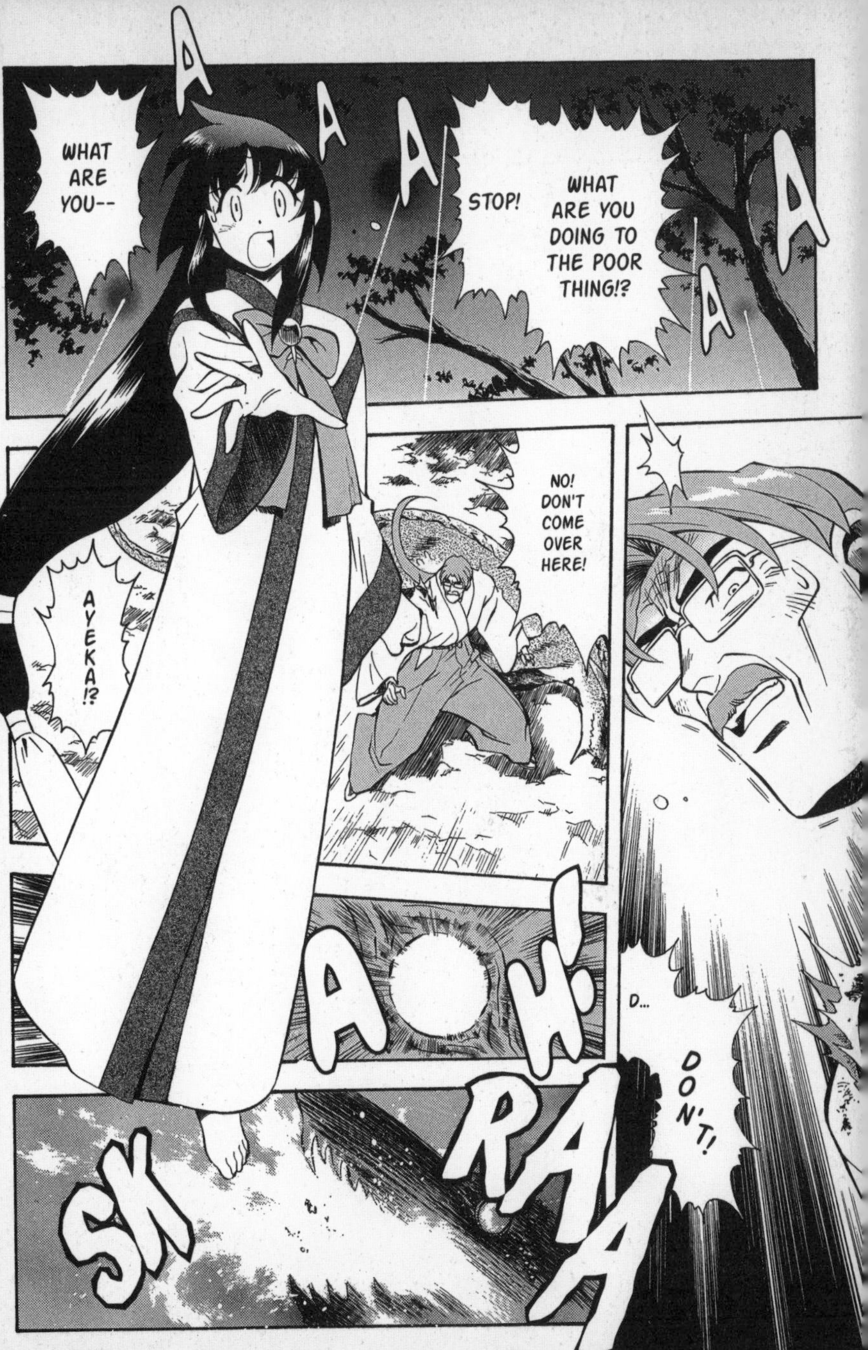

AAAAA
WHAT ARE YOU--
STOP!
WHAT ARE YOU DOING TO THE POOR THING!?
AYEKA!?
NO! DON'T COME OVER HERE!
AH!
D...
DON'T!
SKRAAA

Chapter 4: Many Tears

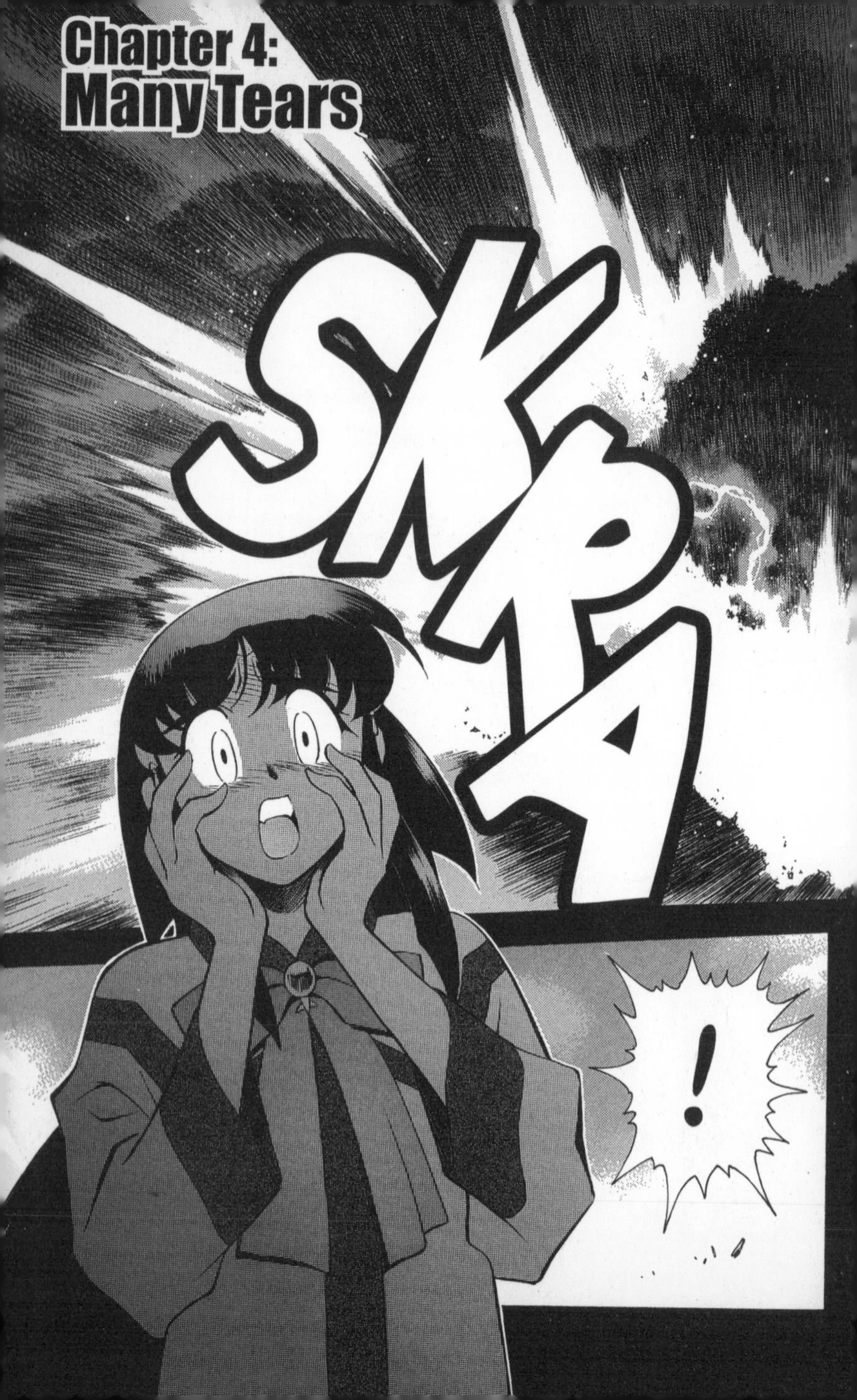
!

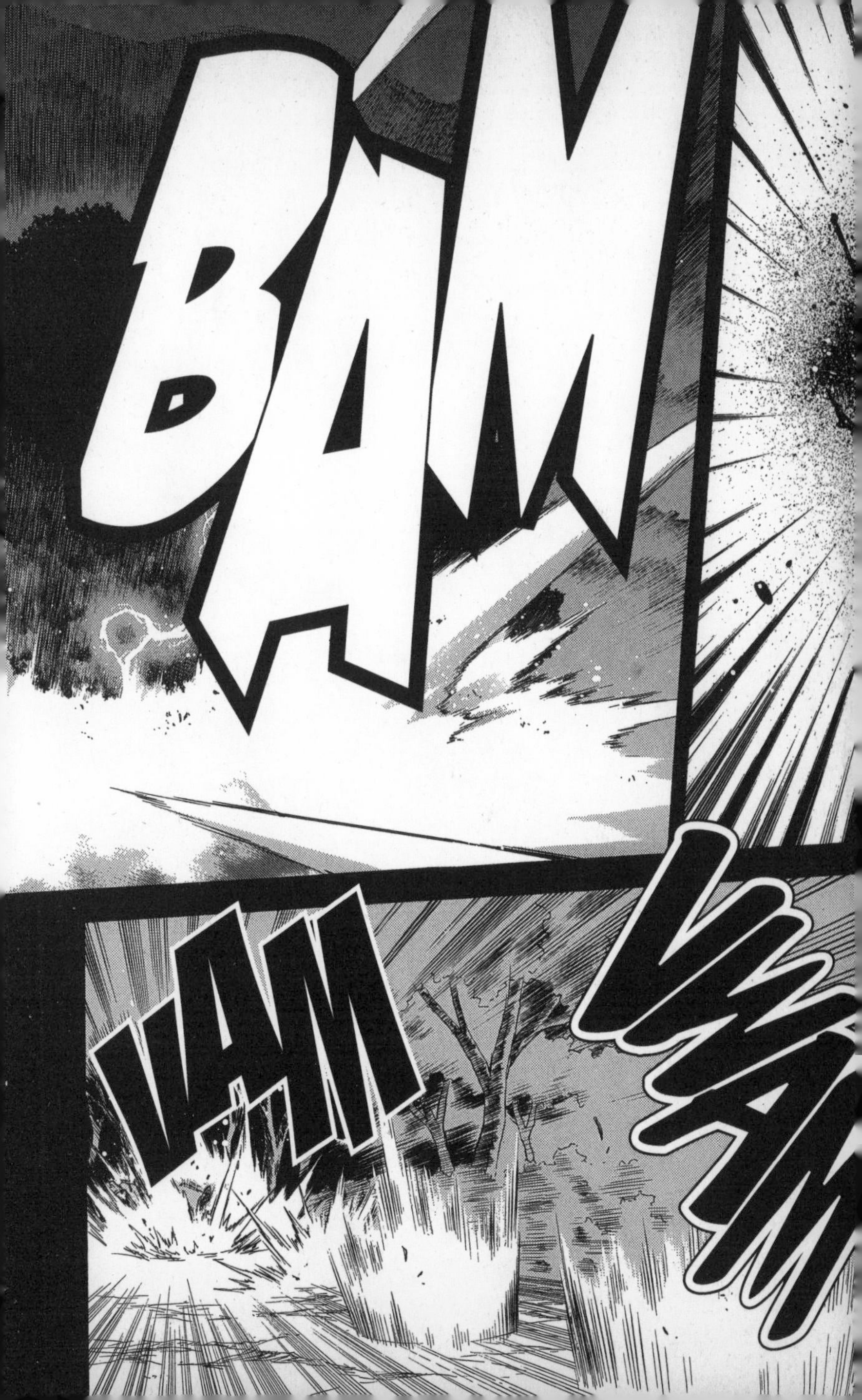
BAM
WAM
WAM

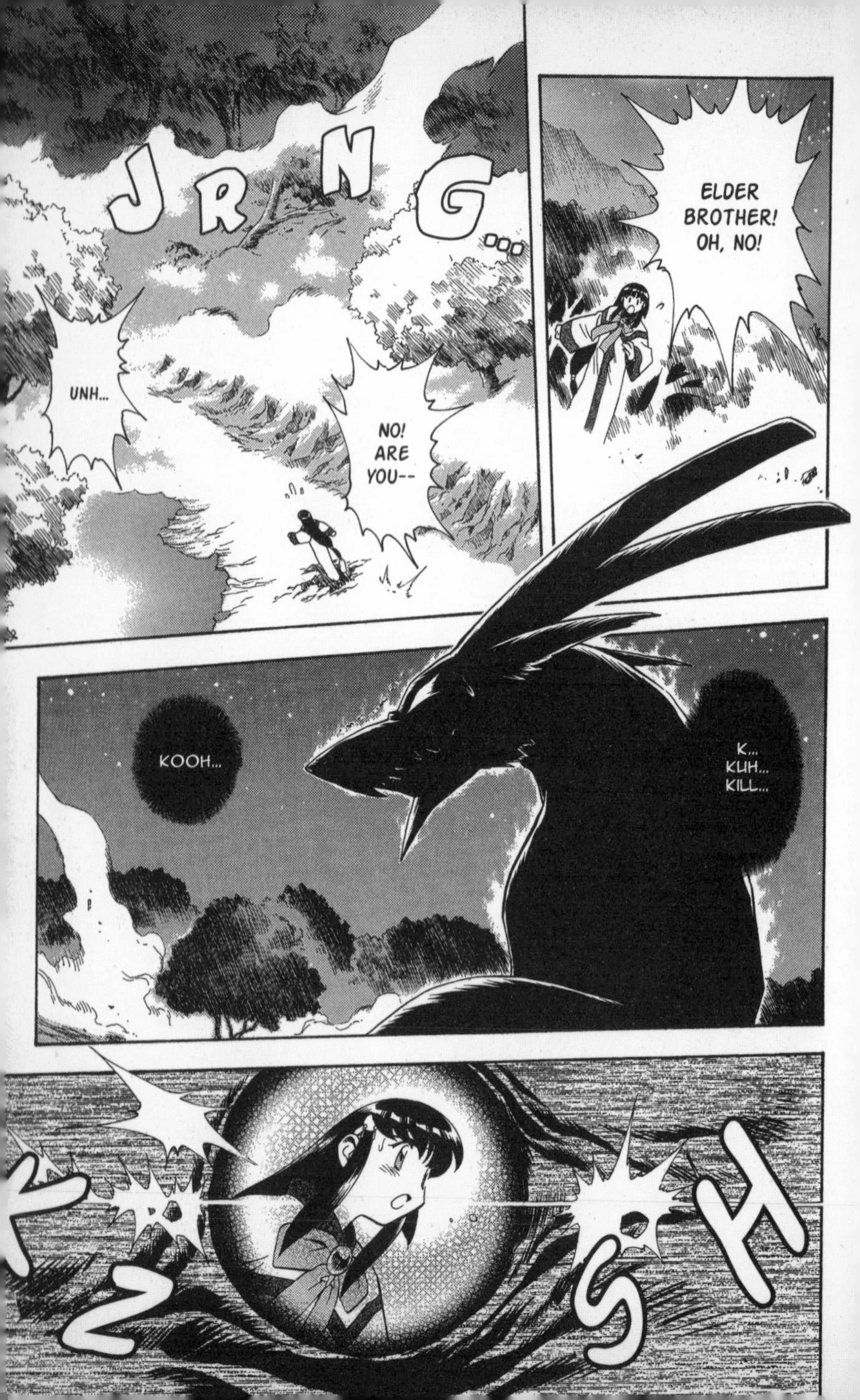
JRNG
UNH...
NO! ARE YOU--
ELDER BROTHER! OH, NO!
KOOH...
K... KUH... KILL...

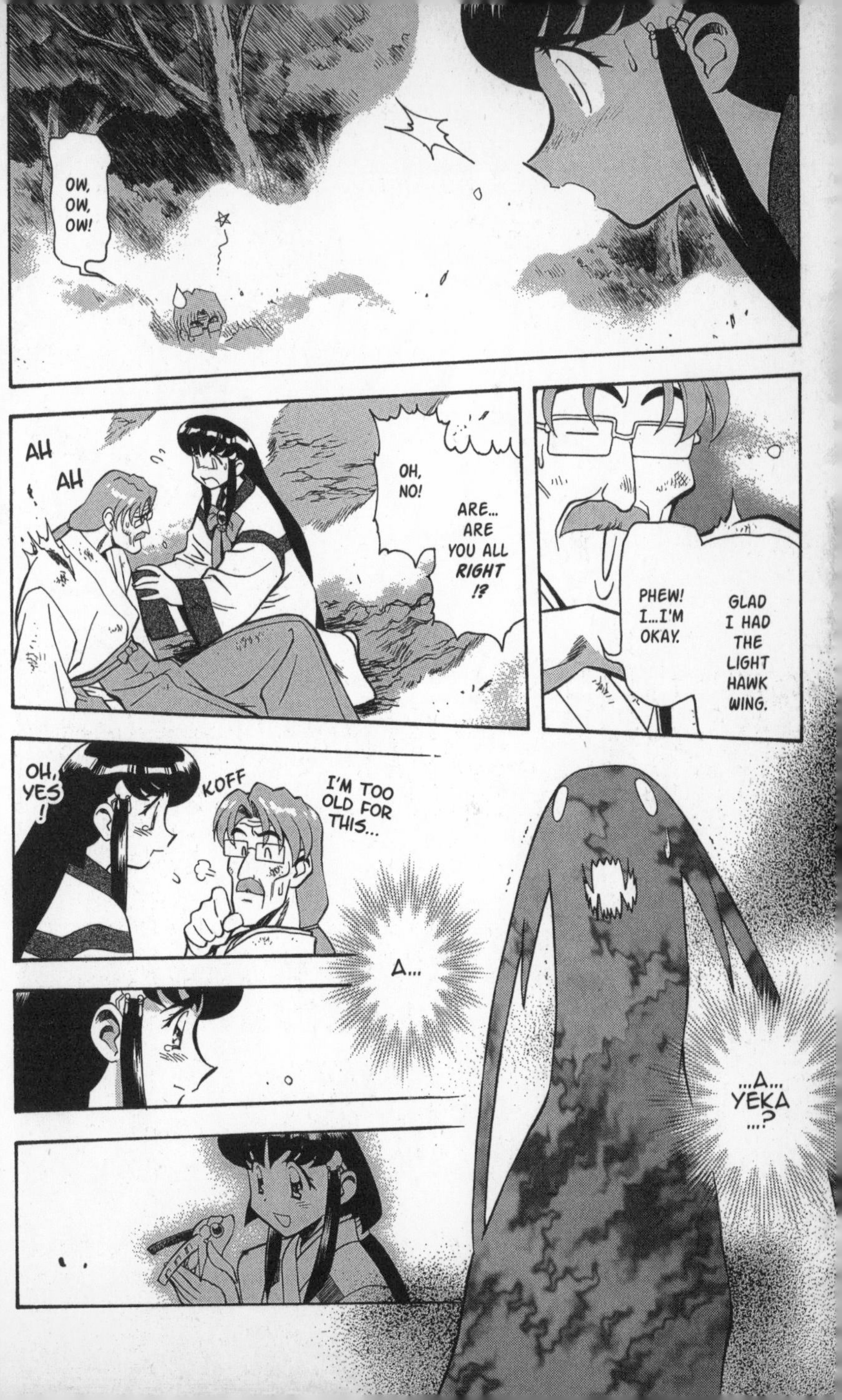
OW, OW, OW!
AH
AH
OH, NO!
ARE... ARE YOU ALL **RIGHT** !?
PHEW! I...I'M OKAY.
GLAD I HAD THE LIGHT HAWK WING.
OH, YES !
KOFF
I'M TOO OLD FOR THIS...
A...
...A... YEKA ...?

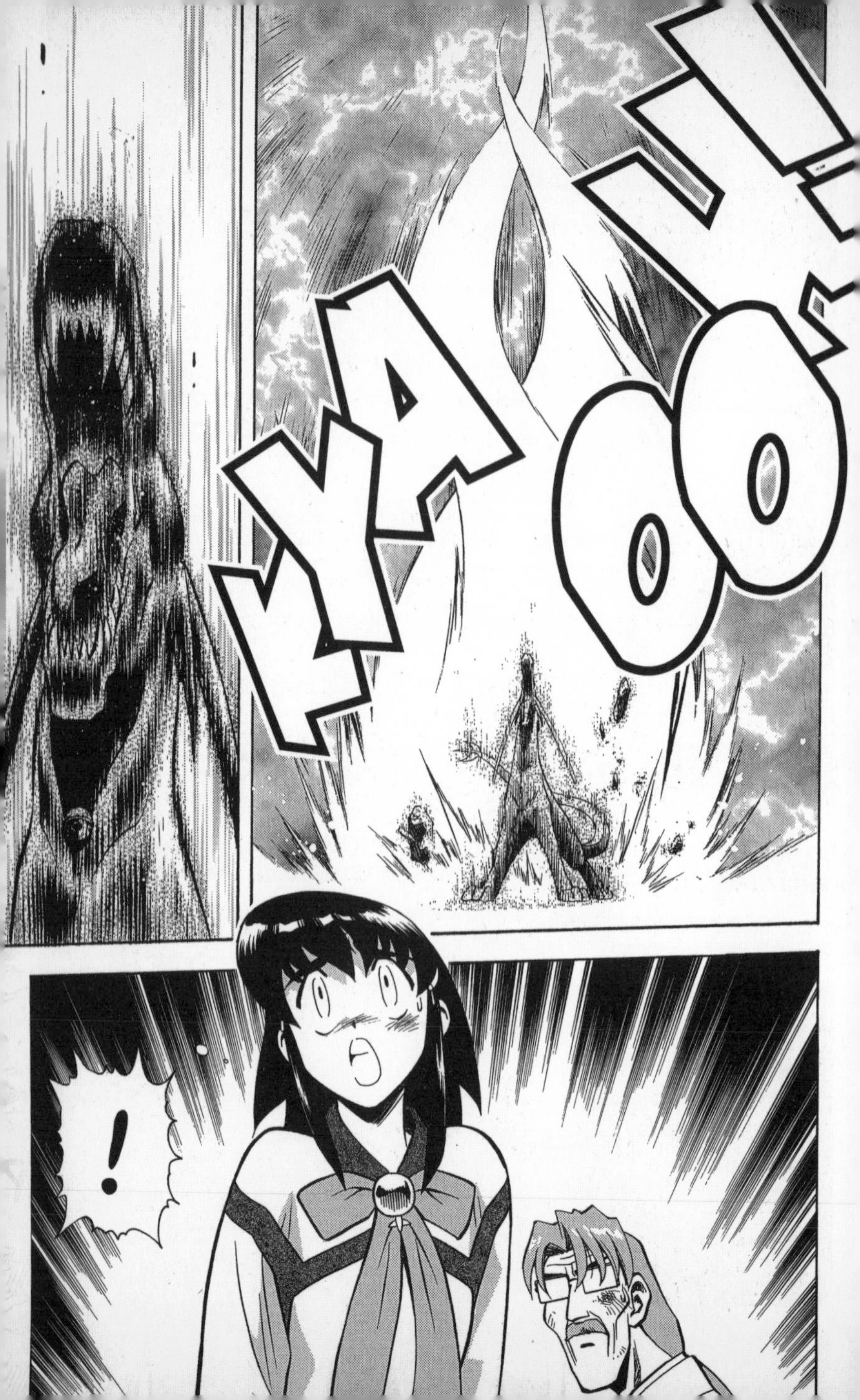
KYAOO!!
!

KOOH...

MITSU ?

SHAAAA

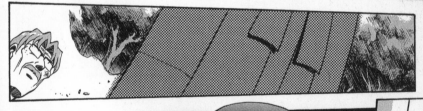

......

TMP

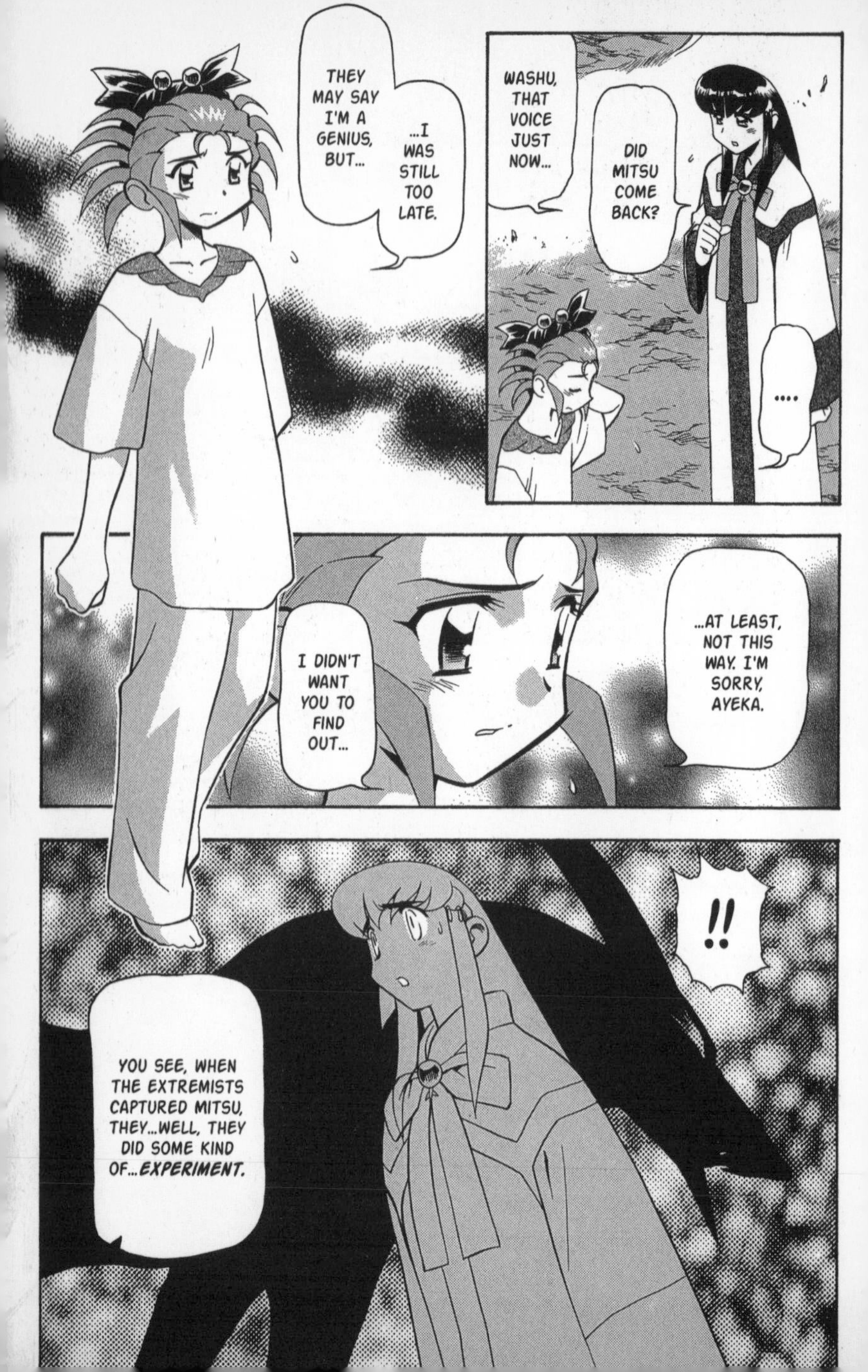
THEY MAY SAY I'M A GENIUS, BUT...
...I WAS STILL TOO LATE.
WASHU, THAT VOICE JUST NOW...
DID MITSU COME BACK?
....
I DIDN'T WANT YOU TO FIND OUT...
...AT LEAST, NOT THIS WAY. I'M SORRY, AYEKA.
YOU SEE, WHEN THE EXTREMISTS CAPTURED MITSU, THEY...WELL, THEY DID SOME KIND OF...*EXPERIMENT.*
!!

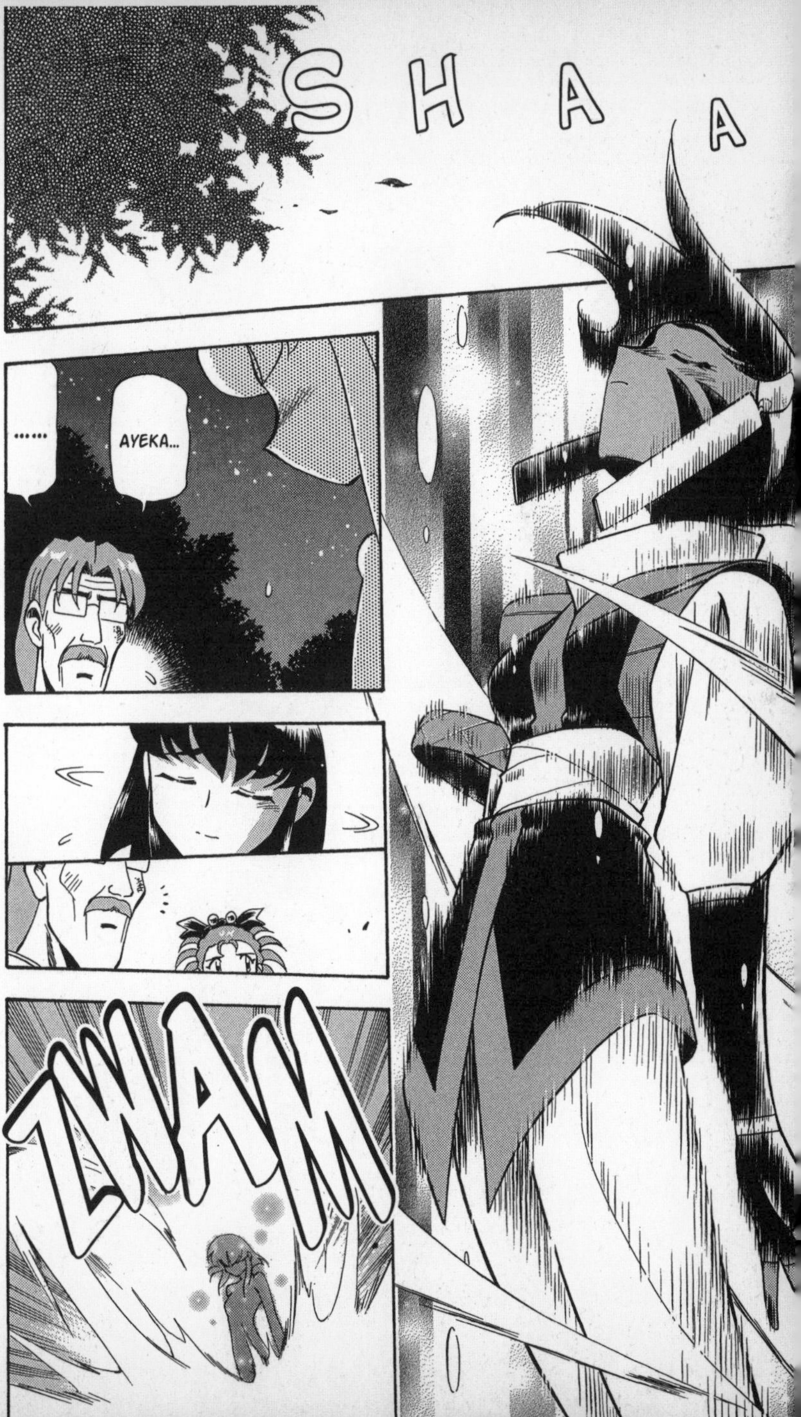
SHAAA
......
AYEKA...
ZWAM

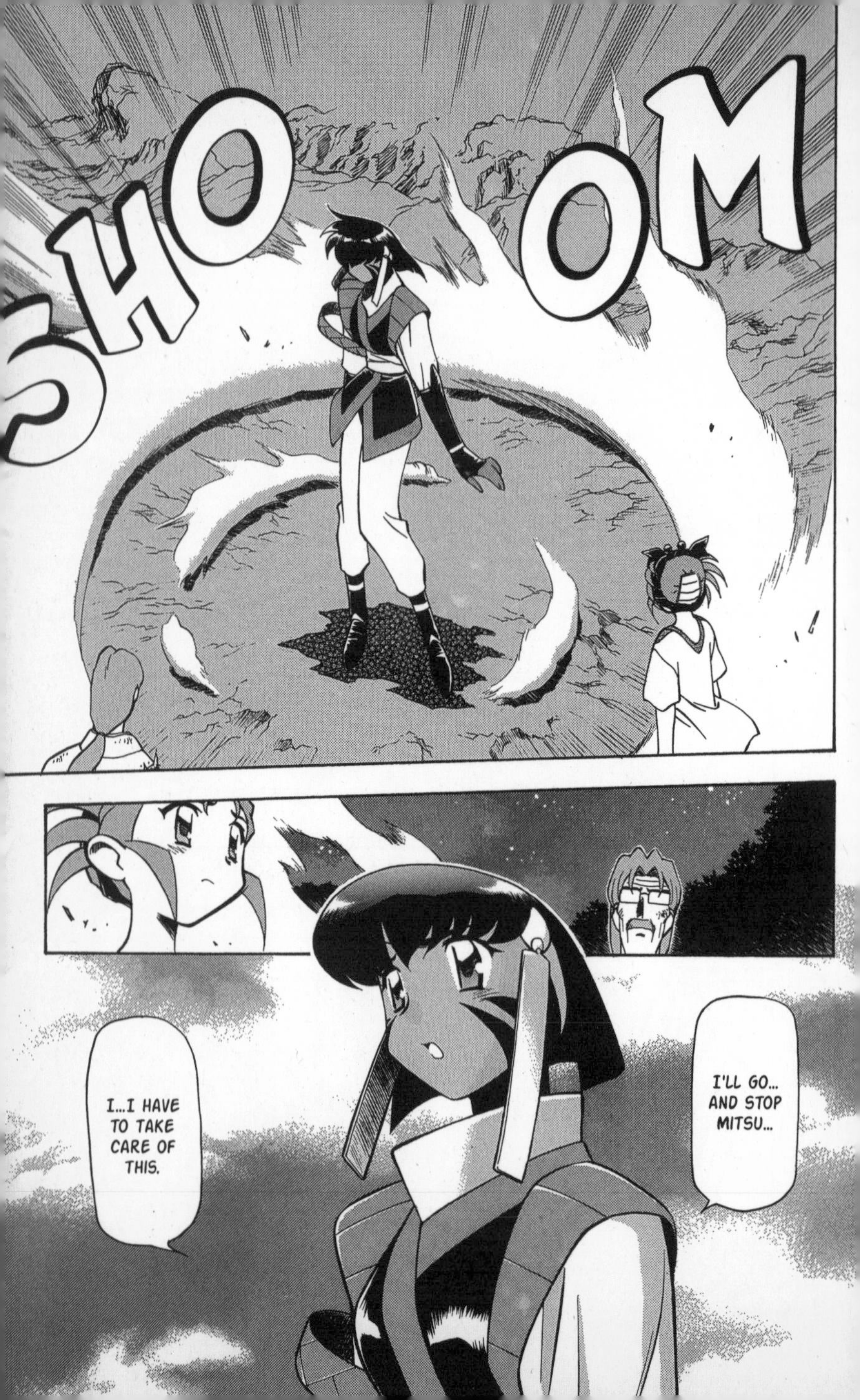
SHOOOM
I...I HAVE TO TAKE CARE OF THIS.
I'LL GO... AND STOP MITSU...

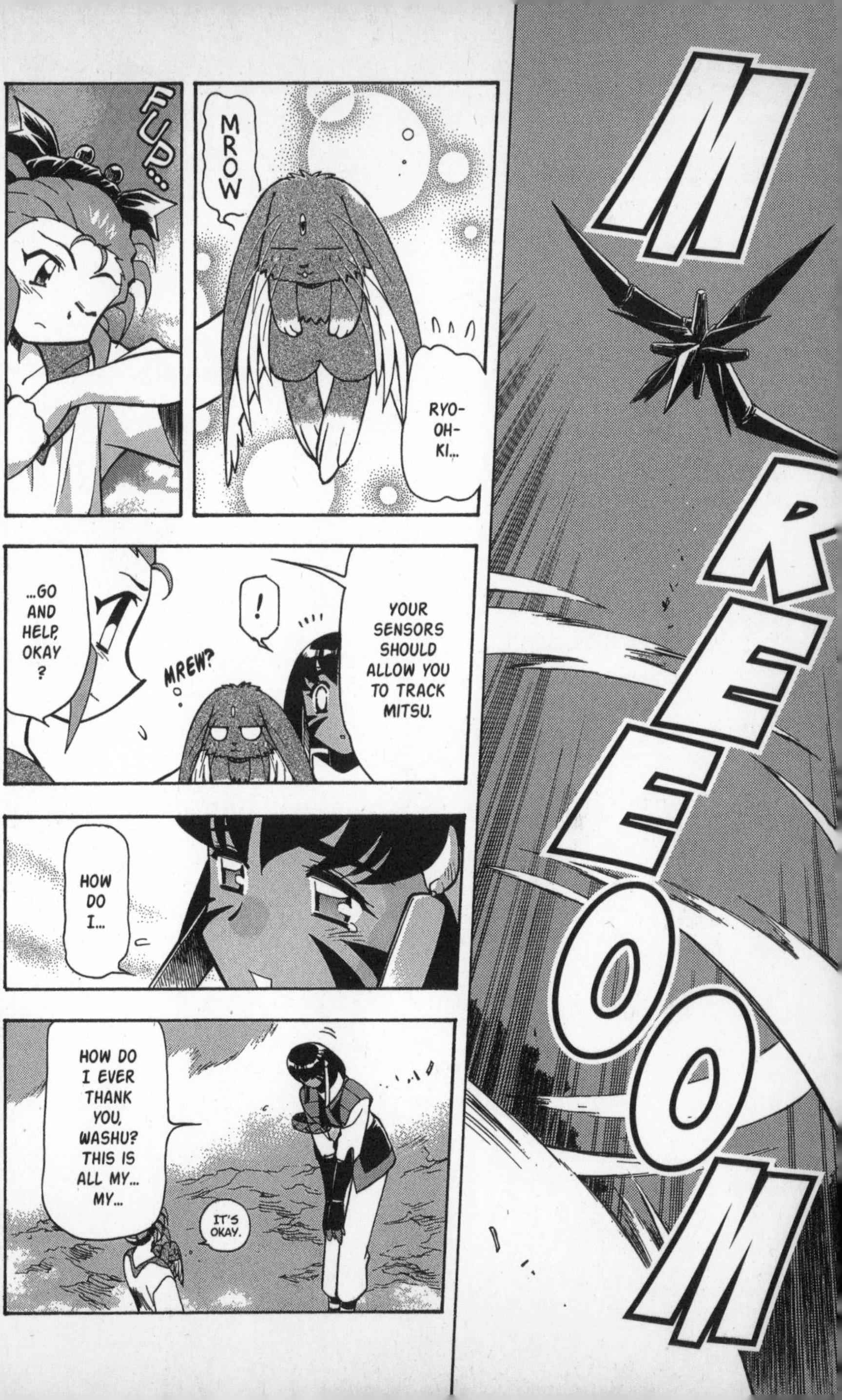

FLIP...
MROW
RYO-OH-KI...
...GO AND HELP, OKAY?
!
MREW?
YOUR SENSORS SHOULD ALLOW YOU TO TRACK MITSU.
HOW DO I...
HOW DO I EVER THANK YOU, WASHU? THIS IS ALL MY... MY...
IT'S OKAY.
MREEOOM

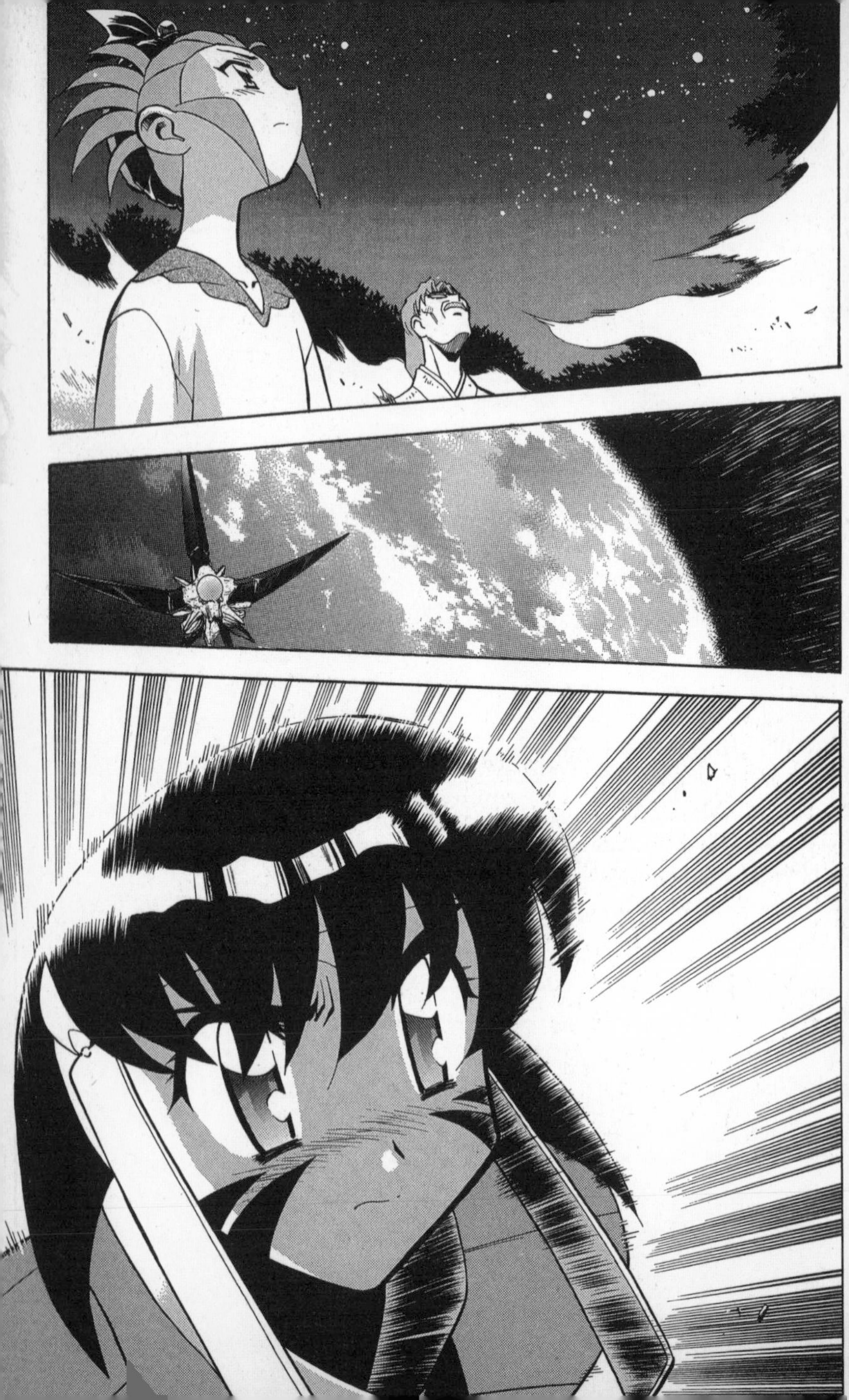

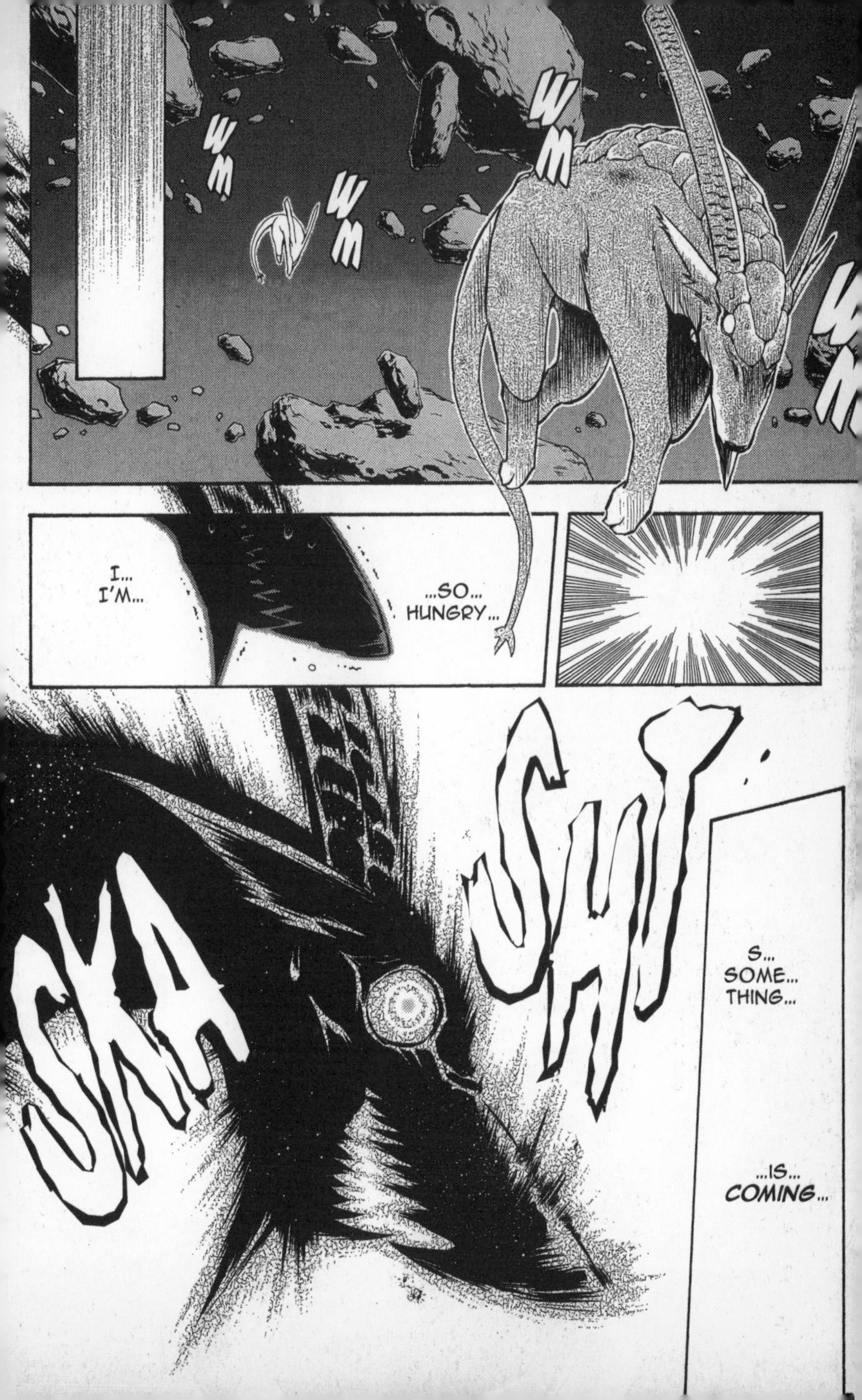
I... I'M...
...SO... HUNGRY...
S... SOME... THING...
...IS... COMING...

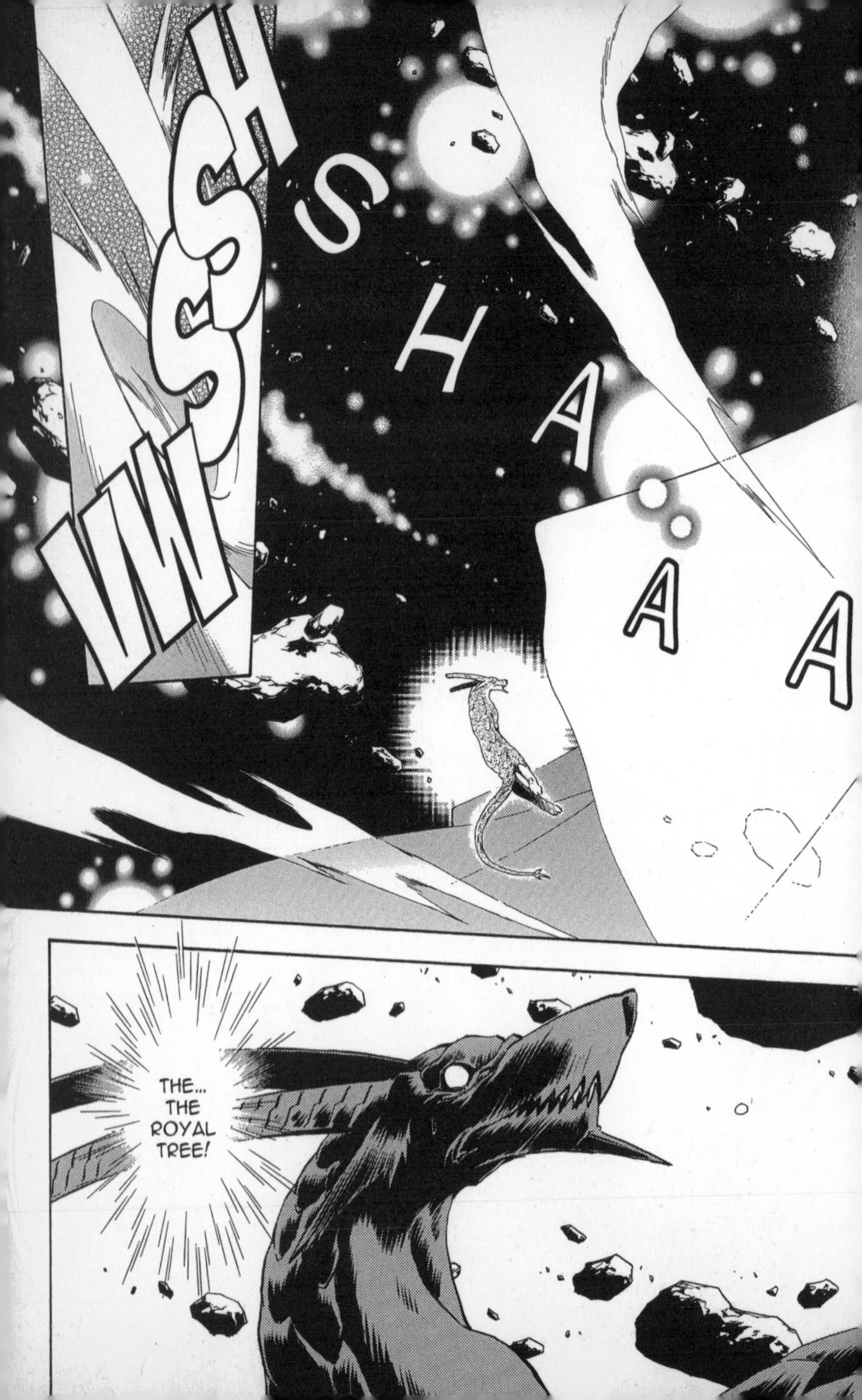
WHSSH
SHAAAA
THE... THE ROYAL TREE!

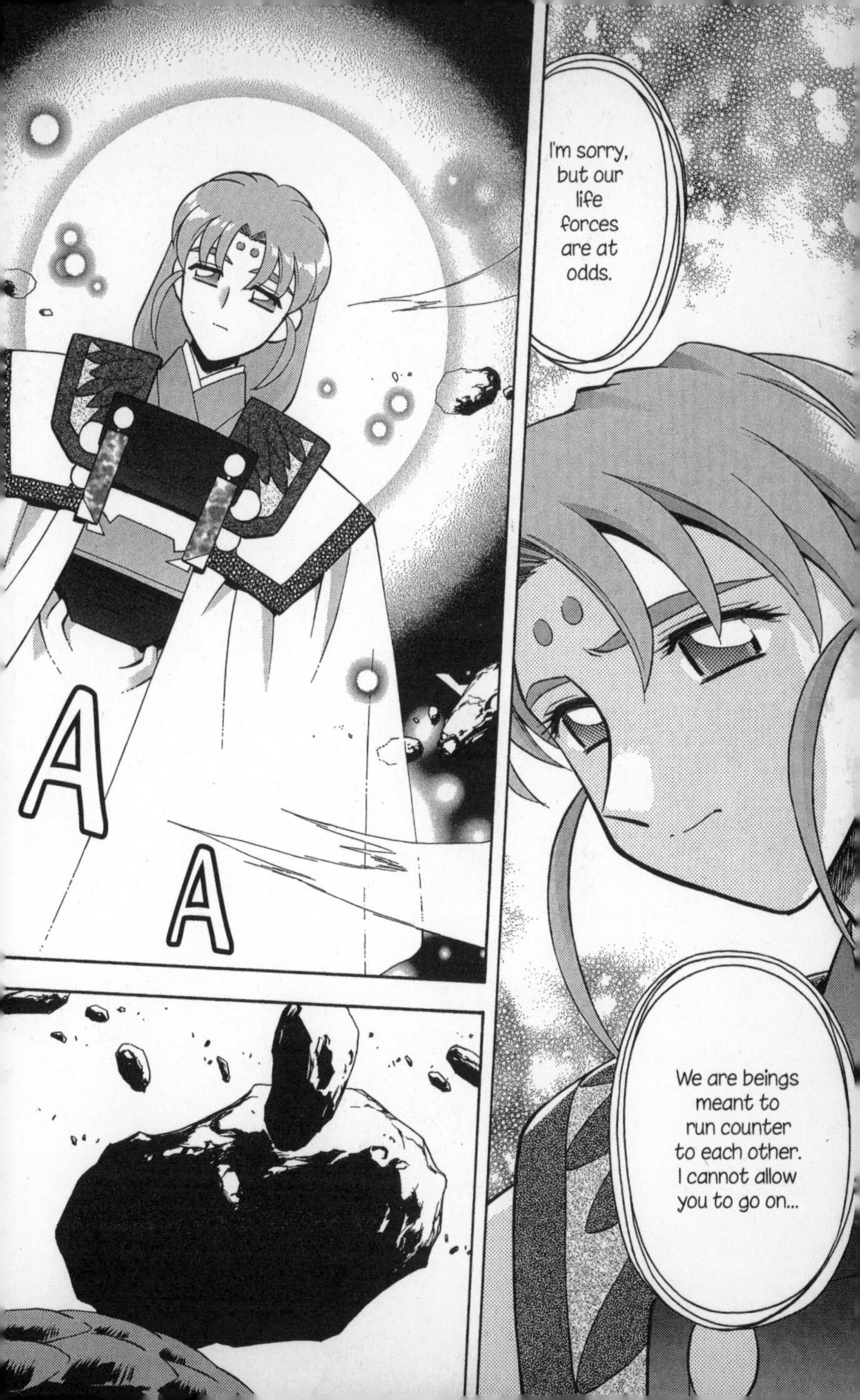
A
A
I'm sorry, but our life forces are at odds.
We are beings meant to run counter to each other. I cannot allow you to go on...

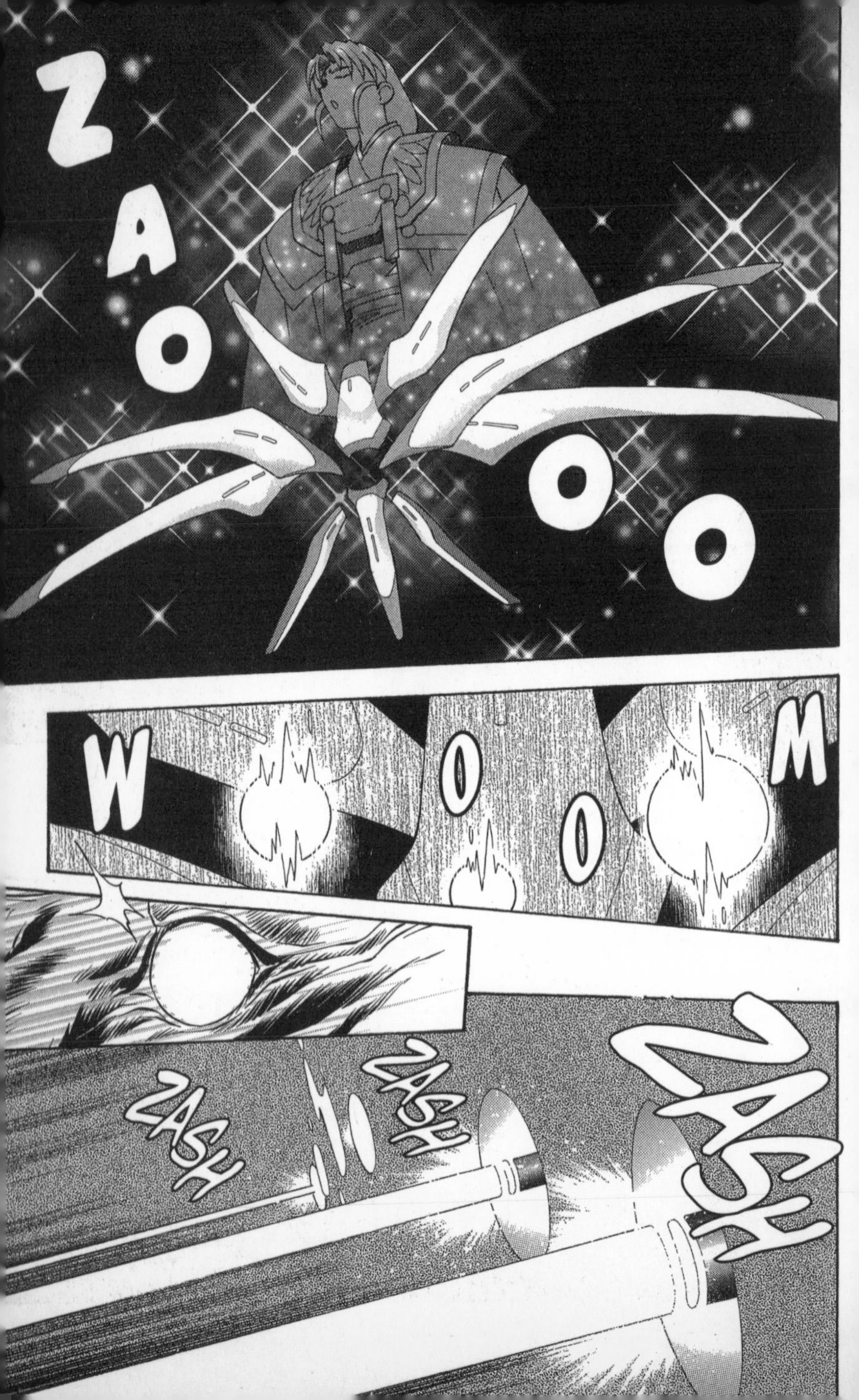
ZAOOOO
WOOOM
ZASH
ZASH
ZASH

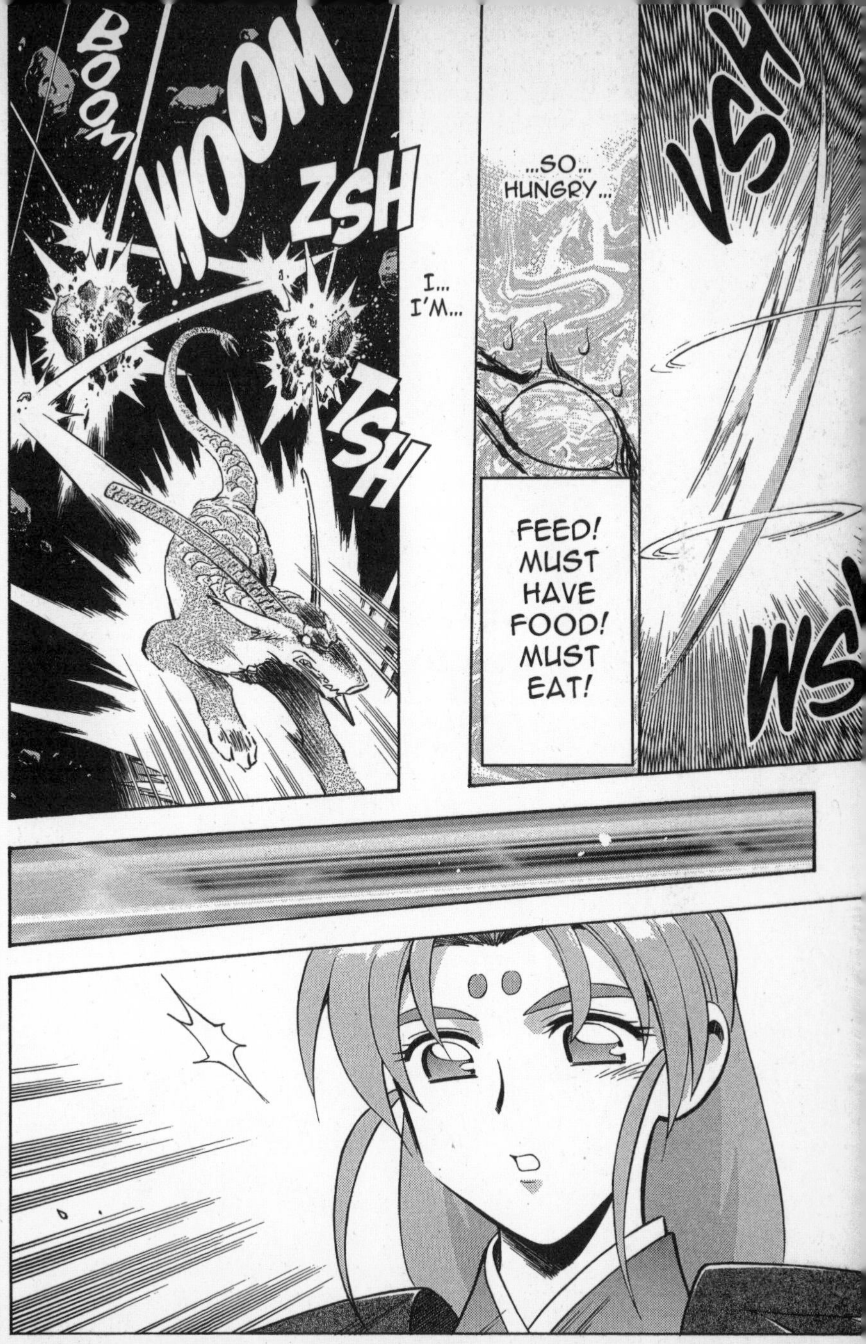
BOOM
WOOM
ZSH
TSH
I... I'M...
...SO... HUNGRY...
FEED! MUST HAVE FOOD! MUST EAT!
VSH
WS

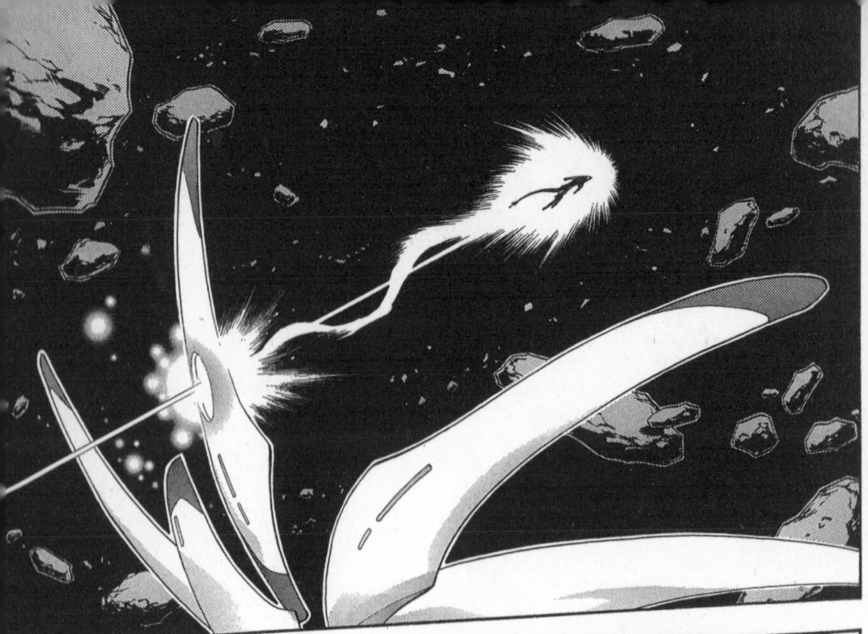

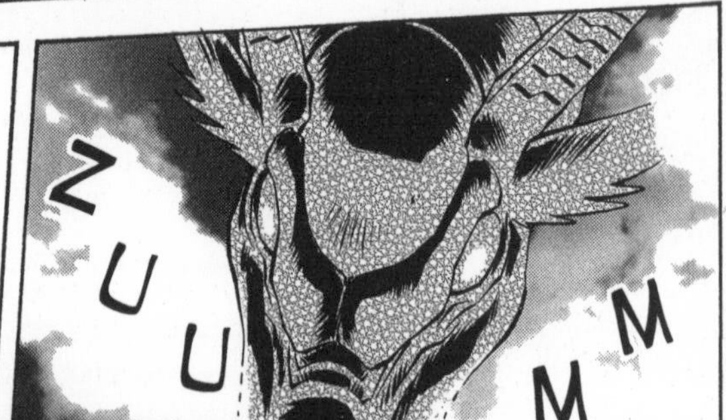
ZUUMM

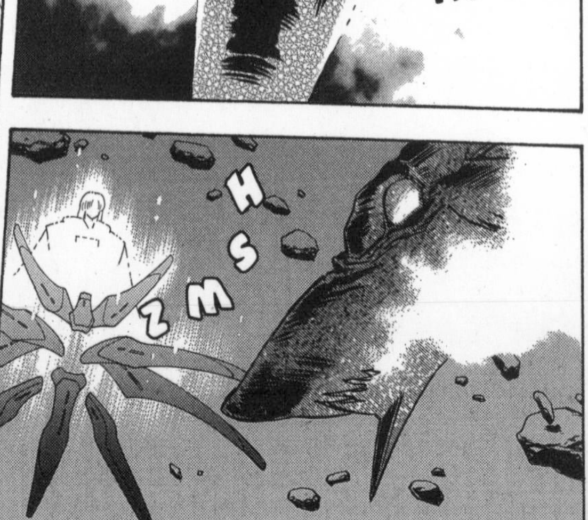
ZMSH

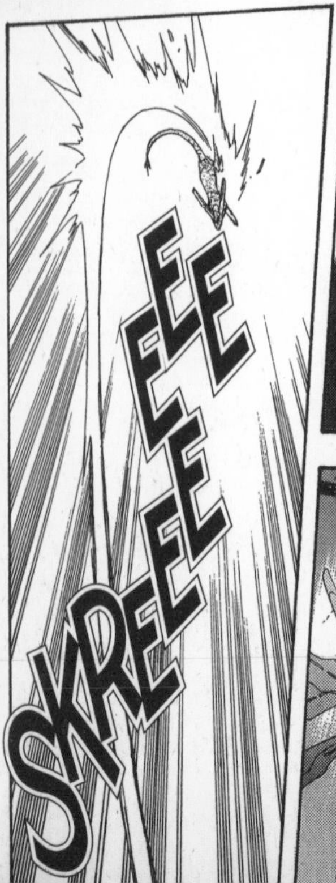
SKREEEEEEE

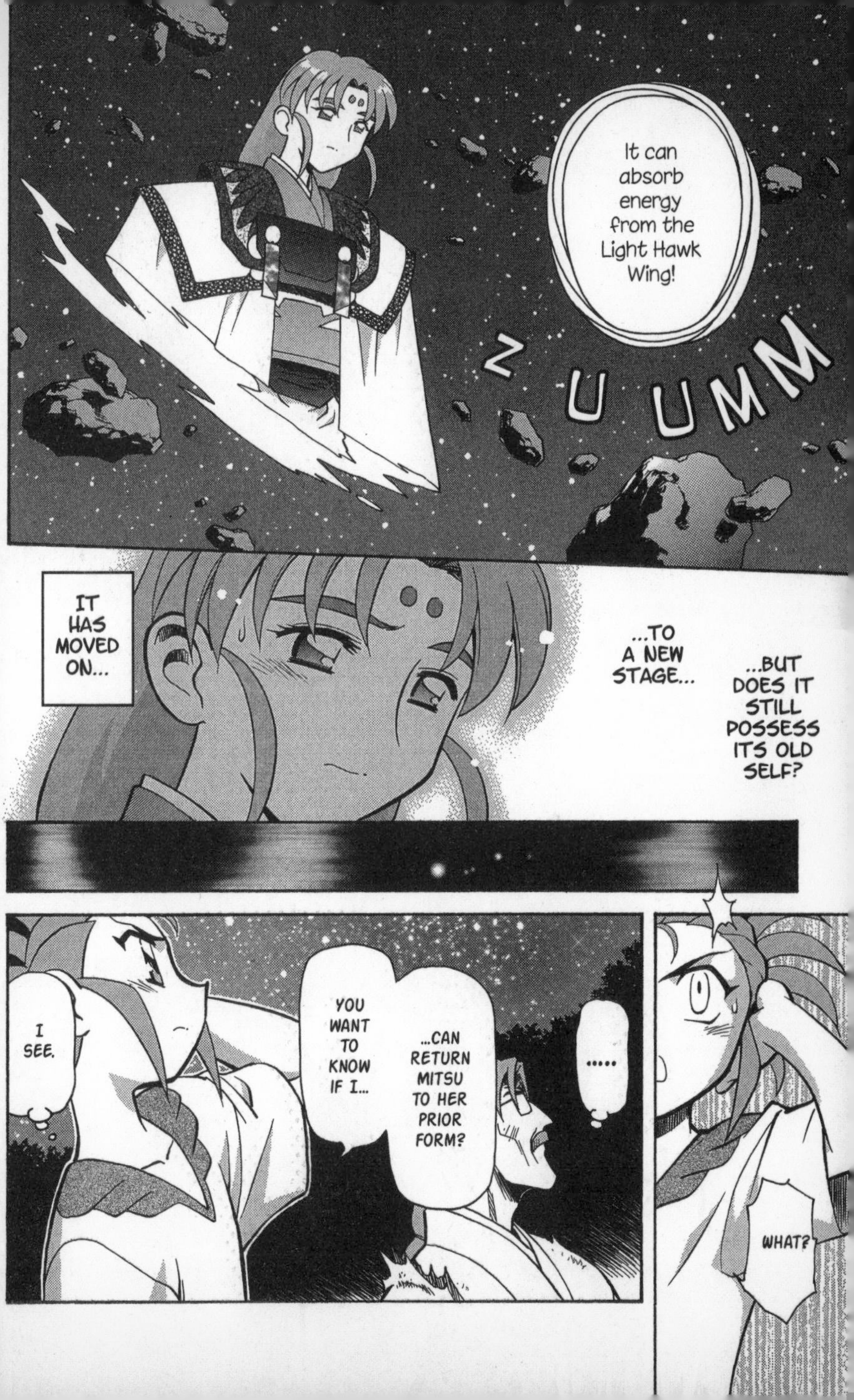
It can absorb energy from the Light Hawk Wing!
ZUUMM
IT HAS MOVED ON...
...TO A NEW STAGE...
...BUT DOES IT STILL POSSESS ITS OLD SELF?
I SEE.
YOU WANT TO KNOW IF I...
...CAN RETURN MITSU TO HER PRIOR FORM?
......
WHAT?

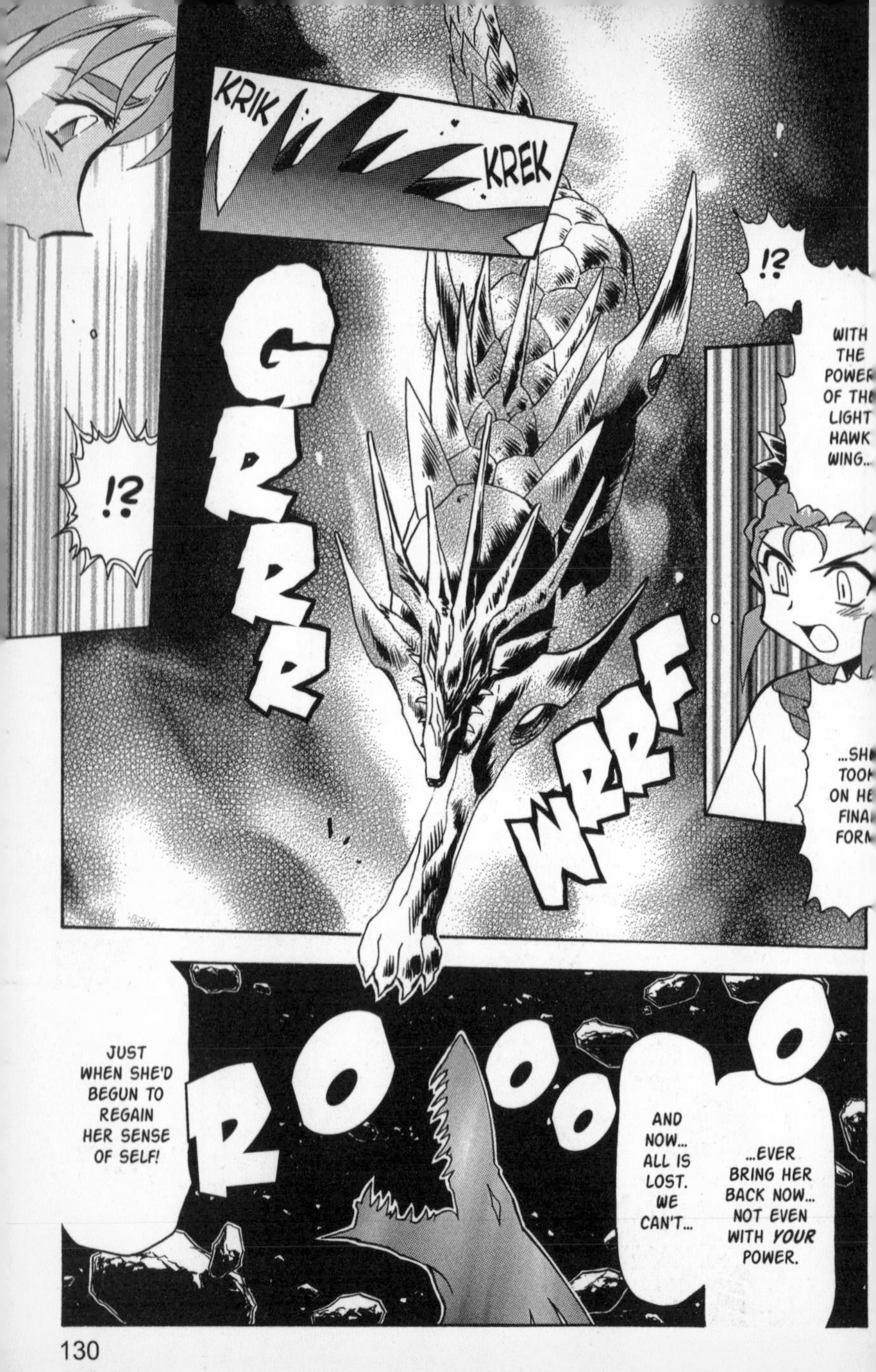
!?
KRIK
KREK
GRRR
WRRF
!?
WITH THE POWE OF TH LIGHT HAWK WING...
...SH TOO ON HE FINA FOR
JUST WHEN SHE'D BEGUN TO REGAIN HER SENSE OF SELF!
ROOOOO
AND NOW... ALL IS LOST. WE CAN'T...
...EVER BRING HER BACK NOW... NOT EVEN WITH *YOUR* POWER.

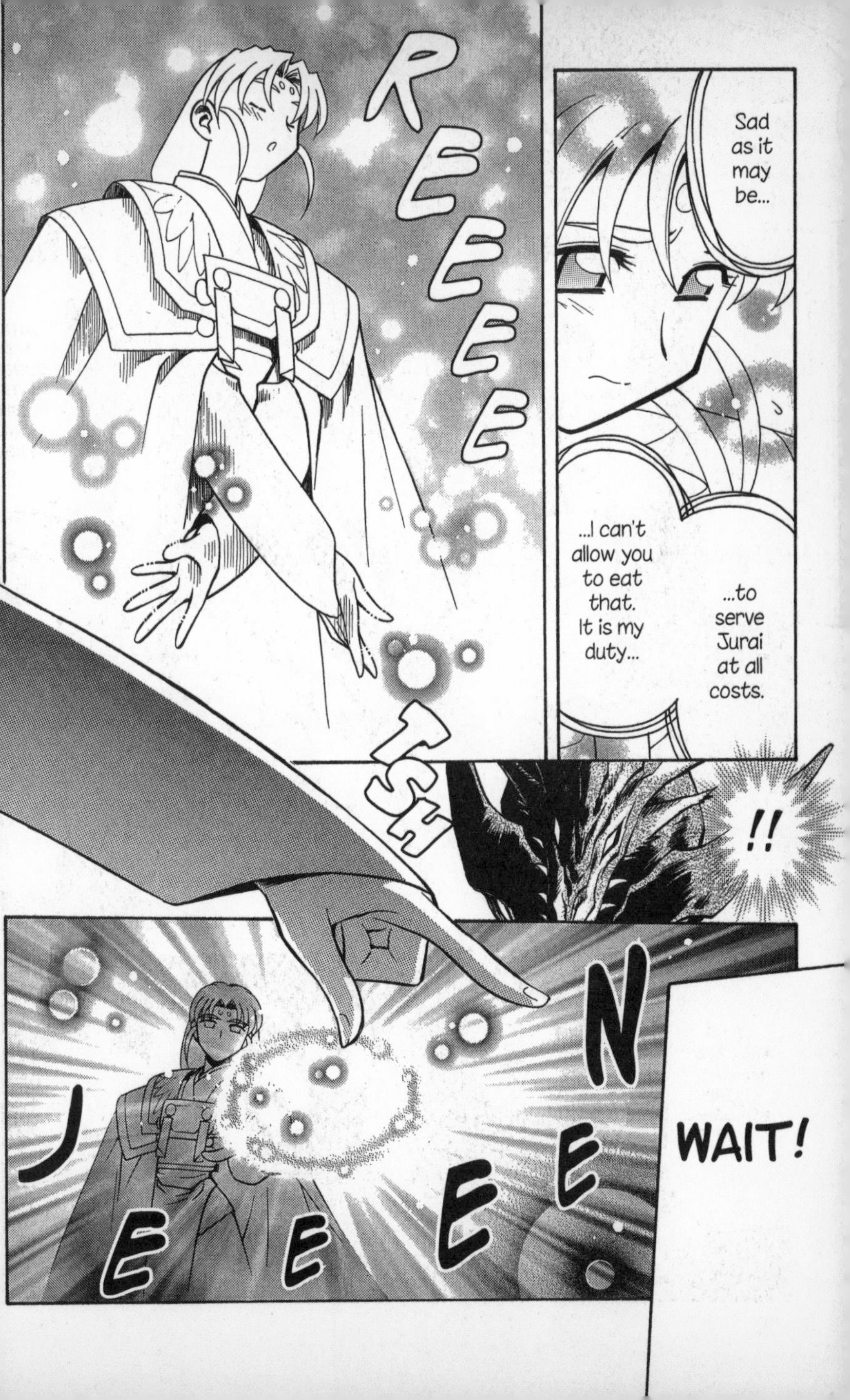
REEEE
Sad as it may be...
...I can't allow you to eat that. It is my duty...
...to serve Jurai at all costs.
TSH
!!
JEEEEN
WAIT!

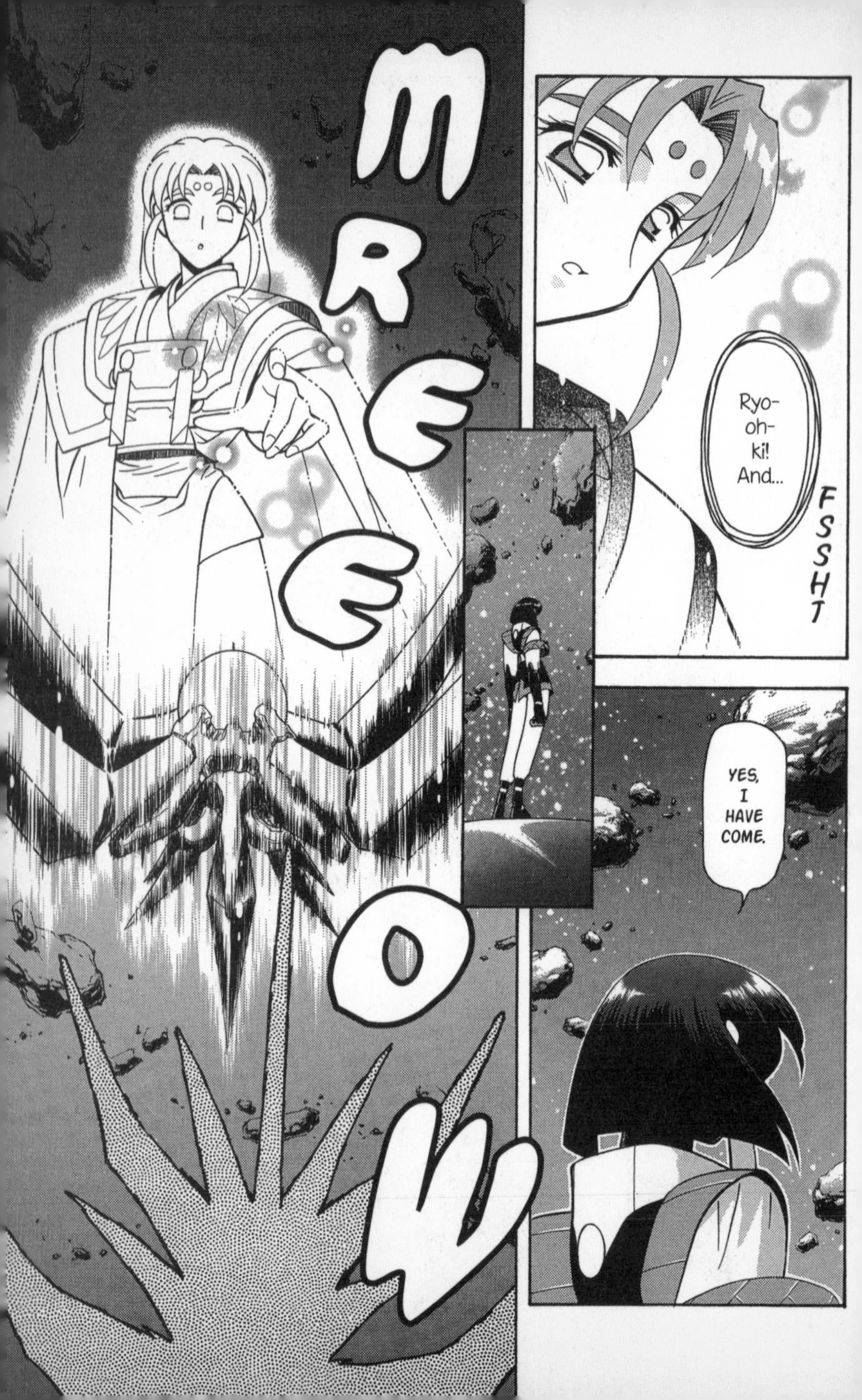
MREEOW
Ryo-oh-ki! And...
FSSHT
YES, I HAVE COME.

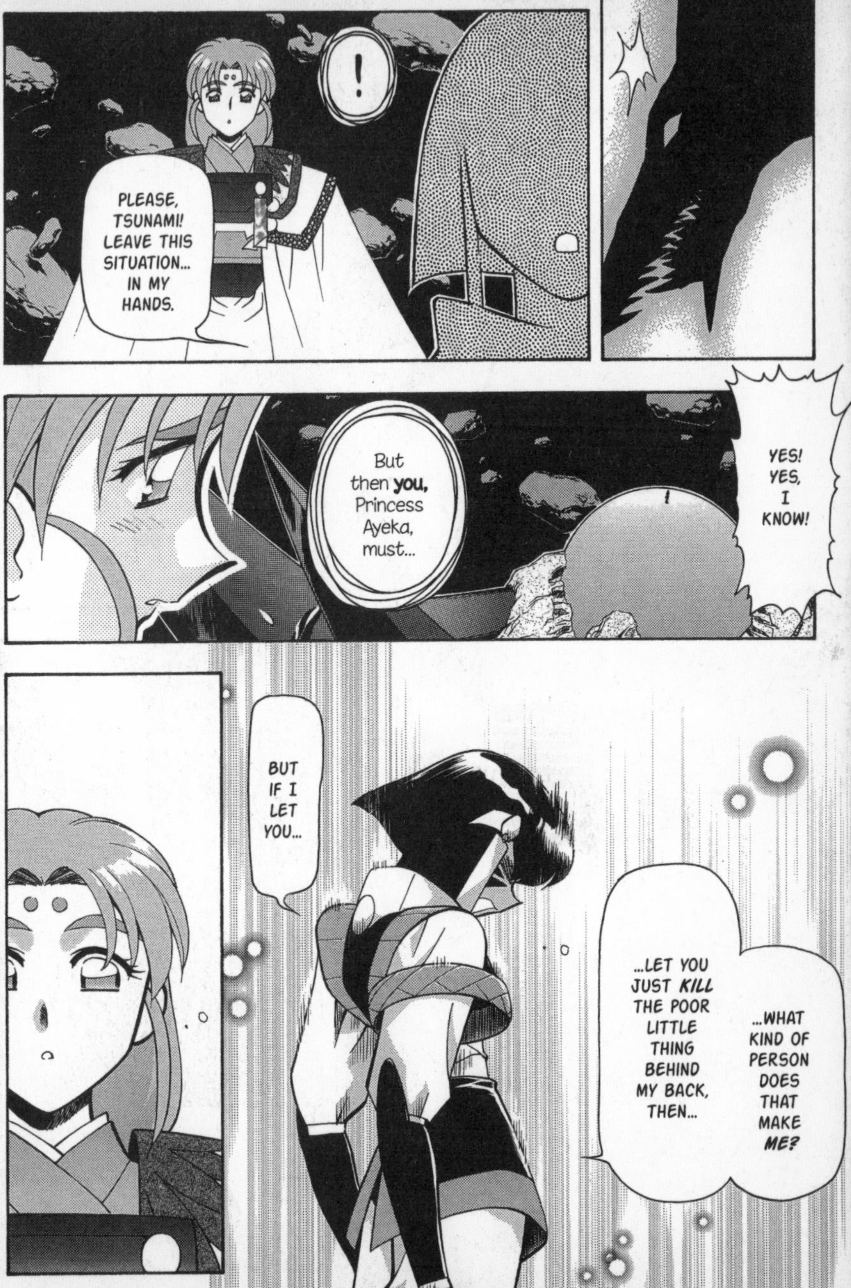
!
PLEASE, TSUNAMI! LEAVE THIS SITUATION... IN MY HANDS.
But then **you,** Princess Ayeka, must...
YES! YES, I KNOW!
BUT IF I LET YOU...
...LET YOU JUST *KILL* THE POOR LITTLE THING BEHIND MY BACK, THEN...
...WHAT KIND OF PERSON DOES THAT MAKE *ME?*

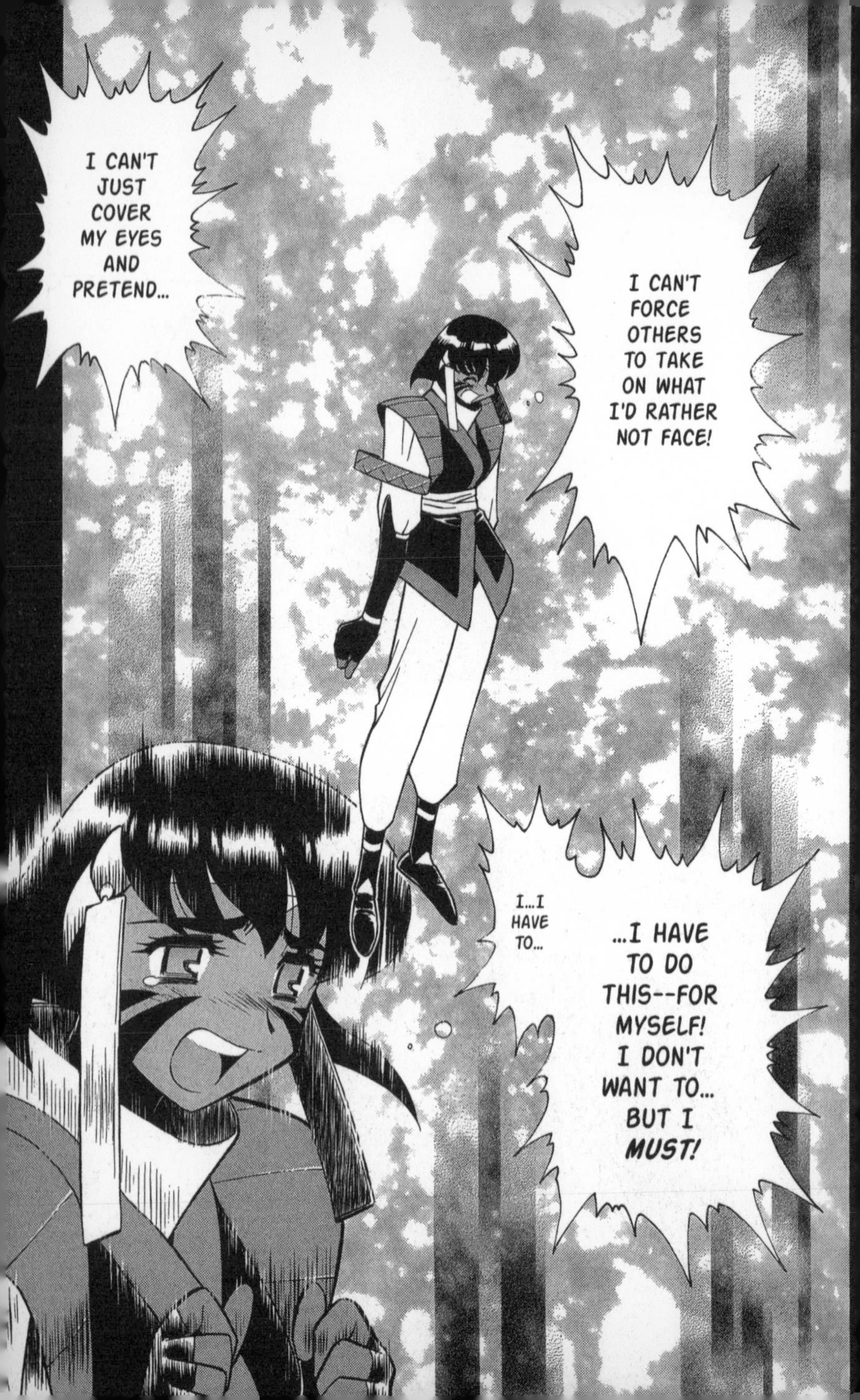

I CAN'T JUST COVER MY EYES AND PRETEND...
I CAN'T FORCE OTHERS TO TAKE ON WHAT I'D RATHER NOT FACE!
I...I HAVE TO...
...I HAVE TO DO THIS--FOR MYSELF! I DON'T WANT TO... BUT I *MUST!*

As you wish.

TH... THANK YOU. VERY MUCH...

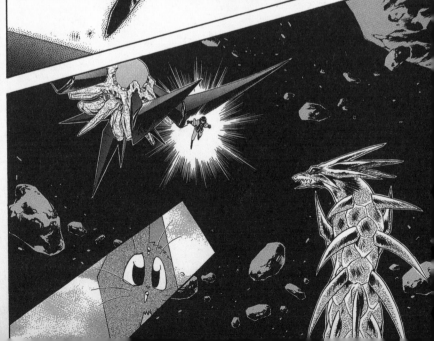

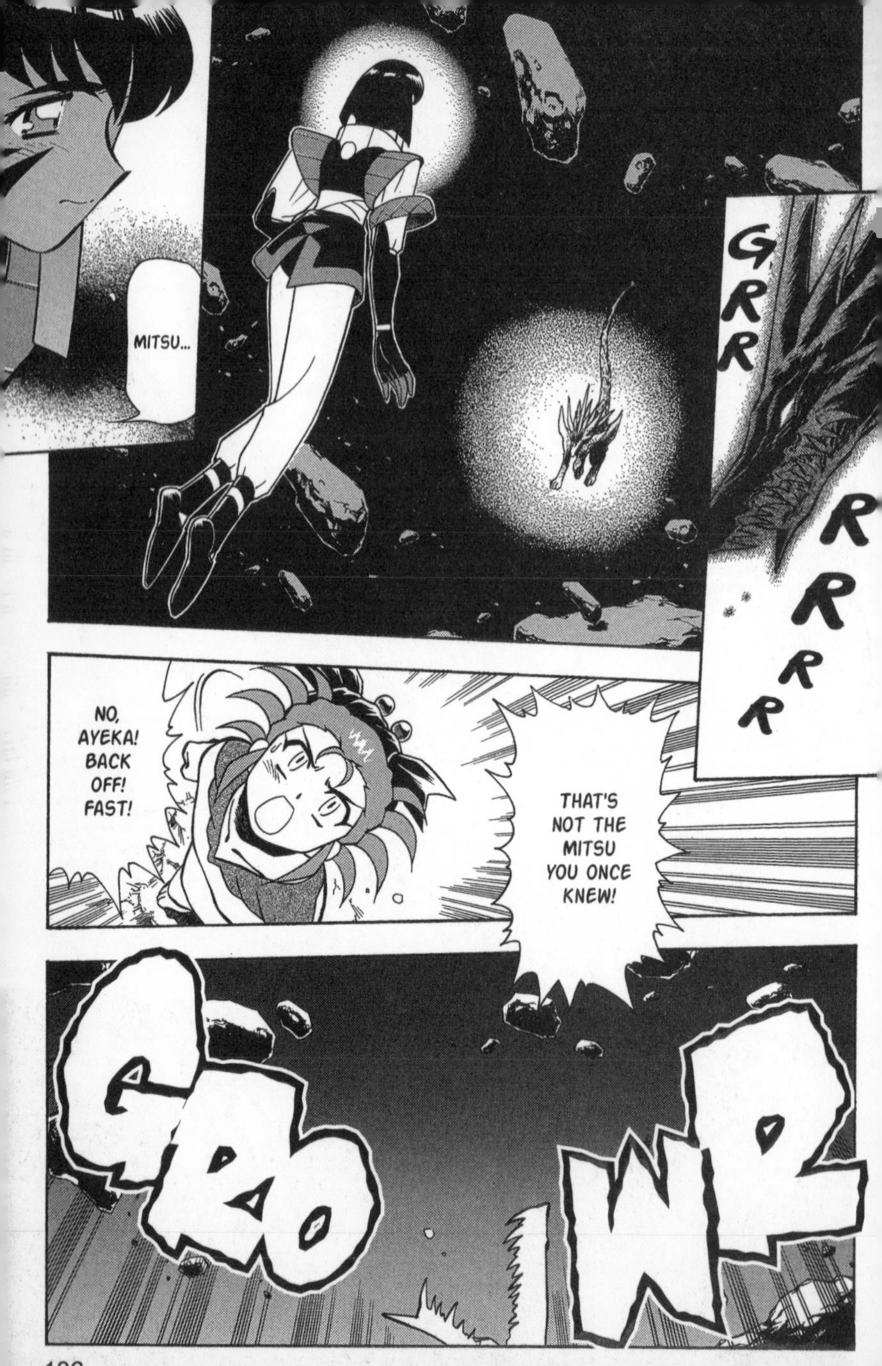
MITSU...
GRRRRRR
NO, AYEKA! BACK OFF! FAST!
THAT'S NOT THE MITSU YOU ONCE KNEW!

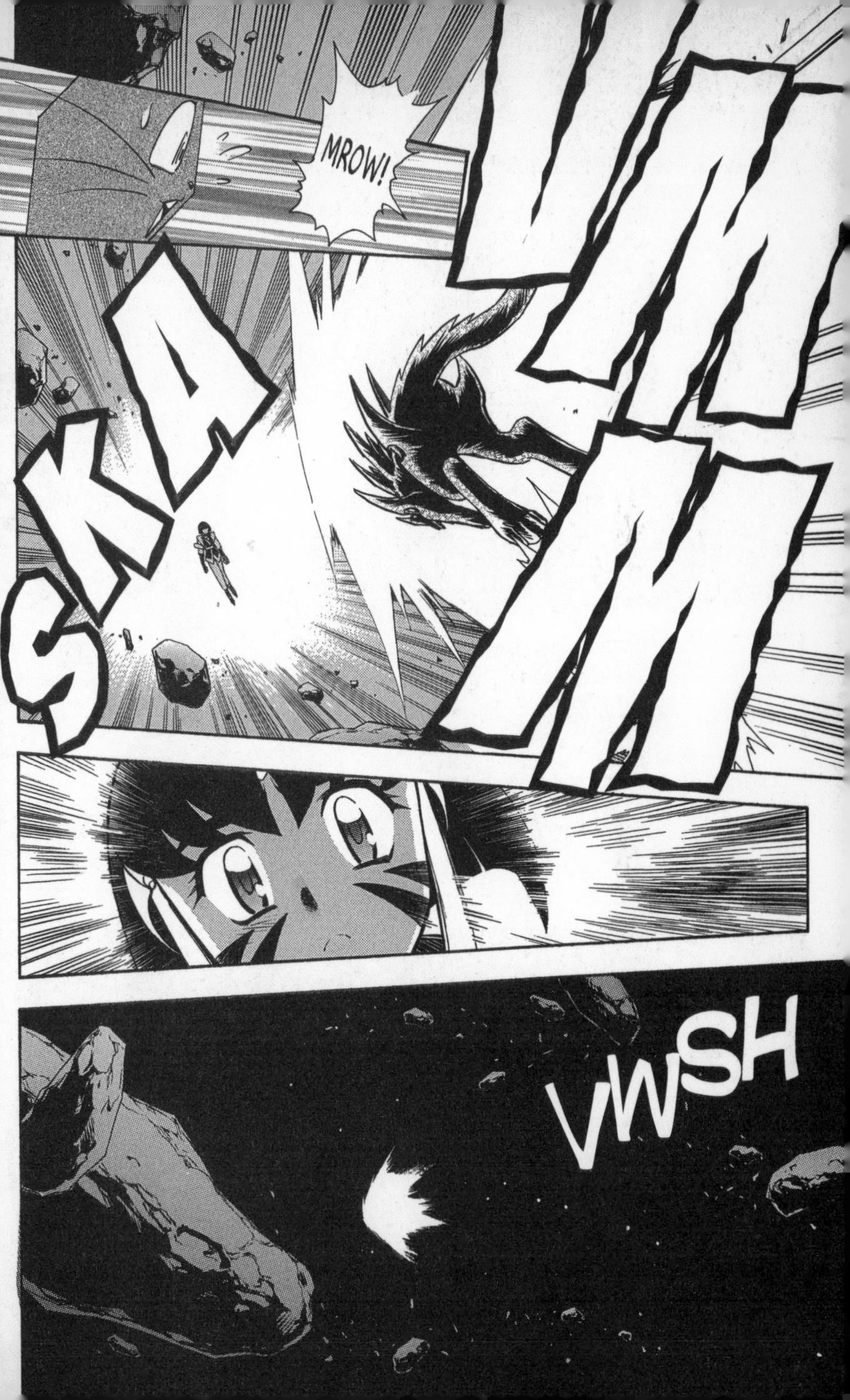
MROW!
VWSH

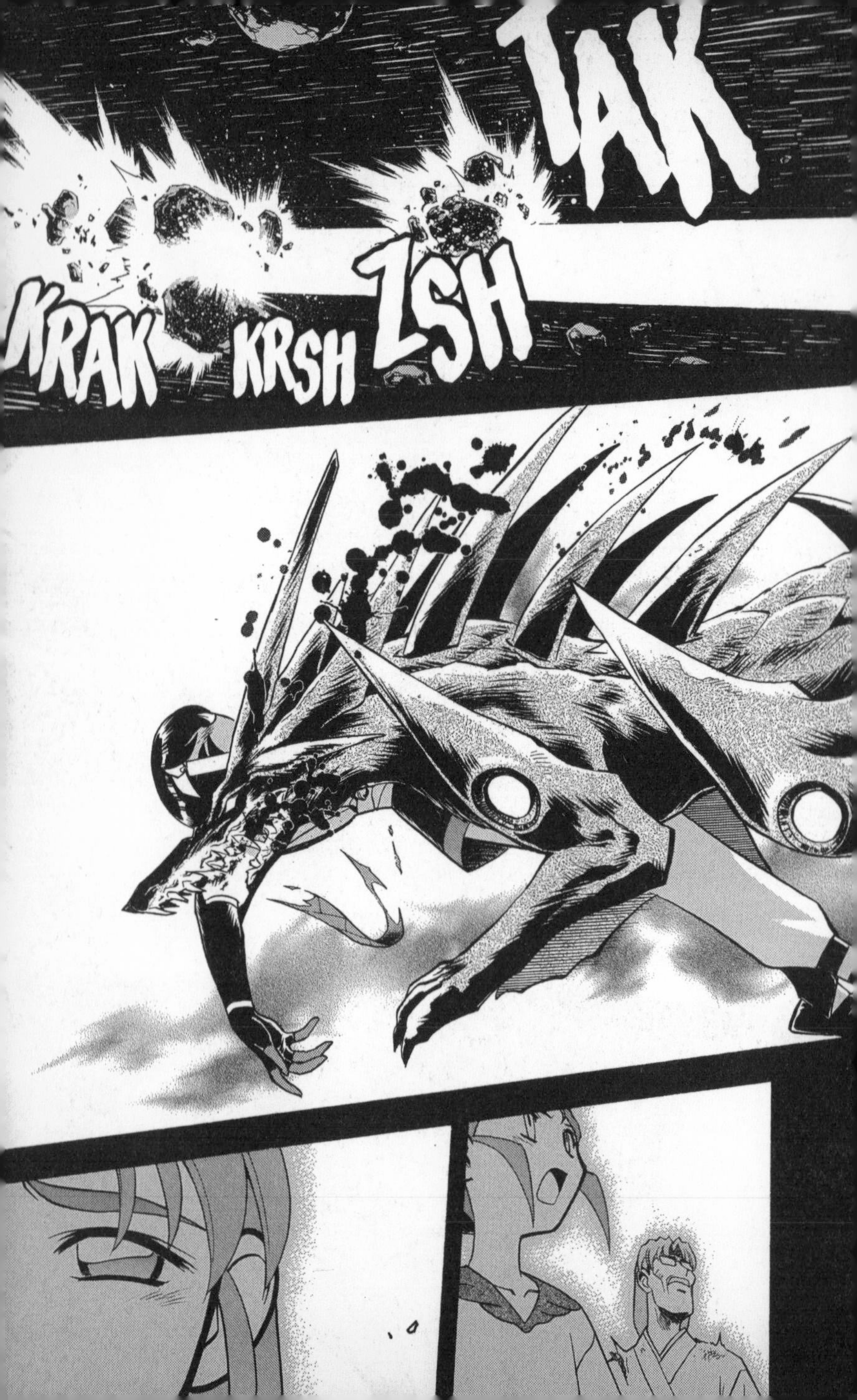
TAK
KRAK
KRSH
ZSH

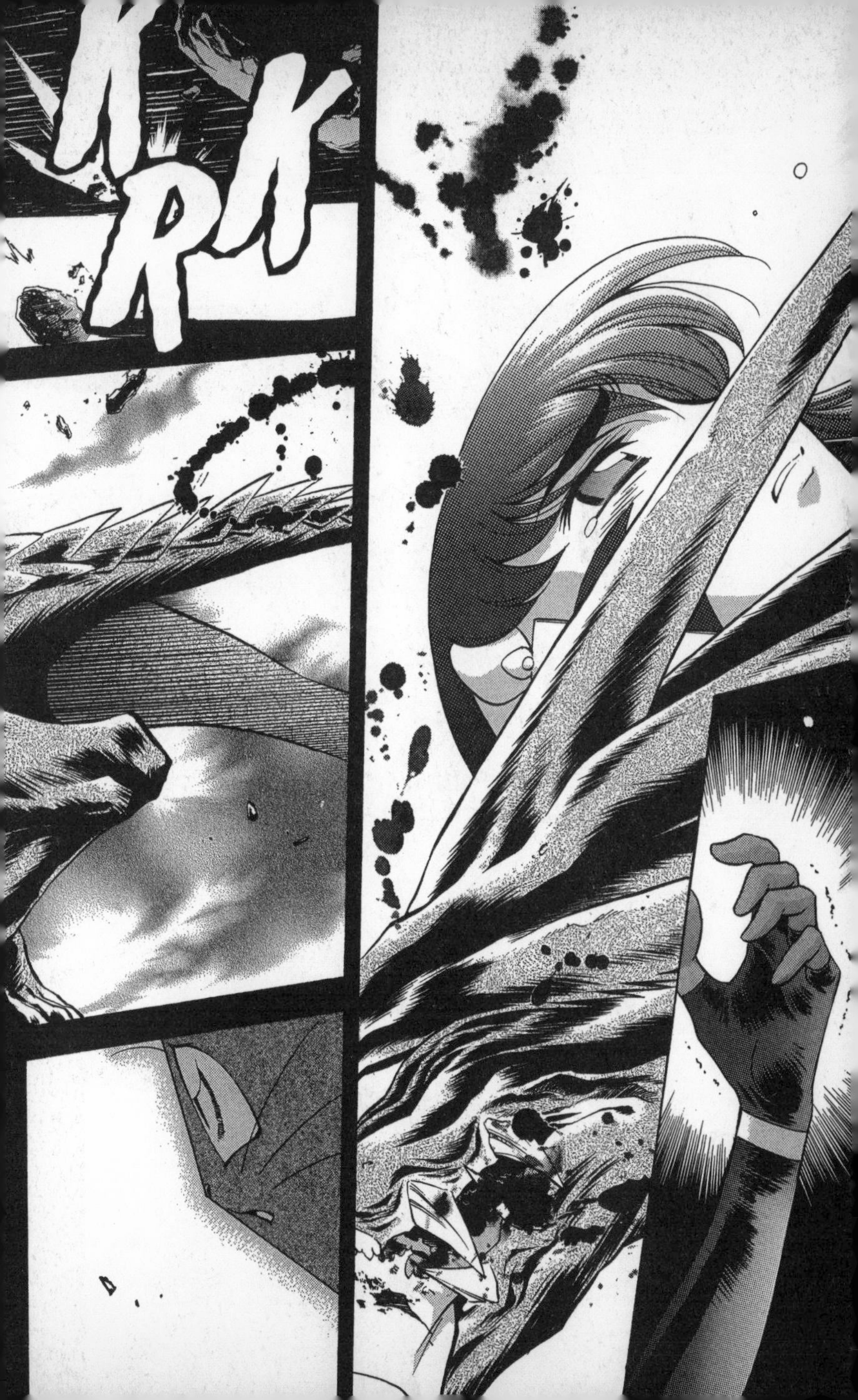

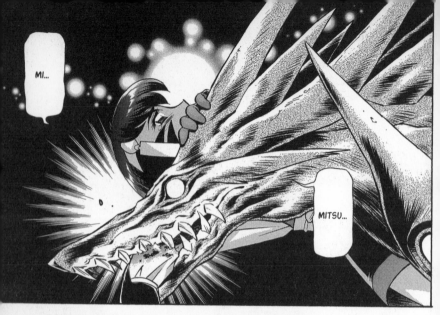

MI...

MITSU...

A...

...AYE...
KA...?

FSH...

FWOM...

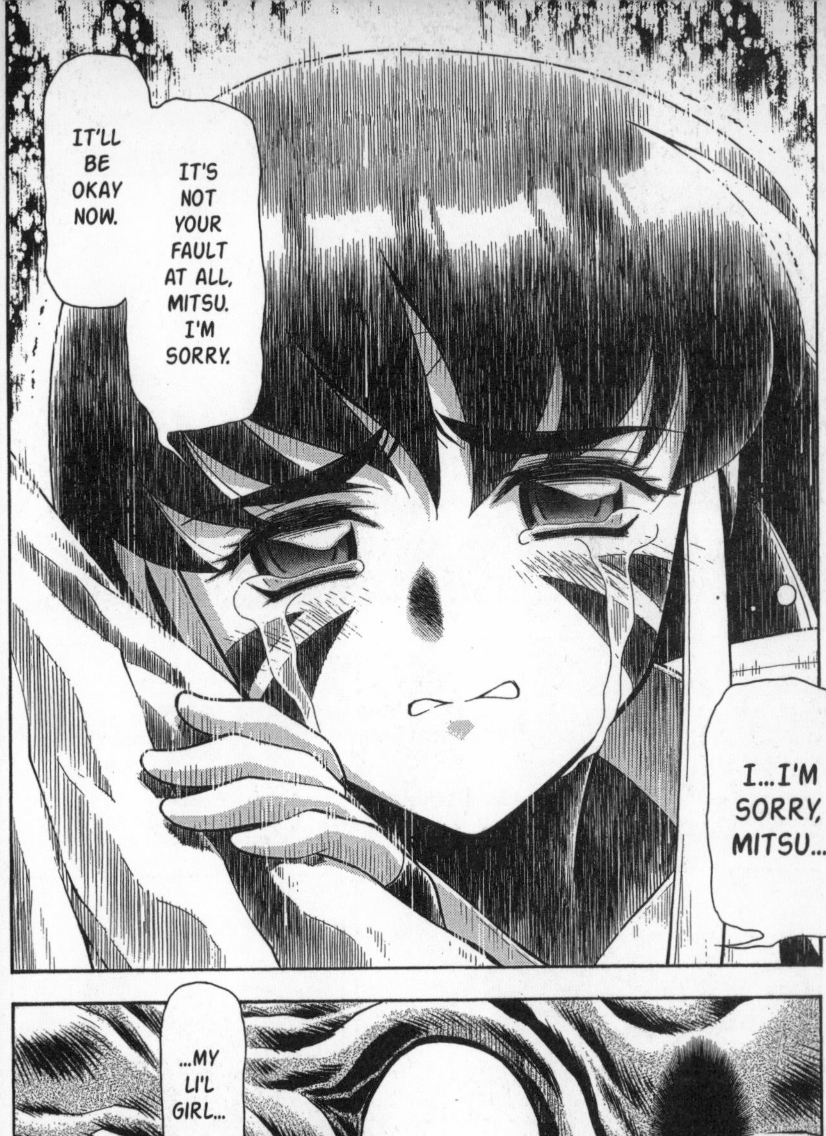
IT'LL BE OKAY NOW.
IT'S NOT YOUR FAULT AT ALL, MITSU. I'M SORRY.
I...I'M SORRY, MITSU...

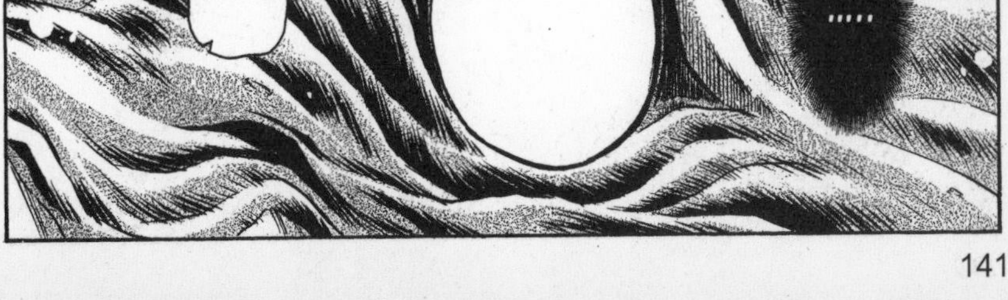
...MY LI'L GIRL...
.....

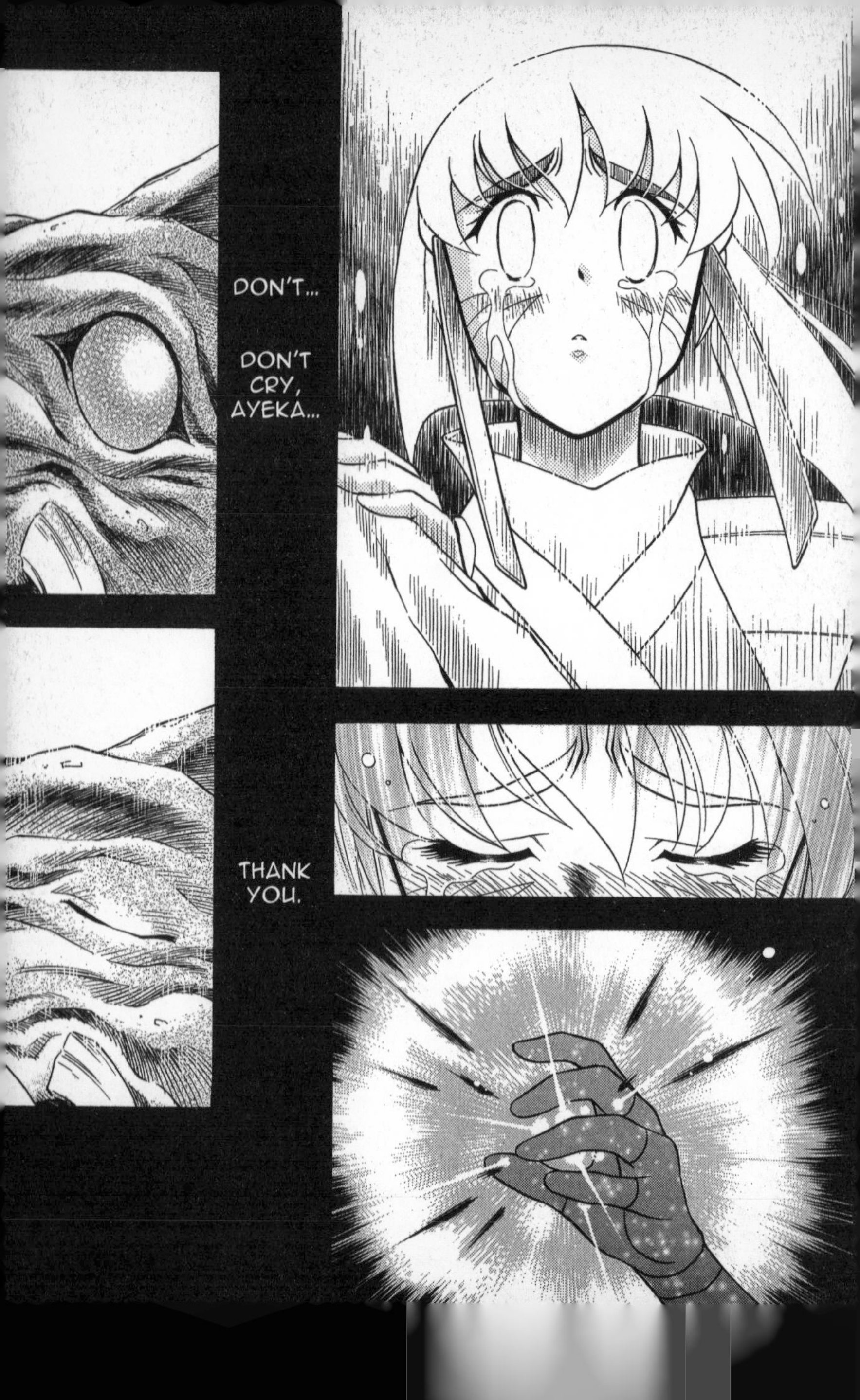
DON'T...
DON'T CRY, AYEKA...
THANK YOU.

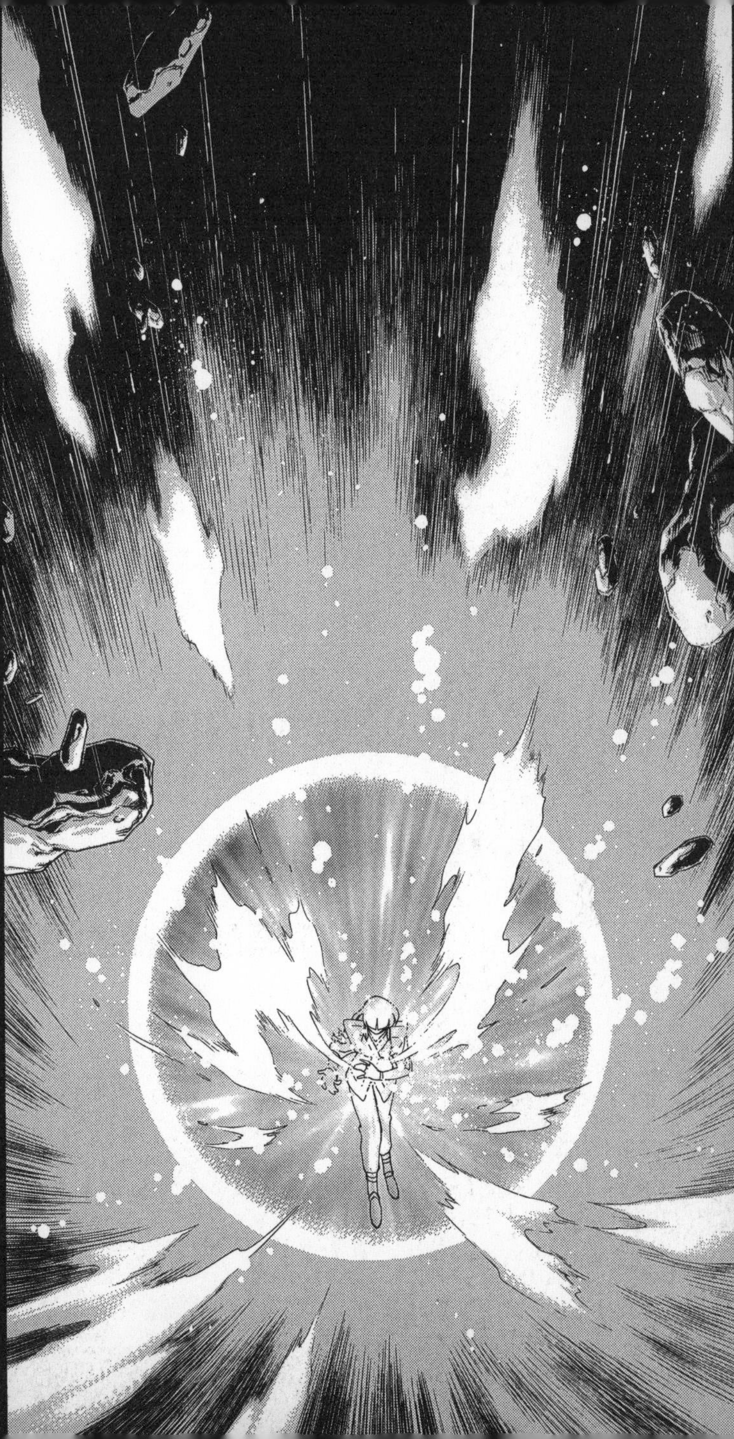

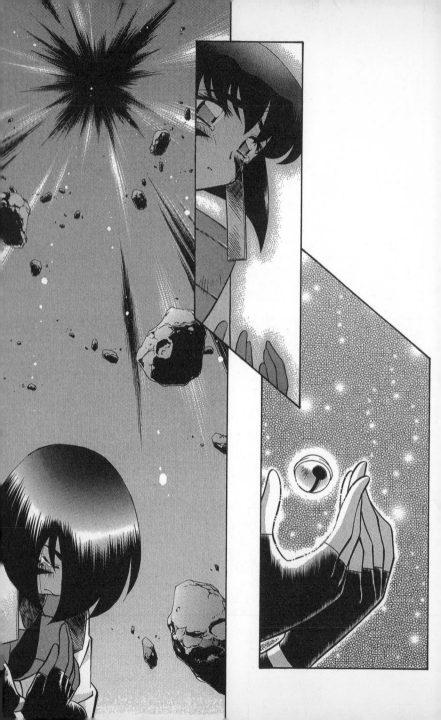

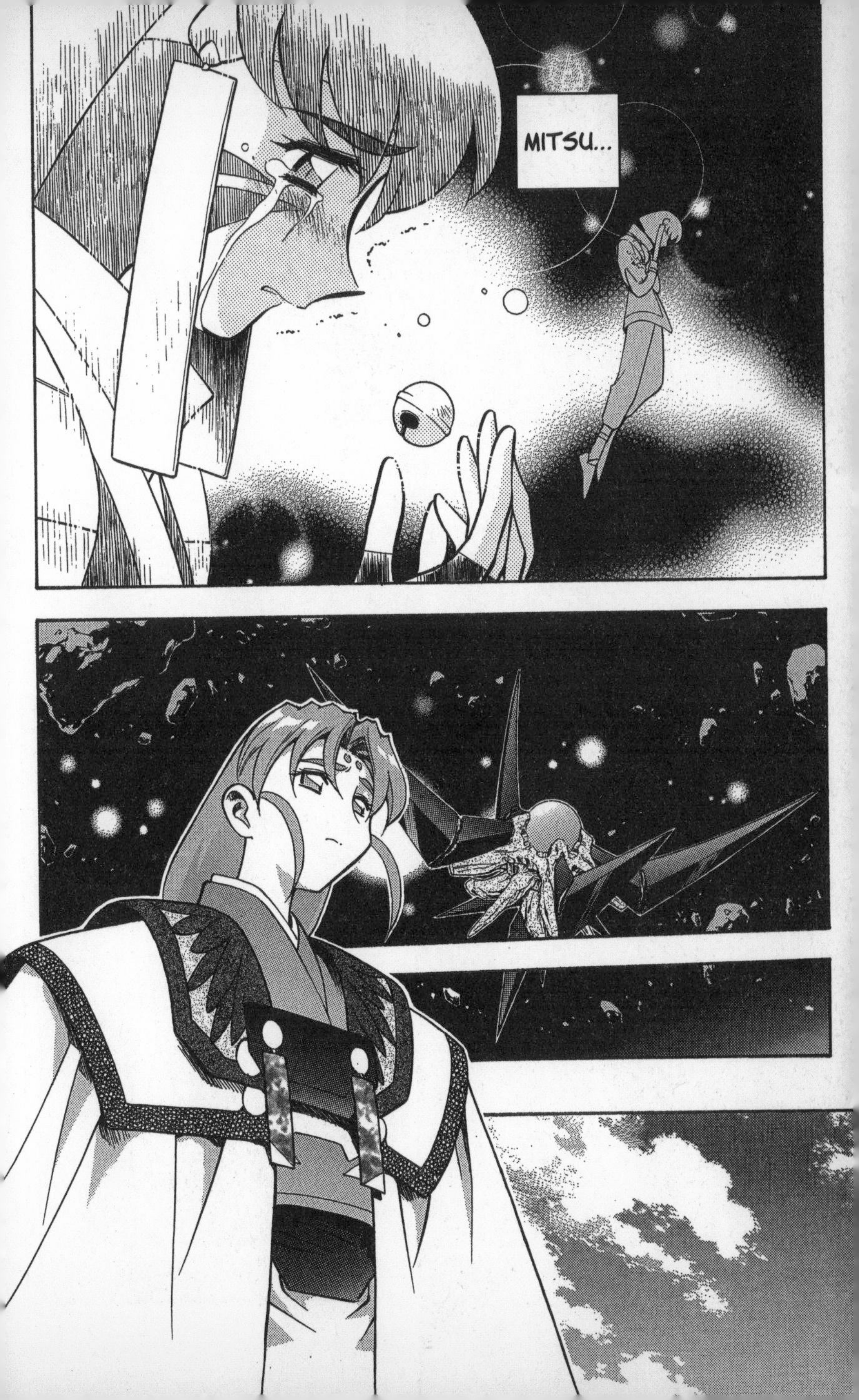
MITSU...

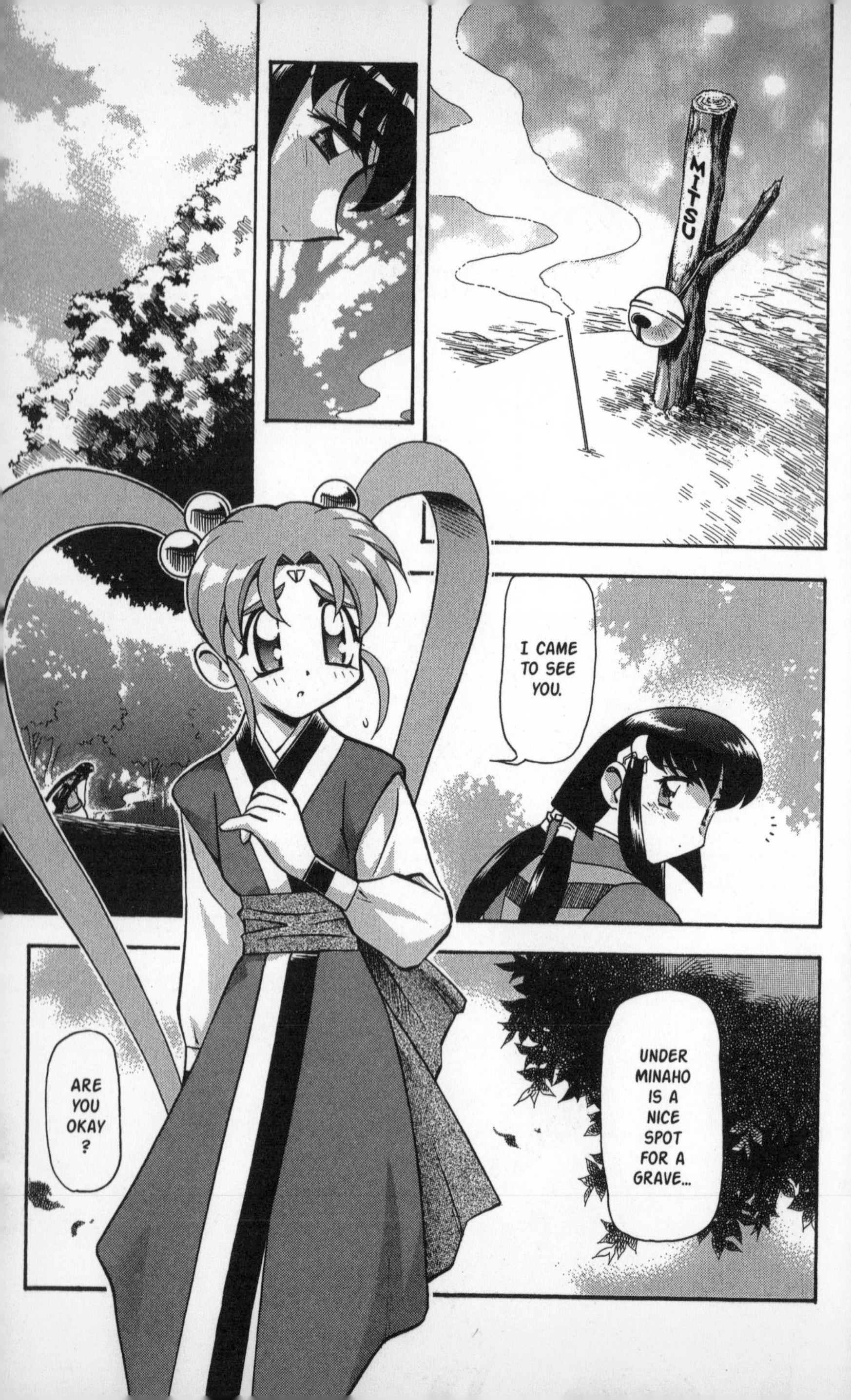
MITSU
I CAME TO SEE YOU.
ARE YOU OKAY ?
UNDER MINAHO IS A NICE SPOT FOR A GRAVE...

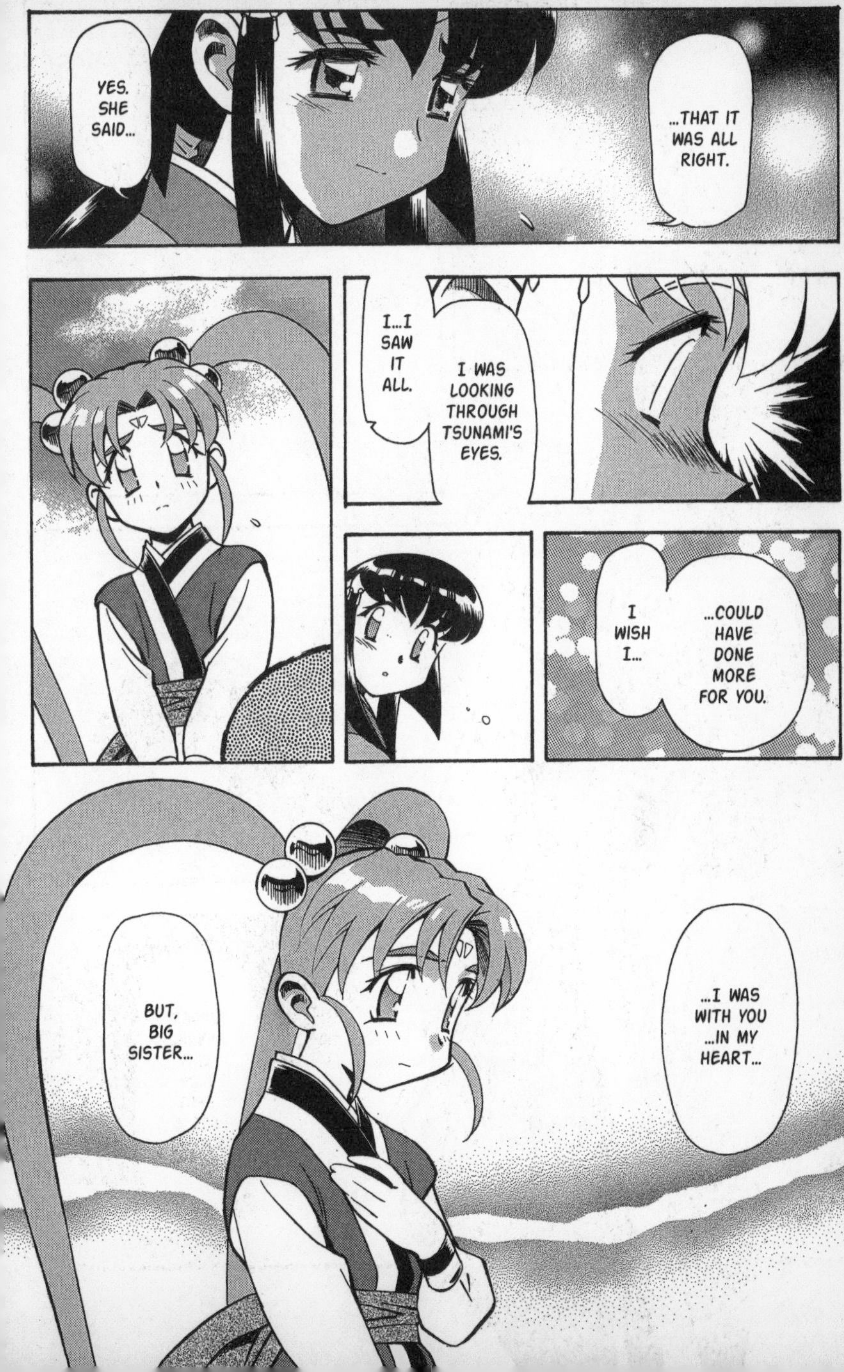
YES. SHE SAID...
...THAT IT WAS ALL RIGHT.
I...I SAW IT ALL.
I WAS LOOKING THROUGH TSUNAMI'S EYES.
I WISH I...
...COULD HAVE DONE MORE FOR YOU.
BUT, BIG SISTER...
...I WAS WITH YOU ...IN MY HEART...

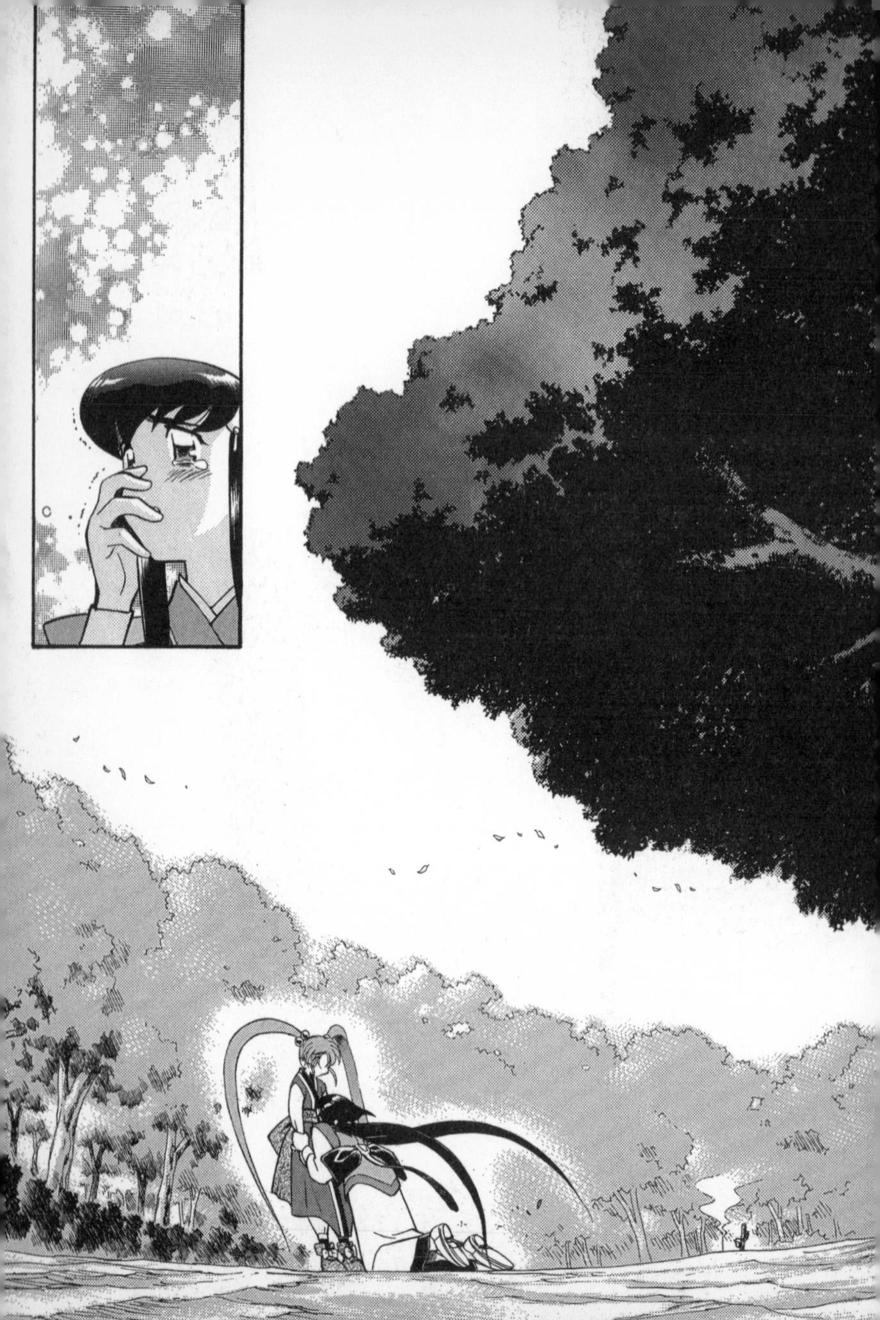

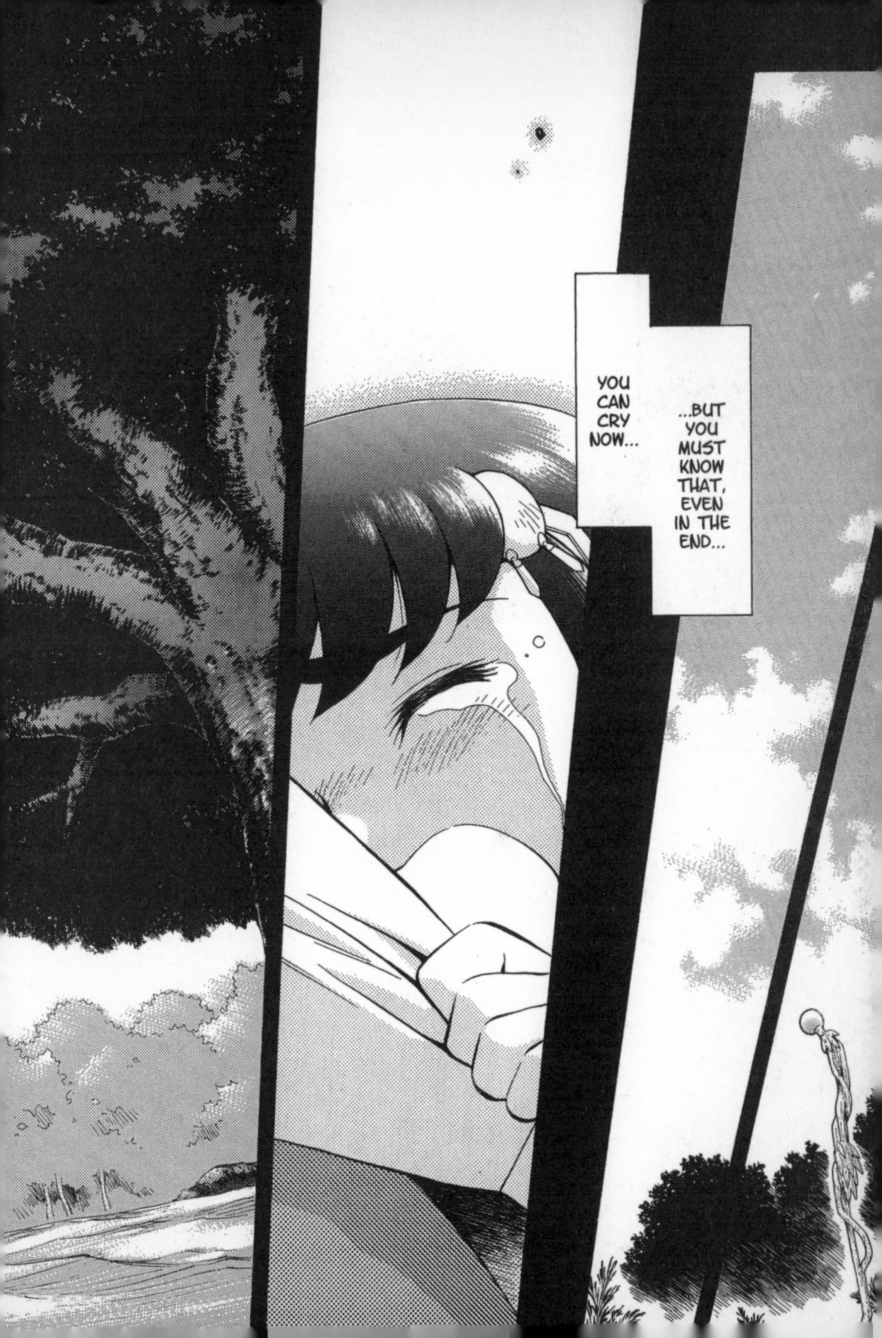
YOU CAN CRY NOW...
...BUT YOU MUST KNOW THAT, EVEN IN THE END...

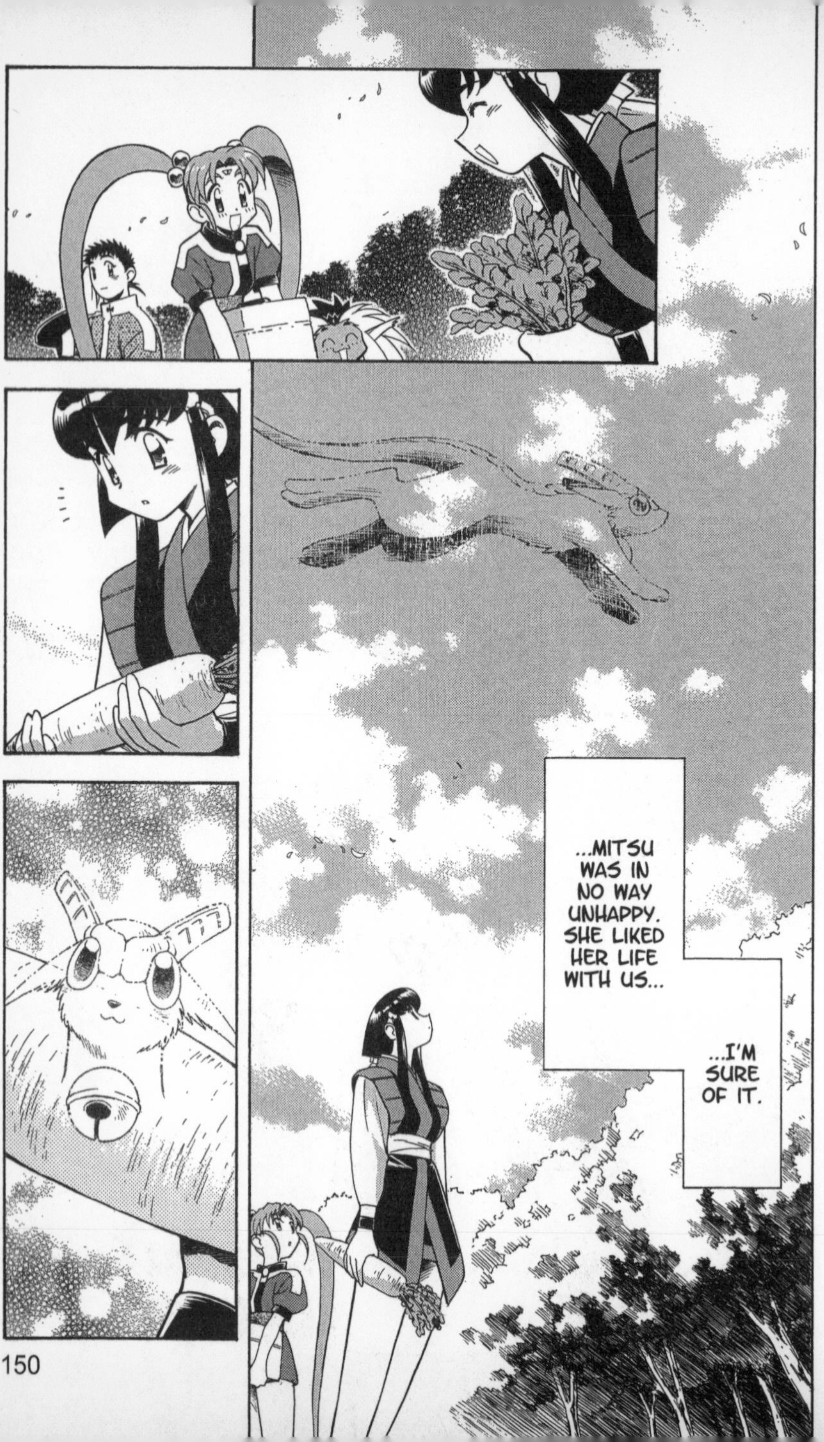
...MITSU WAS IN NO WAY UNHAPPY. SHE LIKED HER LIFE WITH US...
...I'M SURE OF IT.

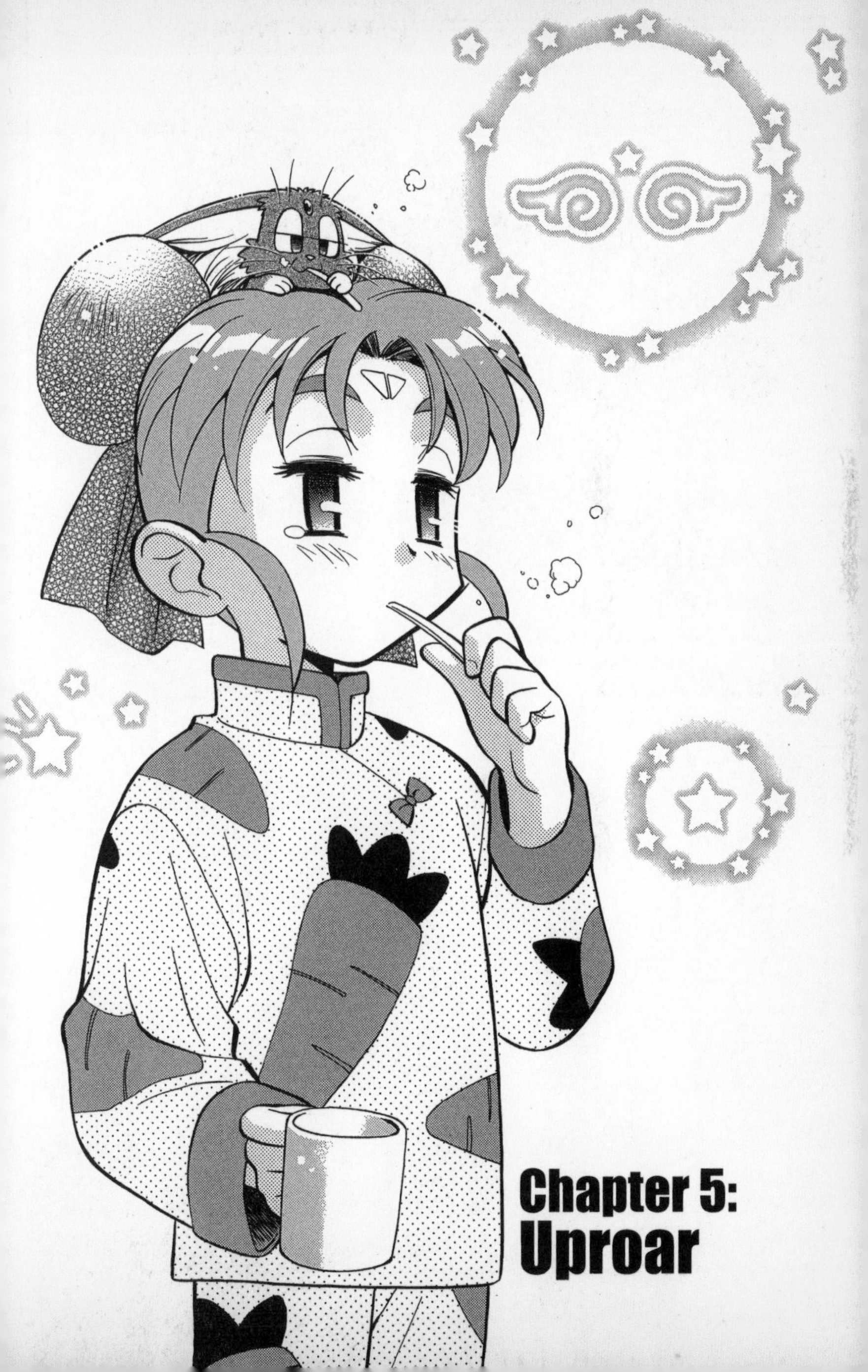

Chapter 5: Uproar

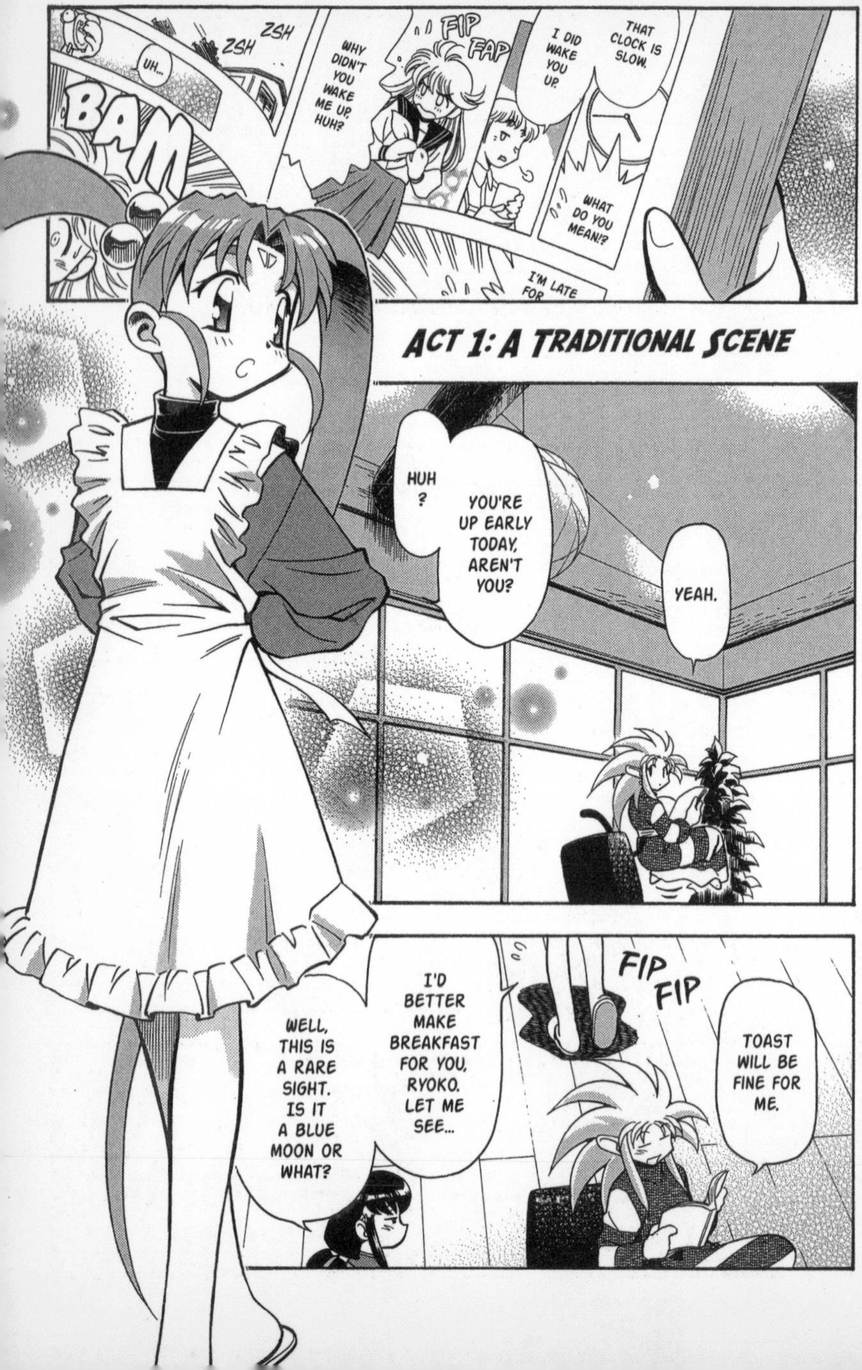
UH...
ZSH
ZSH
BAM
WHY DIDN'T YOU WAKE ME UP, HUH?
FIP FAP
I DID WAKE YOU UP.
THAT CLOCK IS SLOW.
WHAT DO YOU MEAN!?
I'M LATE FOR
ACT 1: A TRADITIONAL SCENE
HUH ?
YOU'RE UP EARLY TODAY, AREN'T YOU?
YEAH.
WELL, THIS IS A RARE SIGHT. IS IT A BLUE MOON OR WHAT?
I'D BETTER MAKE BREAKFAST FOR YOU, RYOKO. LET ME SEE...
FIP FIP
TOAST WILL BE FINE FOR ME.

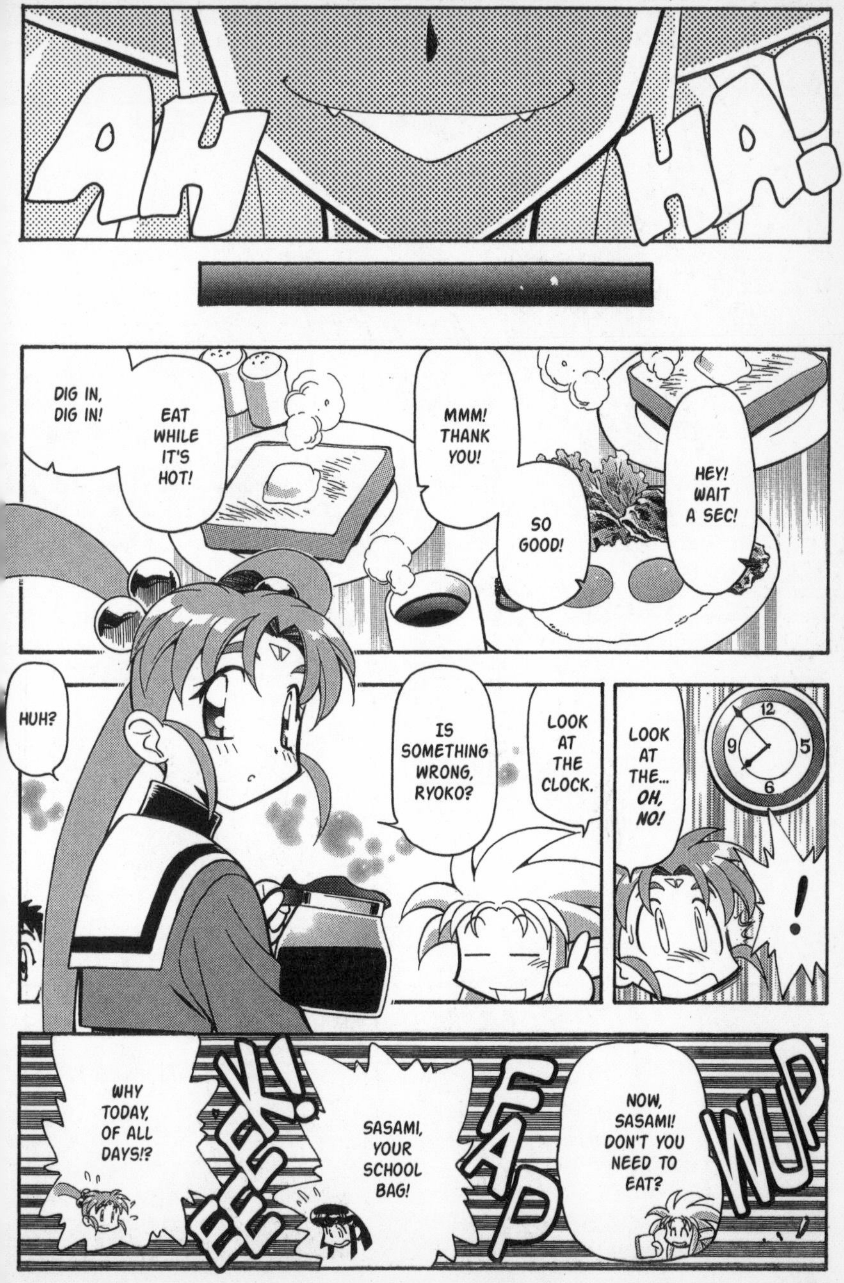
AH HA!
DIG IN, DIG IN!
EAT WHILE IT'S HOT!
MMM! THANK YOU!
SO GOOD!
HEY! WAIT A SEC!
HUH?
IS SOMETHING WRONG, RYOKO?
LOOK AT THE CLOCK.
LOOK AT THE... *OH, NO!*
!
WHY TODAY, OF ALL DAYS!?
EEEK!
SASAMI, YOUR SCHOOL BAG!
FAP
NOW, SASAMI! DON'T YOU NEED TO EAT?
WUP

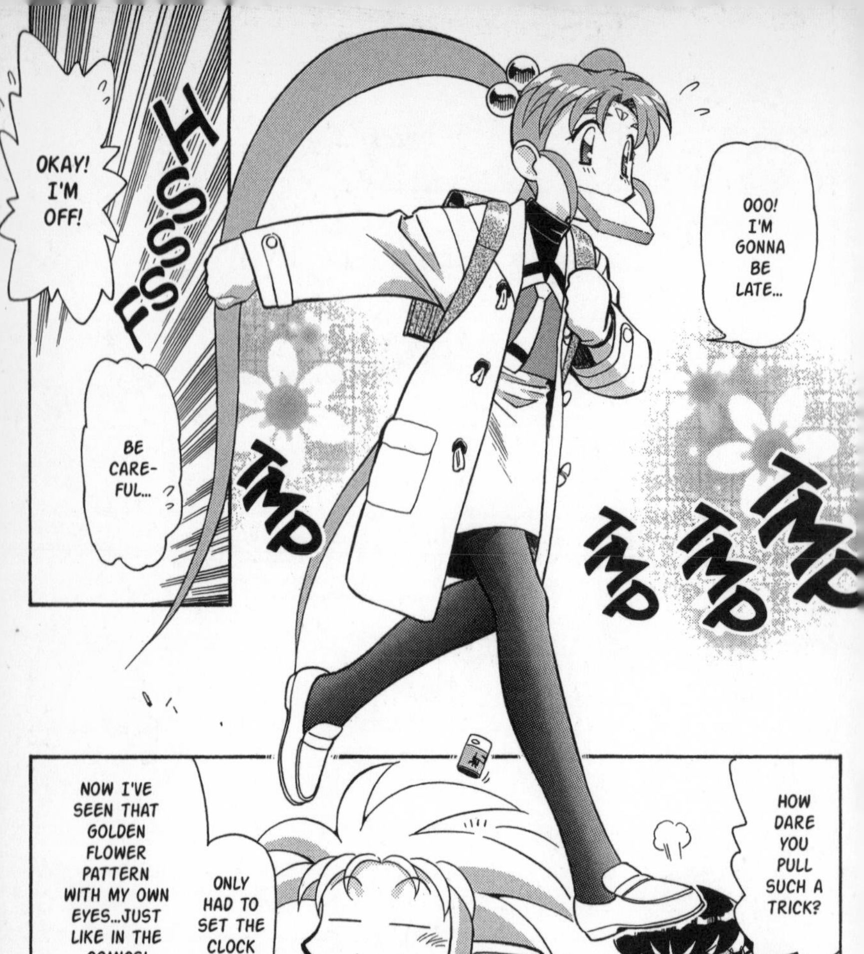
OKAY! I'M OFF!
FSSSH
BE CARE-FUL...
TMP
OOO! I'M GONNA BE LATE...
TMP TMP TMP
NOW I'VE SEEN THAT GOLDEN FLOWER PATTERN WITH MY OWN EYES...JUST LIKE IN THE COMICS!
ONLY HAD TO SET THE CLOCK BACK TO DO IT!
HOW DARE YOU PULL SUCH A TRICK?

ACT 2: MAMAMIYA A-GO-GO

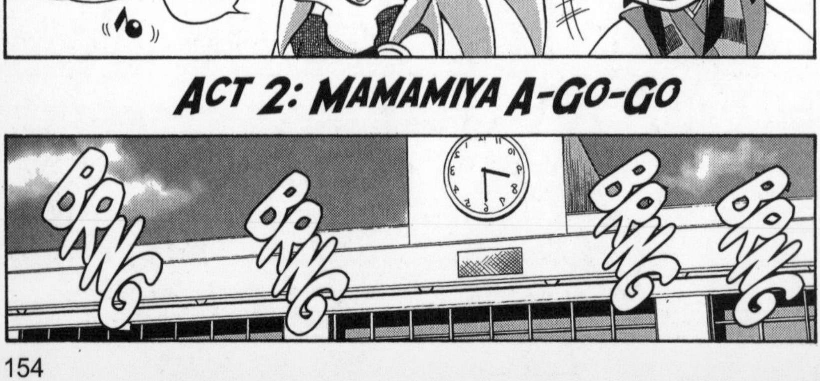
BRNG BRNG BRNG BRNG

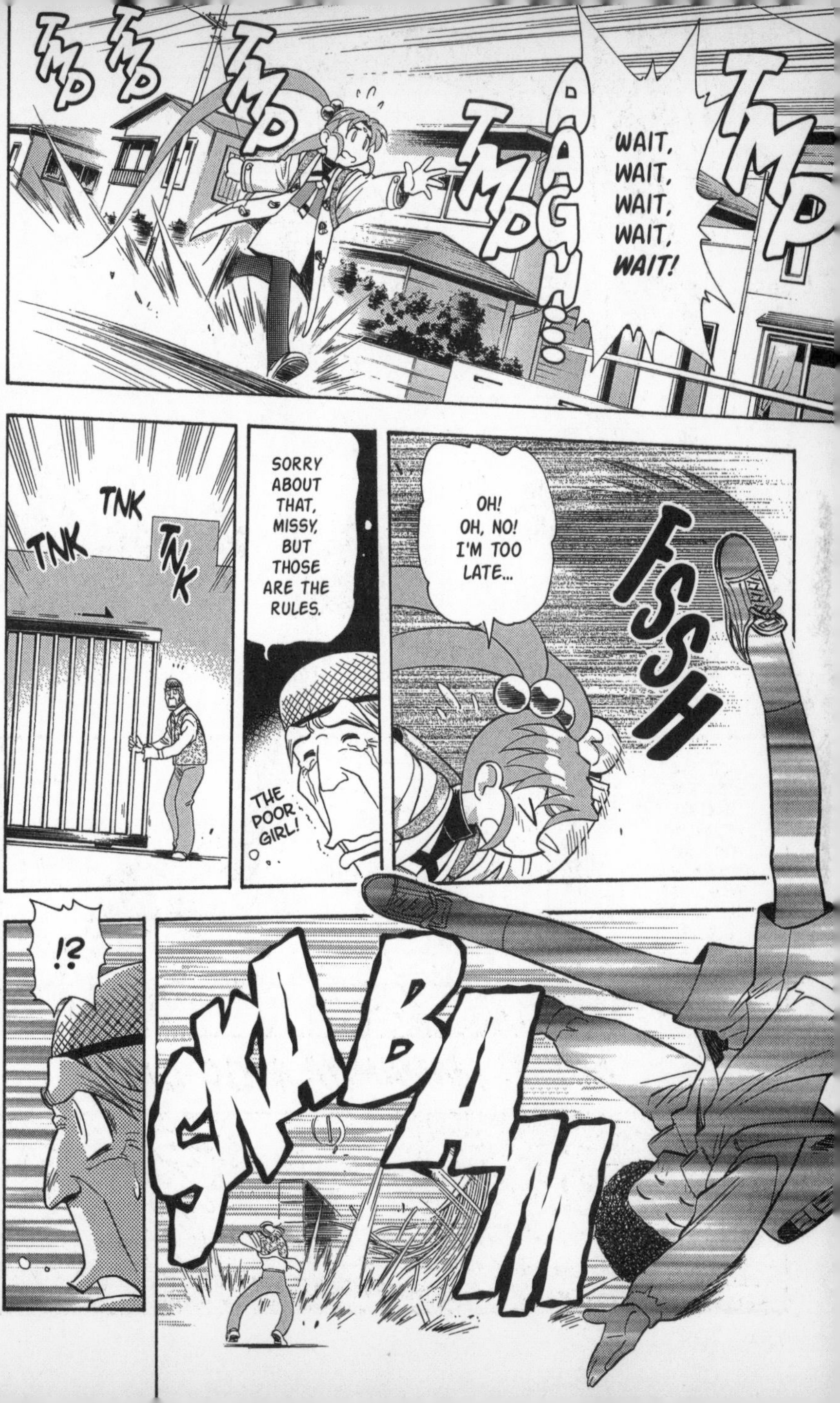
TMP TMP TMP
TMP
AAGH...
WAIT, WAIT, WAIT, WAIT, WAIT!
TMP
TNK TNK TNK
SORRY ABOUT THAT, MISSY, BUT THOSE ARE THE RULES.
THE POOR GIRL!
OH! OH, NO! I'M TOO LATE...
FSSH
!?
SKABAM

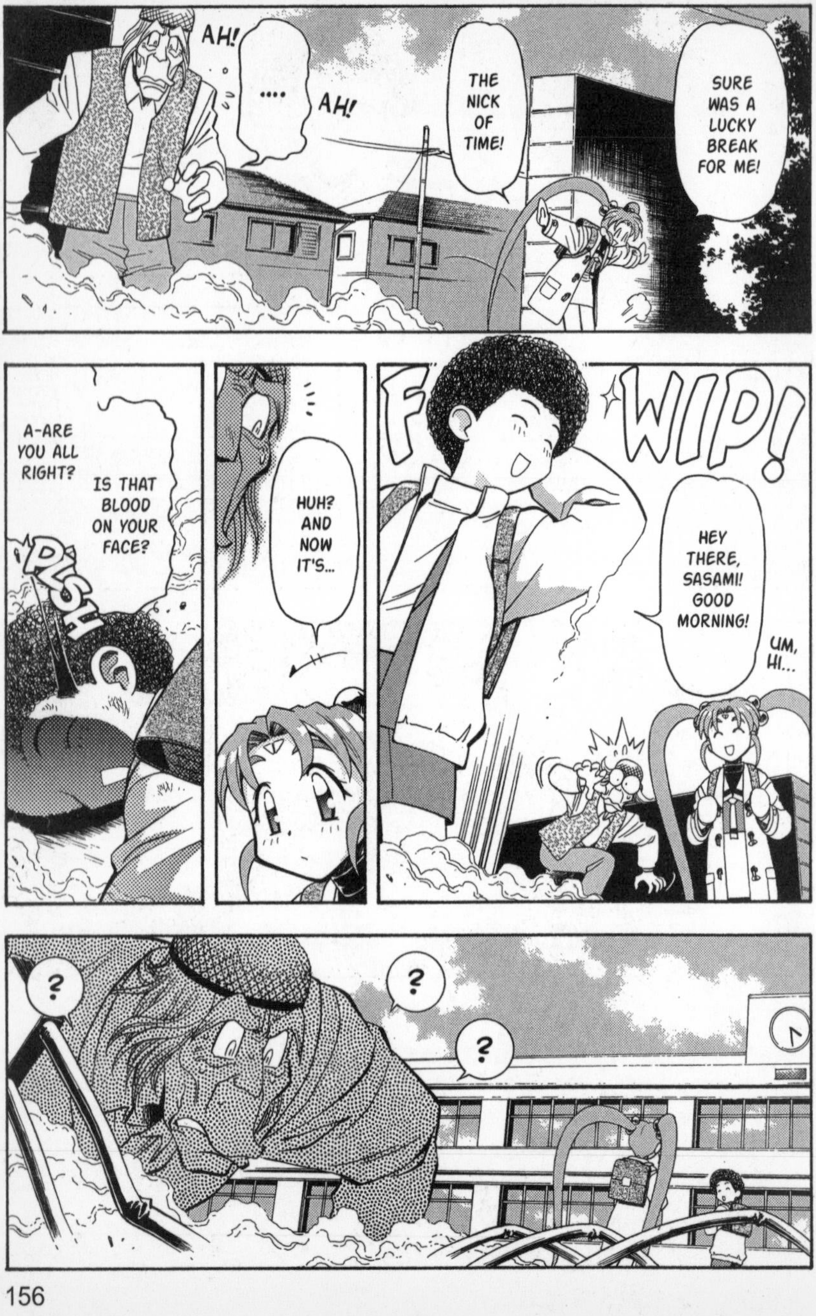
AH!
....
AH!
THE NICK OF TIME!
SURE WAS A LUCKY BREAK FOR ME!
A-ARE YOU ALL RIGHT?
IS THAT BLOOD ON YOUR FACE?
PLSH
HUH? AND NOW IT'S...
FWIP!
HEY THERE, SASAMI! GOOD MORNING!
UM, HI...
?
?
?

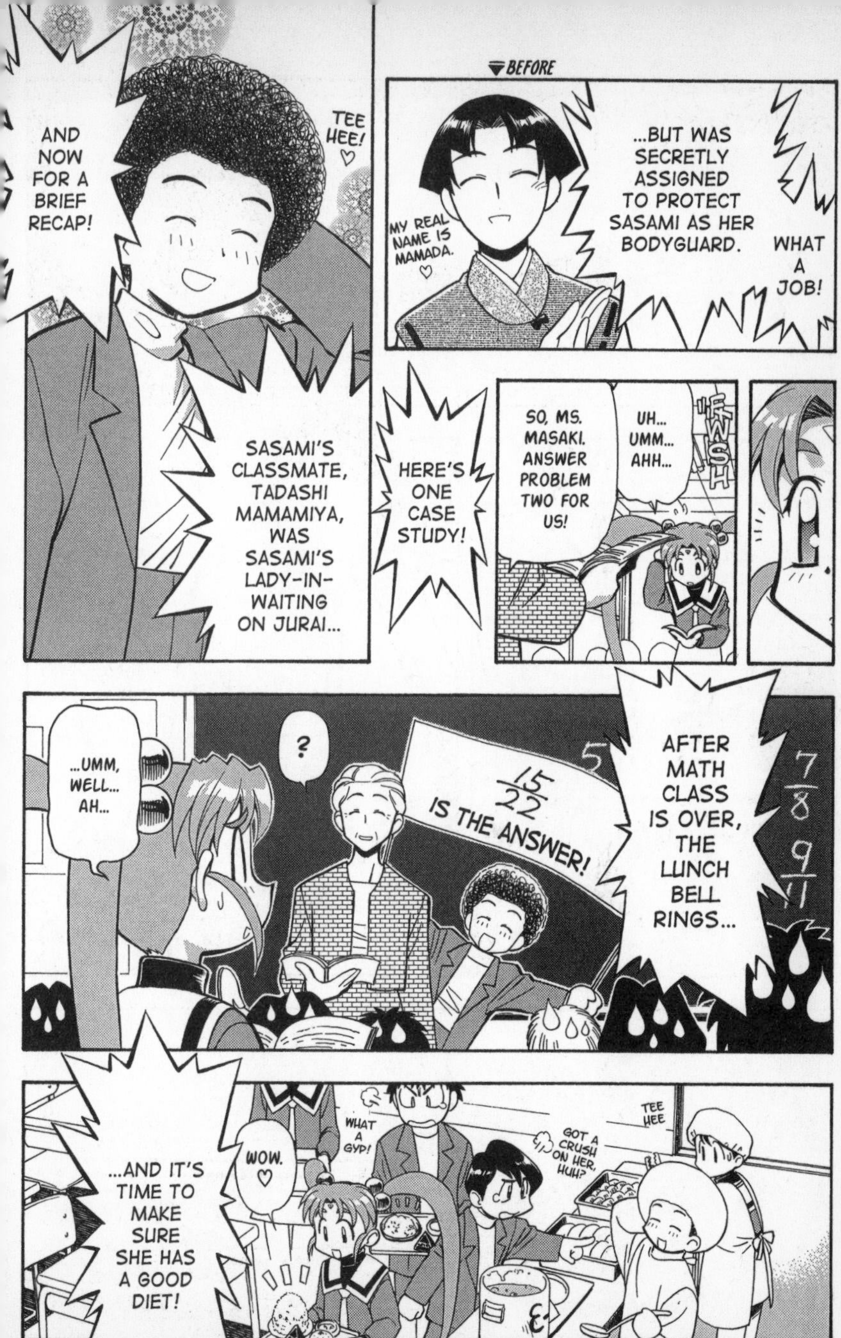
AND NOW FOR A BRIEF RECAP!
TEE HEE! ♡
SASAMI'S CLASSMATE, TADASHI MAMAMIYA, WAS SASAMI'S LADY-IN-WAITING ON JURAI...
BEFORE
MY REAL NAME IS MAMADA. ♡
...BUT WAS SECRETLY ASSIGNED TO PROTECT SASAMI AS HER BODYGUARD.
WHAT A JOB!
HERE'S ONE CASE STUDY!
SO, MS. MASAKI. ANSWER PROBLEM TWO FOR US!
UH... UMM... AHH...
FWSH
...UMM, WELL... AH...
?
15/22 IS THE ANSWER!
AFTER MATH CLASS IS OVER, THE LUNCH BELL RINGS...
...AND IT'S TIME TO MAKE SURE SHE HAS A GOOD DIET!
WOW. ♡
WHAT A GYP!
GOT A CRUSH ON HER, HUH?
TEE HEE

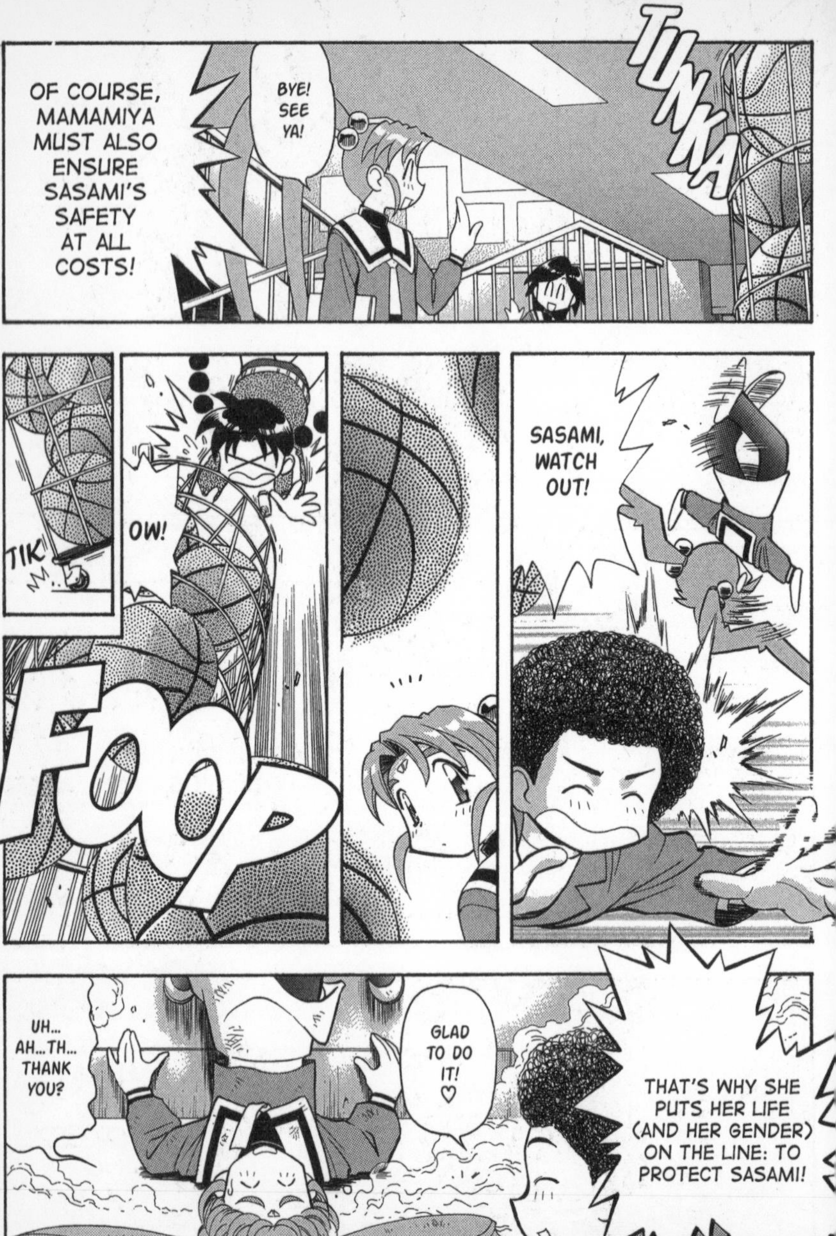
OF COURSE, MAMAMIYA MUST ALSO ENSURE SASAMI'S SAFETY AT ALL COSTS!
BYE! SEE YA!
TUNKA
TIK
OW!
FOOP
SASAMI, WATCH OUT!
UH... AH...TH... THANK YOU?
GLAD TO DO IT! ♡
THAT'S WHY SHE PUTS HER LIFE (AND HER GENDER) ON THE LINE: TO PROTECT SASAMI!

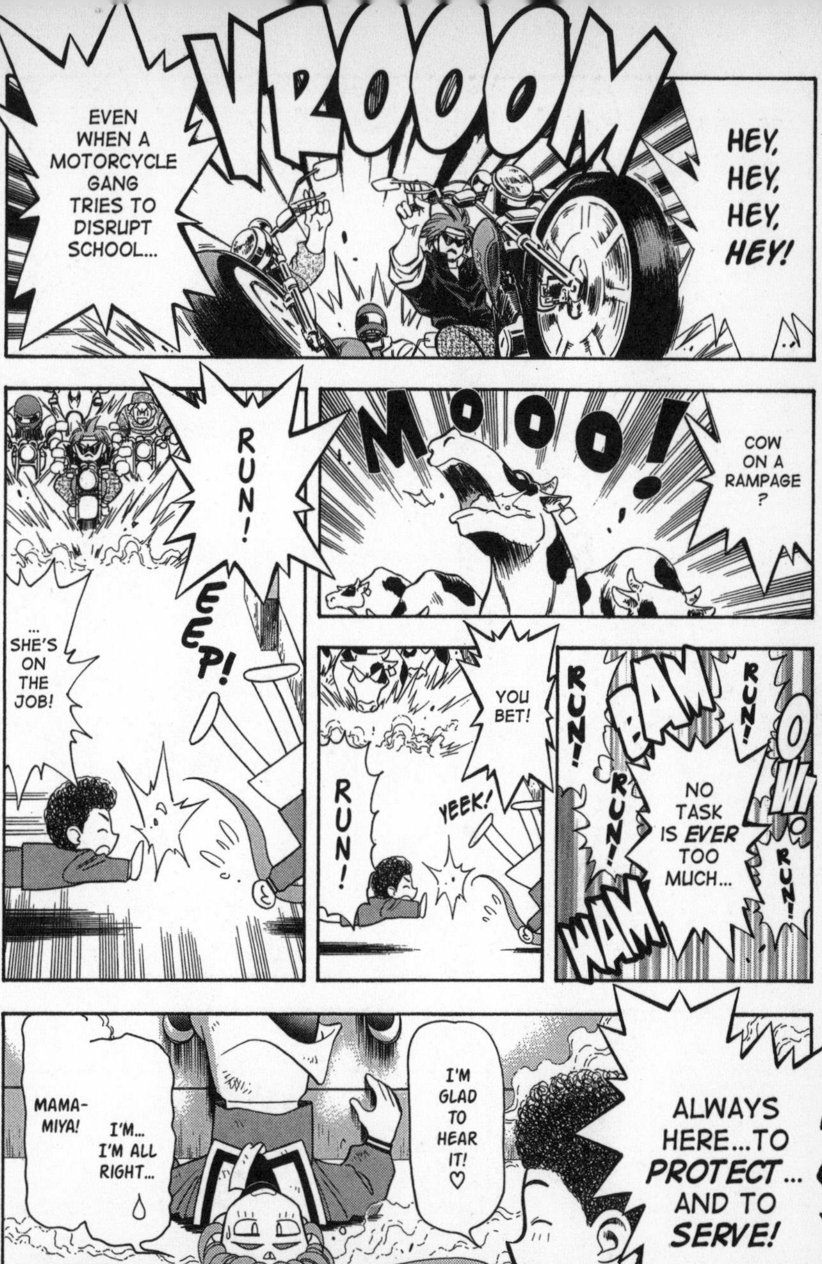
VROOOM
EVEN WHEN A MOTORCYCLE GANG TRIES TO DISRUPT SCHOOL...
HEY, HEY, HEY, HEY!
RUN!
EEP!
... SHE'S ON THE JOB!
MOOOO!
COW ON A RAMPAGE?
YOU BET!
RUN!
YEEK!
RUN!
BAM
RUN!
RUN!
NO TASK IS EVER TOO MUCH...
WAM
OW
RUN!
MAMA-MIYA!
I'M... I'M ALL RIGHT...
I'M GLAD TO HEAR IT! ♡
ALWAYS HERE...TO PROTECT... AND TO SERVE!

Fish stew...sushi...

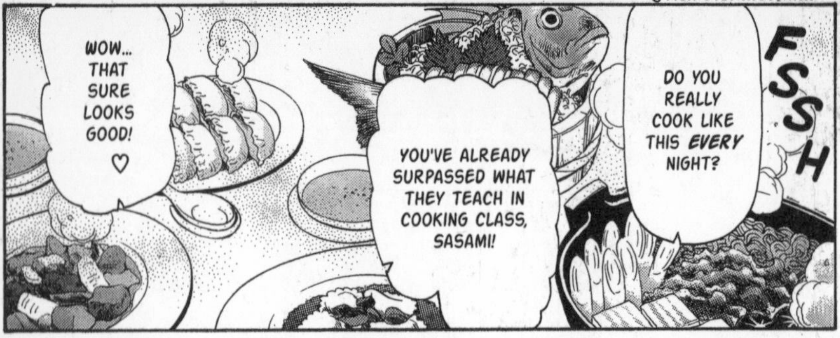
WOW... THAT SURE LOOKS GOOD! ♡
YOU'VE ALREADY SURPASSED WHAT THEY TEACH IN COOKING CLASS, SASAMI!
DO YOU REALLY COOK LIKE THIS *EVERY* NIGHT?
FSSH

ACT 3: WHO'S PAYING FOR THE INGREDIENTS...?

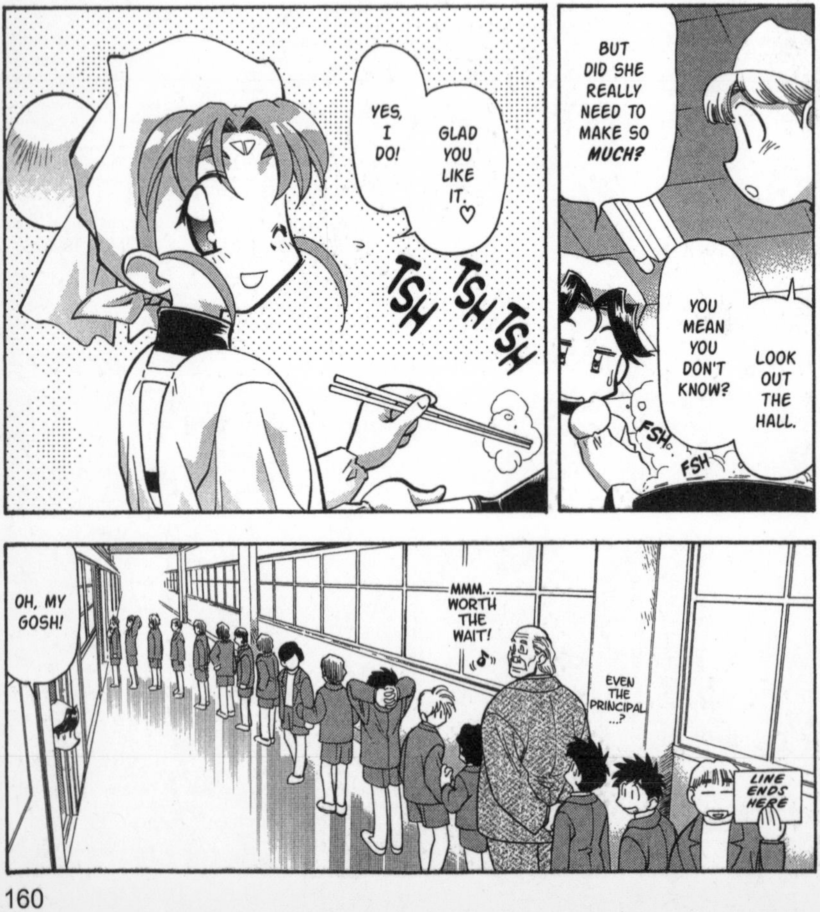
YES, I DO!
GLAD YOU LIKE IT. ♡
TSH TSH TSH
BUT DID SHE REALLY NEED TO MAKE SO *MUCH?*
YOU MEAN YOU DON'T KNOW?
LOOK OUT THE HALL.
FSH FSH
OH, MY GOSH!
MMM... WORTH THE WAIT!
EVEN THE PRINCIPAL ...?
LINE ENDS HERE

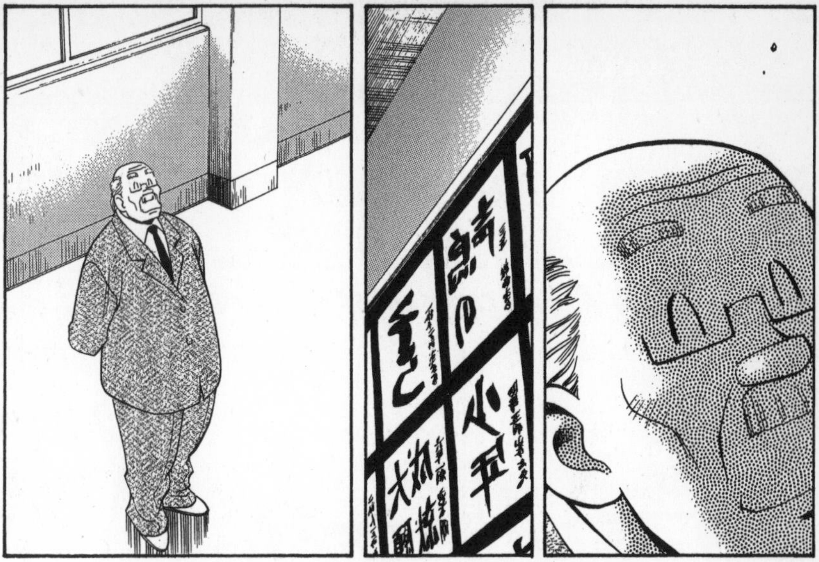

Act 4: Excellent Penmanship...

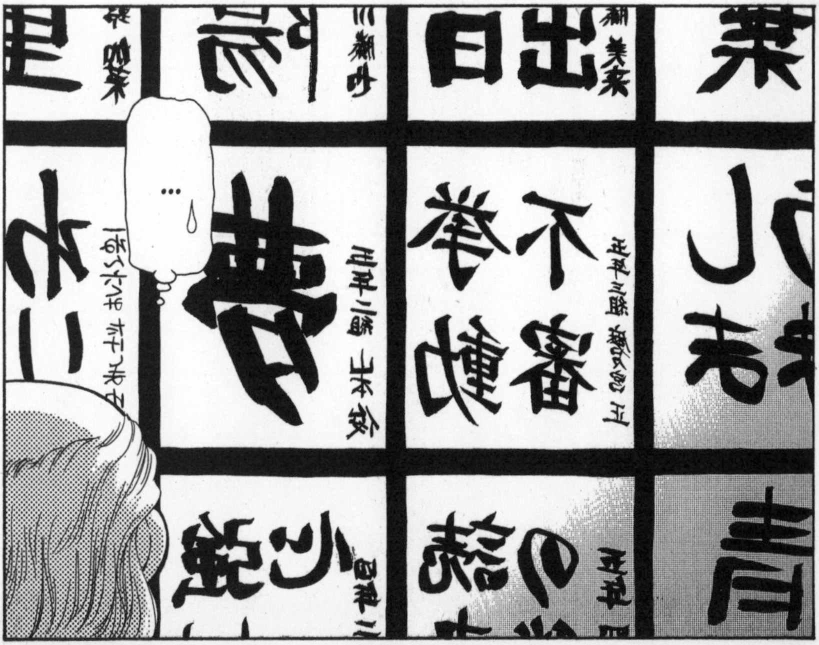
...

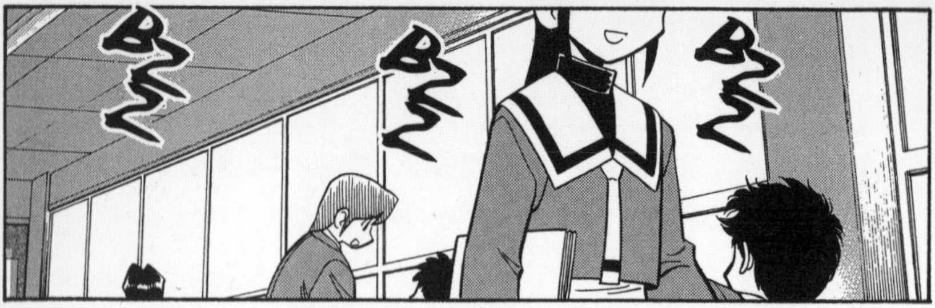
BZZ
BZZ
BZZ

ACT 5: THE IMPISHNESS OF A GODDESS

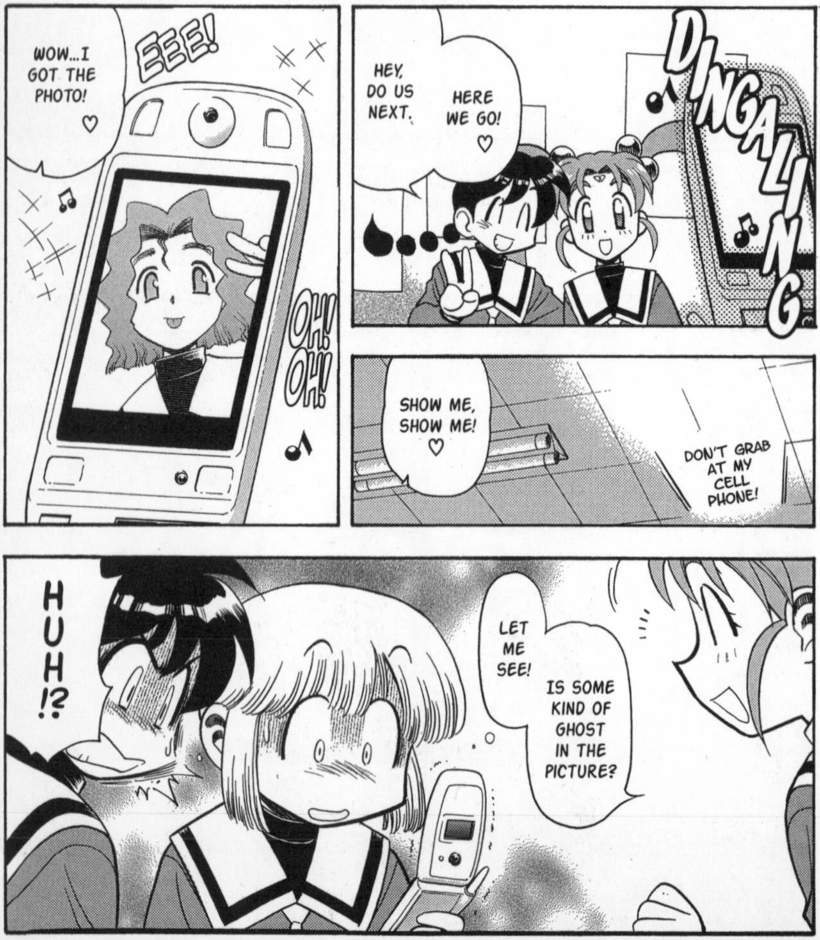
WOW...I GOT THE PHOTO! ♡
EEE!
OH! OH!
HEY, DO US NEXT.
HERE WE GO! ♡
DINGALING
SHOW ME, SHOW ME! ♡
DON'T GRAB AT MY CELL PHONE!
HUH!?
LET ME SEE!
IS SOME KIND OF GHOST IN THE PICTURE?

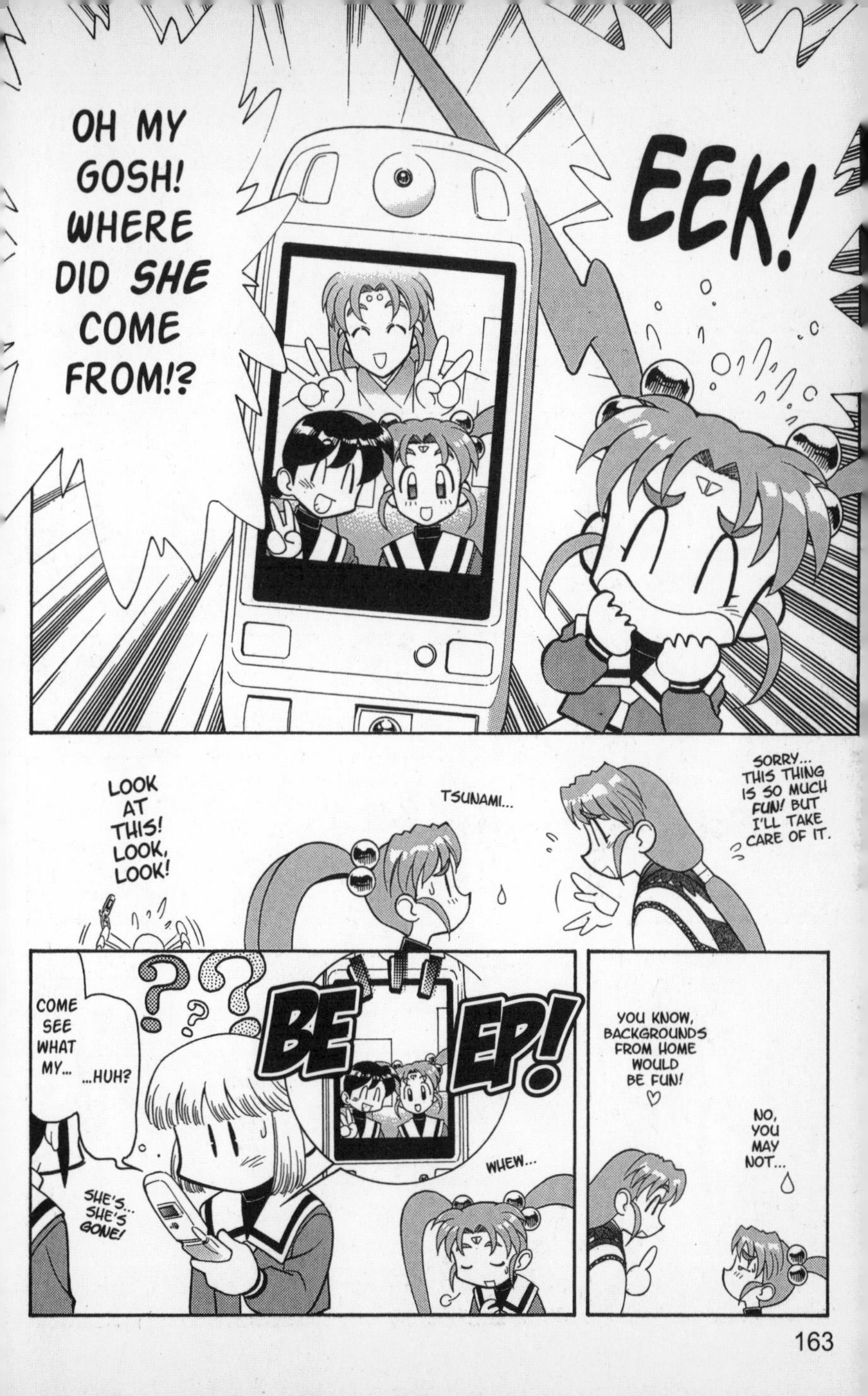

OH MY GOSH! WHERE DID SHE COME FROM!?
EEK!
LOOK AT THIS! LOOK, LOOK!
TSUNAMI...
SORRY... THIS THING IS SO MUCH FUN! BUT I'LL TAKE CARE OF IT.
COME SEE WHAT MY... ...HUH?
SHE'S... SHE'S GONE!
BE EP!
WHEW...
YOU KNOW, BACKGROUNDS FROM HOME WOULD BE FUN!
NO, YOU MAY NOT...

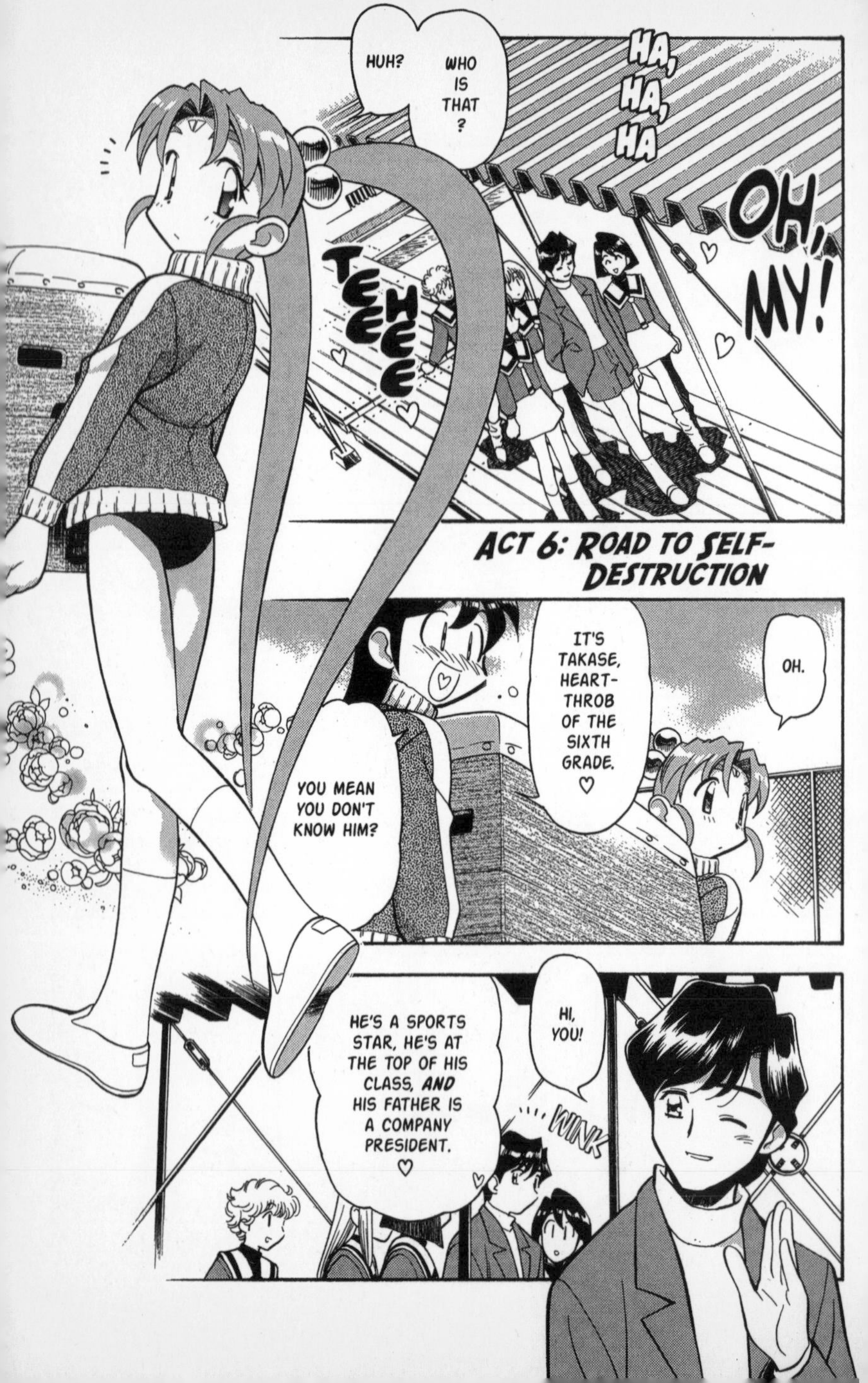
HUH?
WHO IS THAT?
HA, HA, HA
TEHEEE
OH, MY!
ACT 6: ROAD TO SELF-DESTRUCTION
IT'S TAKASE, HEART-THROB OF THE SIXTH GRADE. ♡
OH.
YOU MEAN YOU DON'T KNOW HIM?
HE'S A SPORTS STAR, HE'S AT THE TOP OF HIS CLASS, AND HIS FATHER IS A COMPANY PRESIDENT. ♡
HI, YOU!
WINK

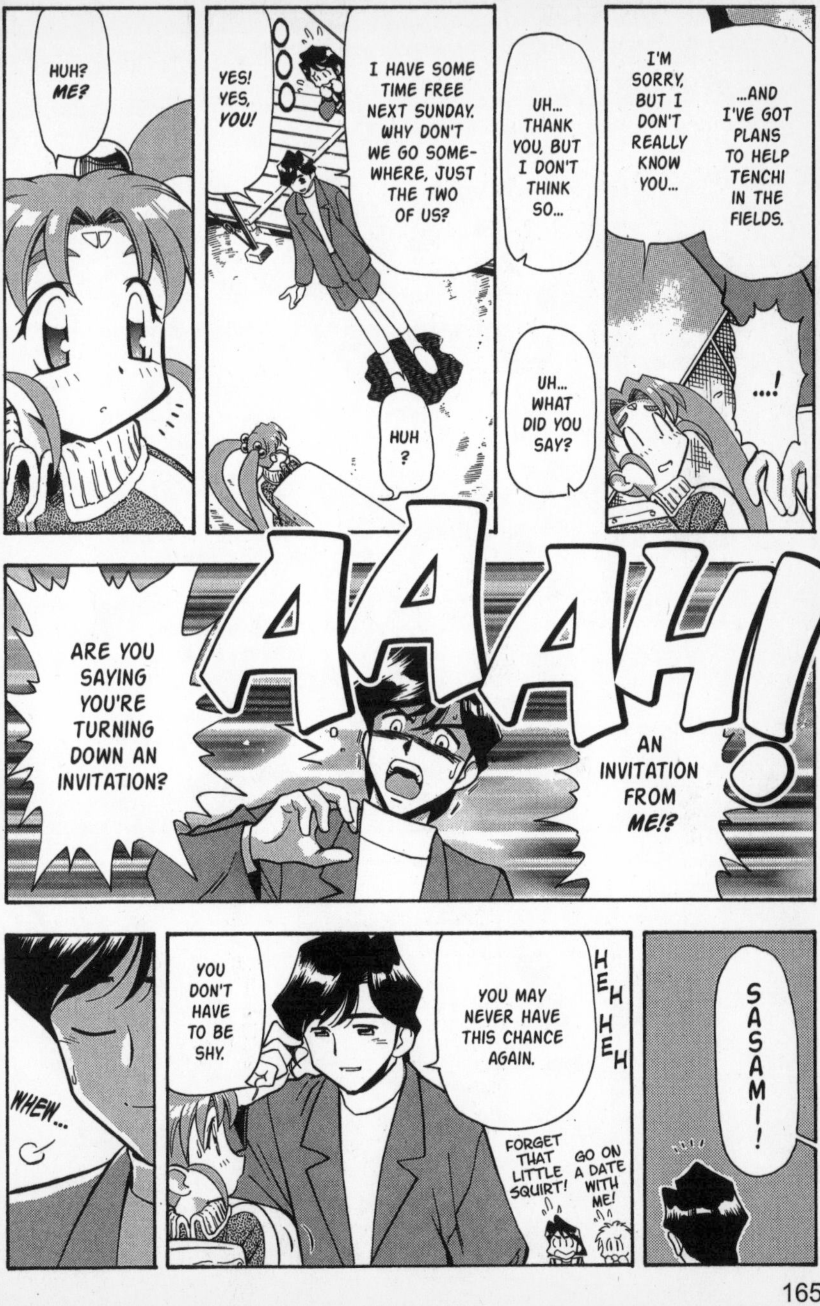
HUH? *ME?*
YES! YES, *YOU!*
I HAVE SOME TIME FREE NEXT SUNDAY. WHY DON'T WE GO SOMEWHERE, JUST THE TWO OF US?
HUH?
UH... THANK YOU, BUT I DON'T THINK SO...
UH... WHAT DID YOU SAY?
I'M SORRY, BUT I DON'T REALLY KNOW YOU...
...AND I'VE GOT PLANS TO HELP TENCHI IN THE FIELDS.
...!
AAAH!
ARE YOU SAYING YOU'RE TURNING DOWN AN INVITATION?
AN INVITATION FROM *ME!?*
WHEW...
YOU DON'T HAVE TO BE SHY.
YOU MAY NEVER HAVE THIS CHANCE AGAIN.
HEH HEH HEH
FORGET THAT LITTLE SQUIRT!
GO ON A DATE WITH ME!
SASAMI!

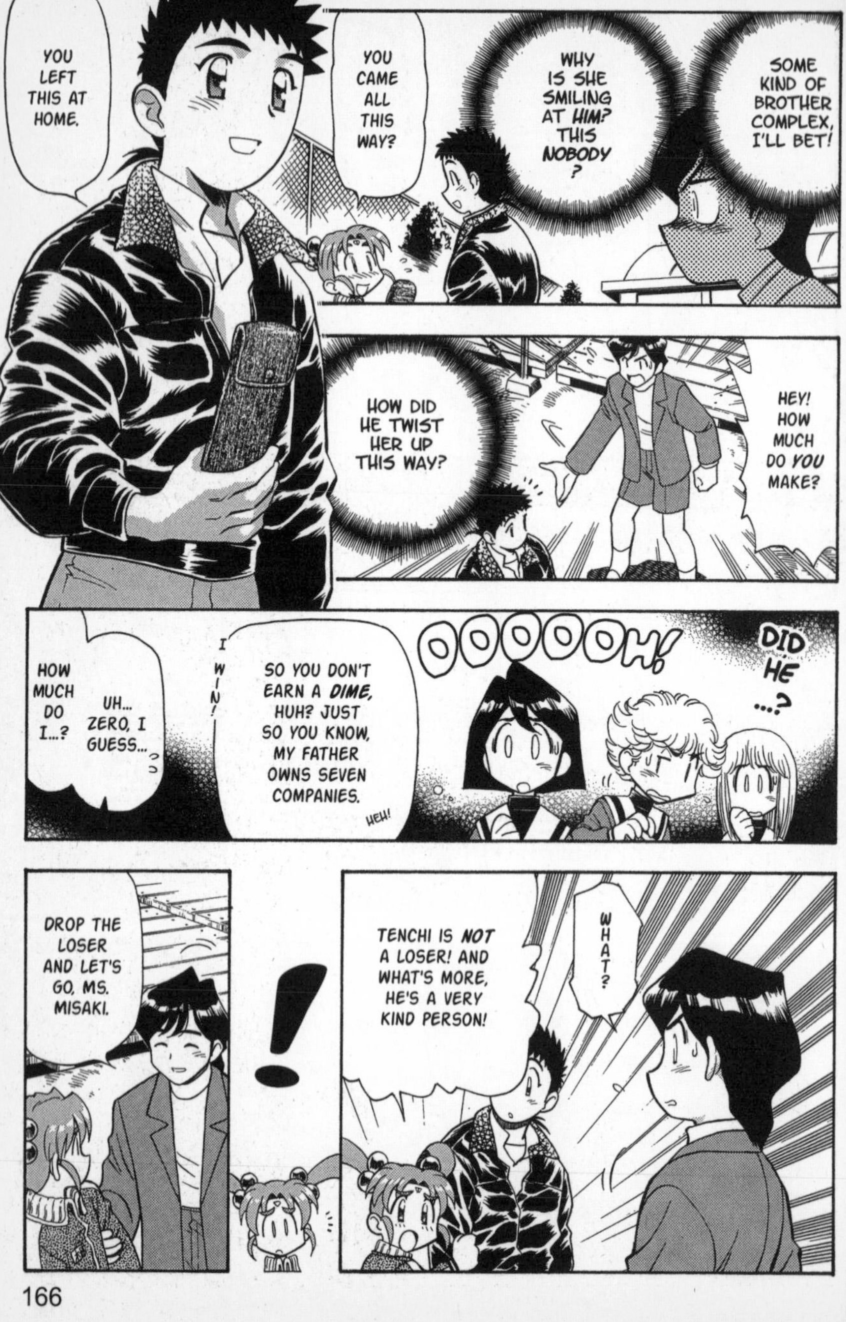
YOU LEFT THIS AT HOME.
YOU CAME ALL THIS WAY?
WHY IS SHE SMILING AT HIM? THIS NOBODY?
SOME KIND OF BROTHER COMPLEX, I'LL BET!
HOW DID HE TWIST HER UP THIS WAY?
HEY! HOW MUCH DO YOU MAKE?
HOW MUCH DO I...?
UH... ZERO, I GUESS...
I WIN!
SO YOU DON'T EARN A DIME, HUH? JUST SO YOU KNOW, MY FATHER OWNS SEVEN COMPANIES.
HEH!
OOOOOH!
DID HE ...?
DROP THE LOSER AND LET'S GO, MS. MISAKI.
!
TENCHI IS NOT A LOSER! AND WHAT'S MORE, HE'S A VERY KIND PERSON!
WHAT?

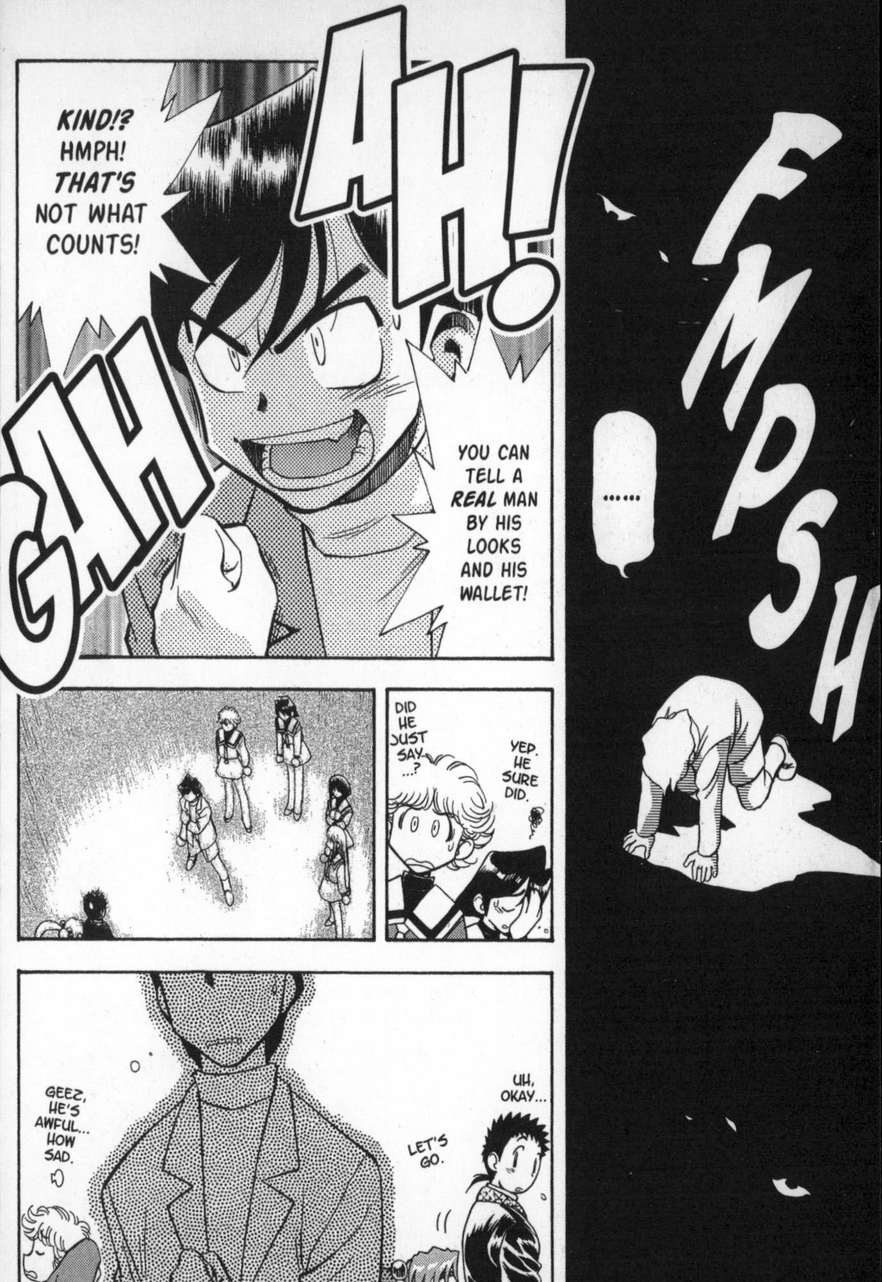
KIND!? HMPH! THAT'S NOT WHAT COUNTS!
GAH
AH!
YOU CAN TELL A REAL MAN BY HIS LOOKS AND HIS WALLET!
DID HE JUST SAY...?
YEP. HE SURE DID.
GEEZ, HE'S AWFUL... HOW SAD.
LET'S GO.
UH, OKAY...
FMPSH
......

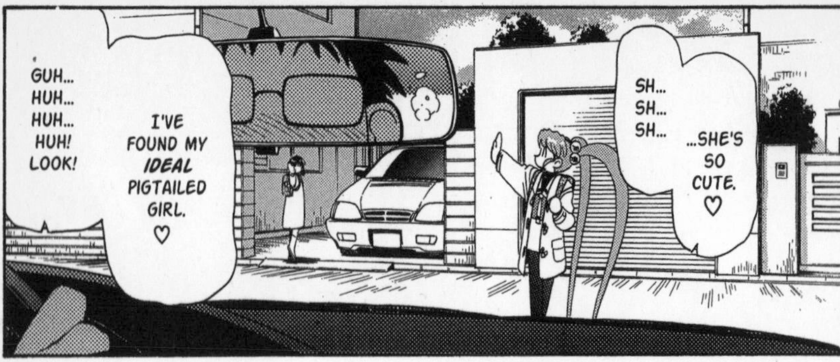
GUH... HUH... HUH... HUH! LOOK!
I'VE FOUND MY *IDEAL* PIGTAILED GIRL. ♡
SH... SH... SH...
...SHE'S SO CUTE. ♡

ACT 7: THAT'S DANGEROUS...

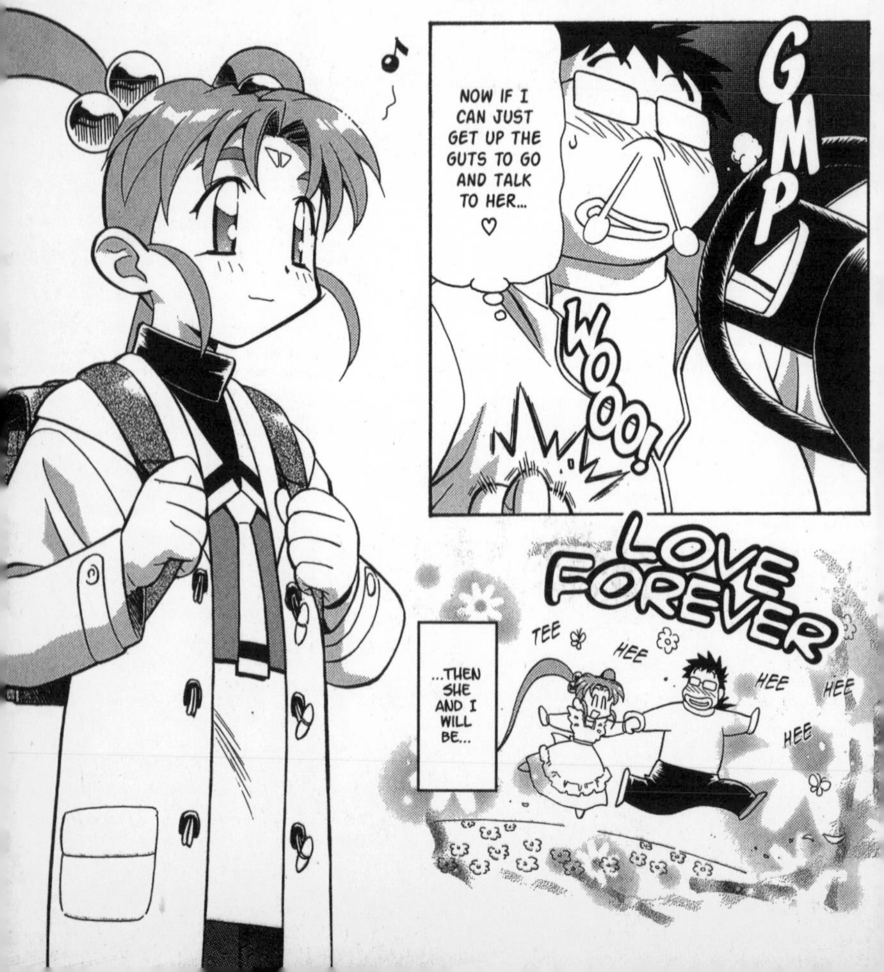
NOW IF I CAN JUST GET UP THE GUTS TO GO AND TALK TO HER... ♡
GMP
WOOO!
LOVE FOREVER
...THEN SHE AND I WILL BE...
TEE HEE
HEE HEE
HEE

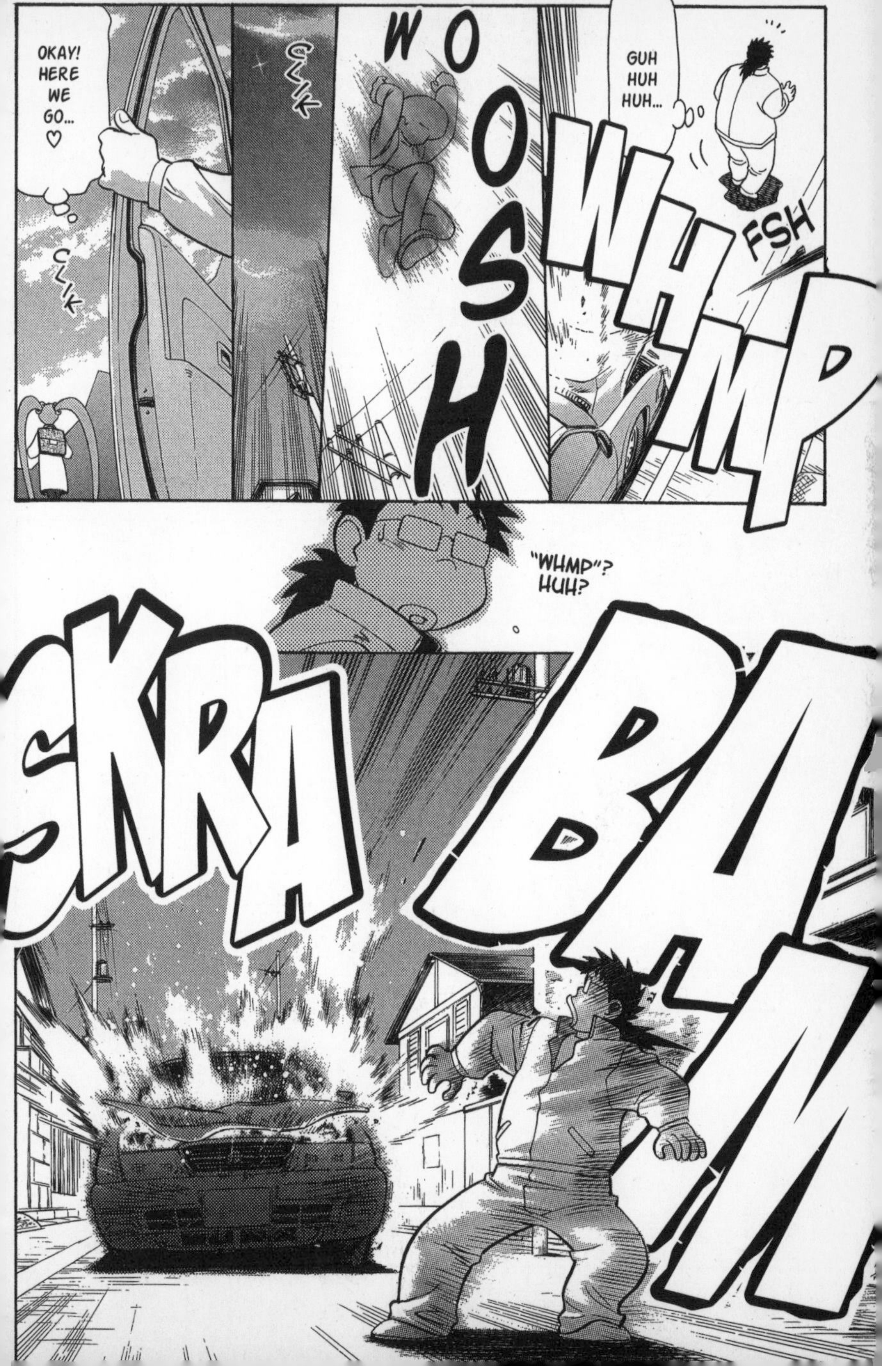
OKAY! HERE WE GO... ♡
CLIK
CLIK
WOOSH
GUH HUH HUH...
WHUMP
FSH
"WHMP"? HUH?
SKRA
BAM

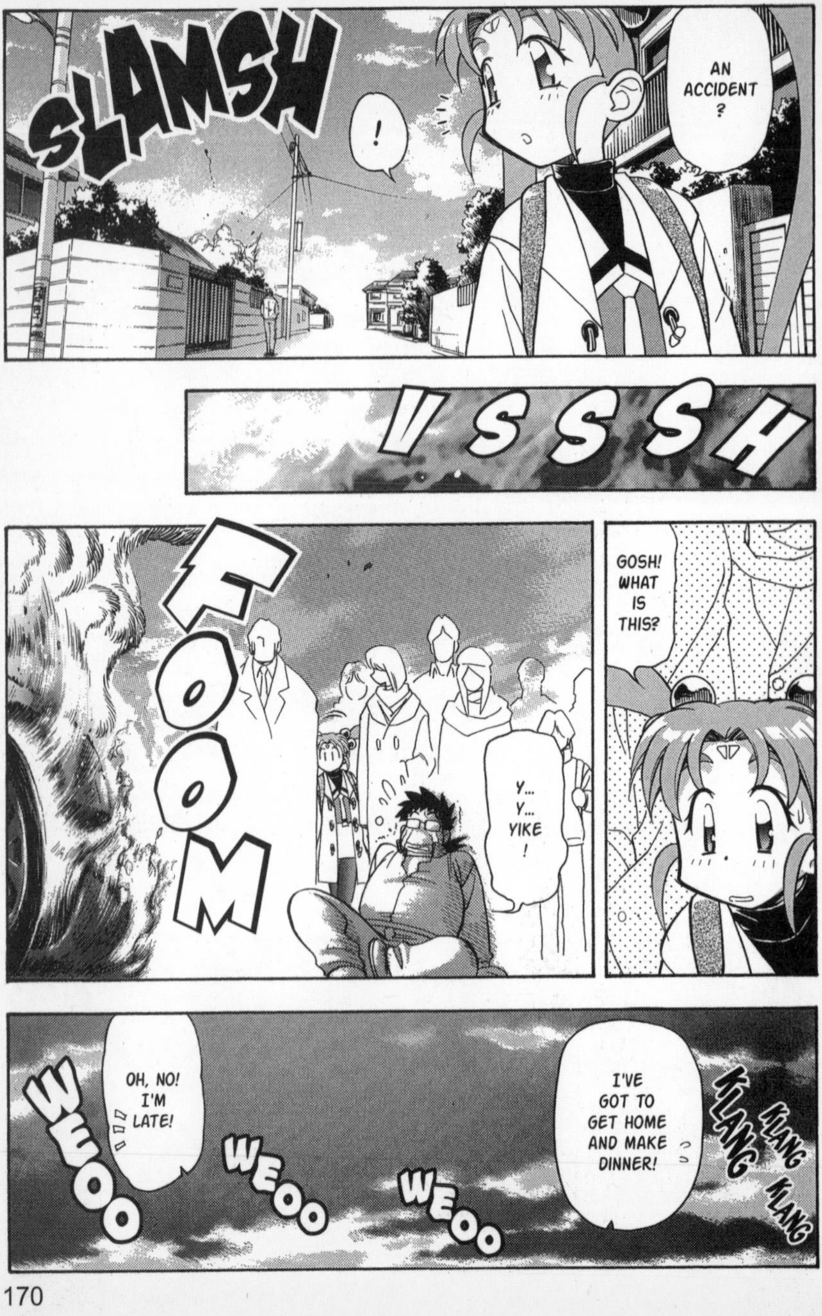
SLAMSH
!
AN ACCIDENT?
VSSSH
FOOOM
Y... Y... YIKE!
GOSH! WHAT IS THIS?
WEOO
OH, NO! I'M LATE!
WEOO
WEOO
I'VE GOT TO GET HOME AND MAKE DINNER!
KLANG KLANG
KLANG KLANG

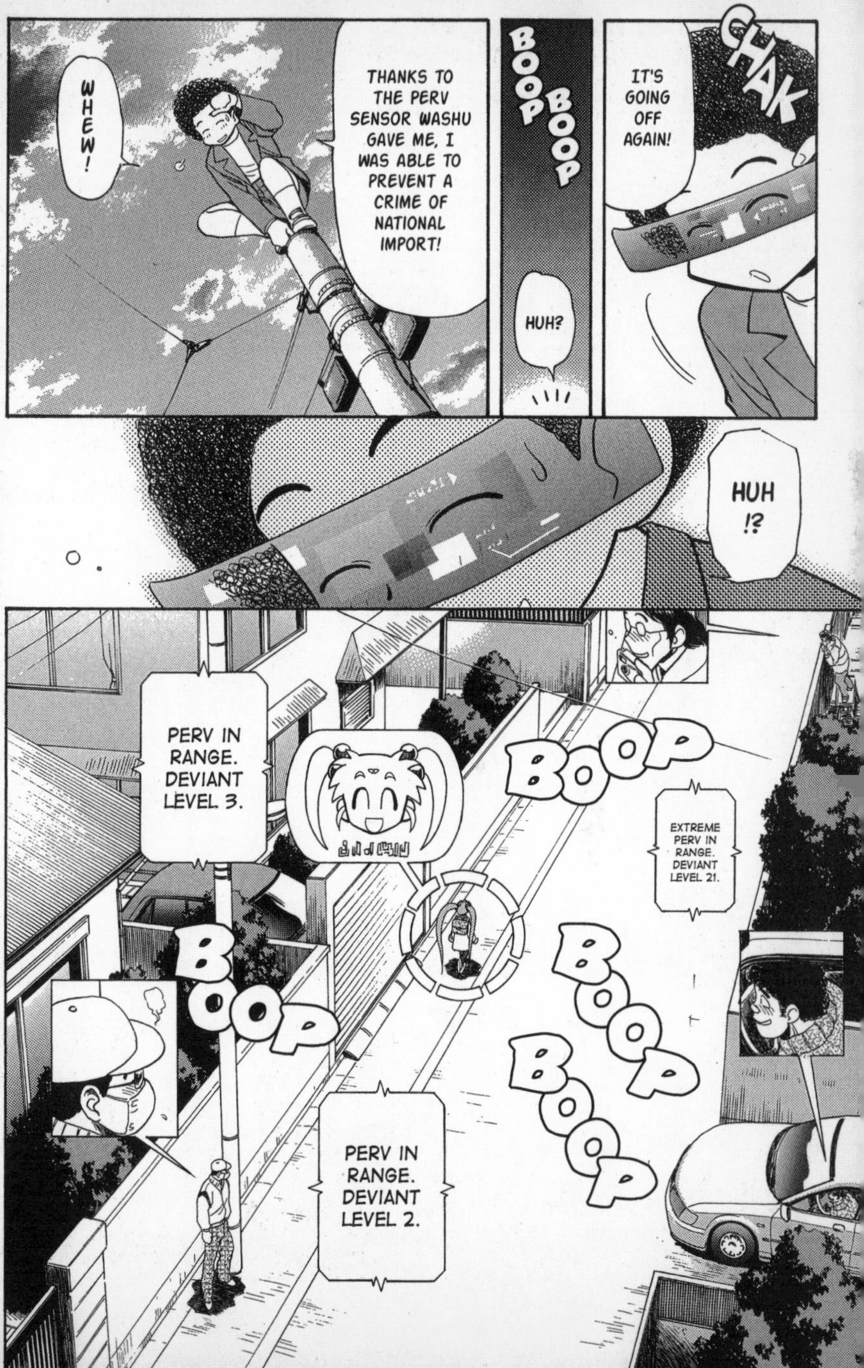
WHEW!
THANKS TO THE PERV SENSOR WASHU GAVE ME, I WAS ABLE TO PREVENT A CRIME OF NATIONAL IMPORT!
BOOP BOOP BOOP BOOP
HUH?
IT'S GOING OFF AGAIN!
CHAK
HUH !?
PERV IN RANGE. DEVIANT LEVEL 3.
BOOP
EXTREME PERV IN RANGE. DEVIANT LEVEL 21.
BOOP
BOOP BOOP BOOP
PERV IN RANGE. DEVIANT LEVEL 2.

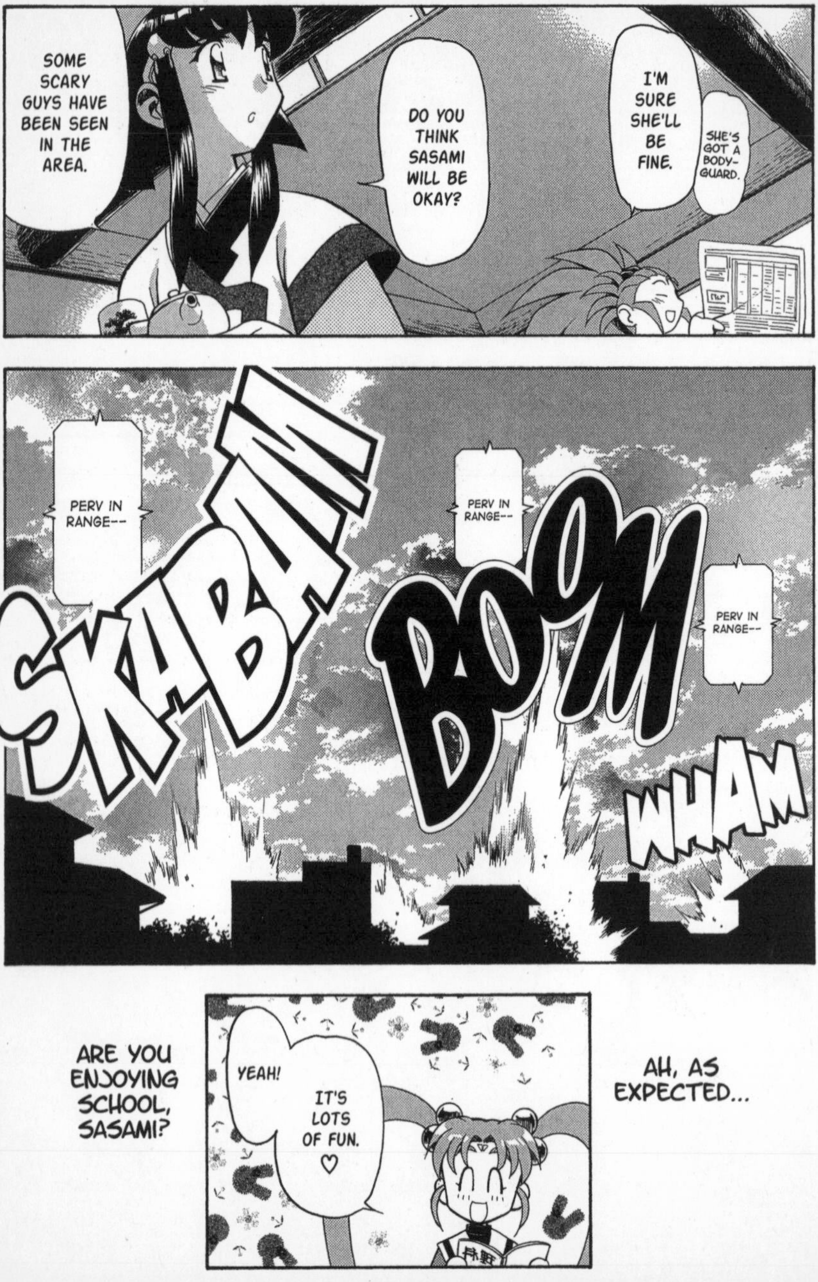

SOME SCARY GUYS HAVE BEEN SEEN IN THE AREA.
DO YOU THINK SASAMI WILL BE OKAY?
I'M SURE SHE'LL BE FINE.
SHE'S GOT A BODY-GUARD.
PERV IN RANGE--
SKABAM
PERV IN RANGE--
BOOM
PERV IN RANGE--
WHAM
ARE YOU ENJOYING SCHOOL, SASAMI?
YEAH!
IT'S LOTS OF FUN. ♡
AH, AS EXPECTED...

Special 10th Anniversary Project

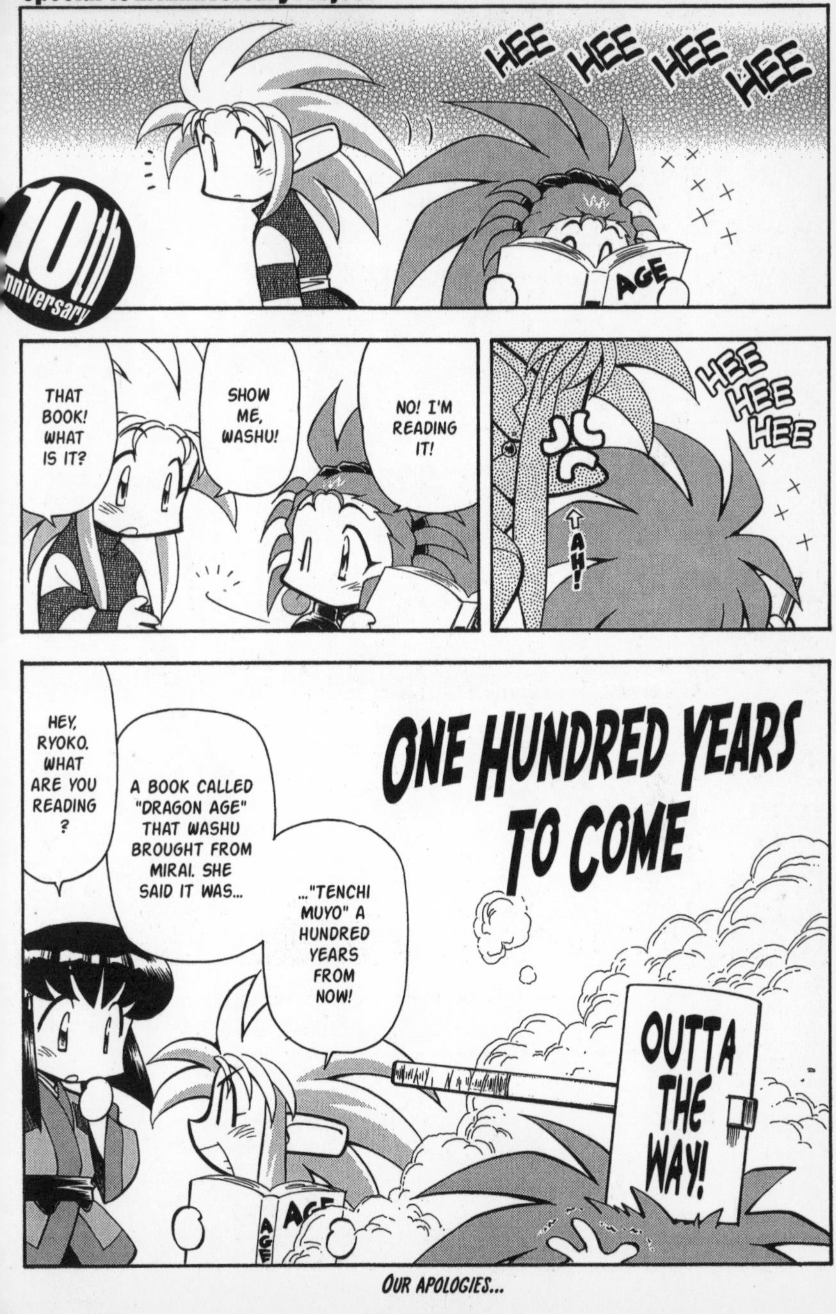
HEE HEE HEE HEE
10th Anniversary
AGE
THAT BOOK! WHAT IS IT?
SHOW ME, WASHU!
NO! I'M READING IT!
HEE HEE HEE
AH!
HEY, RYOKO. WHAT ARE YOU READING?
A BOOK CALLED "DRAGON AGE" THAT WASHU BROUGHT FROM MIRAI. SHE SAID IT WAS...
..."TENCHI MUYO" A HUNDRED YEARS FROM NOW!
ONE HUNDRED YEARS TO COME
OUTTA THE WAY!
AGE

OUR APOLOGIES...

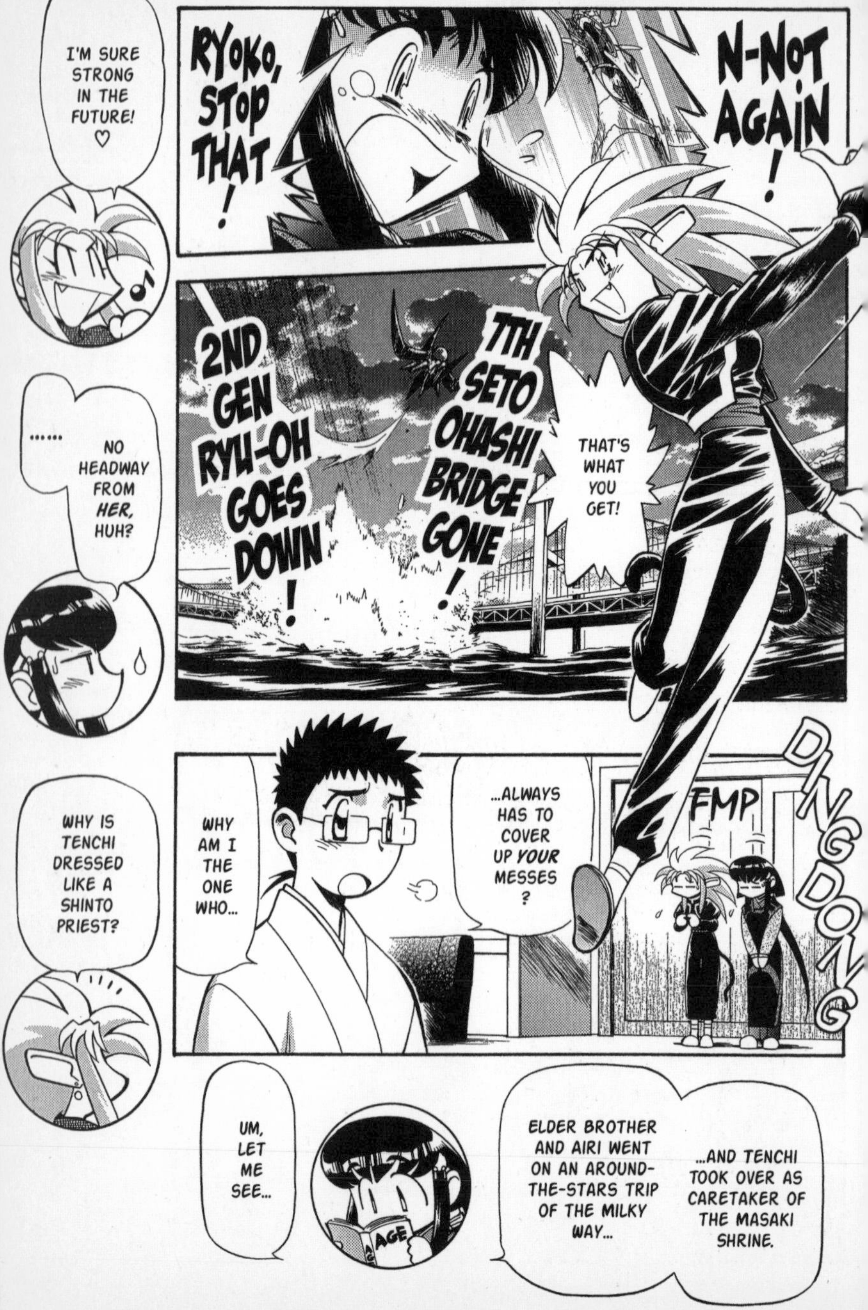
I'M SURE STRONG IN THE FUTURE! ♡
......
NO HEADWAY FROM HER, HUH?
WHY IS TENCHI DRESSED LIKE A SHINTO PRIEST?
RYOKO, STOP THAT!
N-NOT AGAIN!
2ND GEN RYU-OH GOES DOWN!
7TH SETO OHASHI BRIDGE GONE!
THAT'S WHAT YOU GET!
WHY AM I THE ONE WHO...
...ALWAYS HAS TO COVER UP YOUR MESSES?
FMP
DING DONG
UM, LET ME SEE...
AGE
ELDER BROTHER AND AIRI WENT ON AN AROUND-THE-STARS TRIP OF THE MILKY WAY...
...AND TENCHI TOOK OVER AS CARETAKER OF THE MASAKI SHRINE.

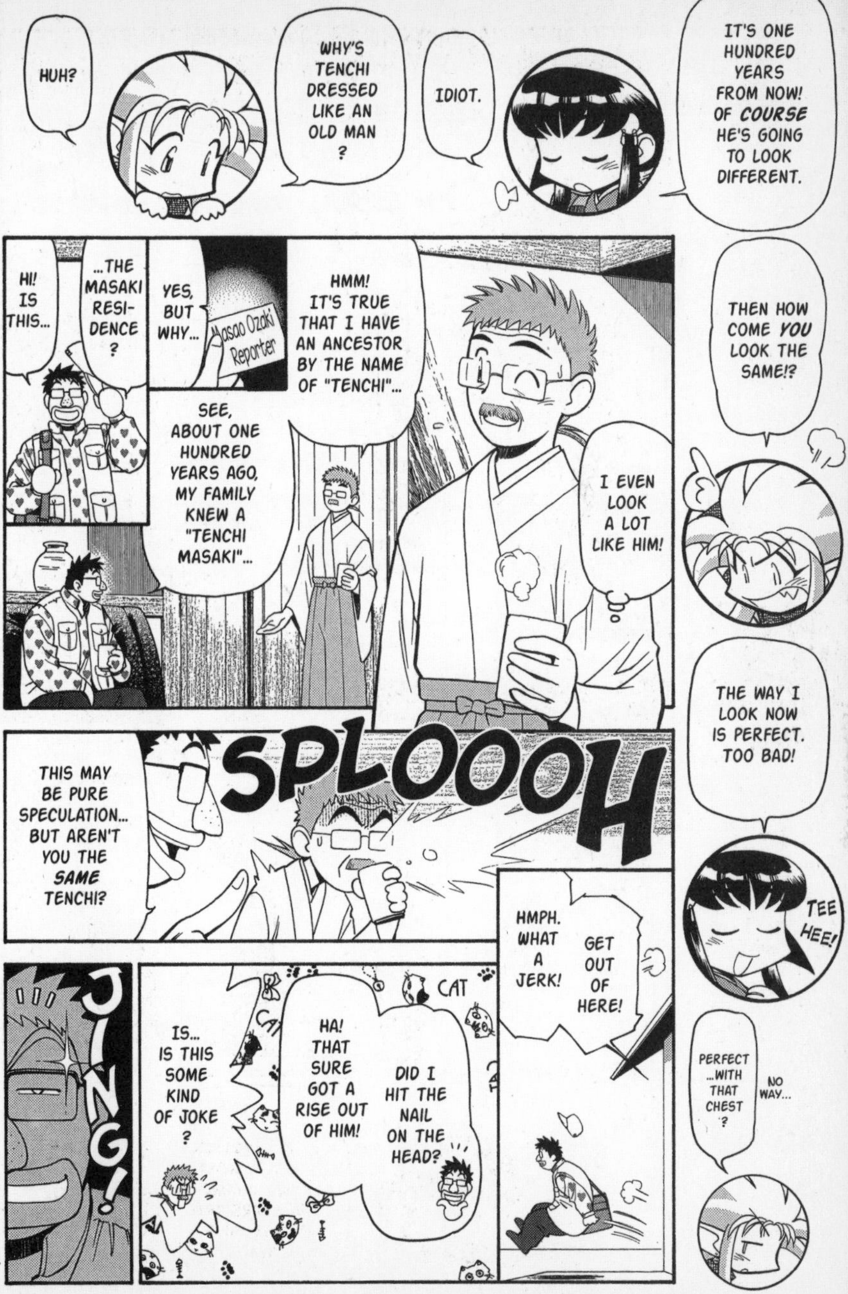

HUH?
WHY'S TENCHI DRESSED LIKE AN OLD MAN ?
IDIOT.
IT'S ONE HUNDRED YEARS FROM NOW! OF COURSE HE'S GOING TO LOOK DIFFERENT.
HI! IS THIS...
...THE MASAKI RESI-DENCE ?
YES, BUT WHY...
Masao Ozaki Reporter
HMM! IT'S TRUE THAT I HAVE AN ANCESTOR BY THE NAME OF "TENCHI"...
SEE, ABOUT ONE HUNDRED YEARS AGO, MY FAMILY KNEW A "TENCHI MASAKI"...
I EVEN LOOK A LOT LIKE HIM!
THIS MAY BE PURE SPECULATION... BUT AREN'T YOU THE SAME TENCHI?
SPLOOOH
HMPH. WHAT A JERK!
GET OUT OF HERE!
JING!
IS... IS THIS SOME KIND OF JOKE ?
CAT
HA! THAT SURE GOT A RISE OUT OF HIM!
DID I HIT THE NAIL ON THE HEAD?
THEN HOW COME YOU LOOK THE SAME!?
THE WAY I LOOK NOW IS PERFECT. TOO BAD!
TEE HEE!
PERFECT ...WITH THAT CHEST ?
NO WAY...

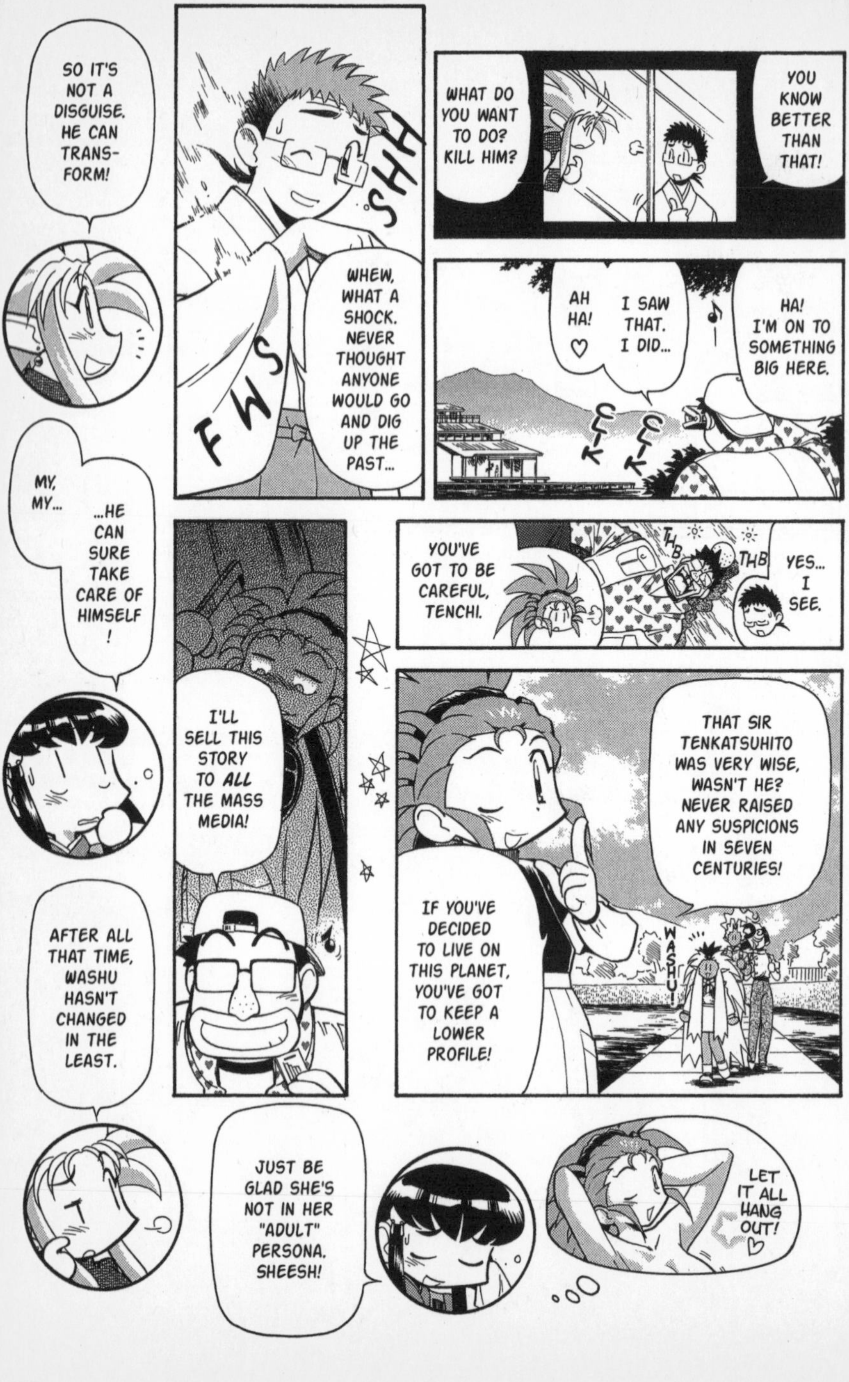
SO IT'S NOT A DISGUISE. HE CAN TRANS-FORM!
SHH
FWS
WHEW, WHAT A SHOCK. NEVER THOUGHT ANYONE WOULD GO AND DIG UP THE PAST...
WHAT DO YOU WANT TO DO? KILL HIM?
YOU KNOW BETTER THAN THAT!
AH HA! ♡
I SAW THAT. I DID...
HA! I'M ON TO SOMETHING BIG HERE.
CLIK
CLIK
MY, MY... ...HE CAN SURE TAKE CARE OF HIMSELF!
AFTER ALL THAT TIME, WASHU HASN'T CHANGED IN THE LEAST.
I'LL SELL THIS STORY TO *ALL* THE MASS MEDIA!
YOU'VE GOT TO BE CAREFUL, TENCHI.
THB
THB
YES... I SEE.
THAT SIR TENKATSUHITO WAS VERY WISE, WASN'T HE? NEVER RAISED ANY SUSPICIONS IN SEVEN CENTURIES!
IF YOU'VE DECIDED TO LIVE ON THIS PLANET, YOU'VE GOT TO KEEP A LOWER PROFILE!
WASHU!
JUST BE GLAD SHE'S NOT IN HER "ADULT" PERSONA. SHEESH!
LET IT ALL HANG OUT! ♡

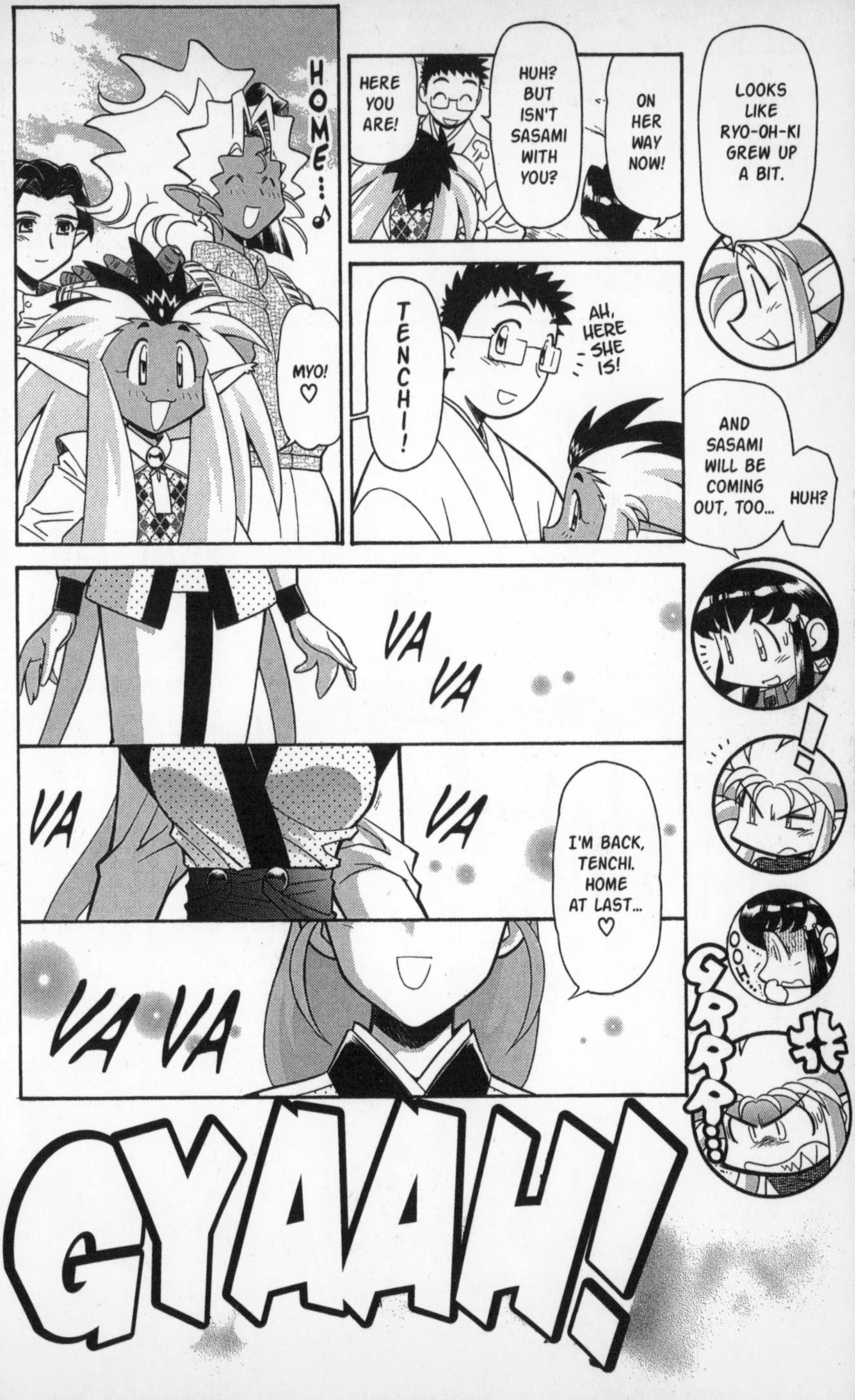
HOME...♪
MYO! ♡
HERE YOU ARE!
HUH? BUT ISN'T SASAMI WITH YOU?
ON HER WAY NOW!
TENCHI!
AH, HERE SHE IS!
VA VA
VA
VA
I'M BACK, TENCHI. HOME AT LAST... ♡
VA VA
GYAAH!
LOOKS LIKE RYO-OH-KI GREW UP A BIT.
AND SASAMI WILL BE COMING OUT, TOO...
HUH?
!
OOH...
GRRR...

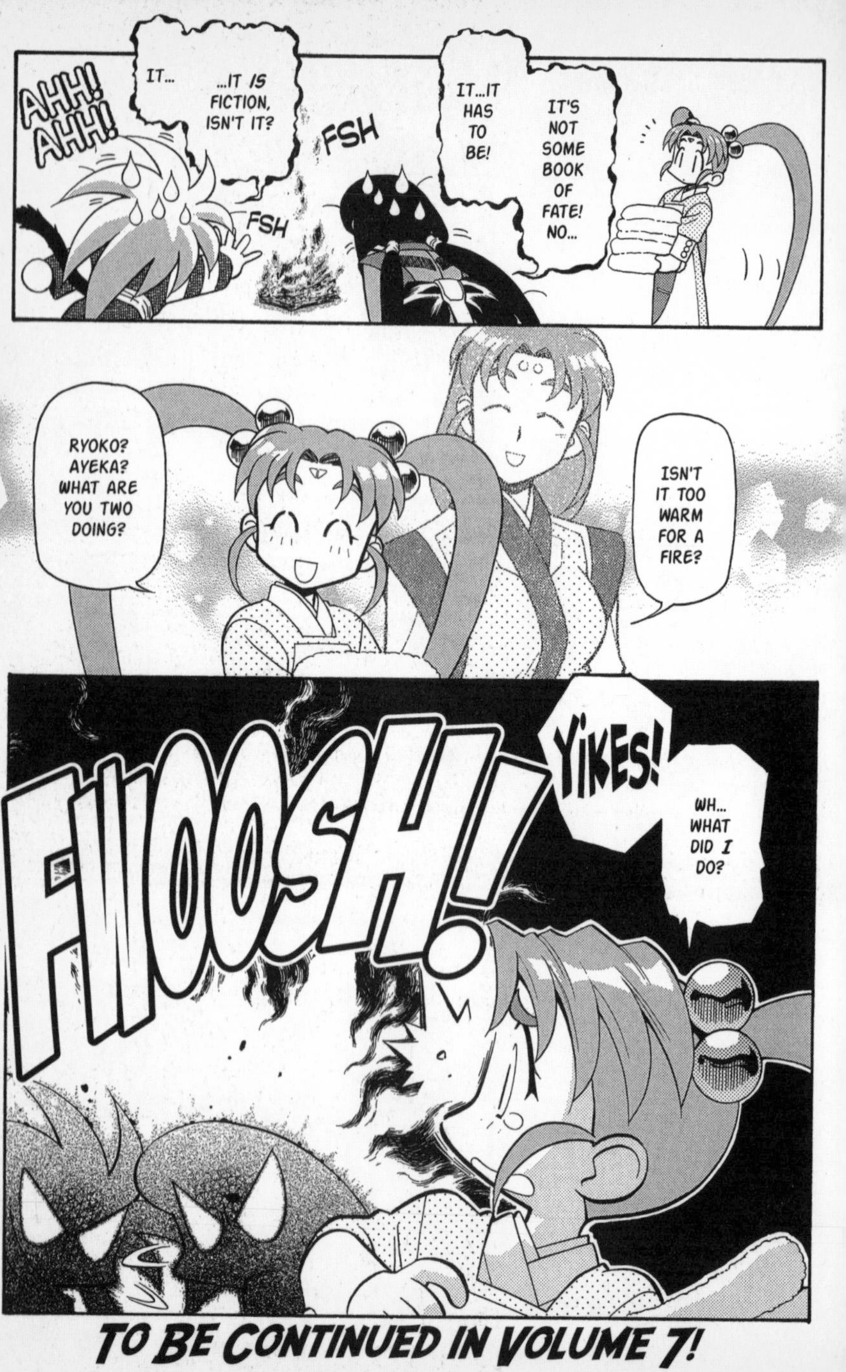
AHH! AHH!
IT...
...IT *IS* FICTION, ISN'T IT?
FSH
FSH
IT...IT HAS TO BE!
IT'S NOT SOME BOOK OF FATE! NO...
RYOKO? AYEKA? WHAT ARE YOU TWO DOING?
ISN'T IT TOO WARM FOR A FIRE?
FWOOSH!
YIKES!
WH... WHAT DID *I* DO?

TO BE CONTINUED IN VOLUME 7!

In Praise of Washu

Allow me, if you would be so kind, to say a few words in praise of Washu. Look at her there on the cover, the very picture of the mad scientist extraordinaire. And, make no bones about it, Washu is indubitably mad. Anyone who's older than human history but chooses to go around being twelve years old forever has got her head in a very strange place.

Given her brilliance, life must sometimes be lonely for Washu. Her friends down at the shrine are, let's face it, not the brightest celestial bodies in the cosmos. However, Washu is smart enough to value friendship above intelligence. She doesn't mind that Ryoko would rather blow up planets than talk about subatomic physics, that Ayeka's mind is firmly fixated on herself, that Tenchi is more entertaining as a lab rat than anything else. Well, maybe she minds a little. But she loves them anyway.

Finally, Washu's healthy self-confidence is admirably true to the spirit of mad science. You can't be a mad genius if you're not willing to stand up and declare yourself the number-one genius scientist in the galaxy, and it helps if you can look cute doing it. Washu carries her brains in style. Mad, they may call her. Mad! But classy.

There's only one Washu, but the Editor's Recommendations in this volume are selected with her mad-science spirit in mind. Enjoy!

Shaenon K. Garrity
Editor of **The All-New Tenchi Muyô!**

Like Tenchi? Love Tenchi?

If so, here are some other books the editor thinks you'll enjoy:

©1994 Gosho Aoyama/Shogakukan, Inc.

Case Closed
Like Washu, Jimmy Kudo is an adult in a kid's body. Unlike Washu, he's not there by choice. Jimmy was a teenage detective until an accident transformed him into an elementary-schooler. Now, taking the name Conan Edogawa (after his two favorite mystery writers, Arthur Conan Doyle and Edogawa Rampo), he attends grade school, searches for a cure for his bizarre condition, and solves one gruesome mystery after another. He may not be the number-one genius in the galaxy, but bold, brainy Conan definitely gives his hero, Sherlock Holmes, a run for his money.

© Yoshikazu YASUHIKO 2001
© SOTSU AGENCY•SUNRISE 2001

Gundam: The Origin
Giant robots fighting stuff. Is there any sweeter way to celebrate the wonders of Science? Of course not. This retelling of the classic Gundam mythos explains how it all began: the mecha, the space battles, the rebellion against Earth. Young Amuro Ray straps himself into the cockpit of a robotic "mobile suit" in a gung-ho effort to restore peace to Earth and its orbiting colonies, not realizing that he's destined to change the course of history and inspire one of Japan's most enduring pop-culture phenomena. This snazzy edition includes all of the color pages that appeared in the original Japanese version. Nice.

© 2000 Hajime Yatate, Hitoshi Ariga
© 2000 Sunrise/Kodansha Ltd.

The Big O
Ever since a mysterious bout of amnesia struck the entire population of Paradigm City, life has been confusing. For one thing, no one knows how to work the giant robots and other hulks of complex machinery scattered throughout town. Happily, wealthy playboy Roger Smith has figured out how to activate an enormous robot called the Big O, which lends a few tons of weight to Smith's arguments as a professional negotiator. The clunky, retro style of Paradigm City's mysterious technology lends *The Big O* a refreshing dash of mad-inventor. Also, it's my friend Rob's favorite Viz manga, and if you don't read it he'll be sad.

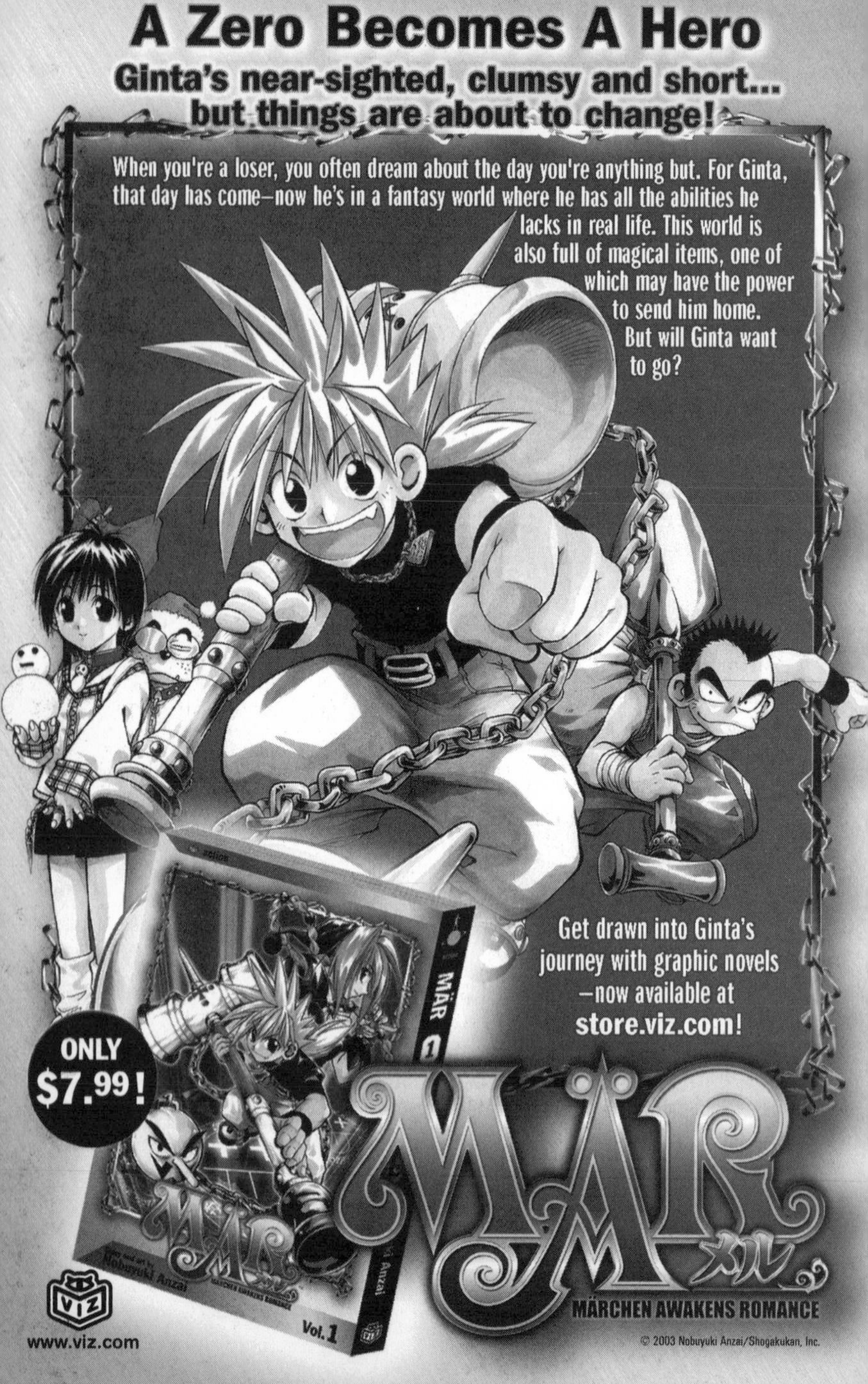
A Zero Becomes A Hero
Ginta's near-sighted, clumsy and short...
but things are about to change!
When you're a loser, you often dream about the day you're anything but. For Ginta, that day has come—now he's in a fantasy world where he has all the abilities he lacks in real life. This world is also full of magical items, one of which may have the power to send him home. But will Ginta want to go?
Get drawn into Ginta's journey with graphic novels —now available at store.viz.com!
ONLY $7.99!
MÄR
MÄRCHEN AWAKENS ROMANCE
Vol. 1
VIZ
www.viz.com
© 2003 Nobuyuki Anzai/Shogakukan, Inc.

COMPLETE OUR SURVEY AND LET
US KNOW WHAT YOU THINK!

☐ Please do NOT send me information about VIZ products, news and events, special offers, or other information.

☐ Please do NOT send me information from VIZ's trusted business partners.

Name: _____

Address: _____

City: _____ **State:** _____ **Zip:** _____

E-mail: _____

☐ **Male** ☐ **Female**   **Date of Birth** (mm/dd/yyyy): ___/___/_____   (Under 13? Parental consent required)

What race/ethnicity do you consider yourself? (please check one)

☐ Asian/Pacific Islander   ☐ Black/African American   ☐ Hispanic/Latino

☐ Native American/Alaskan Native ☐ White/Caucasian   ☐ Other: _____

What VIZ product did you purchase? (check all that apply and indicate title purchased)

☐ DVD/VHS _____

☐ Graphic Novel _____

☐ Magazines _____

☐ Merchandise _____

Reason for purchase: (check all that apply)

☐ Special offer   ☐ Favorite title   ☐ Gift

☐ Recommendation   ☐ Other _____

Where did you make your purchase? (please check one)

☐ Comic store   ☐ Bookstore   ☐ Mass/Grocery Store

☐ Newsstand   ☐ Video/Video Game Store ☐ Other: _____

☐ Online (site: _____)

What other VIZ properties have you purchased/own? _____

_____

How many anime and/or manga titles have you purchased in the last year? How many were VIZ titles? (please check one from each column)

ANIME	MANGA	VIZ
☐ None	☐ None	☐ None
☐ 1-4	☐ 1-4	☐ 1-4
☐ 5-10	☐ 5-10	☐ 5-10
☐ 11+	☐ 11+	☐ 11+

I find the pricing of VIZ products to be: (please check one)

☐ Cheap   ☐ Reasonable   ☐ Expensive

What genre of manga and anime would you like to see from VIZ? (please check two)

☐ Adventure   ☐ Comic Strip   ☐ Science Fiction   ☐ Fighting

☐ Horror   ☐ Romance   ☐ Fantasy   ☐ Sports

What do you think of VIZ's new look?

☐ Love It   ☐ It's OK   ☐ Hate It   ☐ Didn't Notice   ☐ No Opinion

Which do you prefer? (please check one)

☐ Reading right-to-left

☐ Reading left-to-right

Which do you prefer? (please check one)

☐ Sound effects in English

☐ Sound effects in Japanese with English captions

☐ Sound effects in Japanese only with a glossary at the back

THANK YOU! Please send the completed form to:

NJW Research
42 Catharine St.
Poughkeepsie, NY 12601

All information provided will be used for internal purposes only. We promise not to sell or otherwise divulge your information.